# GHOST STORIES OF OLD NEW ORLEANS

# GHOST STORIES
## *of Old New Orleans*

JEANNE deLAVIGNE

*Illustrations by*
CHARLES RICHARDS

*Foreword by*
FRANK de CARO

LOUISIANA STATE UNIVERSITY PRESS

BATON ROUGE

Published by Louisiana State University Press
First published by Rinehart & Company, Inc., New York
Copyright © 1946 by Jeanne deLavigne Scott
New material copyright © 2013 by Louisiana State University Press
All rights reserved
Manufactured in the United States of America
Third printing, 2018

LIBRARY OF CONGRESS CATALOGING-IN-PUBLICATION DATA

DeLavigne, Jeanne.
  Ghost stories of Old New Orleans / Jeanne deLavigne ; Illustrations by Charles Richards ; Foreword by Frank de Caro.
      pages  cm
  ISBN 978-0-8071-5291-1 (pbk. : alk. paper) —
ISBN 978-0-8071-5292-8 (pdf) — ISBN 978-0-8071-5293-5 (epub) — ISBN 978-0-8071-5294-2 (mobi) 1. Ghost stories, American—Louisiana—New Orleans. 2. New Orleans (La.)—Fiction. I. Title.
  PS648.G48D45 2013
  813'.0873308–dc23

                            2013001062

The paper in this book meets the guidelines for permanence and durability of the Committee on Production Guidelines for Book Longevity of the Council on Library Resources. ∞

*To Francis*

In numerous instances, fictitious names have been substituted for genuine ones in these ghost stories. Descendants might not always relish the airing of family phantoms. Old newspaper accounts, interviews, and neighborhood hearsay have been the sources of the tales. It is possible that no one in this old city has ever been able to hear more than one or two of its ghost stories *in toto* before this presentation of them.

—J. deL.

# CONTENTS

# FOREWORD

## Jeanne deLavigne and *Ghost Stories of Old New Orleans*

Jeanne deLavigne's *Ghost Stories of Old New Orleans* is a classic collection of "true" stories about the spirits who haunt people and a variety of old mansions, factories, bridges, and lonely roads. It was originally published in 1946 and has been out of print for many years, hard to find and expensive to buy.

As its title indicates, this book is about the ghosts of New Orleans, a city often said to be full of them and that certainly has produced its share of legends of the supernatural. A website for a company that offers ghost tours in the Crescent City notes that New Orleans "has been called the most haunted city in the United States." On a list of the ten most haunted cities in America produced by the broadcaster CNBC, New Orleans comes in as number 4, after 3) Salem, Massachusetts (a city that, after all, bases a whole tourism industry on the spooky because it is most remembered for its seventeenth-century witchcraft trials); 2) Gettysburg, Pennsylvania (haunted by a host of Civil War dead); and 1) Savannah, Georgia (a ranking possibly influenced by John Berendt's 1994 book about eerie doings, *Midnight in the Garden of Good and Evil*). Author deLavigne herself begins her book with the statement that "there is no place on earth which possesses so vast a reservoir of ghost tales as does Louisiana," with New Orleans alone having "enough of these legends to fill volumes." Whether New Orleans is America's most haunted place or "only" high among the haunted top ten, undoubtedly the city is noted for its stories of ghosts—a fact that deLavigne was able to take advantage of in producing her book. We can only wonder why not many other volumes of New Orleans ghost legends have ever appeared, but there have been few indeed, and in fact this book is one of the few full-length collections of New Orleans ghost stories in existence. It was not till the 1990s that Victor C. Klein published his books of Crescent City ghost tales, *New*

*Orleans Ghosts* and subsequent volumes, and he relies heavily on deLavigne as a source.

Of course some of the interest in ghosts in New Orleans and in general has shifted to the mass media—TV shows about ghost hunters, for example—and to tourism, an industry that now offers an abundance of ghost tours. In New Orleans several companies offer such tours, and they are very popular. More than one company offers tours in the French Quarter almost every night of the year (Christmas and Mardi Gras excepted) and, indeed, twice a night. These tours take place at night to fit in with our notion of ghosts as flitting about in darkness and perhaps also to take advantage of the eerie light. I have often driven through the French Quarter at night and been amazed to see the clumps of tourists spread out along the banquettes (as deLavigne, in the old New Orleans French way, calls the sidewalks here and as some of us still do), listening raptly to animated tour guides telling their tales of ghostly doings. The tour guides themselves are part historians, part actors, and clearly good at spinning out their stories to dramatic effect, often costumed to look like they come from the same past worlds as ghosts, sometimes carrying canes or staffs to add to their personas. Once, years ago, before I made New Orleans my permanent home, I happened to be staying at the Lafitte Guest House on the quiet end of Bourbon Street and headed out from my room to fill a bucket with hotel ice. I opened my door onto a corridor that turned out to be full of ghost-tour goers and a guide talking about the hotel's resident spirits. I rather think that we startled each other. I don't think that anyone took me for a ghost, but personally I was duly impressed by the omnipresence of the tours, this one having even found its way indoors and almost into my room. Interest in ghosts is obviously considerable.

Yet if such tours have taken up the mantle of interest in the spirit world, Jeanne deLavigne was the pioneer and her book blazed the trail. The tour guides like to get their stories from people who claim to have had paranormal encounters with spirits, but I once asked one about her sources for tour material. It was clear that she knew about deLavigne's work and that her fellow guides had originally mined it for its wealth of ghost stories.

But where did Jeanne deLavigne herself get the stories, and how do they fit into the larger world of ghost tales?

Of course there is a long tradition of fictional ghosts in litera-
ture. One thinks of Hamlet's father's ghost setting up the very action of Shakespeare's great play by its appearance in the first scene
of *Hamlet*. In a much later play, the comedy *Blithe Spirit* by Noel
Coward, one of the main characters is an apparition. There are the
Christmas ghosts that whisk Scrooge away to see various scenes
they need to show him in Charles Dickens's frequently filmed sea-
sonal story "A Christmas Carol." And if these literary ghosts are
not particularly frightening ones, other authors have used ghosts
to make their narratives chilling indeed (though their apparitions
may be meant as hallucinations or mere symbols); one thinks of
Kipling's "The Phantom Rickshaw" and Henry James's novel *The
Turn of the Screw*. *Ghost Stories of Old New Orleans* has its literary
side; its ghosts, however, are not intended as fictions. DeLavigne
comes much closer to the world of legend, and in her introduction
she identifies her material as legend.

Orally told folk legends are "true" stories, true in the sense
that they are widely believed to be true or at least presented as recounting true events (whatever skeptics may think), and a signifi-
cant number of legends are about ghosts. We can view ghost legends
as the most fundamental of stories of the supernatural, the "roots"
stories passed on by word of mouth, usually by believers, sometimes
by people who themselves claim to have encountered haunting spirits. It was these stories that Jeanne deLavigne sought out and found.
She got them from reading old diaries and newspapers (New Orleans papers often noticed when local people claimed to be seeing
ghosts; deLavigne said that the old *Delta* and *Crescent* were particularly good sources), from writing "hundreds" of letters to people she
thought knew about ghosts, and from "scores" of face-to-face interviews with people who could tell her ghost tales. Although we don't
have any precise record of her methods, she mentions them gen-
erally in her book itself and spoke about them to a *Times-Picayune*
writer, Marta Lamar, whose article on deLavigne appeared in that
paper on August 4, 1946, just before the book came out in print.

In my trying to find out about her, deLavigne proved to be
a somewhat elusive author, almost a bit of a ghost herself. At the
time Lamar spoke with her, deLavigne, a New Orleans native
whose father was born in France, was living in the French Quarter,
where earlier she may have known some of the Bohemians who had

flocked there. She certainly knew Lyle Saxon's collaborator Robert
Tallant, though she is not mentioned in Faulkner and Spratling's important little book about the group they knew in the 1920s (which
included Saxon), the whimsical *Sherwood Anderson and Other Famous Creoles* (1926). She seems to have been out of New Orleans for
many years but left few traces of herself. After her husband died in
1949 she moved to Franklinton, Louisiana, where she herself died
in 1962, leaving, according to her obituary, no survivors. I discovered her Franklinton residence through copyright sources. An LSU
Press editor located her obituary, which indicates that she was interred in New Orleans, in St. Vincent de Paul Cemetery No. 1, on
Louisa Street—a cemetery once owned by Pepe Llulla, whom Laf-
cadio Hearn wrote about as the "last fencing master" of New Orleans, as if to give deLavigne a final touch of romantic Louisiana
history. I finally found her last resting place in one of the "oven"
tombs here; it bears only her husband's family name, "Scott," and
she was interred therein on June 14, 1962.

Frank de Caro points to deLavigne's tomb in St. Vincent de Paul
Cemetery No. 1, on Louisa Street in New Orleans

*Photograph by Rosan Jordan*

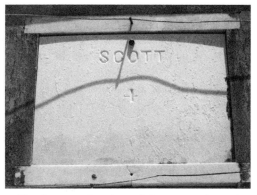

The Scott tomb, where deLavigne is buried

*Photograph by Rosan Jordan*

DeLavigne notes that probably nobody had ever heard more than one or two of the stories she unearthed. This is because ghost legends tend to be very local. Her book includes a couple of well-known stories, like that of the Lalaurie mansion in the French Quarter ("The Haunted House of the Rue Royale," pages 248–258). This mansion is widely known as the Haunted House to residents and tourists alike, and its history of haunting by tortured slaves was probably the only much-disseminated New Orleans ghost story throughout the nineteenth and twentieth centuries. Most ghost legends are known only to a handful of people in part of a neighborhood or perhaps only within a family. These people will speak mostly among themselves about a local haunted house or about ghosts they have encountered or know about, and they may explain to each other the backstory of where they believe the ghost comes from and why it is there. Some people are reluctant to speak seriously about ghosts at all, thus limiting the circulation of stories; deLavigne mentioned to Marta Lamar that she was surprised at how many people believed in the existence of ghosts yet were loath to admit to such a belief lest they be ridiculed because our modern, "rational" world discounts apparitions.

I moved into my present house in the Garden District in 2004. It was built around 1950 and lacks the antiquity of most of this historic area's houses, the antiquity that seems to go along with ghosts.

However, a neighbor, who lives nearby in a lovely nineteenth-century house, informed my wife and me early on that *her* house was haunted, and told us a little about the ghost. I was even more surprised when another neighbor told me that the ghost had been one of her classmates at school. She meant, of course, not the ghost as such, but the now-deceased woman whose ghost it evidently was. It seemed that the classmate had committed suicide in the house and, presumably, lingered on there in spirit. Knowledge of this haunting remains very local, known to only a few, and that is true of many ghosts, as deLavigne discovered.

Ghost stories may arise, then, when someone encounters a haunting spirit (or, if we seek to be more skeptical, let us say when people think they encounter some phenomenon which they interpret as being a ghost). In deLavigne's story "The White Skiff" (pages 292–304), the things seen are the ghosts of the mother of a local tavern owner and the slave who was her lover. However, in 1874 the *New Orleans Picayune* printed a story (April 29, 1874; page 67) by one of its writers of how he and some friends went to the New Basin Canal to investigate a phantom boat that had been spotted there, clearly the same thing that figures in "The White Skiff," whose events deLavigne says took place in the same 1874. In this newspaper story, one of the reporter's companions fires his pistol at the spectral boat only to discover that the boat is quite real and its occupants quite annoyed at being fired upon. The newspaper account takes on a comic tone and seeks to debunk the ghost. Yet we have to assume that *something* that was being taken for the ghostly by some was appearing on the canal; otherwise, the writer would not have gone to have a look. The story that deLavigne tells takes the *something* another way, building on the supernatural possibilities and recounting a story of actual ghosts.

Of course ghost legends take shape in various ways, not just when someone encounters something he or she takes to be a ghost. Because we are usually not aware of a legend until it reaches some sort of final narrative form, it is often difficult to say how the story developed. And legends of the supernatural appeal to us for various reasons. We like to experience the *frisson* of fear that comes from hearing such a story. Or the story gives us a feeling of connection to other worlds beyond our natural one, the world beyond death. It may help us to believe in life after death. Or, if we happen to fear ghosts, it may make haunting spirits more psychologically manageable, for many legends are about how a ghost is "laid"—that is, how a ghost is made to go away, often by determining what has been troubling the spirit in the first place. In both "Warring Wraiths" (pages 277–279) and "The White Althea Tree" (pages 337–346), for example, discovering and moving the bones of the ghost (that is, the bones of the person who became a ghost) to a proper burial place put the haunting to rest.

Jeanne deLavigne, though she certainly hunted for legends, was primarily a writer, not a folklore collector. She co-authored novels and short stories—with her husband, Pennsylvanian James Rutherford Scott, who published as Jacques Rutherford—and worked as a journalist for newspapers in Texas, Georgia, Florida, and Missouri. She gave her legends a literary twist, and the tales in *Ghost Stories of Old New Orleans* read like literary stories. Today, when folklorists can record the stories they hear (on tape or, more likely, digitally), they in effect publish transcripts of actual narrations. Legends as orally told are commonly rather short, almost like summaries; they include the basics, maybe even leaving some things unexplained. DeLavigne may have started with the basic stories she collected, but she develops characters, extends plots, and adds lots of detail. Many ghost stories have in effect a dual structure, an account of or a statement about a haunting, and then a narrative that explains who the ghost is and where it came from. DeLavigne is able to develop the backstory in particular, for usually this is the more involved and intricately narrative part. Her book is rather in the tradition of such writers as Elliott O'Donnell (who recounted a great many ghost stories in books that were published from 1904 to 1958) and Danton Walker (like deLavigne a journalist, he was the Broadway columnist for the *New York Daily News,* and he wrote a popular collection of celebrity ghost stories). Her book is not like the ghost legend collections published by folklorists such as Lynwood Montell, who reproduces exactly what his informants told him.

We can see something of deLavigne's technique by looking at her stories in contrast to more basic legend versions. We can do so by looking at some of the ghost legends that appear in *Gumbo Ya-Ya: A Collection of Louisiana Folk Tales,* the book about Louisiana life and lore produced by the federally supported, New Deal–era Louisiana Writers' Project. The Writers' Project sent out whole teams of employees to collect folklore, and they brought back, among other findings, a raft of ghost stories from throughout the state, including New Orleans, where the project was centered. *Gumbo Ya-Ya* includes some of the same stories that deLavigne recounts. Whether she simply stumbled upon some of the same sources as the project researchers or had access to the project's material is unclear. *Gumbo Ya-Ya* was published in 1945, the year before *Ghost Stories of Old New Orleans,* so deLavigne could have known the book itself, but given the time necessary to publish a book, there might not have been sufficient time for her to see the earlier volume and make use of it. She did know at least one of the editors of *Gumbo Ya-Ya* (a picture of her inscribed to editor Robert Tallant can be found in the photographs he donated to the New Orleans Public Library), so she might have had access through that acquaintance. Or she might have found people who told her the same stories. But undoubtedly *Gumbo Ya-Ya,* which presents rather simple versions of its folk narratives, contains basic recountings of a few of deLavigne's more elaborately told stories.

Portrait of Jeanne deLavigne Scott, inscribed to Robert Tallant
*Louisiana Division/City Archives, New Orleans Public Library*

For example, *Gumbo Ya-Ya* reports the legend of the apparition of a "quadroon slave girl" who appears naked on the roof of a building on Royal Street. This account, only a paragraph in length, says that she was the mistress of a rich young Creole gentleman. When she demanded marriage, he said he would "give her his name" if she spent a cold night on the roof, unclothed. She did so but died from the cold, and she reappears on December nights. DeLavigne's five-page account ("The Golden Brown Woman," pages 29–34, with page 31 taken up by one of New Orleans artist Charles Richards's illustrations) gives the woman a name, Julie, tells how people have climbed to the roof to search for her, gives Julie motivation for seeking an impossible marriage ("Romance filled her strangely blended soul"), provides a few details of her life in her lover's house, uses dialogue to tell the episode in which her lover proposes the rooftop feat, and provides the final words that Julie thinks; it ends with a speculative scene in the lover's bedroom. In her first selection ("The Singing Capuchin," pages 3–15), deLavigne writes of the traditions surrounding Père Dagobert, an early pastor of St. Louis Cathedral, who is said to still haunt the cathedral and to be audible as he sings the sacred songs he loved in his lifetime. *Gumbo Ya-Ya,* in its bare two paragraphs devoted to him, notes his worldly appetites (he loved fine clothing and good food) and that his ghost features him in splendid dress. DeLavigne, though she also notes his attachment to worldly pleasures, ties him in with the events of 1769 when the Spanish assumed control of Louisiana and executed several local French leaders who rebelled against them. When the Spanish governor left their bodies to rot, Dagobert managed to give them a proper burial. DeLavigne's account includes a description of the procession to the cemetery and the burial in the rain. Her account goes on to note the foiled attempts of the Spanish bishop to have Dagobert removed, and it includes the story of his interactions with certain ladies (replete with dialogue). Whether deLavigne was building on oral traditions she collected or simply adding historical material and perhaps material from her own imagination, she creates a much more nuanced account than does *Gumbo Ya-Ya*—indeed a literary presentation of legend.

In several instances deLavigne offers legendary additions to well-known historical happenings. Not only is there her use of the 1769 uprising against the Spaniards, but in "The Mansion That Ghosts Carried Away" (pages 305–311), she plays off the once-famous court case of Myra Clark Gaines. This case stretched on for decades and was heard by the U.S. Supreme Court seventeen times, hence its notoriety. It involved Myra Gaines's having discovered, just prior to her marriage, that she was not the biological daughter of the parents who had raised her but of one Daniel Clark, a vastly wealthy merchant, and a local Frenchwoman named Zuileme Carrière. Myra Gaines sued Clark's estate for her share as a daughter, the case depending on the legality of the union between Daniel and Zuileme. In deLavigne's story, however, the focus is upon Clark's mansion and the "fact" that Zuileme (Zuleme here) is a Gypsy. Gypsy ghosts are dancing in the old house and carrying it off piece by piece because it rightly belongs to one of them. As with many of the stories deLavigne prints, it is difficult to assess what parts stem from actual tradition and where she may have invented (for example, her account of the events involved in the Lalaurie case includes elements—rather sensationalistic elements—found nowhere else). But undoubtedly this story provides an interesting sidelight on a famous Louisiana historical development (the case was noticed because it became so involved and so long-running and had its soap-opera elements, but was important legally because it dealt with the power of federal courts in Louisiana). It provides what might be seen as a "folk" view of this case, suggesting that those who passed on the legend recognized Gaines and her mother as the legitimate heirs.

A bit more puzzling is how deLavigne deals with another historical New Orleans figure, Josie Arlington, and a well-known story about her (not exactly a ghost story, but one certainly about "supernormal" happenings). Arlington was the madame of a reputedly posh Storyville brothel, and when she died she was laid to rest in an expensive tomb she had constructed in Metairie Cemetery. It was widely noticed that her tomb seemed to shine with a mysterious red light, and the joke was made that she was carrying on her old profession after death. Later, the red light was debunked as not of supernatural origin but a coincidental reflection from a traffic light outside the cemetery's fence, but a story also went around that a large bronze statue of a woman seemingly knocking at the tomb entrance (another joke had it that this was a woman looking for work) was seen moving about the cemetery at night. DeLavigne ("The Flaming Tomb," pages 192–197) identifies the tomb's occupant as Josie Deubler (Arlington was, in fact, born Mary Deubler) and says nothing about her Storyville career; the red light comes from actual pink flames. What was important about the tomb to Deubler, according to deLavigne, was that it exactly matched a family tomb in Germany. In deLavigne's version the moving statue is the focus. We have to wonder why she ignores Arlington's notoriety and the more humorous treatment of the story in tradition. Did she come upon a variant of the tradition, or did she consider the usual story unseemly and censor it in her own treatment? We have to wonder, then, to what extent deLavigne changed legend to suit her own writerly needs in general, though it is virtually impossible to say.

*Ghost Stories of Old New Orleans* is of a period when local legends had broad appeal but had to be adapted by writers to make them readable for a wide audience. Jeanne deLavigne did just that (as Zora Neale Hurston did something similar for other kinds of American folklore in her earlier *Mules and Men*), so that what we have are literary adaptations of New Orleans ghost legends. That deLavigne and her publisher were aiming for a general market is underscored by Charles Richards's copious illustrations, meant to give the book further popular appeal. Mississippi-born Richards (1906–1992) originally came to New Orleans in 1927 and first worked as a reporter for the *New Orleans Item,* later reporting for newspapers throughout the country. He had artistic talent, however, and he illustrated some of his newspaper stories with his own drawings and studied art in Paris and with Enrique Alferez in New Orleans. Around 1945 he decided to turn to art full-time, and though he would produce landscapes and figural studies and portraits, he landed the job of illustrating *Ghost Stories of Old New Orleans,* creating illustrations for the book that exude eerie impressions. Richards was a printmaker as well as a painter and sculptor, and his illustrations are etchings (so identified by Richards or the book's designer on those originals owned by the Historic New Orleans Collection), but it is difficult to say exactly what techniques he employed. He may have used some sort of lift-ground technique to achieve his images in white or adapted some relief printing techniques. The talented Richards was particularly fond of doing female nudes, a penchant he seems to have exercised by creating several illustrations that involve ghostly figures without clothes.

Another mark of her times is deLavigne's casually derogatory portrayal of African Americans: her occasional use of the word "darky"; her use of the "n-word"—but only in character dialogue—and her use in characters' speech of exaggerated, fake dialect that no writer today would be likely to employ. DeLavigne was working toward the end of a period when even respected publications printed what would today be regarded as racial or ethnic slurs and falsifications of ethnic and class accents. Despite its limitations in this respect, we are lucky to have a book from this period that records the ghost stories known at the time, stories that in many instances go back further in time and may come down in tradition to the present day. *Ghost Stories of Old New Orleans* is a unique work, a rich collection of supernatural lore made presentable to the reading public of her day by Jeanne deLavigne.

Frank de Caro
New Orleans

## AUTHOR'S NOTE

There is no place on this continent which possesses so vast a reservoir of ghost tales as does Louisiana. In New Orleans alone there are enough of these legends to fill volumes.

Every wall speaks of deeds that have transpired within its protecting confines—grim deeds, ghastly deeds, secret and sinister, most of them very long ago. The emotions, the tragedies, the terrible turns of an inscrutable and capricious wheel of fate—they storm and swarm anew in every quiet courtyard and on every winding staircase in the New Orleans French Quarter. Not a room but what has, at one time or another, sheltered some wraith. Some endured for a season, until their crying desire was appeased. Some still walk, noiseless, unheeding, unseeing, pacing out their mysterious penance, night after night, year after year.

Ghostly feet still tread the old banquettes. Ghostly figures lean over the iron lacework of the old balconies; they teeter on the old slate roofs, they pass in and out through the tall old doors. Even the ancient Cathedral of Saint-Louis has its dim shapes and eerie company, according to tradition. There is not a corner of the city that does not harbor some unearthly visitor in one guise or another. They hug close as feathers on a bird. But they are there all the time—waiting for their little hour, which is so precious and so brief—their little hour of visibility.

Skeptics lay these strange occurrences and manifestations to imagination or threadbare nerves or mental vacuity. Strong men say it is all women's foolishness. Masterful women say it is men's idiocy. Tranquil old ladies and gentlemen who have lived a long time nod tolerantly and murmur, "Maybe, maybe . . ." And as they murmur, their eyes gaze far and far away—farther than any eye ever could see, thinking of the bright morning and blue ribbons and a song by the lake . . . and of Lucie and Tommy and Grace and Rene and little Berta . . . so still, so still.

We of Louisiana are born of the swamps and bayous. Their slow and mighty rhythm, their moist and indefinable sweetness, their laughing languor, their seductive mystery, their inscrutable dreams, their splotches of blazing beauty, their unanswerable magic, their promise of Baal and Circe and the Black Witch and Loup Garou—they ring us round about, they croon to us, they mock us, but they are part and parcel of us, our going out and our coming in—they set our stage and we trip across it with feet as lagging or as light as may be.

Never in this world was a spot where ears were attuned to the music of the stars as they are here in Louisiana. Spanish, French, Italian, Créole, Ethiopian—the blood of each is rich and ripe and warm. There are eyes that can see, where no form riseth; hearts that can hear, where no tongue speaketh; minds that can remember, beyond the realm where memory runneth. It is not . . . and yet it is.

Prince and pirate, noble lady and humble slave, cavalier and courtesan, butcher and baker and candlestick maker—each has his brief turn, his little fling, ere he sinks back into eternal shadows. . . .

GHOST STORIES OF OLD NEW ORLEANS

# (*1780*)   *The Singing Capuchin*

When it rains in New Orleans—a soft, warm, laughing spring rain that makes the violets in the borders blink and gurgle—there are old people who will tell you that the rain sings. Not just a song of glistening marshes and dripping magnolias and rising bayous, nor a song of dancing feet and frilled skirts and young frolicking. But a song which hearts learn to sing, in the fullness of time—a song which rises like slow smoke from the heavy ashes of experience, fanned by the winds of perplexity.

It is a whimsical old tale, and it begins away back in 1745, when New Orleans houses were built of cypress, four to a square, with ditches all around to drain off surface water—to this day there are aged Créoles who refer to a square as an "islet."

It was in that year that a new monk came to the Capuchin monastery, and took his turn at celebrating the Mass in the parish Church of Saint-Louis. Père Dagobert he was, tall and handsome and debonair as any noble at the Court of France. There was a swing of assurance to him which along at the first caused a faint ripple of astonishment among the younger male parishioners, and a sense of apprehension among the older ones. Could it be quite all right, this twinkle in the young priest's eye, as he cast a glance over his flock at the moment of beginning his sermon?

There were no reservations among the members of that early congregation. They worshiped God wholeheartedly, entrusting to their priest every secret of their isolated existence.

3

This young Capuchin from France—surely he was not a day over twenty-five!

And yet, when they were girded for stern criticism, there was his friendly hand held out to them at the church door, his fine eyes smiling at them as though he could read every thought in their craniums, his clear voice sending a blessing after them. How could you sit in harsh judgment on a man like that?

Oui, he had a voice, to be sure. Even the grandmères stopped saying their beads when young Père Dagobert began singing the Mass. The grandpères sighed a little, and wiped their watery eyes. The silly jeunes filles knelt enchanted, their mouths open, rising to their feet like slim young machines at the proper time—fascinated, entranced, hypnotized! **And the** prim, placid mesdames, those cool-headed young matrons who kept so firm a hand on the reins of their several households, whose judgment was so sound, whose scheme of life was so precise and so beautifully ordered—were they quite as cool and unemotional as they made out?

The sunshine was very golden and lovely. The River dappled and shimmered. There were mocking birds in the magnolias and the live oaks. The orange trees were in flower, and the mint and sweet marjoram were fragrant in the borders. There was jasmine pouring over green lattices, and peach blossoms and scarlet pomegranate blooms. The world was a wonderful place, and Sunday was a wonderful day, especially early in the morning . . . when young Père Dagobert was singing the Mass.

But gradually the newness of things wore off, and the handsome Capuchin drew his people gracefully into his way, without their realization or protest. Père Dagobert was like no one on earth. He was Père Dagobert.

Sometimes he was pastor of the parish Church of Saint-Louis, and sometimes he was not. Occasionally one or another of the friars would take the services, while Père Dagobert lolled luxuriously on the shady galleries of the Capuchin plantation up the river. Returning, he would speak pridefully of the fine growths of indigo and oranges and figs.

Did he soil his hands in the rich loam which His Catholic

Majesty, Louis XV, and le bon Dieu had conferred upon the Order of Saint-Francis? He did not. He stretched himself lazily in a long chair under the cool vines of the gallery just outside the refectory, and sipped choice wines and French brandy, and coffee strong as lye. When the sun sank, he strolled under the bearded live oaks, singing softly and helping himself now and again from a jeweled snuffbox, like any worldling.

Did he fast on Fridays and other regulation seasons? He did not. He stuffed himself with roasted veal and delicate slabs of lamb and juicy pink beef—not to mention brochettes de rognons and foie sauté and langue de boeuf braisée and ris de veau piqué aux champignons and fromage mou. Too much—very much too much. And he said, shameless as he was, "Today I shall eat. Tomorrow—maybe—I shall go without, and doubtless that will make up for today's gorging." Not that he felt that there was the least occasion for apology on account of the gorging.

Nor did his vast and constant appetite savor of vulgar gluttony. Indeed not. His manners were perfect. His wine-bibbing never was carried beyond polite bounds. He grew neither gross nor fat, sluggish nor dull. The capacity of the man was incomparable. And his flock followed him like the amiable and delightful sheep they were.

In 1756 they were his by right—he came into the full and permanent duties of pastor. Eleven years had cemented them to him like the skin on an apple.

No girl in the colony would have consented to marriage if Père Dagobert could not perform the ceremony. In death he must be there. At births, he was the first to be told. If a youth were perplexed he sought out Père Dagobert. If a man were worried he knew Père Dagobert could think of a way out. Money was nothing—it poured into the church coffers.

Wherever there was a merry gathering, a feast, a celebration, an anniversary, a reception, a bout of private theatricals, a girl's début, a picnic, a boating party, a crab roast, a chess tournament—there was Père Dagobert in the midst. Not as the parish priest, the godly example, the pillar of righteousness—but with costly silk hose on his well-shaped legs, a costume of satin and velvet and lace and gold embroidery, if you please, not to mention the fashionable three-cornered hat which sat so jauntily on his handsome head, or snuggled gracefully in the crook of his arm.

His people were used to it. They liked it. What was joy for, except to be experienced? And when that golden voice rose on the trembling air, it could warble a tender love-ditty as effectively as it could chant a *Te Deum* or a *Sanctus* or a *Kyrie*. It was like liquid honey, with the power of a tempest and the throbbing of a world newborn, and the delicacy of a waterfall at evening.

And yet, with all the frivolity—with all the peepings at Père Dagobert's priceless gold snuffbox with its encrustation of diamonds and sapphires—never was such devotion offered in any parish church as those French colonists brought to the little Church of Saint-Louis.

Oh, to be sure, the handsome friar had eyes of his own. There was Mademoiselle Louise Mignone de la Chaise, with her russet hair and violet eyes. There was her younger sister, black-haired Mademoiselle Marguerite; and little Madame Michel Fortier, and Madame Antoine Philippe de Marigny, to mention a few. Their gentle hearts beat wildly at his mere approach. How could they help it!

He knew all the pretty words in the French language— all the soft words, all the graceful words, all the words that meant music and laughter and tenderness and response. Of course he did. And spoke them whenever occasion permitted, in season and out of season, and always into ears eager to hear.

They gave him ancestral laces for his altars, jewels for the church's sacred vessels, books bound in velvet and ivory and silver filagree, cases of delicate china, rolls of shimmering brocade. The ladies prepared scented wax for his candles. They packed hampers of jellies and fruit cakes and game and clotted cream, and posted them to him by slaves. And Père Dagobert smiled his thanks, bowed low . . . and sang like an archangel.

A year or two after he had assumed full charge of the parish, Mademoiselle Marguerite de la Chaise came to confession. Her voice was soft as velvet, deep in her throat, and heavy with questioning. The widower, Nicolas Chauvin de

Lafrénière—he of the eloquent tongue and brilliant intellect—
had asked her hand in marriage. Her parents were even now
making arrangments for an early wedding; an order for rosewood furniture had been dispatched to France, another for
silver, and a mountain of linens was being hemmed. But of
course there was already a houseful of these things, Monsieur
de Lafrénière having kept up his own establishment.

"There is no question of the suitability of such a match,"
Père Dagobert mused, humming a little tune under his breath,
there on the other side of the confessional wicket. "You are
happy, of course, my child?"

"Oh," she murmured, with a little sob, "how can I be
happy? Only one man has ever lived in my heart—you must
know, you must know!"

"Oui," he replied, "I have eyes and I can see. But it is not
permitted that a priest shall love a maid and keep her from
mating with another. I have nothing to give, you see—I am
already given, so I am no longer my own to bestow.

"God is very wise . . . there are so many lovely ones in
the world, and love is due them all. I may love, but I may not
wish. Only the wish is sin. Marry Monsieur, my child—and my
heart goes with you. Besides, your home will be no very great
distance from our plantation. I can play chess with Monsieur,
sing my songs to you—and a little later baptize your babies."

He laughed lightly as they stepped out of the confessional.
Old black Melisse was waiting for her charge just outside the
door. And like a hot wind sweeping over a vineyard, he bent
and kissed the fair penitent full on the lips, crushing her close
for an instant.

"God go with you, my child!" he whispered, and pushed
her gently toward the door.

A few months later he blithely married her to Nicolas
de Lafrénière, and drank to her health from a very large
silver goblet.

Little Mademoiselle Louise, of the russet hair, came next,
in the summer of 1759.

"I am troubled," she murmured, her blue eyes heavy.
"It is that I must marry. My father has promised young Joseph

de Villeré that I will marry him in the autumn. It does not seem that I can."

"Non?" the priest queried. "Little girls are like young lambs—they never know what they want, and they are afraid of any fold except the home one. Young Joseph is a good boy. Why are you afraid?"

"I am not afraid," she faltered. "But I cannot divide my love in two. One man lives in my heart—one man only. He sings my soul into heaven—and I cannot live without him!"

"There is no need, my dear child," Père Dagobert replied softly. "I have read dreams in your eyes these many months. I know your need, and I know your secret worship. Marry young Joseph, my child—he will make you a tender husband and a true lover. A priest cannot be a husband, although he can live in a heart as long as it beats on earth. There are so many hearts—God has put them in the world to be as roses to lonely souls. So, as a sweet rose, I shall carry you in my bosom always. Go in peace, dear child—I shall not forget."

And, as they stepped from the confessional, they stood for a moment in the shadowy church. One lingering kiss her young lips gave him. On the twelfth of October of that year, he married her to Joseph Roy de Villeré—and their son became the first Créole Governor of Louisiana.

Still Père Dagobert sang. His brother monks were jealous and proud by turns. They did his bidding, they ran the plantation, they kept still tongues. Sometimes they did grumble among themselves, saying it would be a mercy if His Holiness were to take a trip to this forgotten corner of the world and catch Père Dagobert playing ducks and drakes with the Church calendar and his vows of obedience. To whom was he obedient, except his own precious whims and comforts? And yet, if one of them were perplexed or disquieted or ill, it was Père Dagobert who helped him happily out of his dilemma. The man was at once a curse and a blessing.

"That man!" Frère Étienne groaned one day, picking worms from the cabbages. "Sometimes I think he is Lucifer incarnate, with his silk stockings and his canary velvet coat and his diamond snuffbox! And then, when my spirit is sad and sorry, he comes and lays his finger on my wound, as gentle

*"Kyrie eleison, kyrie eleison . . ."*

as a healing Christ. Nom de Dieu, how can one deal with such a puzzle!"

"Humph!" Frère Hypolite muttered. "One cannot deal. One can but hope for the best. He sent us three sucking pigs this morning, all dressed and stuffed and ready for the fire."

"They always feed him well," grunted the other. "Come, let us make haste about the roasting. It is well that he forgets today is Friday. There are ripe peaches—and yams and almonds and good wine. Three sucking pigs will make a pretty platter, mon ami. Le Père likes his dinner best before sunset."

"Oui, and not a bouchée left over to nibble on tomorrow, when we must set every shred of the leavings out for the poor at sunrise. Such a waste!"

"Mais, Frère, we ourselves were once poor—it is difficile to walk the straight path when the belly cries out for food. We ourselves now always have a plentitude. And it is Père Dagobert's way, after he has stuffed himself richly, to give the remainder away to the poor who have never enough."

"Oui, and it does seem that when he walks in the garden, lilting like a nightingale straight from the throne of God, that he calls all the poor on this strange continent. They do not know their exceeding good fortune—the scurvy Jesuits, who are forever scheming to gnaw a way in, would not feed them as we do."

"No, with them it is always starve and slave and suffer. An austere and ugly Order. They are like rats in a pantry— grab and carry off, all for themselves."

"Their eyes are sharp, Frère."

"And their teeth, too. Sometimes I have the gloomy apprehension. It is far to Rome, and the Jesuits have a cunning tongue."

But in 1763, the Jesuits were ousted bodily from New Orleans, and all their sacred vessels turned over to the Capuchins. Père Dagobert smiled contentedly, and took dinner three days in succession with Monsieur Antoine Philippe de Marigny, Monsieur Rochemere at his right hand, and Monsieur d'Estrehan across the table, to recount the vicissitudes and the triumphs, the vituperations and the spicy glories of the last decade.

Silver and crystal and satiny damask—turkey, terrapin and oysters—pompano and capons and cress—Madeira, champagne, and marvelous drip coffee—cakes and tarts and bombe glacé —a pinch of snuff with the gentlemen, a taste of bonbons with the ladies, a sip of eau sucrée with the small folk—after all this, a French chanson sung with all the delicate abandon of a fairy prince wooing a dryad. And when it rained, his golden voice took on a magic quality which drew his hearers straight into a heaven of perfumes and pearls and delights which promised favors beyond the limits of mortal imagination.

But slowly rumors were creeping in that the clutching Spanish claw was edging nearer and nearer. In 1764 Louisiana was ceded to Spain. The gay French still sparkled and laughed, but sometimes Père Dagobert walked late in the monastery garden, planning instead of singing.

A stranger priest had been to look over the church records, which Père Dagobert kept with scrupulous accuracy. The stranger's face was long and dark and melancholy, and he would partake only of crusts and dried fish. His teeth were yellow, his fingernails were dirty, and his clothing reeked with the unpleasantly intimate odor of his unwashed body.

And the next morning, while Père Dagobert was singing the Mass for a congregation that had flocked from all over the colony, this sour-visaged one had knelt by himself in a corner, his bare feet caked with the dried mud of Nouvelle Orléans, and his Latin responses carrying a strong Spanish accent.

Several years slipped by. The rumblings from Spain had grown into deafening thunder. Don Antonio de Ulloa came and went—March to September. The French still laughed and danced, but they set their teeth and dug their gay toes a little deeper into the moist clay of Louisiana. The eloquent tongue of Attorney-General Nicolas de Lafrénière was busy. His associates were tugging at the new and unwelcome bonds which Spain had fastened onto the colony.

And one July day in 1769, Spain swooped like a vulture. Don Allesandro O'Reilly came sailing up the river, landing like an octopus, with all his sucking tentacles outstretched and hungry for prey. Who had been doing all this talking? Who had been rousing the colonists? Who had been lighting the continual little fires which were eating away the structure which Spain was at such pains to build up? Who was guilty? Out with him!

But O'Reilly soon learned that this direct method never would do. He must bridle his Irish tongue and employ the more subtle Spanish tactics. He would invite certain popular colonists to call upon him. A little wine, a little of the cunningly directed conversation, a little patience—they would all be in his basket, and the troubles and annoyances would be at an end. He had men, he had authority, he had skill and experience and the callous malevolence of the Devil.

He sent out his spies—to mingle, to listen and to watch. And as they returned, each with his drop of poison, O'Reilly filled the hemlock cup to the brim.

On the morning of October twenty-fifth, 1769, he sent forth his messengers, each with a smoothly-worded invitation. They went to ten Frenchmen—Nicolas de Lafrénière, Jean Baptiste Noyan, Pierre Caresse, Pierre Marquis, Joseph Milhet, Hardy de Boisblanc, Jean Milhet, Pierre Poupart, and Messieurs Ducet and Masan. As they arrived at his headquarters, the barracks facing the rue du Quai, they were arrested and hustled into a rear apartment.

Then came the outrage which still rouses a spark of madness in the breast of every true Orleanian. At three o'clock in the afternoon, after a mockery of a trial at which O'Reilly presided as both judge and jury, five of these men, the flower of French Louisiana, were lined up against a brick wall and shot. So the Patriots fell—Lefrénière, Noyan, Caresse, Marquis, and Joseph Milhet. The remaining five men were sentenced to life imprisonment in Morro Castle. Joseph Roy de Villeré was bayoneted on board a Spanish frigate.

The populace was in an uproar. Spanish soldiers were everywhere. The bodies of the five Patriots still lay where they had fallen—no one dared touch them, and O'Reilly was too busy to bother about their disposal. In agony, dark-eyed Madame de Lafrénière—she who had been Marguerite de la Chaise—dragged herself to Père Dagobert.

"My Nicolas—my Nicolas—they have murdered him!" she cried. "They will not let me have even his poor body! But you—you can do this thing! You are a priest—surely they will let you take him away! To let him lie there like a sack of meal—and the horrible rain—and my sister's husband floats dead in the river! Père Dagobert, I went to you once with my heart its own confession—you must save now, somehow, the remnant of my reason! I am widowed, bereft, hounded at every turn by those Spanish ruffians—hide me if you can, and I will pay you in whatever coin you ask!"

Père Dagobert hummed a little tune, but it was not one of the light French chansons which the ladies so adored.

"My child," he said, his eyes very still, "wait here until night. I have a great deal to do. Spain is on us like a wolf pack. Do not venture out, for any reason whatsoever. Tell your beads, and sleep a little if you can."

When he left her, he closed the door and locked it. But he came again after dark, many times. And each time he brought a breathless, sobbing woman, and sometimes terrified children. Yet, with all this sorrowing company, there was a funeral stillness about the Presbytère. No light flickered at any window. The wine and the milk and the bread which Père Étienne brought in were scarcely tasted. So the widowed and the fatherless waited, they knew not for what.

Then, near two o'clock in the morning, Père Dagobert opened the door. He held a lighted candle in one hand, and with the other he beckoned to them. The little procession crossed the wide alley to the Church of Saint-Louis. Shading the candle with one hand, he led them to a row of still figures stretched on the floor, each covered with a dark cloth. They were the six Patriots whom O'Reilly's men had slain. How the priest had contrived to spirit the bodies to the church, no one ever will know.

And then, through the blinding rain, those brave women, with the help of Père Dagobert and Père Étienne, somehow bore the bodies of their dead to the cemetery—we know it today as the Old Saint-Louis Cemetery Number One.

There Père Hypolite awaited them. And in the rain they laid their dead in the deep pit which Père Hypolite had dug, Père Dagobert singing snatches of the burial service softly under his breath as best he could, as the soggy earth was spaded in to cover them. Finally it was but a heap of brush and rubbish. The morning light revealed no trace of boot or burial.

But at Mass, Père Dagobert's clear voice rose sweet and powerful as ever. The Spanish monk who crouched in a rear pew had nothing amiss to report. Where were the bodies of the five? Who had fished Villeré from the river and whisked his body away in the darkness? Among the careful records of Père Dagobert not one word ever gave the secret away. But he went oftener to the cemetery, walking in green aisles and singing a requiem as he walked. Always when it rained he went there, unless other church duties pressed him.

And all that dreary, puzzling winter, with never an eye to a window nor an ear to a door, the widows and children of the Patriots lived at the Capuchins' plantation house. No one guessed, nor would have meddled if they had. In the spring they crept away, one by one.

On Dumaine street lived a quiet, white-haired woman whose name had once been Marguerite de la Chaise—she called herself Madame Boisclair now. Away down on the rue Royale, in a tiny house, lived little Madame de Villeré, with her small son. Père Dagobert comforted them all, singing gentle songs and teaching them prayers from ancient French breviaries, giving their growing children wise advice, helping them to plan life and build it up anew.

"Ah, well," Père Dagobert learned to say, "le bon Dieu made Spaniards as well as Frenchmen, although it seems scarcely possible. Heaven frowns on friction. Let us have peace and quiet. In that only can we prosper."

Came Bishop Cirilo de Barcelona, Spanish Auxiliary Bishop of Havana. He supped and he spied, in growing consternation. And, finally, he wrote to the head of the Capuchin Order, complaining bitterly of Père Dagobert. The unobserved fast days, the worldly clothes, the jeweled snuffbox, the Papal Bulls which for thirty years had not been read to the congregation, the ladies whom he loved—there were even references to certain quadroon women, too much wine, too much of everything except devotion to Mother Church.

So investigations were made. The parish—nay, the whole colony—stood solidly behind the beloved priest and swore he was without spot or blemish. Bishop Cirilo was recalled in something very like disgrace.

And when Père Dagobert died, in 1776, they buried him in a crypt under the altar, in the Church of Saint-Louis. A hundred women found their lives suddenly empty. The gentlemen missed a gay and wise companion. The poor missed a constant friend. The children missed the priest who could solve all their difficulties. No more did the glorious voice throb with honeyed melody through the morning Mass.

And yet . . . came a time when an awed whisper began to go the rounds. One heard it, and another heard it. And when it rained, they gathered on street-corners—between the church and the cemetery. Faintly it would drift at first— "*Kyrie eleison, kyrie eleison*"—then rising in a golden swell like a tide of honey and flame, rich as amber, it carried up and up until the universe seemed to quiver in response. And a form seemed to pass along the way—sometimes a man's figure in glistening satin and lace and embroidery, sometimes in a somber cassock and cowl. But always singing. Always from the church to the cemetery, as though he could not keep away.

So it has grown to be a New Orleans tradition—this wraith of Père Dagobert, beloved of his people. They will tell you, the old Créoles, to watch for him any morning, at the hour before dawn. They will tell you to listen, with reverence and faith, when the rain comes down in a silver torrent. And there you will see Père Dagobert—perhaps in a courtly coat of canary velvet, with a cascade of lace at his throat and wrists, and a jeweled snuffbox in his hand—his handsome head upraised, singing like an archangel—"*Kyrie eleison, kyrie eleison*" . . . God rest him . . . .

# (*1860*)     *The Mystery of Madame Vaquer*

The news was out. All along Customhouse street (which is now Bienville), eyes peered cautiously from V'd shutters, ears listening eagerly for a fresh morsel of luscious scandal, and tongues wagged in an incessant whispering. It was thus-and-so, such-and-such actually had taken place, somebody had heard something else, maybe the other thing was true. . . .

And amid it all, Madame Jean Vaquer, small and gray-haired and precise, walked to the French Market and returned with her basket of greens and yams and sweet herbs. Sometimes there was a poulette in the basket, or artichokes and wine and oil. Madame did not herself carry the basket, of course. That was borne on the head of young Sara, Madame's slave.

Madame did not know about the whispering. But the black girl did. It had been going on for a week or more now, and Sara was daily contributing her mite. Indeed, it was this mite for which the gossipers waited and hungered, figuratively licking their chops after each tasty crumb. It was Sara alone who knew exactly what was going on in Madame's house—and Sara alone who could tell them.

True, Sara had but one confidante—Debby, Madame Furin's slave cook. Debby's tongue was infinitely more industrious than her hands. Every slave in the neighborhood knew all that Debby knew. And what the slaves knew, the mistresses presently knew also.

It all had to do with Rosine, a slave of eighteen years or thereabouts, belonging to Madame Vaquer. This Rosine had been purchased in February of that year—1860—from one

Jacques Derviche, a Saint-Jean Baptiste parish planter, who had guaranteed her to be sound and healthy. Madame had bought Sara at the same time, considering the two of them a good bargain.

Very shortly, however, Rosine began to grow listless and thin. She ate ravenously; but one day, late in April, they found her lying dead in the courtyard.

Miss Abigail Mason, Madame's friend and paying guest, was the one who quieted the hubbub, saying that, after all, it was only a dead nigger. The commotion arose, she observed, because there was no man at the head of the household. A man never would have tolerated such nonsense—he would have had the carcass scooped up and carted off and buried, and that would have been the end of the matter. Miss Abbie, as the neighborhood called her, smiled calmly through it all.

But Madame was not satisfied to let the Negress' death go unaccounted for. She had paid good money for Rosine, with the guarantee that the slave's health was perfect. She had been cheated. She would sue Jacques Derviche for damages. So, in order to establish her claim, she sent for Doctor Leclerc, her family physician. He must examine Rosine's body, and furnish her with his written statement as to the ailment which had caused death.

The doctor announced that, while the dead slave seemed extraordinarily light for a wench of her size, there had been apparently nothing specific the matter with her. Quite likely she had died of a sudden heart attack, for which no one was responsible. There was a queer sort of birthmark on her back, he added—a white, hook-shaped mark, just between the shoulder blades. Madame reproached herself for not having inspected the wench's back herself, before buying—she could have compelled Monsieur Derviche to throw off something on account of the blemish.

Sara was caught listening at the door when Madame and the doctor emerged from the gallery room where the body lay. Madame cuffed her ears soundly, and hate boiled within the slave.

That night she managed to get a word with black Debby. She told a weird tale of Madame's having sizzled Rosine's poor

back to a crisp with hot irons, as punishment for laziness. She
told also of Rosine's having been starved until she dropped
dead—punishment inflicted by Madame for wasting food. She
added that when Rosine died, Madame was frightened lest the
facts become known—therefore she had called in her doctor
to make a statement that Rosine had died of heart failure.

The tales spread with lightning-like rapidity. The white
folks of the neighborhood heard them almost as soon as the
slaves did. Miss Abbie could not be consulted—she, of course,
was away sewing every day. It was a pity to have to get everything at second hand, but it was the best the gossips could do.

When Madame Carriere, who lived next door, heard of
it, she sniffed audibly.

"Impossible!" she snapped. "Madame Vaquer never tortured a slave in her life. As for starving, I have seen that
Rosine stuffing herself between meals, time and again. I lent
my Josie to Madame one day, and she came home and said
she never in her life saw a nigger eat as much as Rosine did.
Don't let me hear another word of such drivel!"

One morning Madame Vaquer came down to breakfast
racked with pain in her shoulder blades. She descended in a
distinctly ill-humor because Sara had not brought the usual
cup of steaming black coffee up to her six o'clock. She found
the breakfast table not yet laid. The kitchen was in an uproar
—dishes smashed, pots and pans on the floor, and furniture
overturned. A jar of cream spilled in the midst had not
improved matters, for its rivulets were black with ants.

Sara was nowhere to be seen. A prolonged search revealed
her crouched in a coal-box in a building formerly used as a
stable. She was wild-eyed and ashen, and declared a ghost had
appeared on the stairs when she started up with Madame's
morning coffee. She said it waved its arms and pointed at her,
and then wrecked the kitchen as it chased her out into the
courtyard. It was the ghost of Rosine, Sara declared, her teeth
chattering.

Madame snorted, and would have given the wench a flog-
ging had breakfast not been of more importance just then.
Evidently Miss Abbie had had to go to her work without
breakfast, rather than disturb her friend.

The pain in Madame's shoulders grew so acute during the morning that she called Sara upstairs and told her to apply liniment to the cramped muscles. When the slave had pulled Madame's gown down sufficiently at the neck, she gave a wild whoop of terror and dropped the bottle of liniment.

"It's de hook-mawk!" she squalled, when Madame ordered her to stop her yelling, slapping her in fury. "De same hook-mawk what de doctah man done found on Rosine's back—on'y dis yere mawk am red an' raw!"

"Do be quiet!" groaned Madame. "You had not the business to listen at the door. Besides, you misunderstood Monsieur le Docteur. There was no such mark on Rosine."

Madame knew she spoke a lie, but it was best to keep Sara in the dark about such things. So she sent the slave downstairs, and thought to apply the liniment herself. She was a modest woman, but the thing that Sara had screamed out about a hook-mark on her back made her wonder. She bolted her chamber door, slipped down her bodice and underthings, and twisted herself before her mirror so that her bare back came partially into view. The silvery surface of the looking glass showed her a hook-shaped mark, just as Sara had described it—red and angry and terrifying enough.

No wonder her shoulders ached! What in the world could have made such a mark? She threw on a dressing robe and rushed down the hall, hoping against hope that her friend was merely sleeping late and had not yet left the house. But the gallery room was deserted. A great hook high up on the door casement caught her eye, and she shivered. The hook had been there always, and it was nothing to shiver about. She felt weak and ill this morning. That matter of the miserable Rosine had given her a case of nerves—and no wonder!

After an hour's rest she went downstairs to see how Sara was progressing with the morning's work. All seemed serene enough. When Miss Abbie came home in the evening, Madame asked her to rub some liniment on the painful back.

"My back—it does not appear of a redness or—or anything?" Madame queried.

"No, it's quite all right," replied her friend. "Probably you have caught cold in it. You should have Sara rub it for you."

"Oui, oui," nodded Madame vacantly. "Oui."

So there was no mark on her back now. Doubtless a wrinkle in her chemise had been responsible for it. She had glimpsed it herself, oui—but some days all people are fools. How the liniment smarted!

The next morning, no black coffee being forthcoming, Madame descended to the ground floor in mounting disgust. Her smoothly-running, well-ordered household—how disjointed it had become! No morning coffee, Abbie leaving the house at dawn, one slave mysteriously dead, the other slave grossly disobedient—what, indeed, was the world coming to?

Her shoulders still ached cruelly. They gave an extra twinge as she craned her neck to behold fresh havoc wrought in the kitchen. There on the floor was her best violet-bordered china, teapot and all, broken to bits. The cunning cups, the adorable little bowls, the treasured tea plates—all a tragic ruin! Ashes strewed the place; and out in the neat courtyard, with its oleanders and night jasmines and the clump of feathery bamboo in one corner, lay a great stick of half-burned firewood, still smoking viciously. Where was Sara, who was supposed to be in the kitchen at this moment?

"Mon Dieu, that Sara—she is the answer to all this damage!" raged Madame. "I should have known it yesterday, had I not been blind as la taupe! That young demon, with her lies and her play-acting—what she shall have is a good whipping! Sara, Sara—come here this minute!"

But no Sara responded. Madame stamped out to the old stable, but Sara was not in the coal-box. She was, so far as her mistress could ascertain, nowhere on the premises. That story of a ghost and her great fright—what a lie! And what a custard-head had been Madame to believe it, she reflected wrathfully. Every nook and corner she searched, without result.

Her mouth stiff with resolve, Madame donned her black silk and her small, cream-colored Paisley shawl, and made a call at the police station. No runaway slave had been taken in charge, she was informed. Whereat she gave a detailed description of the decreant Sara, and posted a reward of ten dollars for her arrest. A bit mollified at this last flash of inspiration, she returned home.

As the day advanced, Madame set herself to the task of putting her littered house to rights. She had barely begun when a bucket of soft soap was overturned on the washroom steps, to come rolling down in a slimy tide over her feet. Her back was turned at the moment, and her voluminous skirts swished into the stuff before she saw what had occurred.

When she hurried upstairs for a change of shoes and clothing, several chamber doors slammed, a raised window fell with a bang, and her own small night lamp came crashing through the doorway of her room, missing her head by an inch. The carpet in her chamber had an ugly gash in the middle, and a bucket of ashes had been dumped into her snowy bed. Her clothes had been ripped from the armoire hooks, and lay trampled on the floor. Worst of all, her best bonnet floated in a washbowl of grimy suds. Madame was beside herself with rage and despair.

So many strange things happened in la maison Vaquer that day that Madame feared a physical collapse. She was nearing sixty-five, and when dusk came she felt almost too weary to eat the dinner she was preparing. Suddenly she remembered that the banquette had not been swept all day, and she hurried out with her broom.

Madame Carriere had just stepped out of her house next door, and Madame Vaquer almost embraced her. What surcease from the day's perplexities a friendly chat would be!

"Bonjour, Madame," greeted her neighbor. "And how goes life for my dear friend?"

"Ah, life has become indeed a thousand riddles!" exclaimed Madame. "Me, I am the victim of ghosts—no less! Oui, oui, you may scoff all you wish, but you should have spent this day in my terrible house." And she launched forth with a detailed account of her miseries.

Officer Boullosa chanced to be passing, and he paused to inquire as to whether or not Sara had yet returned. He had received instructions from headquarters to be on the lookout for the runaway.

"No—the worthless black vixen!" snapped Madame. "And on this day, of all days, when I needed help so sadly! Think of me, at my age, down on my poor knees polishing the stairs!

Mon Dieu, it has been enough to make one's very bones rattle, to hear and see all I have seen and heard this day!"

"Are you sure the slave is not somewhere about the house?" asked the officer.

"Me, I have searched everywhere," Madame wheezed. "There is not a crack big enough to hold a cockroach that I have not peered into. No, no, she is gone."

"Would you permit me to search your house?"

"Oui, of a certainty," returned Madame. "But you will find nothing, nothing. That no-account wench is nowhere about."

A group of firemen were passing, and the officer hailed them, asking their assistance. Madame led the men into her house, and the search began. A fly brush came hurtling down from the second landing, grazing Officer Boullosa's ear. He bounded up the stairs, but no one was there.

Finally the party came to a tightly-fastentd upstairs door.

"That you cannot open," warned Madame. "It leads into the house next door, which I own. Madame Carriere is in residence there. No one ever uses this door—it must not be opened. It is used only as a convenience when the other house is unoccupied."

Nevertheless Officer Boullosa gave the door a mighty wrench, and open it came. Behind it, in the clothes closet of the house next door, lay the shameless Sara—sound asleep on Madame Carriere's best black velvet mantle!

"A-ha!" growled the policeman, dragging her forth by one ear. "Is this the way you serve your mistress, you worthless wench? Get you down to the kitchen before I beat you myself —and I hope Madame whales the life out of you!"

"Me, I yearn to do that very thing this moment!" spluttered Madame, almost speechless with amazement and chagrin.

"No doubt this is the ghost which has been smashing your dishes and frightening you half to death," Boullosa continued. "You will do well to lay on a few extra lashes for the mental discomfort you have undergone. As to that small matter of the reward you offered, I believe you will agree that I have fairly earned it."

"Oui, oui, certainly," Madame hastened to nod. "If you

will excuse . . ." She retired to a corner, turned her back chastely, and raised the front of her skirt so that she could reach the pocket in her flounced petticoat. She handed the ten dollars to Officer Boullosa without a word.

When the policeman and the firemen had gone, Madame turned to her slave, whom she still clutched by one black arm.

"You shiftless vixen!" she stormed. "Why did you do those unspeakable things? You should be killed—I have a mind to cut your empty head off! Messing up my kitchen and my bed-chamber—ruining my clothes—wasting my food—destroying my dishes—spoiling my sleep—mon Dieu, I think you are possessed of a devil! You ought to be thrown into the parish prison, to rot and eat mule hoofs!"

Sara was weeping copiously.

"Ah ain't did nuffin', Madame!" she wailed. "Ah wa' comin' into de kitchen one night wid a candle, an' sumpin' done grub me by de back an' smack me on he haid an' stawt cay'n me off! Ah yells oncet, an' de Fing it whack mah haid wid a ham bone. Dat am all Ah knows, sho's Gawd, 'cept Ah wa' flang in dat dar closet an' de do' locked—an' mah back it ached pow'ful bad—it ache pow'ful bad right now!"

"It should ache—me, I am glad it aches!" her mistress scolded, shaking her until her teeth clicked together. "You are a worthless, lying wench—and I paid a good price for you, too! After this I shall tie you up at night, and then we shall see how much damage is done! Now go and lay the table for dinner, and mind that the potage does not scorch!"

At that moment a potted begonia came crashing down the stairs, the soil scattering and the plant crushed and broken. Followed a small chair and Madame's hand mirror.

"Oh Madame!" quaked the slave, cowering against the white woman. "Ah wa' meanin' to tell you—I done had a awful dream 'bout dat dar big white hook-mawk on Rosine's back—a awful witch-dream it wa', 'bout Miss Abbie an' all— Ah sure wa' meanin' to tell yo' . . ."

"What's that about Miss Abbie?" smiled that lady, coming in through the front door. "Dear me—more confusion and mess?"

Madame was beside herself with anxiety and trouble.

"You are my only comfort, Abbie!" she cried. "I beg you, have patience with this house—it is bewitched! Me, I must finish the dinner while this wench clears away this fresh discouragement!"

"Ah, yes," the paying guest assented, picking her way daintily up the stairs. "I shall be seeing you presently, dear Madame."

Madame sighed jerkily. Her poor brain felt as though it were churning in her skull. She, too, had suffered from a frightful dream in which Miss Abigail Mason figured prominently. But a dream is only a dream, and one's good friend is one's good friend. Poor Abbie—certainly she had received little enough attention of late.

During the next few days Sara grew more and more listless. When she fell in a faint, Madame was frankly terrified.

"It must be the worms!" she muttered. "I can think of nothing else. Monsieur le Docteur could find nothing in Rosine —and now this one is going on the same way. She will be dying before I know it. Two wenches lost in three months— I shall be bankrupt! Surely it must be the worms in her liver. I shall dose her with oil and calomel!"

Over by the pantry door a strange shape was hovering— a shape tall and angular, wrapped in a luminous glow, swaying and swaying like fog in a river wind. In a moment Rosine's old shoes were flung into the middle of the kitchen. The stove door flew open, hot ashes showering onto the lye-scrubbed floor. A blue china cooky jar tumbled from a high shelf, and a bucket of rainwater was dashed in at the open window.

"Mon Dieu, mon Dieu!" cried Madame, wringing her hands and remembering her frightful dream. "It is the ghost again—the ghost of that accursed Rosine! Before she came into this house, never did we have any of this terrible trouble, and never did I have the frightful dreams about my dear Abbie. Such things are of an outrage!"

"Dar she am—dar Rosine am agin!" shrilled Sara, coming out of her fainting spell. "It am 'cayse Ah tole lies 'bout her an' 'bout yo', Madame! Ah's gwine die, lak Rosine she tell me las' night—Ah's gwine die, 'less Ah tells yo' de trufe! So dat am de trufe—Ah done telled lies on yo'!"

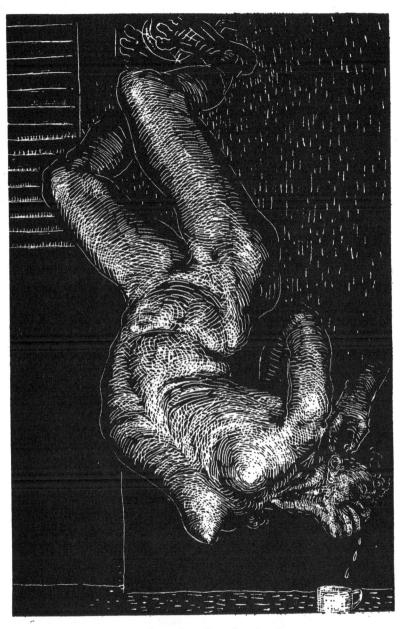

*. . . was hanging by the heels . . .*

"Hush, you bad one!" Madame blustered in her tempestuous French way. "You and your lies—Rosine and her ghost—you are all of a pack! I wish I never had bought either of you. Trouble, trouble—that is all I have had with the both of you!"

But, for all her storming, her heart stood still with terror whenever she thought of the ghost of Rosine. Was it waiting for a chance to throttle her? Her shoulders could still feel the rake of horrible claws, as in the awful dream. Still, it had not been Rosine who clutched at her in the dream . . . It had been Abigail Mason.

She gave orders to the revived Sara to prepare certain things for dinner. Then, being excessively tired, she went up to her chamber for a brief rest. She slept. And yet she dreamed again the terrible waking dream which had overtaken her so often during the last few weeks.

She dreamed that Abigail Mason came and stood in her chamber door and gave her a wordless summons to rise and follow. This she did, and back they went to Abbie's gallery room, the ghost of Rosine following obediently. Sometimes she could see Rosine's thin black face, with its empty eye sockets and shriveled lips. Sometimes it was only the filmy form, and the ever-reaching black hands against the white film. But always there was that soft, crafty smile on Abbie's smooth face.

Then there was black Sara, too, there in Abbie's room. Black Sara was nude, and was hanging by the heels from that ghastly hook in the casement. Abbie had a little penknife in her hand. She bent down, and the point of the narrow, glittering blade slid up in one side of Sara's nose. Abbie held a bottle under it . . . drip, drip, drip. . . . Sara's blood was dripping into the bottle. Abbie's gloating eyes watched it fill. Finally she drew the bottle away and stoppered it. Then she dipped a small swab into a squat jar, and drew a hook-shaped mark on Sara's naked back. There was a sudden smell of scorching flesh. Madame could not move. She had a strange, baffled feeling that her head was being pulled about, her brain dominated, her eyes forced to see what another willed. She was like a spirit in a glass case, unable to be herself or to return to what she had once been. . . .

When Madame awoke she was in her own bed. She felt weak and languid, as though her own body had been drained of its blood. She heard her small clock strike one . . . She had had no dinner . . . No one had called her . . . Why had Abbie not come and spoken to her at dinner time? Where was Sara? . . . How her shoulders ached!

She arose with difficulty and stepped into the hall. The moonlight was streaming in through the window. She was wide awake—yet she could smell that odor of scorching flesh, persistent, nauseating. There at the top of the stairs was the Thing she called Rosine's ghost. Something must be done immediately. Supposing she spoke to the apparition . . .

"Rosine," she said, "if it is that you have something to tell me, show me the way to understand you. If you are only fog, go back to the river where you belong, and leave us alone!"

The shape moved backwards along the hall towards the gallery. Madame followed—and stumbled over Sara's inert body lying outside Abigail Mason's door. But Miss Mason was nowhere to be found.

Madame dragged the unconscious slave into her own chamber and bolted the door. With the lamp held close, she examined Sara's flat nose. It was as she feared—a line of dried blood made the dream too real for question. It was a witch-dream, surely—only a witch could gain so great a power over any mortal as to will what should be done, and be obeyed; only a witch could accomplish such hellish things, with innocent mortals rising from their beds to assist, yet having no voice and no will of their own with which to protest, and retaining but a vague memory of what had taken place.

When Madame opened the door, the shape beckoned to her and she followed it out into the warm night. Through the dark and muddy streets she went. Then there were no streets, only a sodden rough road. They came to a low shack in a wood, somewhere between Bayou Saint-Jean and the Lake. The shape pointed, and Madame stretched up on tiptoe to peer in at the latticed opening which served as a window.

Flaring candlelight . . . naked black bodies she saw, circling to a delirious chant about a tub in the center of the place. In the tub a great snake was coiled, its ugly head lolling from side to side. There was a white priestess, half naked and twisting in horrid contortions. And that priestess was—*Miss Abigail Mason!*

Even as Madame gazed, Abbie raised a glass bottle high above her head—a bottle of blood—the same bottle which had played its part in Abigail Mason's gallery room earlier in the night. Its crimson contents spattered out over the writhing black bodies, over the snake in the tub, over the revolting priestess herself.

Then suddenly the snake came to life. It raised itself in a slimy column for an instant, and then it hurled itself onto Abigail Mason's naked back. It coiled about her body and wound itself about her neck, crushing her and strangling her. And then it shot its hideous head into her open mouth— wriggling, pushing, jamming its way down her throat. Madame could see the white woman's neck and body swell, as the reptile descended into her belly. She sprawled on the mud floor now, the snake her master and possessor . . . filling her, sucking her lifeblood into its own stomach, devouring her as its proceeded inward. . . .

Abigail Mason never returned to her room at Madame Vaquer's house. She had gone to live with relatives in Charleston, Madame told the neighbors when they inquired. Sara never asked. She was growing strong and well, and doing her work faithfully. She was a good slave.

And that other slave—that glistering, white-wrapped, misty shape? It never was seen again in Madame Vaquer's orderly house. Madame had the terrible hook taken down from the casement in the gallery room. And one day she traveled out to Chalmette, and threw the hook into the river.

# (1800) *The Golden Brown Woman*

In the seven-hundred block of rue Royale stands an old mansion built more than a century ago. It rears its solid bulk on the uptown river corner of Royal and Sainte-Ann streets, and in the long ago was the domicile of a wealthy widower.

But along with its heavy ancient bolts and its fan windows, its old-world archways and its vine-hung courtyard, it has a ghost. Not a pale, feminine wraith with snowy hands and chalk-white countenance, nor yet the phantom of some tall young swain bled ashen in a duel for love's sweet sake. Not these. And not when the blaze of summer sunshine has left all things hot and breathless. Nor when the spring rains fall. Nor when the waters of the river creep like hungry tongues, licking higher and higher up the straining levees. Not then.

Only in December, when the winds whistle bitter about the square old chimneys of the Quarter, does this ghost walk— the golden brown woman whose feet tread so lightly along the edge of the slanting roof. She is naked, they say—her round, sleek limbs graceful as whips, her bosoms like plump oranges, her lithe brown back glistening in the moonlight, only the gold double-hoops in her small ears clinking like fairy bells.

On December nights, when it is very, very cold, this golden brown phantom rises from the narrow old staircase which leads from the attic to the roof. Around and around the edge of the roof it walks, swaying and bending against the icy wind, teetering around the perilous corners, shivering in chilled misery, wrapping its arms about itself for protection, struggling and stumbling, hour after hour, night after night. Then, when comes that still and awful hour just before the dawn, the brown woman bends lower and lower, her feet grow heavier and heavier. And finally she sinks slowly to the roof, a forlorn heap, desolate and beaten.

Certain sane and callous watchers, talking glibly and planning sagely, have immediately climbed the winding mahogany stair and come out at the narrow door opening onto the roof. They have searched minutely with flashlights every inch of the silent old roof—and not a scrap of anything have they found. Yet the next night the lithe, naked brown woman has again taken up her walk round and round the roof, shaking and shuddering in the biting wind.

Who was she? Why does she choose bleak December nights for her eerie promenade?

The story is that the rich widower who lived in this house so long ago owned many slaves. To him they were merely property. They served him, did his bidding, made his great establishment possible.

But there was one slave, Julie, whose nature ran to dreams. Romance filled her strangely blended soul. She was an octoroon—seven streams of white blood, one stream of black. But her spirit cleared the black barrier at a single leap. She fell in love with her master—passionately, hopelessly, without reason or reserve.

The master accepted her gift, laughing because she was, after all, merely something he had purchased and which he could sell again when he wearied. He humored her because it suited his fancy to do so—set her at the head of his household, gave her a spacious and beautiful apartment adjoining his own, bought more slaves to wait upon her, loaded her with costly trinkets and clothed her in silks and velvets and delicate laces.

Only, of course, when his friends came to call or to visit, Julie was shunted severely into oblivion. Not a glimmer of her must appear—not a breath of the heady perfume she so loved, nor a clink of the jewel encrusted ornaments with which she loved to deck herself. The doors to her chamber were locked and bolted, and the windows were barred and shuttered. Still, whispers began to drift around. Female cousins and sisters-in-law can be intensely inconvenient in such circumstances.

*She is naked, they say—*

Then one day the bewitching octoroon faced the man she loved and demanded that he make her his wife. It had come to be her one thought, her overwhelming ambition. Why not his wife? Only one thin stream of Negro blood against seven that were white! What did one little stream of Negro blood matter? Was not she, Julie, the "fountain of gardens," the "well of living waters?"

She remembered his reading a book to her one glamorous day—a big book it was, full of quaint pictures and decorated letters and pages of writing inside the front covers. Julie could not read. But her master had opened the great book whimsically and read passages to her, while he laughed indulgently— "Thy teeth are like a flock of sheep that are even shorn, which come up from the washing . . . Thy lips are like a thread of scarlet . . . Thou hast ravished my heart . . . how much better is thy love than wine! . . . The smell of thy garments is like the smell of Lebanon." Then there had been another line— "I sleep, but my heart waketh: it is the voice of my beloved. . . ."

But days like that one seemed never to come again. If he married her, he would not dare to tire. So one day, when something of the old warmth seemed to spring again to life between them, she put the proposition to him. She was his, he was hers—would he stand the test?

"Yes," he responded, catching her closely to him. "I'll marry you, Julie. I'll marry you tomorrow. But you must do one thing for me, to prove that you are worthy of so great a favor. You must take off all your clothes tonight, and go up onto the roof and walk until morning."

"But the cold—it is December! I shall freeze to death!" Julie cried aghast.

"Love is warm," he mocked merrily. "You do not have to go. Only if you wish me to marry you."

"But I shall be seen!" she whimpered.

"As you please," returned the master coldly. "I am not the one who is set on matrimony."

"Oh, but I shall do it!" the octoroon declared. "It is a test—love will preserve me! I shall not feel the winter wind!

And tomorrow I shall be your bride—you have given the promise!"

The master knew he was safe—he knew the girl never would go through with such a thing. As darkness came on a driving rain began to beat against the shutters. The house fairly shook in the wind, and the master ordered the fires replenished in every room, it grew so cold. A friend came, and the two men played chess until far into the night. Julie was forgotten.

But Julie herself did not forget. She waited until near midnight, when the storm bellowed and crashed. Then she removed her clothing and crept up the stair to the roof, shivering miserably before she stepped out onto the streaming slates. Out she went, the sharp rain pelting her sensitive skin like lances, the bitter wind tearing at her like surging hosts of angry beasts. Somehow she would endure it—somehow she would pay the price he required!

Sometimes she slipped, sometimes she fell to her knees, clutching in mad terror at the enshrouding darkness, sliding downwards, always managing somehow to recover her balance, always the terrible wind shrieking and pushing and buffeting her this way and that. But to be his bride tomorrow . . . to be Madame instead of merely Julie! How much more of tonight's furious punishment could her soft body withstand?

Julie thought of the comfortable fires in the rooms beneath her—the luxurious cushions, the perfumed furs, the steaming foods, the fiery wines, the couches of down and satin. But most of all she thought of the man who had promised to marry her tomorrow.

She leaned against a chimney a moment, the rough bricks tearing her tender flesh, her feet a mass of raw wounds.

She shook with cold, and her ears began to hear strange sounds above the roar of the wind and the torrent of the rain. Then a strain of music drifted to her, clear and sweet, and words that the master had read out of the staid old book . . . "I sleep, but my heart waketh . . ." Julie was slipping down and down, but she had forgotten the pounding rain and the demon wind. A brown wet heap at the foot of the chimney, cold and stiff and lifeless. "I sleep, but my heart waketh . . ."

And every December, Julie walks that terrible roof. Her golden brown body bends against the freezing wind, her breath comes short and painful. And then, when the night grows old and weary, she sinks at the foot of the chimney, to walk no more until the next night. "I sleep, but my heart waketh. . . ."

The occupants of the house admit that the queer things do not all happen on the roof. When the house is quiet and deserted, there are footsteps in the chamber which used to be Julie's. Four footsteps at a time, as though someone were going from one window to another—peering out, perchance, upon a world which she had thought to face with her white lover.

And in the master's bedroom a ghostly chessboard appears sometimes on a table at night when it is cold and rainy. Do ghostly hands move the phantom pieces, as they were moved that terrible night? None shall know. Only that golden brown figure on the steep roof, fighting the dreadful cold, December after December. "I sleep, but my heart waketh. . . ."

(*1865*)     *The Soldiers Who Could Not Die*

On the woods side of Constance street, between Race and Orange, stands a mansion built about 1820. The rooms are spacious and high-ceiled—so high that, although the house has only two stories, it is a tall, imposing place. Heavy brick pillars support the front from ground to roof. In these years it has been turned into a lamp factory. But time was when the favorites of fashion danced on the polished floors and smiled into its huge, gilt-framed mirrors.

Nowadays the place is viewed with a wary eye by the people of the neighborhood. They hear things and they see things, and at night they hurry by on the opposite side of the street. Not one of them would enter it after dark, even though it might be lighted from one end to the other. The Negroes prefer to go a block around, rather than pass the place after dusk.

What do they see and what do they hear? They see two white-faced soldiers in blue uniforms, staring out of the upper windows—they hear them babbling a strange and muddled jargon, such as never was on land or sea. They peer cautiously around corners, these curious ones, and see the two soldiers waving their arms, their faces lined with despair, their eyes dark with foreboding, their lips set, grim and determined.

Sometimes the watchers see the two clasp hands, their white foreheads glistening with sweat and their breath coming hard. Sometimes they lean against the old casements, stark and terrible. Sometimes they pass up and down the hall—up and down, up and down, muskets over their shoulders and little blue caps on their heads. Sometimes they sing in thin, high, faraway voices, like music heard in dreams . . . "Mine eyes have seen the glory of the coming of the Lord . . . And his soul goes marching on"—or, "Hang Jeff Davis on a sour apple tree. . . ."

The lamp factory now has its display rooms on the second floor. In December of 1936, one of the Negro helpers was prevailed upon to work at night, as Christmas orders were heavy and many customers did their buying after supper.

At about ten o'clock, while they were locking up, this boy, Calvin, was putting things to rights in the showrooms. Suddenly the proprietors heard a terrified shriek, and beheld Calvin plunging down the stairs, his black face ashen gray, scream after scream issuing from his throat. Out the door he dashed, and up the street. He raced six squares before anyone could induce him to slow down. Asked what he had seen, he finally related the following tale:

"Ah wa' fixin' to go home, an' Ah wa' 'rangin' de lamps all straight lak fo' mawnin'. Ah wa' in de front room, an' Ah jes' trun round to stawt downstays. Ah heerd sumpin', an' Ah seed de do' ob de back room openin', slow an' queer lak. Ah wa' skeert right dat minute, an' mah laigs dey begun to kind o' crumple at mah knees, weak lak.

"De front room wa' still all lit up bright, an' Ah sees a pair o' boots walkin' tru de do' from de back room, an' anuddah pair o' boots walkin' jes' back ob 'em—long, shiny boots dey wa', black an' smoove. Dey wa'n't no laigs in dem boots, an' dey wa'n't no feet an' no nuffin, but dey wa' walkin' right fo' me, dey wa'.

"Dey wa' walkin' an' laughin'—kind o' chucklin' lak—an' den Ah heerd a man a-singin'—'An' his soul goes mawchin' on—Glory, glory hallelujah!'—an' Ah jes' makes fo' de stairs—an' down Ah goes, an' dem boots prancin' aftah me, sho's Gawd—"

Nothing could induce that colored boy to return to the haunted house. Even the promise of increased wages failed to move him.

When the proprietors first took possession of the place, they came especially early one morning to unpack materials before the help arrived. They were standing in the front hall talking, when a huge concrete block was hurled at them from the head of the stairs.

"It didn't fall," Isadore Seelig said. "It was thrown. It never struck a stair as it came, and it landed just where we had been standing. My brother saw it coming and pushed me out of the way. It would probably have killed us if it had hit us. We never had seen it anywhere around here, and there was no one except us in the building at the time. The upper windows and doors were locked, and when we went upstairs no one was there, and no one had been there. No such blocks had been used in any of the repairing around here."

Some years ago, although it had seemed impossible to get tenants for the house, a widow moved in. She had been there for a while, and all seemed serene enough. Then one day she sat sewing in the second room upstairs. She felt something dropping on her arm; when she looked, she saw it was blood. Drip, drip, drip—warm and red and sticky. It seemed to come from the ceiling, and she sprang from her chair. When she had washed her arm and grown a bit calm, she got a stepladder and examined the ceiling. No trace of blood or anything else could she find.

Deciding that she must have scratched her arm, she again sat down at her sewing. She could hear someone singing, and she thought it was some man passing on the banquette— "Mine eyes have seen the glory of the coming of the Lord . . . And his soul goes marching on."

And suddenly the slow dripping began on her arm again. While the blood splashed onto her white apron she sat there watching it, frozen with fright and horror. Then she found her voice, and she began to scream. Down the stairs and out of the house she ran, shrieking like a mad woman. Nor would she go back. Relatives packed her household effects for her and moved them to another house. They encountered no dripping blood. But when they were locking the front door, two soldiers appeared at a window—two soldiers in the old blue uniforms that the Yankee troops had worn in the War Between the States.

Who is it that peers out through the windows? Who opens

and shuts the old doors? Who sings the rolling battle hymn of the North, and tramps up and down the hall with ghostly feet?

The story is that when the War Between the States cast its dark shadow over the land, and Ben Butler came to New Orleans to strut and swagger and bluster, he ordered his officers to settle themselves in whichever mansions of the city they might choose. Captain Hugh Devers and Quartermaster Charles Cromley took over the great house on Constance street, and immediately sent for their wives. The two Boston ladies arrived in due course, and were conducted to the mansion in which their husbands were quartered. They unpacked their trunks, hired servants, and started housekeeping. All went well for a time.

When the money arrived with which to pay the Yankee bills in New Orleans, it was too great a temptation for Quartermaster Cromley. So he and Captain Devers devised a plan to divide the money and give out a story of its having been stolen. The wives, of course, were completely deceived and exceedingly worried about the missing cash.

But General Butler was not so easily hoodwinked. A spy, secreted in the Constance street house for two days, heard enough to know what had been going on, and reported accordingly. A whisper ran round, and reached the Captain's ears. After dinner that night he called the Quartermaster into the library.

"Old Ben knows we weren't robbed of that money, Charley," he said in a low tone, closing the door. "But he knows *he's* been robbed."

"I was afraid of it," Cromley replied. "Careful as we were, there are too many eyes and ears. We ought to have waited a while—only one never knows what's going to happen these days. What had we better do?"

"There's only one thing left to do," Captain Devers said. "They'll arrest us tomorrow—you know how gentle and sympathetic Old Ben is likely to be. It's disgrace for the girls and cold lead for us, Charley. We've been fools, but that can't be helped now. We're all supposed to dance at the Colonel's house tonight. We'll send the girls on ahead, to wait for us at the Fenlons' house—tell them we'll join them there in an hour if we can—and if not, to go on to the dance. They've gone with the Fenlons before when we couldn't get away. We'll get rid of black Sam. And then . . . we'll go together."

The other nodded. In an hour's time the ladies were on their way to the Fenlons' house. Black Sam had been sent to town on an errand.

The two officers dressed themselves immaculately in fatigue uniform, striving to act cheerful and unconcerned. "Mine eyes have seen the glory of the coming of the Lord—" sang Captain Devers, adjusting his sword carefully. The Quartermaster went on with the verse. "And his soul goes marching on," he finished, his tongue dry in his mouth.

They were in the second upstairs room, and they bolted the door and stretched themselves side by side on the white bed. There was a wrinkle in the heavy lace counterpane and Cromley reached down and straightened it.

"Polish your boots, Charley?" Devers asked, laying his head squarely in the center of the pillow.

"Yes," the Quartermaster answered. "They look pretty fair."

They raised their heavy army revolvers, and each muzzle pressed a man's side, just over his heart.

"Good-bye, Hugh," the Quartermaster said steadily.

"Good-bye, Charley," the Captain returned. "Now . . . ready—aim—fire!"

Two shots, so close together that they sounded like one. The room grew very still. The smoke from the revolvers rose to the ceiling and hung there like a silver veil. Drip, drip, drip . . . through the mattress . . . thick red drops . . . onto the floor . . . drip, drip, drip. . . .

They found them in the morning, side by side on the lace-covered bed, cold and still and stiff. And though they have been buried three-quarters of a century and more, they still inhabit the Constance street house. Still they walk and walk, opening the old doors and peering out through the old windows . . . "Mine eyes have seen the glory of the coming of the Lord. . . ."

# (*1852*)     *The Specter on the Shell Road*

Early in September of 1852 word went round the bawdy houses
that a ghost was haunting the Bienville street Shell Road. In
those days, the outer reaches of Bienville street were flanked by
swamps and thickets. Oyster shells had been laid down; and
these, crushed by hoof and iron tire, made an acceptable
roadbed.

That section was, at the time, given over at night chiefly
to lights o' love who drove out in carriages for the purpose of
drumming up trade. It had come to be a notorious stretch of
road, referred to by male Orleanians with grins and knowing
winks and tittering references to Tiny Toots or Big Annie or
French Lou.

The cabmen, jogging along with their painted and perfumed fares, began to look twice at the dim, approaching lights
of other cabs. It was rumored that such lights frequently proved
to be no cab at all, but a being which swayed across the white
shells with ever-increasing malevolence, frightening even the
tired cab-horses and sending the vehicle into the ditch.

The story was that this white-swathed apparition haunted
the spot where a certain old man had met death at the hands
of robbers the preceding winter. This man was known to be a
Californian who had reaped a fortune during the great gold
rush of Forty-nine. He had been reputed to carry his wealth
mostly on his person, and the thugs decoyed him to this lonely
spot and murdered him.

The strange part of it was that shortly after the discovery
of the body it disappeared. Though a thorough search was

instituted, the mystery was still unsolved. Lacking the physical evidence of the crime, the authorities were powerless to proceed with the case. The thugs were still at large, and likely to be until apprehended for some other atrocity.

The murdered man had been, at the time of his death, about seventy-four years old. His throat was cut from ear to ear. Now it was said that he appeared nightly on the Shell Road, waving ghostly arms and pointing ever to his bloody, gaping throat, moving across the road and back again, across and back, across and back, like a wild animal pacing its cage.

The loose women who saw it immediately went into wild paroxysms of hysterics. The cabmen whipped up their snorting nags and made for town. The madams cursed the returning whores and called them drunken fools.

And then one Wednesday night a truculent policeman, Officer Bolonsa, drove out along the Bienville street Shell Road, armed with two pistols and a club and a bottle of holy water, and arrested an escaped lunatic whom he found wandering on the edge of the ditch. This was the famous ghost, Officer Bolonsa laughed—a poor, addled creature who fancied he owned all the land between the river and the woods and was merely trying to chase off "trespassers."

But, it appears, even with the lunatic locked up, the ghost with the bloody throat continued to haunt the Shell Road. And there are those in this old city who can tell you why.

It seems that, early in 1851, there was a druggist's clerk named Mentor Quigley. At that time cooks used vanilla beans for flavoring, along with orange and lemon peel. It was the dream of young Quigley to perfect extracts of these which would be of commercial value. His wife, Délie, was a young Frenchwoman who had assisted with the pastry-making at one of the better restaurants. She was as enthusiastic about the flavoring extract venture as was her husband. The chief problem was lack of money.

Still, the matter of formulating the extracts was not yet wholly settled in Quigley's mind. He was in the habit of taking long walks on Sunday—his only day off—in order to work out certain details and arrive, if possible, at some definite plan.

On a certain Sunday he started out Bienville street. He

was so occupied with his own reflections that he did not realize how far he had gone until he heard a great crunching roar beside him. It was a heavy carriage with a span of bays coming along the Shell Road. The carriage tires grated and rumbled, and the horses' hoofs smote the shells with a loud clatter. Quigley kept to the path, heedless of the ribald greetings of the female passengers.

As darkness began to close down the young man was still walking towards the woods, his thoughts busy with chemical formulae. Suddenly he heard a shuffle of feet behind him, and something struck his head a heavy blow. He went down without a cry.

When he came to himself it was very dark. He sat up, wondering where he was and what had happened. His head ached blindingly, and he reached for a handkerchief. Every pocket was turned inside out, and his keys and wallet were missing, as well as his watch and ring.

As he sat there in the wet grass he saw someone coming down the path with a lantern. The man paused and bent over him, and Quigley could see that he was very old. His eyes were a sparkling blue, and his beard was white as wool.

"Better git up, young feller," he advised. "Yer head's bleedin'. Been in a fight?"

"No . . . no," Quigley responded, his tongue slow and heavy. "I . . . I've been robbed, I think. I was walking along, and something hit me."

"H'm," grunted the old man, holding his lantern high. "You don't tell me! The cussed world gits tougher and tougher, don't it? You look kind o' peaked. H'ist yourself up and we'll git you to my shack. It's a piece up the road. You lean on me, young feller."

Though his head swam giddily, the drug clerk managed to reach the shack with his rescuer. The old man dressed his wound, sponging it with neat alcohol.

Then he asked, "What might yer name be, young feller?"

"Mentor Quigley," was the response.

"You don't tell me!" beamed the old man. "I don't calc'late yer father's name is Matthew, is it?"

"Yes, it is."

"You don't tell me! But I don't calc'late yer grandfather was named Israel, was he, now?"

"Why, yes," Mentor smiled. "And he had a brother named Adam."

"Well," chuckled the old man, "I calc'late I'm Adam, then. That's my name—Adam Quigley. I had an only brother named Israel, and he had an only son named Matthew. Jumped from Genesis right through all the kings and commandments to the New Testament. Israel and me, we was both raised in Connecticut. But he went south and I went into Californy. I've only been here in this town about a month. But I calc'lated I'd begin lookin' him up purty soon. A feller's got to git rested up some, after a hard trip like me and Nelly took. Nelly's my burro—come here, Nelly, and meet a relation."

From a corner of the shack ambled a little burro, soft-eyed and long-eared. She nuzzled against the old man's sleeve, and he scratched her neck affectionately.

"How's Israel?" he inquired.

"Oh, Grandfather died more than fifteen years ago," replied Mentor. "In 1836, it was. I remember I was nine."

"You don't tell me! And Matthew—is he dead, too? I've never seen him, of course."

"He's still living. But he's pretty bad off. He has a cancer on his face."

"You don't tell me! Well, I may outlive the whole cussed family yet." His blue eyes twinkled, and he chuckled as though he had just cracked a huge joke.

Such was the beginning of the reunion of the Quigleys. Old Adam spent many a joyous hour regaling his afflicted nephew with tales of his travels and his California prospecting. He would chuckle gleefully and observe, "Nelly and me, we done purty well out there in Californy. Purty well."

But he never told how much he had made, nor where he kept it. And none of them ever asked him. When he came to spend the day with them, as he frequently did, Délie made the crab gumbo of which he was so fond.

"I've et goats and I've et woodchucks and I've et slippery elm and wild onions," he would ruminate. "I never did think I'd git as low as crabs—but, damn it, I like the cussed things!

I never was much on fish, but nobody couldn't resist Délie's core-beyond. I calc'late I'd walk twenty mile for a mess o' that."

So, if he came to visit on a Friday, court bouillon he had. Often he stepped over to the big family Bible on the parlor table and left a ten-dollar bill tucked in the Gospel According to Saint Matthew. Mentor always handed it to his father, who duly thanked old Adam. And Matthew always gave it to Délie, who he knew would put it to good use.

One day Adam confided to Mentor, "Matthew ain't goin' to last long. So I calc'late all I've got'll go to you, young feller, when my time comes. Don't go countin' on it, though—I may live to bury the whole cussed kit and caboodle of the Quigleys."

He flatly refused to come and live with them.

"I'm an outdoor critter," he chuckled. "I like to feel the grass under me and see the stars over me. That's what Nelly likes, too. Me and Nelly, we bunk together. She ain't got so low as to be likin' crabs and fish-messes, same as I do—but I calc'late she'd eat 'em if I was to offer 'em to her."

One day in December, Mentor read in the newspaper that an old Californian by the name of Adam Quigley had been decoyed down the Shell Road and murdered for his money. It went on to tell of the disappearance of the body before the arrival of the police. Two men swore they found the old man lying beside the roadway with his throat cut from ear to ear. They knew the spot exactly, for workers had the day before finished repairing a bad place in the road.

But the police could find no trace whatever of the body. They searched the shack. Nelly, the little burro, lay dead behind it with her head almost severed. There was nothing in the shack except a few tin dishes, a small stove, a bench, a rude bunk, and a battered old felt hat.

Matthew went to the police immediately, but there was nothing more to be done. He himself went to the shack later, and searched every inch of the premises. He found nothing.

Just once had old Adam referred to his money. That was to Mentor, after a Friday dinner, when they were sitting on the gallery outside Matthew's room. A mocking bird was singing in a fig tree.

"Some day I calc'late to bury my gold," the old prospector had chuckled, patting his stomach. "I've got a purty good idee where, but I've never told nobody 'ceptin' the beetles and the cussed little angleworms. Nelly knows, of course, but she's part o' me. They's a mockin' bird in a cypress tree back of my shack—he wrastles with me night and day to git my secret out o' me, but he ain't goin' to git it. I'm fair lined with that cussed gold, young feller—but I ain't tellin' nobody nothin'.''

Once when Mentor had called at the shack, the old man had jerked his thunb towards the jug of alcohol sitting on the floor by the bunk.

" 'Tain't to drink," he grinned, his face puckered with mirth. "It's for hardenin' purposes. You'll know some day—I calc'late to tell you when I git ready. Alky's fine to keep yer hide like a cussed leather saddle-flap."

Mentor remembered these things now, but they made no more sense than they had before.

Then came the tales of an apparition on the Bienville street Shell Road. Terrified beholders spoke of a bloody throat, slashed from ear to ear. The Thing appeared at the spot where the two men claimed to have found Adam Quigley's body.

Mentor Quigley began to wonder. Délie's time was occupied with caring for her sick father-in-law, and he hated to bother her with speculations regarding a ghost. Then Officer Bolonsa captured the lunatic, and Mentor was thankful he had not mentioned the matter to his busy wife.

But he was not satisfied. What had become of his grand-uncle's body? He entertained no doubts about the murder. Old Adam had, of course, been done to death for his money. And some day the body would be found. There was real grief in Mentor's heart, for the old man had been lovable in many ways.

Again came persistent rumors of a ghost along the Shell Road. Mentor Quigley consulted with Délie, and one Sunday she got a colored girl to stay and take care of Matthew. They hired a horse and buggy from a livery stable, and packed a lunch in a big basket. Délie told the Negress that she was tired out and a spell in the country would do her good. A large square of heavy sailcloth was folded and put with the basket, along with a lantern and a paper-wrapped spade.

They drove out the Shell Road until they came to the abandoned shack. They led the horse back into the underbrush and tied him. Waiting in the shack until nearly midnight, they finally started walking along the path by the road, carrying the unlighted lantern. Often they stepped aside almost to the ditch, as a carriageful of boisterous merrymakers passed. Occasionally a cab trailed slowly along, a painted face peering from the window, a discordant ditty drifting out upon the night.

"This is the place, I think," Mentor whispered, as they paused near a hump in the road. "The road menders left this. The shells seem newer here, too."

The night was pitch-dark, and the two huddled close together. They could hear a vehicle coming from the direction of the woods, and voices in high converse.

"Another pack of streetwalkers with their night's catch, I suppose," remarked Mentor.

The carriage approached, and suddenly stopped. The horses strained backwards, plunging madly when the driver wielded his whip. The women shrieked and the men cursed. Out in the roadway, directly in front of the team, a white shape was moving. It shone clearly, as though the moonlight were upon it—but there was no moonlight. Back and forth it wove, across the white shells. There seemed no movement of lower limbs—just that weird gliding, across and back again.

The white-bearded shape held its head well up. The throat was slashed from ear to ear, gaping horribly, the blood pouring out in a red torrent—yet it never soaked into the draperies or the snowy beard, nor stained the white shells of the road. But a stench came down the wind, as of a thousand corpses rotting on a battlefield.

Suddenly the apparition seemed to melt into the shells. One moment it was there, and the next moment it had vanished utterly. A mocking bird started to trill in a nearby tree, and the carriage went careening townward. Délie Quigley clutched at her husband's sleeve.

"It was old Uncle Adam!" she gasped. "They killed him,

Mentor—and I believe they buried him right here under this hump in the road!"

"But this hump was here before that," he rejoined.

"Then it should have been worn down level by now," she persisted.

"Supposing we wait here for an hour or two," Mentor suggested. "Everybody will have passed by that time. Then we'll light the lantern and look carefully."

The mocking bird was still singing. After a time the moon rose, and the road grew deserted. They held the lantern close to the shells at the edge of the road.

"Look!" whispered Délie, pointing. "Here is a line of little black beetles . . . Where are they going? Down into the shells. Don't you remember what Uncle Adam said about telling the beetles?"

"I'm going to dig up the hump in the road," said Mentor.

The moonlight was bright as day now. The shells came off in quick spadefuls. Under them the dirt was surprisingly loose and light. Perhaps two feet down, the spade struck something hard—a steel box. It was so heavy that it took the two of them to hoist it out.

When they pried it open they found it packed solidly with gold coins. A folded paper rested on top of them: "I, Adam Quigley, being of sound and disposing mind, memory and understanding, do hereby give and bequeath unreservedly and forever to my grandnephew, Mentor Quigley, and his wife, Délie Dupree Quigley, jointly, all that is in this box, and whatever else I may die possessed of, including Nelly, my burro. Also the mocking bird that sings in the cypress tree, if they can catch him, and all the bettles and angleworms in the world."

And there was Adam's scrawl of a signature, followed by those of six witnesses. The date was a month before the murder.

"He did it up brown," Mentor observed. "And I happen to know that at least three of these men left town right after Uncle Adam was killed. H'm . . . I wonder if the other three left, too? Hoodlums aren't the only ones out committing murder."

"But," Délie returned, "they didn't find the box. He must have buried it right away after making his will—and they never would think to look under the Shell Road. Dig a little farther, Mentor. Maybe. . . ."

They hid the box under the long grass near the ditch, and Mentor resumed his digging. Again the spade struck something hard—a man's heavy boot, perhaps three feet away from where the box had lain. And, after a time, they unearthed all that was left of Adam Quigley.

"The newly repaired road," Délie mused, turning her face away as Mentor heaved the mud-caked body up onto the square of sailcloth. "But they didn't find his gold. It looks as though he was guarding it, even then. They never dreamed how close they were to it."

The night was nearly done.

"We must hurry," Mentor warned, spading the dirt and shells back into place. "We have still to get *this* into the shack. I never thought a body would be so heavy. It's like lead."

They gazed at each other queerly a moment. So heavy. . . .

"What are we going to do?" Mentor asked, when they were safely in the shack, with the bundle wrapped in sailcloth. They had stowed the box into the back of the buggy, and covered it with a linen duster. "We must remember that this is the body of a dead man. No matter how innocent we are or how truthfully we might explain, we surely would be accused of his murder. Otherwise, it would be argued, how could we possibly have known that he was buried under the Shell Road? There are at least six persons who know that he made a will in our favor. They would be the first to accuse us, especially if they were the ones who put him out of the way. Now, what is the best thing for us to do?"

A breeze shook the door, like someone knocking. Délie opened it, her face blenching as a small sheet of discolored paper blew in. Mentor picked it up. It was the flyleaf of an old book. On it, in faded ink, was written, "Under the skin some men are yellow. Look under the skin for . . ." There had been more, but water had washed the words away.

"Yellow," pondered Mentor Quigley. "Could that mean anything? Oh, it's just a bit of paper that's been blowing around. It doesn't mean anything, of course."

But as he tossed it into a corner, the breeze shook the door again, angrily, impatiently.

"He was so heavy, you said . . ." murmured Délie.

"Go outside, Délie," Mentor growled. "I'll find out if there's anything . . . to see." She knew it was not temper that made him so abrupt.

After a long time he called to her.

"I found out," he said. "It was a terrible thing . . . He must have done it safely by means of the alcohol. He had slit his own skin into little sections—hundreds of them—from shoulders to knees, wherever he could reach, and slipped gold coins underneath it. Then he had sewed the slits up again. He was like hundreds of small pockets, leathery and tough. That's what made him so terribly heavy. I've taken out all the coins and tied them in the horse's feed bag. The body's light now. But we can't leave him here, Délie, and we can't bury him in the swamp. He's Uncle Adam, you know."

They spoke together for some minutes. Each could hear a faint chuckling sound, over by the bundle of sailcloth. They gazed at each other aghast.

It's the wind," Mentor said.

"In the cypress tree," added Délie.

But each knew it was neither the wind nor the cypress tree. Suddenly Délie spoke again. She had a plan.

"How did you think of it?" asked Mentor.

"It came to me . . . when I heard the chuckling," she replied.

"But you cannot walk all the way in to town," he objected.

"Oui—I walk much farther than that at home every day, my dear," she smiled.

"But without a hat. . . ."

"I can say it blew into the lake."

So the buggy started toward town. The side-curtains were buttoned on, and Mentor was driving. Beside him was a figure wrapped in a linen duster, wearing Délie's hat . . . but its face was only sailcloth, and the laprobe was tucked securely around its awful knees. . . .

Mentor drove home, turning into the yard and stopping close to the back door. He tied the horse, and lifted out the still figure. As the first streaks of dawn showed in the still sky, he carried the long bundle up to the garret. Then he went down and got the box and the sack. He locked the garret door and put the key into his pocket.

An hour later he paid the colored girl and told her she might go—that Mrs. Quigley was very tired and was sleeping late. He sent a note to the drugstore by a neighbor, saying he could not get down that day because his father was much worse. During the forenoon Délie arrived, and he took the horse and buggy back to the livery stable.

That day he sealed old Adam's body in sheet lead.

Matthew died the next week. Délie laid him out herself, as was the custom in those days. When she and Mentor had lifted him into the coffin, she asked the neighbors and friends to go home. Mentor would sit up with his father that last night —he wished to do so. The poor face had been covered with a napkin, so that none could see how the cancer had eaten it away.

And that night, Adam and Matthew were housed in one coffin, and it was sealed. Délie could not bear, she said, that anyone should see her father-in-law's terrible face at the funeral.

Just at dawn a misty shape gathered beside the dead man . . . chuckling, chuckling . . . and then it disappeared.

"It was . . ." began Mentor.

"It was Uncle Adam," Délie declared fearlessly. "He is pleased at what we have done—and that is all I care. He would have enjoyed fooling them. It is our own business, but I should want him to be pleased."

"The drugstore is for sale," Mentor nodded. "I shall buy it soon—but not too soon. I have perfected my formulae for the extracts. Now we can launch them. But we must remember that Uncle Adam dug for his gold, and we dug for it. It was hardly and dangerously come by both times. We must respect it."

"Oui," agreed Délie, satisfied. "That is what would please Uncle Adam."

Every time they visited the cemetery they left double wreaths at the tomb, remembering two men where they were supposed to be remembering but one.

After a long, long time, they had names carved in the marble slab at the front of the tomb. You can see the place today, a trifle sunken and surrounded by small, friendly ferns. Among the names are these two: MATTHEW QUIGLEY—*born 17 July, 1803, died 20 October, 1852.* ADAM QUIGLEY—*born 8 March, 1777, died 27 December, 1851.*

And they say that when the breeze rises, just before dawn, there is a great chuckling in the little chinaball tree which grows close by.

# (*1893*)    *Le Néant*


Aubévie Brou walked slowly down Royal street on a night late in May, 1893. He crossed Esplanade and made his way to his own door, in the middle of the square.

His twin sister, Edvige, a maiden lady of fifty-six, was dozing by the window in her cretonne-covered chair. Auguste, the tomcat, dozed beside her, plump and sleek and tiger-striped.

Edvige roused with a faint snort as her brother entered. Auguste yawned and stretched and blinked an eye in welcome. The china clock on the mantel struck one crisp, accusing note.

"Mon Dieu!" the lady exclaimed, clutching at the black lace shawl which draped her ample shoulders. "How you frightened me, Aubévie! Is it then so late?"

"Monsieur almost managed it tonight," her brother replied, seating himself with a sigh and mopping his damp forehead. "Twenty of the guests arrived—I saw them myself. And then, as usual, some meddlers sent for the police. I am of a disgust."

"Ah, poor Monsieur!" nodded Edvige, adjusting the artificial brown ringlets which adorned her broad brow. "It must be a year now, and never a moment's rest. He must be of a weariness. Every day I pray for his success—he should have quiet rest by now, the poor man."

"You say truly 'the poor man.'" Aubévie sighed, blowing his nose. "Twenty friends—only five more to come. Monsieur waiting, the cards waiting—and then only the small word, the imperceptible sign—and a lifetime's misery wiped away. But no, it is too much to expect!"

"The terrible police!" moaned Edvige, struggling with her

great fan and dropping it in the midst of Auguste's round stomach. "Mon pauvre enfant—I am so clumsy! Come, come, Auguste, mon petit chou, you are not quite killed. In a moment you shall have a saucer of crevettes. Tell me, Aubévie, what happened?"

"Monsieur was summoning his guests—the twenty-five who were at that first astounding game. They were coming through the dark, from wherever they are—I counted them, twenty of them—and Monsieur waiting at the window with his lighted candle, his heart calling and crying to the girl he adored—ah, poor Monsieur!"

"And you spoke of the police—"

"Nom de Dieu, oui! Pardonnez-moi, Edvige, but my tongue is full of fury, as well as my heart. The police came, stamping and shouting and banging with a stick—you know how they do."

"Non, Aubévie, I never have seen the police bang with a stick—naturally. But, all the same, it is a pity that poor Monsieur Tounoir cannot be let alone, even when he has been dead more than a year. It would seem that the police could be on a better business."

"Humph—they understand nothing of these more delicate matters. Monsieur will have to be trying again and again. And if someone desires to rent the house, it will make the long and dreary postponement."

"No one will desire to rent the house, mon frère," soothed Edvige. "It is far too big and much too dirty by this time. You have never even had it dusted. I always have said you should."

"Ah," grunted Aubévie hopefully. "Doubtless . . . doubtless."

Truly, the night had seen strange doings. The day before had been Sunday, and there had been a neighborhood dancing party at a house on Royal street, between Sainte-Ann and Orleans. Shortly after midnight some of the guests were on their way home, passing the massive old mansion known as the Lalaurie house, at the uptown river corner of Royal and Hospital (now Governor Nicholls).

One of them glanced upwards and saw the tall white

figure of a man standing in one of the windows on the second floor, with a lighted candle in his hand. As the rest of the party stared, white shapes began to gather on the balcony, and the sound of hurrying feet came from within the house.

The woman who saw the figure screamed, as something clutched her arm and jostled her off the banquette. The air seemed to move with rushing forms, although nothing could be seen on the ground floor. The windows were close-shuttered, and the great front door was guarded by tall iron gates.

"Oh!" cried another of the ladies. "There's somebody in the haunted house! I can hear them groaning—can't you? Maybe somebody's been murdered in there! We ought to call the police."

They did call the police, but not until the next day. Sergeant Schomaker of the Third Precinct Station detailed Officer Perrier to watch the place. At a little after nine o'clock at night, the policeman began to hear strange noises within the house. Someone was groaning heavily, as though in the last stages of torment. Footsteps raced hither and yon. Suddenly a thin beam of light glowed above the curving staircase.

Officer Perrier ran across the street so as to obtain a view of the second story, above the balcony railing. He saw a white figure standing at a window holding a lighted candle. The face was waxen, and long wisps of white hair straggled about the sunken cheeks. The eyes glared out into the night like lamps, peering this way and that. The officer shivered involuntarily, but gathered himself and hurried back across the street. A crowd was beginning to form.

"Lalaurie ghosts or no Lalaurie ghosts," he grunted to himself, "I'm going into that there house! If hell's loose, I'll just have to take the consequences. But I'd about as soon face the Devil as that old bugger up there in the window! He looks too much like that old Tounoir what died there last year."

Setting his jaws, he pounded on the iron gates with his nightstick. To his surprise, they swung ajar. The door opened at his touch. He entered and started up the stairs, the crowd at his heels.

As he reached the top of the staircase, just at his left, he saw what looked like a roomful of weaving white shapes. A fire was crackling in the fireplace, though the night was warm. The figures moved and swayed like heavy fog. Their eyes were like fish eyes, round and blank and unblinking. A queer, nauseating odor pervaded the place, like dry bones newly dug.

"Hi you, git out o' this!" Officer Perrier bellowed, his handkerchief held tightly to his nose. "Do yer masqueradin' some place else—this here house is private property and you're trespassin'!"

The shapes gathered into a white clump, and began to ooze through the door leading onto a rear gallery.

"I'll cart you off to jail, that's what I'll do!" Perrier went on, realizing that it was his job to make an arrest whenever and wherever possible. "Come back here, you in the sheets!"

But the last white shape was through the gallery door. Pell-mell went Perrier in pursuit—down the stairs, into the old courtyard and out the gate onto Hospital street. He could see something white in the distance. Along Hospital street he sped, turning on Chartres—a square on Barracks, and over onto Decatur. Seeing nothing suspicious there, he paused for breath.

Ah, there was a man running! Perrier caught up with him and grabbed him by the collar.

"Got you!" he yelled. "Go breakin' into houses, will you? What did you do with your sheet? Where did your pals get to? Talk, I tell you!"

The man protested that he had no sheet and no pals, that his name was Charles Rousset, and that he never had stepped foot into the haunted house on Royal and Hospital until he followed the policeman in, to see what was going on.

"Well, you've saw," Perrier told him, and marched him off to jail.

The next day Judge De Lebretonne sentenced Rousett to serve twenty days or pay a fine of ten dollars—for disturbing the peace and violating Ordinance 5046. But the man still maintained that he had followed the officer into the haunted house, and that he knew nothing whatever about any persons who might have gathered there. . . .

Let us go back to the year 1822.

We should see a beautiful drawing room in Paris, brilliantly lighted, with perhaps two dozen people playing at cards.

The laughter was gay, the gowns were rich, the jewelry was
magnificent. The men were courtly and clever, the women
were beautiful and accomplished. Probably no choicer group
of minds and manners could have been gathered in all the city.

In an alcove two young men were discussing an all-im-
portant subject. One was twenty-three and the other was
twenty-four.

"I still maintain that it is I whom Mademoiselle Avequin
favors," declared Étienne Tounoir, who was the younger.

"We shall see," smiled Armand Lestauche loftily. "I am so
certain it is I whom she favors that I am willing to risk a
game of cards on it. If I win—which I shall—you must agree
not to pay court to my little Leda. Should I lose—which is not
possible—I shall abide by the same terms. This continued
bickering is useless and undignified."

"It were more undignified to play cards for a lady's favor,"
sneered Tounoir. "I would not insult her by such an arrangement. There is nothing to prevent my asking for her heart
and hand at once—and winning them both."

"Nothing whatever," sneered the other, in his turn, "except
the fact that your father is suspected of selling Government
secrets."

"Ah," rejoined young Tounoir in a voice of ice, "you know
you speak a lie—my father has already been vindicated. I will
play your damned game of cards, and watch you lose your
lady!"

They parted the curtains and entered the drawing room.

"I am sorry I spoke as I did of your father, Étienne,"
Lestauche said. "I did not mean it—you know my miserable
temper. Say that you forgive me—or, rather, as evidence of
resumed friendship, let us play the game we invented—the
little game we used to call Néant. What do you say?"

Tounoir gazed at his companion a speculative moment.
It had ever been so—sharp words, a hateful retort, and abject
apology. However, was not this last a degree too much? . . .

"Very well," agreed Étienne slowly. "Néant it shall be.
Deal the cards."

Every hand went against him. At the end, he was the loser

by many points. But he had lost more than the game. His opponent's dark eyes were sparkling with triumph.

"Leda is mine!" Armand said, under his breath, as he arose.

"If she will have you," added Étienne dryly.

He went home at once, striving to realize that honor forbade him ever to speak again to lovely Mademoiselle Leda Avequin, except to exchange the vaguest commonplaces. So sweet, so desirable, so responsive—how could he make up his life without her? One hope alone remained—she might not find Armand Lestauche to her taste.

The days which followed were empty and difficult. Leda married Armand that same year.

"Néant," Étienne brooded bitterly. "The little game which means 'nothing'—because in those days we had nothing to lose. But through it I have lost everything. It is my life that the word now stands for!"

Paris became a torture to him. Always his carriage seemed to meet the one carrying the Lestauches. Always they were gay and laughing. He would have wanted that, of course, seeing they had married, but. . . .

With a heavy heart he left Paris and came to New Orleans.

"I will live with the ruffians and the savages," he told himself. "Paris has cheated me of everything I would have loved to possess. It does not matter what becomes of me now."

To his amazement, he found New Orleans delightful. The men were frank and hearty and the women pretty and sensible. The houses were comfortable and he seemed welcome wherever he went.

Suddenly, the next year, he married Mademoiselle Félicie Janin, a New Orleans girl. He felt certain he never would hear again of Armand and Leda. He grew wealthy. His two daughters married happily and brilliantly. Madame his wife died in 1855. One daughter lived in Boston and one in Quebec. So he was again alone—and fifty-six years of age.

His married life had been tranquil. He had had little sense of happiness or unhappiness. A home and family had been his. Now he had an empty house, a large fortune, and very little else. Yes . . . he had still the beautiful memory of Leda Avequin.

He began to pretend to himself that she never had married Armand Lestauche. That she was still girlish and lovely, ready to respond to his caresses. He took to playing Réussite, which is very like the English game of patience and our American solitaire. Always he pretended that Leda was looking over his shoulder, giving him enchanting little pointers now and then about the cards.

"I am an old fool," he would say to himself sometimes. "Leda is a grandmère by this time, and ugly as sin."

But in his heart he never acknowledged that Leda could possibly grow ugly. To him, she still dressed in the fashion of 1822. He went over each charming detail—her blonde curls, her delicate hands, her small lace handkerchief, her tiny slippers, her filmy flounces and the little rosebuds she affected, her dainty fan, the faint perfume she used, the blue stars which were her eyes, the intoxication which was her laugh, the heavenly benediction which was her voice.

And one morning he knew he must go back. The ache rent his spirit asunder.

"Hélas!—one can stand only so much," he groaned within himself. "Voila qu'on m'appelle—always I hear her voice! Oui, vraiment, I am an old fool, and daily I grow more foolish. But I am alone and I am human. Perhaps when I see her, with three chins and a dozen sons and daughters, I shall be cured. Maybe my thoughts will then dwell more ardently on Félicie, who stayed slender and amiable to her last hour."

Tounoir sold his house, and Dominique packed his trunks. The voyage took six weeks. But at last he trod the streets of Paris. It was a new Paris. He had been gone so long . . . thirty-three years. He arrived on March sixteenth, 1856, as the city was celebrating the birth of the prince imperial, son of Napoleon III and the Empress Eugénie. There were strange new customs. All of the old rendezvous had changed hands. The entertainments seemed to him bizarre and flat. The gaiety sounded forced.

He could not find the Lestauches. They seemed to have vanished from the earth. At last a new acquaintance told him, with a titter, that they had been separated for years. Nobody knew where they lived now—maybe Lucerne, maybe Vienna, possibly Venice. Once Armand had gone to that terrible South America. Once Leda had spent a season in St. Petersburg, where some prince was mad about her.

And then Tounoir saw her entering a shop. Could it be possible? . . . She was dainty as ever, a trifle faded, but he would have known her anywhere. And yet—she was nearly fifty-four years old! She was wearing black velvet and pearls. He caught himself wondering what she used on her hair, to keep it the same burnished gold it had been thirty-three years earlier. . . .

He followed her into the shop. Would she remember him? She did not. He even had to explain a trifle, humiliating though it was. Thirty-three thousand years would not have wiped from his heart the vivid memory of her.

"Oui," she smiled presently. "I think now I remember. There was some scandal or other concerning votre père, I believe. And you went away and lost your fortune—that was miserable luck, wasn't it?"

"Oh, but . . ." Étienne checked himself. She believed he was beggared. Very well. Let her continue to believe so. These women were always after money. Doubtless she had grown like the rest of them. He could discern a speculative glint in her blue eyes. No, he would not invite her to lunch . . . just yet. She told him she lived in a small apartment on the rue Sevin —at that time a most exclusive and outrageously expensive thoroughfare. Leda must have money . . . or else . . . Étienne checked himself again.

She was at home on Tuesdays, she added. What was the matter? Were his clothes provincial? He was glad they were. If she had know how rich he was, he reflected, she would have fished for an invitation to dinner and the opera that very night. Was he growing cynical and sour? This was Leda, whom he had worshiped from the first moment he ever saw her— and here he was analyzing her, pulling off her wings as though she had been a moth. It was horrible. Everything was horrible.

He was giving her his address. He was glad it was so modest a place. Let her think he was poor. He could feel the sweat trickling down his spine . . . There never had been any children, she was telling him, warming a trace. Armand always had disliked children. They had lived together only a year— a very long and unpleasant year.

"I remember you well now," she was saying, toying with her pearls. "At one time I fancied perhaps. . . ."

She never finished. She had not forgotten him, then. But she still twitted him about the Government scandal in which his father had briefly figured. The old raging tempest possessed Étienne Tounoir for an instant. Why had he ever come back to Paris!

The modiste was exhibiting laces for Madame's selection. The slim fingers were rippling through the filmy lengths. This one . . . this one . . . Étienne felt himself to be de trop, and made his adieux with what grace he could muster. What a hell one golden-haired woman could make of a man's life!

On Tuesday he called upon her, having sent a box of roses on before. Not too large a box.

"Ah," she told him, "you should not have wasted money on me! I expect you are going without dinners for a week, in consequence. It was sweet of you. But you must always remember that Armand is still the head of my house. We never have been divorced. I can think of you only on the sly—as I should like to think of you, that is."

Was she playing with him?—with this man whom she supposed had nothing, except the memory of her exquisite youth? He could see a network of fine lines around her eyes and mouth now. And a collar of pearls covered the once flawless throat. There were many faint wrinkles around her white knuckles. She applied rouge a bit too lavishly.

"Oui," he heard himself observing coolly, "the game of love is always amusing. Only to us middle-aged ones it occasionally seems a trifle dull, because we have played it so many times."

"I have heard," she murmured, "of a queer little game called Néant. I wish you would teach it to me."

A roaring fire leaped in Étienne Tounoir's bosom. Néant! Then she knew! She had known all along!

"Néant—what is that?" he asked smoothly.

"It is a little game where lives and destinies are tossed about like volants, bon gré, mal gré. A very cruel game, I should call it."

"A very ancient game," he said.

"And I am very ancient, too," she sighed, seeming to wither and shrivel all of a sudden.

"No, Leda," he whispered passionately, hearing footsteps in the outer corridor. "You will never be old. You were like a rose in my heart—you always will be my lovely rose. Honor and pride—they are damnable qualities! But for honor and pride, you and I would have lived a long and ideal life together, Madame!"

Well, it was said. Perhaps it was a good thing. Someone was coming in at the door. There was music starting in the other room. Voices, a burst of laughter, somebody telling a bit of ridiculous gossip.

"There are other lives . . . beyond this melancholy one," she murmured, and turned to her new guests.

Was she wise, or merely shrewd? Was her graciousness from within or was it purposeful—like everything else nowadays?

Étienne Tounoir was walking down the rue Sevin before he realized he had left Madame Lestauche's drawing room. He had not even said farewell. He must be entering his dotage, he thought.

He never went to see Leda again. The torture would have been too exquisite. He did not want a mistress. He could not make her his wife. She baffled and perplexed him.

She died that same year, on her fifty-fourth birthday. Armand died in Egypt a month later. But quietly, like a gray spider in a hole, Étienne lived in Paris thirty years longer. When he was eighty-eight he foolishly bought himself a decoration. When Grévy resigned, because of the great decoration scandal, Tounoir packed his trunks and sailed for New Orleans. He was through with Paris forever.

"She spoke of other lives," he muttered, pacing the steamer's deck. "I hope they are not all as long as this one."

He was still tall and straight and clear-eyed. He was still

enormously rich. Dominique had died years ago, and Bertin now served in his place.

When he arrived in New Orleans he purchased the musty old mansion at the corner of Royal and Hospital streets. They called it the "haunted house."

"I have been haunted for sixty-five years," he told himself grimly. "In that length of time ghosts grow monotonous."

Bertin attended him. Black Bella cooked for him. He surrounded himself with massive old rosewood and mahogany, and lived solitary. Again he took to playing Réussite. He would sit far into the night, matching his cards, and go to bed too fatigued to sleep. Nobody remonstrated with him.

Only one friend he had—Aubévie Brou, who had stopped to talk one day when Tounoir was moving into the haunted house. Brou was thirty-eight years his junior, but one could talk to him. To old Étienne, the younger man was a rare treat. Aubévie would sit for hours watching him play Réussite and never once interrupt. When conversation was in order, he proved to be an understanding soul.

Little by little, Tounoir told his friend the whole story. Brou pieced it all together, like a jigsaw puzzle, each scrap in its proper place. Then he went home and told it to Edvige. She told it only to Auguste, and that when he was sound asleep. Only one thing did the old gentleman keep to himself— the matter of the decoration which he had bought. Of that he was intensely and bitterly ashamed.

One day he said, "I have seen Armand again. I saw him last night."

"So?" Brou returned. "You dreamed, Monsieur?"

"No, I did not dream. He came to me. His ghost came to me."

"Ah, yes, I see."

"No, you do not see—you think I am old and that I imagine," the old Frenchman retorted. "But it is not so. I was sitting exactly where I am now, playing La Réussite, as usual. Armand came in at the door, smiling as he used to smile. He was young, as he was when he married Leda, and he was wearing the same sort of clothes."

"He spoke?" inquired Aubévie gently.

"Yes. He asked why I played a silly old-woman's game like Réussite. I told him it was all there was left for me to play. It seemed to hurt him. And then he said to me, 'We made a mistake, you and I, playing that last game of Néant. I did not really want the girl. I merely wished to prevent you from having her. I told her many lies—all I could think of, in fact. I told her especially that your fortune was a myth, that you cheated at cards, that you kept two mistresses, that you were in debt to everybody, that you already supported a bastard son. But she found me out. The baggages always do.' "

"He confessed that?" gasped Brou in amazement.

"Oui. I would not have believed him, only it accounted for so many things which had for years perplexed me. It answered all my questions. But there was something else. We made a bargain."

"A bargain? With a ghost?"

"Oui, with a ghost. For I myself shall be a ghost when the bargain is completed. It concerned a game of cards, but two ghosts must play it. The game is to be the old Néant, but this time there will be no cheating. We shall play—Armand's ghost and my ghost, while the ghost of Leda looks on. We shall play, and I shall win—this time for all eternity. But you—you are the one who will make it all possible."

"I?" Aubévie was all attention.

"You are vitally necessary," nodded Tounoir, adjusting his pince-nez. "I am going to bequeath this house to you. After I die, you must keep watch. That is part of the bargain—there must be a living witness. I shall come back here, from wherever I am. And every night I shall send forth a call through the universes. Every one of the twenty-five must hear—the twenty-five who witnessed that game of Néant. And they must come in answer to my summons.

"They will come here to this house, I say, and you must count them, to make sure they are all present. I myself shall always be present—I shall stand in the front window of the hall over there, and summon them."

"Oui. And then?"

"When every one of them is here, I shall send forth my last call. Armand will come then; and lastly, Leda. Think of it,

mon ami—she will be here in this house! She will stand beside
the table, and watch every card that is played. And this time
I shall win her—my soul will at last be satisfied, and Armand's
soul will at last be clean. It it not clever?"

"Very. I shall help you all I can, Monsieur."

"I am sure of it. Promise me you will keep faithful watch!"

"I promise, Monsieur."

"I shall give you a sign," the old Frenchman nodded
slowly, smiling at something which he did not put into words.
"Remember, Aubévie—I shall give you a sign."

"I shall remember," responded his friend.

Étienne Tounoir died in 1892, at the age of ninety-three.
And Aubévie Brou kept watch, as he had promised. It was not
a pleasant task. Often his hair rose stiff on his cold scalp. He
saw things and heard things which terrified and revolted him.
It seemed that the old house was a rendezvous for all the mali-
cious and unclean spirits in creation. They shrieked and
groaned and groveled and squalled and fought. They prayed
and wept and begged and babbled and booed. They laughed
and danced and staggered and swaggered and swore. They
mewed and growled and bawled and tittered and cat-called.
And, through it all, Monsieur Tounoir stood at the upper front
window, sending out his desperate silent summons for twenty-
five spirits who once long ago watched a foolish game of Néant
in Paris.

Orleanians were more terrified of the haunted house than
ever. They seemed always calling the police to put somebody
out of it, or to hunt down somebody they fancied was in it.
They told all sorts of tales about it—many of them true.

But every night, Aubévie Brou watched in the great
second drawing room. Twenty spirits had already responded.
Only five more!

One night, a week later, it rained torrents. Aubévie built
a fire in the second drawing room fireplace. In spite of umbrella
and coat, he was very wet and glad of the blaze, although the
weather was hot. The old house was damp and close.

It was nearing midnight when the tall phantom that had
stood so many nights in the window entered the room. He spoke
no word. But he set his lighted candle down on a rosewood

table, and it sputtered and went out. Behind him trailed a company of misty shapes. In spite of their eeriness, they were beautiful. They smiled and bowed and seemed to converse with one another, but not a sound escaped them.

Then came a young man, dark-eyed and debonair—but he was only a wraith, like the rest. As he seated himself at the table a girl appeared behind him, smiling over his shoulder at someone who sat opposite. And Aubévie Brou knew that that someone was the wraith of Étienne Tounoir when he was young. The fine brow, the steady eyes, the well-set head, the graceful shoulders, the shapely fingers—ah, it was something to see old Monsieur Tounoir as he had looked when he was young!

It was all a rare sight indeed. The game began. The ghostly company drew nearer. surrounding the players at the table. Aubévie counted . . . twenty-five. It was not a long game. Monsieur Tounoir held up two cards, face outward.

The other young man smiled a sickly smile and rose. He seemed very tired, as though he had been playing for a century. Then he bowed low, spread his arms open before ehe company, and vanished quite away. Dimmer and dimmer grew the twenty-five witnesses. Finally only two of them all remained —the ghost of Étienne Tounoir and the ghost of Leda. He arose and took her small hand, bowing before her. Then they glided slowly to the door.

Only once did Étienne glance back. And then Aubévie Brou saw the face of the old man he had loved lighted by so celestial a happiness that the younger man turned his eyes away, lest he intrude.

"You are sure you did not dream, Aubévie?" asked Edvige, when he told her.

"Certainly I did not dream!" Aubévie felt distinctly outraged, "I wait a year, I keep faithful vigil, I dodge the police— and then she asks me, did I dream! Mon Dieu!"

"The terrible police," Edvige sighed. "They never would understand. Tell me about the young lady, Aubévie. What was the perfume like—the perfume she used, that Monsieur always mentioned?"

"Something between musk and heliotrope, I think," her

brother replied. "I am very tired, Edvige. You will not mind if I retire at once?"

"Of course not. I shall go to bed myself as soon as I have fed poor Auguste some cream—he has had nothing since dinner, have you, mon chérubin?" She patted the sleeping cat fondly.

But in his own chamber, Aubévie Brou took from his pocket a miniature, framed in a circle of great pearls. It was a portrait of Leda Avequin, done in 1821, when she was eighteen beautiful as Juliet, sweet as Marguerite, appealing as Ophelia. He had seen it only once before the ghostly Monsieur Tounoir turned to face him, there at the last moment. Then suddenly the miniature had been in his hand. "I shall give you a sign," he had said, when he lived.

Aubévie remembered a paragraph in the old Frenchman's will.

". . . all this, on condition that said Aubévie Brou place in my dead hand the miniature which he shall find wrapped in silk in a drawer of my safe. It shall be buried with me, in my right hand . . ."

So it had been done. And now, Aubévie's fingers again touched the circle of pearls. He wondered. . . .

Turning up the lamp, he looked closely at the sweet painted features. What a lovely, lovely face it was! Then slowly it began to fade. Breathlessly he watched it disappear, pearls and all. He could hear the rain tapping softly at the blinds of his bedroom. The night was very still.

"I am glad I did not tell Edvige about the miniature in the first place," he ruminated. "One never can tell what a ghost is going to do. . . ."

## (1867-87) The Ghost of the Headless Woman

It has always been a pet human theory that love is stronger than death. On the downtown-woods corner of Josephine and Rousseau streets, a house stood for generations. And that house saw a series of gruesome incidents proving the old belief.

It was a house of two stories and an attic with dormers, built in 1840 by Charles Vesey for his bride. They went there to live in May of that year. Alice Vesey planted morning glories so that the vines crept up like lace over the windows. And she made curtains, although her husband disapproved of the frivolous ruffles on them. When she tied them back with pink ribbons, his frown was so dark that she grew silent and frightened—but she did not remove the pink bows.

Two little ones came, and Alice cooked and sewed and washed and ironed and scrubbed and scoured. Frequently her husband urged her to hire help, although he was not overly anxious to spend the extra money. He saw her growing worn and old. She had been twenty when they were married. At twenty-seven her beautiful golden-brown hair was streaked with gray and had lost its youthful luster. Her face was faded and lined, and her hands were knotted and hard. Her deep blue eyes were dull and tired—too deathly tired for twenty-seven.

But she said to herself, "I shall hire no help. If I do not have the hard work, I shall have time to think and to remember. I have put the past away, and my youth along with it. I must never remember."

For Alice Vesey, when she was Alice Miner, had loved a

man—a young man with delicate features and slender fingers and eyes which saw more than there was in heaven and earth to see. This youth, Jeminy Crews, came of a good family but refused to apply himself to the estimable pursuit of making a living. His people urged him to study for some profession. Very well—he would study art. But, his family objected: art was not a profession—it was an avocation, something to play at when more serious and important work was completed.

Jeminy went through the first few motions of studying law. For several months he attended medical school. A little later he dabbled in theology. Once he took part of a course in chemistry. But he always ended up in a small rear room on the top floor of his father's spacious house, painting frantically and sitting up all night composing verses.

That was bad enough.

Then it became known that he and Alice Miner were hopelessly in love. How could a boy like that support a wife? The Miners were of the same severe opinion. Jeminy only painted the more furiously, and covered endless sheets of foolscap with sonnets to his ladylove. Everybody said Alice was too good for a shiftless fellow who refused to work. And Alice herself began to wonder what they were going to live on.

When the Crews family finally informed Jeminy that if he didn't fit himself for some definite work that would support a wife and family he would have to find other living quarters, he was a trifle aghast. But he recovered his poise, slouched down in a deep velvet chair and took a long draft of gin. The family would come to its senses, of course. There was plenty of room. His sister-in-law and his brother James lived in the east wing. Why couldn't they be decent about it, and let Alice and him live in the south wing?

But the family refused to see things in that light. James was an architect, and paid his way. Soon he would be in his own house. Well then, Jeminy grinned, all the better—he and Alice would take James' quarters, and everything would be perfect. But even Alice seemed to be viewing him with a slightly critical eye. After all, gin was the only true friend he had. And so he grew more and more devoted to gin, while Alice and his own family grew more and more aloof.

Finally Alice told him coolly that she had decided not to marry him. He listened to her calm tones quite gracefully, acknowledging that she was doubtless wise in her decision. Only it was a pity, for they could have written such marvelous verses together . . . Oh well—nothing mattered very much these days.

So Jeminy Crews soaked himself in gin, and Charles Vesey came along and married Alice Miner. But for both of them, Alice and Jeminy, it was as though every rose had been burnt out of the world. Jeminy wrote no more verses. The pictures which he painted were weird and horrible—headless women and crawling monsters, and castles whose every frightful tower was a giant maw wherein lolled and drooled a loathsome tongue.

Alice Vesey never say Jeminy. She had not seen him for years. Not seeing him, she fancied she had forgotten. But one day she met him on the street. She was piloting her two children, and her arms were full of groceries and vegetables. Somehow she was ashamed and maddened. She had meant to spoil her hands and spoil her pink-and-white complexion. But suddenly her spirit rose in strange revolt—Jeminy would know nothing of her hard resolve: he would think of her merely as having grown into a slovenly drudge!

Although it did not matter what Jeminy might think, she stole to a mirror when she reached home. She saw there a woman who looked all of forty—a faded, discouraged woman, hard of eye and tight of lip. The picture did not please her. Jeminy had been looking well—tall and and straight and trim, his dark eyes serious and a grave sternness about his mouth. He must have stopped drinking long ago, by the looks. Nobody had told her that Jeminy had his own atelier in Paris, where his queer work had become much more than a vogue.

Alice looked down at her full skirt of coarse black cloth, and the blue gingham apron which she wore from morning till night, at her ugly hands and clumsy shoes. Where were the silks and the laces and the high French heels and the fetching little curls that she used to love?

Just once, during the weeks that followed, did she open a chest in the attic and deck herself again in girlish finery.

But her figure had grown too full for the delicate satin gown of an earlier day. The white slippers with their seed pearls were a torture. And the old face which looked out over the dainty, knife-pleated lace at the throat was a scourge and a mockery. Alice stuffed the clothes hastily back into the chest and banged down the lid.

But up there in the still attic, where the dormer windows let in narrow shafts of light, she wanted to say things. There were beautiful, tempestuous phrases to which her tongue longed to give utterance. Her spirit was full to the brim.

So she set a great wooden box on end before a dark corner, drawing the old chest behind it in grateful seclusion. A candle, a pot of ink and a quill, a little stack of white paper—and she was writing the verses she had not dared to formulate even when Jeminy Crews was helping her to build a house of dreams.

Every day she went there while Charles Vesey was at his office in town. The verses she wrote were not good poetry. They were only the outpourings of a starved and miserable heart. One day, grown bolder than usual, she penned a passionate letter to Jeminy Crews. She did not intend ever to send it to him. But the temptation to write it was greater than she could withstand. And that was the day Charles Vesey drove home early and found her there, among all her verses of adoration and desire.

The War Between the States flared and raged and subsided. Others came to live in the Vesey house. Twenty years after that ardent letter was written, a girl by the name of Wilhelmina Walter climbed the stairs to the upper chamber to make the beds. Suddenly she saw a woman standing directly in front of her—a mature woman dressed in a full dark skirt, and wearing a blue gingham apron. The hands were fumbling with a quill pen and a pad of white paper, fluttering and writing as though in great alarm lest some important message be not expressed. But above the low collar of the coarse bodice there was no head! The phantom moved towards the girl, who fled shrieking down the stairs. That was in 1867.

In 1887, Katie Lanegan, a young bride, was one day ascending the stairs with a pitcher of water. When she reached the second floor she saw coming towards her the same headless woman—full dark skirt, blue gingham apron, and the pad and quill pen, as though she were writing. Screaming in terror, Mrs. Lanegan dropped her pitcher of water and ran from the house.

In 1907, a girl of seventeen, named Alma Valentine, who was working for a Mrs. Messina at the time, was told to hang the last of the day's washing in one of the dormer windows in the attic. She reached the top of the steep stairs with her basket, and there she saw the headless woman coming forth from a corner. The ghost glided into the shaft of light which slanted from the narrow window. The girl noticed the full black skirt and blue gingham apron, and the hands busy with their pen and pad, writing something which seemed urgent.

But Alma did not wait to see what might be written on the pad. The clothes basket tumbled onto the attic floor, while she plunged down the narrow stairs and out onto the street. Her shrieks brought the neighbors running. Controlling her hysterics as best she could, she told them what she had seen—what she still saw, for that matter, for the headless phantom had followed her and was weaving in and out among the assembled women, as though struggling vainly to make them understand something or other.

Informed of this, several of them rushed home for holy water, and sprinkled it liberally on Alma and the banquette and the stairs and wherever the girl declared she had seen the apparition moving. The neighbors were unable to see the headless woman, although Alma saw her quite distinctly for more than an hour.

What was the message the phantom wished to impart? If it were a warning, there may have been reason why it should have been heeded. Wilhelmina Walter married, and died young. Mrs. Lanegan died soon after seeing the headless woman. Alma Valentine was seduced by the grocer's clerk and died in childbirth . . . Or was it merely that Alice Vesey came back to find Jeminy Crews, and tell him that she loved him still?

Although each witness described the apparition minutely, giving precisely the same picture, not one of them had previously heard of the ghost. The fashion of the clothing never changed. The three witnesses never knew each other, having lived at different periods.

Why did Alice Vesey come back in her full black skirt and blue gingham apron? For come back she certainly did.

That afternoon when Charles Vesey discovered her in the attic she was paralyzed with fright. He picked up a few of the foolish verses and read them. Then he read her freshly penned letter, while she hid her burning face in her shaking hands. And suddenly he reached for a blunt old ax which leaned in a corner of the attic, and struck her down, beating her head to a pulp.

Recovering momentarily from his fury, he threw her body down the stairs. When he called the police, he told them he had found her so upon his return from his office. The tale, however, was too thin. Charles Vesey was arrested for his wife's murder, and later confessed and was hanged.

The little ones died shortly afterward. Jeminy Crews was killed at Appomattox. The story goes that Alice Vesey's poor head was so mashed that it was impossible to do more than scrape up the oozing mass and do away with it. So she came back, headless, to the house which had held her and her mockery of a marriage—came back every twenty years (which was her age when she married Charles Vesey), to warn one of her own sex of death which follows in the wake of love.

The house burned in 1927. Some who saw the fire declared that they glimpsed a headless female standing on the flaming staircase—a woman in a full black skirt and a blue gingham apron, writing on a pad which she held in her work-scarred hands.

# (*1899*)     *Between Worlds*

On a night in August, 1900, three men—Steven Biddle, John Garsten and Allen Gregg—sat in the latter's courtyard. The banana palms rustled in a slight breeze, and a tree toad chirped in the vines on the wall. There had been a shower during the day, and a moist fragrance rose from the flower beds.

"Such nights as this always make me think of a cemetery—the smell of flowers and fresh earth does it, I suppose," Biddle observed, lighting a cigar.

"Do you mean ghosts?" smiled Garsten, leaning back more comfortably in his chair.

"Perhaps—although I dislike the word," replied the first speaker. "I always think of disembodied spirits as a species of force, each retaining its own earthly individuality. As to whether they have any true power over those here on earth who have not yet passed the mysterious portal of Death, I do not know. One hears all sorts of bizarre tales—but are they true? Do souls, having shed their fleshly sheaths, return to meddle with mortals who have not yet finished their earthly existence? And if they do, why?"

"I believe they do," put in Allen Gregg quietly. "And while it may not be possible for finite minds to analyze spiritual motives and phenomena, I know there are forces really at work, and that these forces pursue definite methods and perform definite tasks. I can cite at least two instances which have occurred in this vicinity during the last year."

"Tell us about them," his friends urged.

"The first had to do with a young man by the name of

73

Alfred J. Mutt," Gregg acquiesced. "His people lived in Carrollton, but he had for some months been doing carpenter work in Lafourche parish. About a year ago he came home quite suddenly and handed his mother a sheet of paper on which were several lines of handwriting. It was a message from himself to his family, telling them that he had been stricken deaf and dumb.

"'I must consult a doctor at once,' the note read. 'There must be help for me, but the wall seems very thick.'

"The parents, of course, took him immediately to the family physician, who examined him carefully and questioned him at length. Having had a good education, he wrote detailed answers to all the doctor's written queries, although this method was necessarily slow and tedious. The young man grew more and more restive and nervous, and the doctor advised the family to consult a specialist.

"Several specialists were visited, but not one of them could discover a single symptom—only the bare fact that Alfred was certainly stone deaf and absolutely dumb. They tried every test of which they knew, even firing a revolver when his back was turned, but he never so much as blinked an eye. It was perfectly clear that there was no imposture about it, and there was no response whatever to their various treatments.

"He was taken to the best hospital the specialists could recommend, and there he was given every attention—electricity, massage, sunshine, medicines, baths, diets, ointments—everything. But through it all he remained deaf and dumb. However, he grew increasingly nervous and irritable. He began to spend long periods in what was apparently deep thought. Then he began to call for city directories, old and new, going through them endlessly. Quite evidently he was searching for some name which he could not find. But what that name was, or why he sought it, he refused to divulge.

"The parents had communicated with various people in Lafourche parish, in an endeavor to learn if anything had occurred to shock their son and induce his deplorable condition. But they learned nothing of importance. They were told, among other casual statements, that Alfred had been attending Spiritualist meetings which had been held in the neighborhood, but nobody took a second thought about that. Everybody went.

"Upon further and more persistent investigation, it was learned that at these meetings several of the young people permitted themselves to be used as subjects. At the last meeting which Alfred had attended, it seems that one of the so-called 'mediums' had persuaded him to participate in their program. He was told that, in a state of trance, certain spirits would enter his body and use it as they would their own, speaking with his tongue, and by means of his voice conveying messages to loved ones whom they had no other means of reaching.

"Alfred agreed to this, and he did enter the trance state. Either no message was given him, or else he was stricken dumb before he was able to transmit it to whomever should have been the recipient. Nobody realized that he emerged speechless from the trance, as the meeting broke up quickly, and they all started for home. One woman did notice that Alfred said nothing, but she laid it to thoughtfulness on account of his experience. She said they were not in the habit of quizzing subjects afterward, and that Alfred had had no message to give while in the trance state.

"It seems that when the young man first discovered his inability to hear or speak, he was frantic. He thought only of his physical self, and the idea never occurred to him that the trance had had anything to do with his affliction. His one plan was to get home as speedily as possible. He relied implicitly upon his parents' judgment as to what should be done to restore his two lost senses. When the doctors failed, he was more alarmed than ever, believing that paralysis must have robbed him permanently of speech and hearing. He began to look forward to endless years of utter silence, an object of pity to friends and relatives, and a monstrosity to strangers.

"Then one day, after he had been in the hospital for some time, he began to collect his scattered wits. The troubled waters of his mind grew calm, and a species of resignation crept over him. Thinking back quietly—instead of ahead to turmoil and disaster, as he had been doing for weeks—he began to dissect the various phases of that Spiritualist meeting.

"They say that the subject remembers nothing that takes

place while he is in a trance. His actions, his utterances, whatever thoughts may travel through his brain during that time, are wiped out when he again descends to the lower, or entirely finite, state.

"But there was something which Alfred did begin to recall —a faint glimmering of some sort of message which he had been commissioned to deliver as soon as the medium's hypnotic influence was withdrawn. He remembered a name quite clearly. 'Clement,' it was. But whether a given name or a surname, he could not recall. He went about repeating it mentally, struggling for something more definite—something that he knew must be more than a mere name.

"One morning just as he was awakening, he seemed to read it against a curtain of fog—'Clement Ware.' And then, as though a voice spoke, repeating something that he had heard before—'Tell Clement Ware that his brother Howard says to look in the family Bible for the lost papers. As many chapters as there are in the Book of Isaiah and the Book of Job—at that number on Baronne street he will find my old trunk, and in it the papers he needs.'

"Alfred was so impressed that he immediately wrote this down. The next thing was to look for Clement Ware, if there were such a man. At first Alfred thought this man must be in Lafourche parish. But, in his piteous state, he had no way of getting there. To pass the time, he began searching through New Orleans directories, which the hospital supplied. Finally, in an old one, he came upon the name, and wrote a letter. After some days Mr. Ware called at the hospital, the letter having been forwarded and re-forwarded.

"The moment he stepped into Alfred's room, the young man felt a sort of tickling along the muscles of his neck and jaws. Suddenly he knew that the nurse was telling the visitor that the patient was deaf and dumb, and would have to carry on any conversation in writing. But he heard the name quite clearly—Clement Ware.

"At once he began to speak. He said afterward that he felt as though he were some sort of machine, and somebody were turning a crank to keep his tongue going. He said that a skeleton seemed to be turning the crank, with its empty eyesockets yawning at him and its hideous fleshless jaws champing and drooling. Then it seemed to change to a corpse, bubbling and oozing from its shroud like brown jelly, and giving forth a stifling odor of animal decay. He thought for an instant that he was fleeing in terror over bogs and swamps and the slimy backs of water monsters. But what he was really doing was repeating the message he had been instructed to give to Clement Ware.

"Ware had, it seems, been in great perplexity. His brother Howard had died a while earlier, and left his property to Clement. There were deeds and bonds and policies and a number of other vitally important papers missing. Though they had searched everywhere, the family could not locate them.

"Following instructions, Clement hurried to 108 Baronne street. There, among a mass of junk piled into a small cubbyhole at the rear, was an old rusty tin-covered trunk. True, it had once belonged to Howard Ware, and it must have been disposed of as worthless and beyond repair. How it got to Baronne street nobody seemed to know. But under an old raincoat at the bottom of the trunk, tied up with a pair of worn-out rubbers, was the bundle of missing papers.

"From that moment, Alfred Mutt regained his powers of speech and hearing. Nor has he ever, so far as I know, had the slightest recurrence of the difficulty. The matter was taken before the Orleans Medical Society, but that body had no explanation to offer. Physicians can diagnose the ills of the body, but they are unequipped to cope with the complexities of the spirit."

"Pretty gummy," observed Steven Biddle, running his fingers through his hair. "Is the other example you spoke of—"

"Worse, if anything," smiled Gregg.

"Let's have it, Allen," Garsten chuckled. "I'm not afraid of any spook coming at us from over the wall."

"This second account," resumed the host, "concerns a boy of about eighteen, named Ernest Snider. A group of young folks near Donaldsonville, where he lived, thought it would be great fun to invite a Spiritualist medium to a party, with a séance as part of the entertainment. The medium was not told that she was only a part of a program, and came in good faith. She selected young Snider as the subject for a trance.

"At first he was merely hypnotized, going through the various silly antics usually directed by the hypnotist. He took on the attributes of a dog, barking excitedly and so on. And then he was a circus performer, jumping through hoops from the backs of chairs. Finally he swallowed a quantity of salt and cayenne pepper, believing it to be sugar, and apparently enjoying it as such.

"Presently, however, he sank into a deep sleep, and all the efforts of the medium failed to arouse him. In great alarm, they removed him to his home, where he continued to slumber soundly.

"As time went on, he would wake partially now and then, but he did not speak and did not seem to hear anything that went on about him. A number of physicians were called, some of whom resorted to drastic treatment. But the boy slept serenely on.

"As a last resort, he was brought here to a boardinghouse in St. Charles street, and a strict regimen was mapped out for every hour of the day and night. Several nurses were engaged, but Ernest failed to improve.

"One morning the day nurse was called away temporarily, and another nurse came in her place. Although the boy never responded, the family always talked to him as though he could understand. When the new nurse came in, his mother said to him, 'We have Miss Dominick today, Ernest, and I'm sure you'll be pleased with her.'

"Ernest roused at once, propped himself on an elbow, and stared at the nurse. 'Is your name Pinky Dominick?' he asked, speaking clearly but with visible effort. 'Oh no,' the young lady replied, 'My name is Erna.' The sick boy seemed stunned for the moment, but kept gazing fixedly at her. 'Do you know anybody by the name of Pinky Dominick?' he demanded suddenly. 'Not now,' she answered, 'but I did have an aunt named Frances, and we always called her Aunt Pinky. She died a week ago today.'

" 'No, she didn't die!' Ernest cried. 'I was at a party one night when I was called away from the world, and I have been away ever since. I have been away searching for a woman called Pinky Dominick. She came to me that night while I was in a strange land, and told me who she was, and that she wanted me to tell her people that she had been buried alive, and that they must hurry and get her. I think you had better hurry now, for she is still alive and waiting!' And with that he began to weep hysterically, crying out that the nurse must hurry, or the rescuers might be too late."

"Well," asked Garsten, "what did they find?"

"They found the woman alive in her tomb, just as Ernest Snider had said. Catalepsy, you know, produces rigidity closely resembling rigor mortis, and the heart seems to have ceased beating. This was an extreme case, otherwise the woman would have died from suffocation in the tomb. Fortunately, she had not been embalmed."

"But," Biddle protested, "the woman wasn't dead when young Snider received the message, was she?"

"No," replied Gregg. "But it seems that that same night she was hypnotized also, and that she remembered nothing of her experience. It might be argued that she had some means of foreseeing the tragedy which was to befall her, and sent out her call for help."

"Is this woman alive now?" inquired Garsten. "Are you sure?"

"Yes," nodded Gregg, "I'm sure. She happens to be my wife's cousin."

# (*1840*)    *Up From the Sea*

The sea hath its dead. But how well it holds them is another matter.

There is the Seamen's Bethel on Saint Thomas street. This property was acquired by the Presbyterians in 1860 and adapted to its present use. Before that one of its buildings had been a private residence.

Shortly after it had been renovated and furnished for the accommodation of sailors, whispers began to go the rounds— weird tales of mysterious shapes and sounds, the coming and going of ghostly feet, and a strange and puzzling pantomime. Seamen told of two vague forms—and occasionally not so vague —that climbed the stairs and went in at each chamber door, as though they were searching desperately for someone they never could find. Lodgers awoke in a cold sweat, to see two shifting Somethings bending over them, swaying and twisting and giving off a smell of rotting fish and bitter salt. Some thought it was fog, and got up to shut the window. Some thought it was smoke, and aroused fellow sleepers. Some thought it was moonlight; but when they turned over for another nap, there came a tugging at the bedclothes, and two queer faces peered down out of the still darkness, the mouths agape and the eyes like shining shells.

There began to be tales about two misty shapes passing up and down the stairs, and from one end of the hall to the other—back and forth, back and forth. Sometimes there was faint music—a boyish soprano very far away, but moving with the shapes. Doors opened and closed.

And then one night a seaman, bolder than the rest, watching the two uneasy wisps of vapor moving round and round his bed, cried out to them, demanding to know their mission or their grievance. At once came the reply, in a thin, faraway wail.

"Mother, Mother! Where's Mother?" the voice called. "I've brought Julian back to Mother! Mother, where are you? I never can find you—Mother, Mother!"

Then, as the sailor raised himself on an elbow, the two visitors stood before him clear and plain—a young seaman in dripping oilskins, and by his side a slender boy with seaweed for clothing. A moment they tarried, then vanished.

"I looked on faces of the dead," the sailor told himself. "They spoke to me, because I was not afraid. All these other ninnies have been too scared to find out what the ghosts wanted!"

He recounted it to his comrades the next morning, laughing loudly and bragging at his own bravery. But at noon he died. They said he choked to death, staring terrified at Something which the others could not see.

One there was who made it his secret business to inquire and remember and piece together. He learned that about 1840, when the house was built, a newly married couple by the name of Weaver came there to live. During the ensuing decade they had five children. The youngest was a boy, named Julian. When he was between four and five he was spirited away by some stranger, and never was seen again. In frantic grief the family searched the country over, but to no avail. The mother always clung to the belief that he would come back, no matter how long he might be away.

Later the eldest son, Edward, went to sea. His ship, the *Steven Gaunt,* was wrecked, and of all the crew and passengers but one survived. That one sailor came to New Orleans and established a home. He it was who related, when storms roared and rains spattered down the chimney, the story of young Edward Weaver who shipped on the *Steven Gaunt* and discovered his long-lost brother as cabin boy. They were inseparable, these two, going over and over again the joyful story they would have to tell when they returned home. How happy they would all be again—and Mother would bake a great cake, with all the candles it could hold, because Julian, who had been away forever, would never be lost again! They used to play at the various ways she was to be told the glorious news, rehearsing this speech and that, laughing and joking and planning gifts with which to surprise her.

But they never lived to come home. Only after the sea had claimed them, mauling them and summoning its fishes to the feast, did they make their ghostly way back. Certain members of the family recognized them—even spoke to them, welcoming them warmly. But the mother had grown strangely hard and skeptical—God had cheated her, stolen her sons, wrecked her hopes and spoiled her whole scheme of life. She would not listen when her daughters spoke of the brothers who had come back at last in spiritual guise.

But when she locked her door, the two went in, just the same. They stood beside her bed, waiting for the word of welcome which she refused to give. And because she closed her heart to them, they were unable to speak. Only their pitiful hands reached out to her, their wistful eyes begging for a word of love.

Sometimes they would stand all night outside her window. Sometimes they would perch on the roof, beside the chimney which led to her fireplace. Sometimes they would crouch beside the front door, and passing neighbors would see them and run shrieking to their own safe homes.

The sisters could do nothing. With all their loyalty and their affection and their belief in the two apparitions, it was the mother whom the ghostly visitors adored and whose communion they sought. Finally the neighborhood was roused to such terror that the Weaver family moved away. But the phantoms continued to haunt the house, as though they did not understand that any change had taken place.

When the Seamen's Bethel was opened, the neighborhood breathed a sigh of relief. Surely now the ghosts would give up! But it remained for one bold sailor to speak up and call forth an answer—pitiful petition that it was—though he paid dearly enough for his audacity. That moment of articulation, however, appears to have brought an end to the whole matter. No ghost ever came again to the Seamen's Bethel.

# ( *1874* )   *The Gay Caballeros*

Away down in the lower part of the city known as the Third District, stood many years ago a large and imposing mansion, called La Casa Rosa, built in 1770 by Don Juan Luis Angula, a native of Barcelona, Spain.

A reporter, scenting a spicy story for his paper, made a trip to La Casa Rosa early in 1874. He was a young man, tall and straight, dark-eyed and fresh-complexioned—a youth of cultivated manners and exceptionally pleasing appearance. La Casa Rosa was that day his oyster. After his visit, he wrote only half the tale for his paper. The other half—by far the more astounding portion—he reserved for his diary.

To give the incident in its entirety, we shall begin at the moment when the reporter, William Dawson, ascended the crumbling brown steps of the mansion. He had previously rung the clanging bell set in the rusty iron gate. After waiting an interminable time, and ringing twice thereafter, the wide front door had opened a crack and a withered brown countenance had appeared. After some parley, during which young Dawson had employed every persuasive quality he possessed, the old creature had crept down the steps and unlocked the gate, permitting him to follow her inside.

The moment he stood in the big gloomy hall, the mulatto woman slammed the door shut and drew two enormous iron bolts into place. Then she dragged a heavy chain across the door and dropped a link of it into a thick hook fastened into the casement.

"We has to shet 'em out," she croaked in a queer singsong.

"Dey comes a-rompin' an' a-ravin', hull comp'nies ob 'em, when dey takes de notion. Sometimes it's one at de fust, lak yo' comes —an' de res' dey trails right 'long, an' squeezes in 'fo' Ah kin git de do' bawd. Yo' sho' yo' am 'lone? Yo' am sho' tellin' de trufe? Ain't no foolin' 'bout de res' what'll come flockin' in attah yo'?"

"I'm all alone, Aunty," Dawson assured her. "I'd like to see Miss Angula, if I might."

"De Señorita," corrected the servant. She spoke with a certain hesitant caution. Then, "Yo' wants to see de young leddy, Ah specks."

"Oh—is she young?" Dawson had understood otherwise.

"Ah sees her young," the crone replied, swaying her old head as though to some inner rhythm, her beady eyes resting on the caller. "Yassuh, Ah sees her young. But she done be old, Ah specks. She gwine on ninety-five dis yeah, yassuh. Ah's on'y ole Zimena—she wa' thirteen when Ah wa' bawned. Mah mammy wa' ole Bautista, an' she wa' sebenty when she die, way back in 1838. Mah gran'mammy she wa' ole Pedra—she wa' bawned 'fo' ole Mawstah. She die ten yeah 'fo' mah mammy die, an' she wa' sebenty-seben den. Yassuh, dey all be bey'd out dar in de yawd nex' de wall. Right good place, out dar nex' de wall, yassuh."

A droll, crafty smile puckered the old brown face into knots. There was a glint in the slits of eyes, and Dawson felt a shiver run along his spine.

"*Awk—awk!*" It was a strange and terrifying sound which echoed along the dark old paneling of the damp hall. "*Awk—awk—awk!*"

"It's de Señorita," sighed Zimena, "She am wantin' me. Yo' kin come 'long, suh, still an' quiet, an' Ah tell her yo' am callin'. Yassum ma'am—Ah's comin'."

"*Awk—awk!*" The sound was fretful and impatient, like some animal caught in a trap, imprisoned but not hurt.

"Come on upstays—de Señorita she cain't git down no mo'. Her eyes dey am failin' some, an' de steps dey's steep. Ah kin climb 'em—ain't nuffin gwine stop ole Zimena— he-he-he!"

The old cypress staircase was deep in dust. The baluster

rail was cold and gritty to the touch. Dawson followed the old mulatto woman down a musty upper corridor to an open door. He wondered momentarily how many of these dozens of rooms were actually occupied nowadays. The whole place was icy cold.

"Zimena!" came a cracked old voice. "Where are you? I feel a draft—have you been opening a door? You know I'm afraid to have a door opened—everybody coming in, nobody knows who! You haven't let anybody in, have you? I'll kill you if you have—you know I've told you I'd kill you if you ever let anybody in!"

"Yassum, Ah knows," wheezed the servant, unworried. "Dis yere nice young man, he come to pay his respecks to yo', ma'am. Yo' sho' don't want to miss conversifyin' wid a nice young man, Señorita."

Dawson stood in the doorway, hat in hand. His eyes sought the direction from which the harsh voice of the Señorita seemed to come.

In a great ragged velvet chair was bunched a soiled feather-bed, and in the midst of this was crouched the figure of a frail woman who might have been a thousand years old. Her skin was like yellow leather, so wrinkled that it looked as though it had been wadded tightly in some great hand and then tossed onto a framework of human bones. A slate-colored vein bulged in the middle of the seamed forehead, and the eyes were mere watery depressions. The head was entirely bald, save for a thin tuft of white hair over each crumpled ear. There were no eyebrows, no eyelashes. The mouth was sunken and misshapen, the lips purple and cracked. The bare neck was a horror.

But there was more.

The ancient creature was huddled in a voluminous dress of scarlet silk, frayed and spotted with grease. Around the terrible old neck was a massive necklace of diamonds and sapphires. On the shapeless arms hung bracelets set with flashing-stones. From the withered ears depended heavy diamond earrings. On the hairless scalp was arranged a pearl and emerald coronet. Half a dozen great priceless brooches decked the front of the filthy gown. The crooked old fingers were literally loaded with flashing rings—rings tied on with dirty twine, the loose ends of which this noisome creature sucked. A wave of almost overpowering perfume caused the reporter to catch his breath.

"Ah, Señorita," he bowed, "I am indeed charmed to find you at home. I trust I do not intrude?"

The strange old woman eyed him cloudily, the pouches of dry brown skin making her face seem more than ever like some decaying vegetable.

"You come about the jewels?" she inquired, with a halting little squawk, wetting her stiff old lips.

"No, Señorita. I came to talk with you about beautiful things—the flowers in your garden, the birds you love, the music you remember, tales your father used to tell, the pictures you enjoy. These are the things worth talking about. You agree with me, Señorita?" Young Dawson had struck his stride. He knew instantly that his appeal had found its mark.

"H'm," the old creature grunted, hitching herself about in the midst of the featherbed. Her long, lean nose dripped unheeded onto the breast of her stained scarlet gown. "I never talk of such things now. I have no one to talk to. No one remembers the things I remember. No one but Zimena, and she's only a black devil. Zimena, you go away—go downstairs and wake up that dead man under the steps, and tell him he can have his silly snuffbox. The jewels on it are paste—he doesn't think I know that. But I know diamonds, when I see them close enough—I never did think he was worth asking here. Tell the Don I said that, Zimena—although he'll probably beat you for it."

"The Don he been daid mo'n sebenty yeahs, suh—the Señorita she fergits, suh," excused the mulatto woman in an uneasy whisper at Dawson's elbow. "She finkin' ob ole Pedra, what use to ca'y all de messages back an' forth 'twixt her an' de Don, when dey wa'n't speakin'. Yassum ma'am—Ah tells him right off."

"Let me see," the Señorita went on, ignoring the servant's mumbling, "you are Señor—"

"Dawson," supplied the reporter, with another bow.

"H'm, yes. Señor Dawson. It seems that I ought to recall you. Doubtless I grow stupid, with my father away. We have estates near Barcelona. I had a letter from him the other day. He reports a prosperous journey. There was the young Señor Restez . . . there was some difficulty concerning the transfer of property, it appears. He was very rich—and he looked a trifle like you . . . But we got the property.

"I remember Señor Miguel Blenco—there was a difficult youngster for you! He found me quite to his taste—and ah, the rubies that young man had! They were in the family vaults in Valencia—he went all that way for them, and had his own mother poisoned in order to get them for me. A gracious, valiant boy, he was, though he died easily. The rubies were worth tens of thousands. My father was intensely pleased with me. I stole all the rubies I dared to—my father never missed them. I have hampersful of jewelry that he never missed. It really was quite amusing. . . .

"Señor Villesca—he was a pretty one. Never have I seen such eyes, nor felt such kisses! He was not made for commerce and the deft plottings of moneylenders. He totally misunderstood values—he was rich in emotions, and it seemed a pity to let him waste so wonderful a thing as money. He gave me everything he had . . . My father was really clever at such transactions. But I'd rather not have seen him after his back was broken . . . Thoroughly unpleasant. . . .

"Did you by any chance know Señor Cristoval Morin? No—he would be older than you—quite middle-aged, in fact. A most insufferably stupid man, opposed to perfume but fond of parrots. Indeed, it was the squawking of a Cuban parrot which he mistook for something quite different when he tripped and struck his head with such violence that he died instantly. Poor Señor Morin—I had that evening accepted his proposal of marriage and he had deeded to me all that he possessed, which was a great deal.

"My father was far cleverer than I—his guests journeyed from across the seas to drink his health and court his daughter. But he always arranged matters so that they left our house by daylight, so that everyone saw them go. That they returned shortly, upon one pretext or another, no one suspected. It was a pretty trick . . . Life was graceful in those days. . . .

"The Don will be returning in a month's time, I should

think. I cannot remember precisely what it was he said in his letter . . . Where is that letter!—Zimena, you old vixen, where are you? *Awk—awk—awk!*" The cry rose to a shrill scream, like the squalling of hungry gulls.

"Niggers are so trying," the nauseating old Señorita sighed, rocking herself about in the dirty featherbed, clawing at it with her grimy, discolored old nails and sniveling weakly. "She's away down in the kitchens, I suppose, stuffing a goose or something. We never can keep help—poor Zimena has to do everything. They all die—old Pedra died, and then Bautista died. Just contrariness, of course. One of these days that old Zimena will pretend she is sick, and then we shall see her cold and stiff and useless. Well, that is the way life is. . . ."

The loathsome old creature babbled on, her toothless gums giving her words a peculiar champing hiss. The Spanish accent was strong, too—the only musical note in the whole tirade.

Dawson stood still. Not for all the gold of Ophir would he have seated himself in any of those chairs. For one thing, he had noticed the vermin which crawled over the dirt-caked bald head of the Señorita. The perfume was already stifling, but the old mummy in the featherbed grasped a fat bottle which stood on a table beside her and soaked a filthy rag with a further supply. Dawson wondered how long he could weather this fresh blast.

"I exist on roses," the hoarse whine continued. "Doubtless you brought me flowers . . . they always did that at first. One could scarce expect more, along at the first, could one? I must ask Zimena about it. The old demon must put your flowers in water . . . It is always so dark here that I can't see what she's done. I shall move presently to the sunny side of the house, where I can look at the garden . . . The garden has been of infinite use. No one suspects a garden. We have lived very gracefully, Señor, conducting our ways profitably, selecting our guests carefully, never permitting any friend to graft himself into our affections—ah, that is the mistake, Señor.

"The gold of the heart—what is it? A puff of smoke, a reflection in a lake, a foolish illusion. But the real gold— hard and bright and yellow—ah, that is what counts! You can feel it and see it and taste it and live by it. It never

deserts you. It works for you, night and day. So long as you
have it, you are a power, a master.

"How old am I?—thirty, forty—oh, I forget how old I am.
But always I have had gold. I always shall have gold. It is
enough to have. It doesn't cheat you and lie to you and break
your heart. That Zimena—where has the she-devil gone?"

She pounded the table with the perfume bottle, her dreadful "*Awk—awk—awk!*" shrilling through the dusty stillness of
the high-vaulted apartment and out into the dim halls. The
mulatto woman came creeping up the stairs like some crippled
old chimpanzee.

"Sí, Señorita," she murmured in her broken squeak.

"Tell the Don we shall dine at eight, as he requests," the
hag in the big chair directed, feebly dipping an end of the
twine into the perfume bottle and sucking it noisily. "Have
the servants lay the cloth that was used on the Pope's table, and
the Carlos III silver. If Fernando dribbles the wine he shall
have hot irons applied to his armpits. If the crystal does not
sparkle like gems, Zoé shall have red-hot irons run up her nose.
If there is a wrinkle in the linen, Luisa shall have lye poured
in her ears. Go down to the kitchens and say that these are
my orders, Zimena.

"I shall wear the cloth-of-gold and emeralds. See that Señor
Dawson is seated in front of the arched door—that is always
the smooth and convenient beginning . . . eh, Zimena? Tell
Pedra the coffee must be strong, strong—and then half cognac
—Courvoisier, I think . . . Afterwards we shall dance. . . ."

She shrank back into the depths of the stained featherbed,
and it was then that Dawson noticed that her feet were bare.
Broken brown claws they were, shapeless as lumps of driftwood
. . . "Afterwards we shall dance" . . . He knew that she could
not walk—had not walked for years, probably. She had closed
her eyes and was snoring loudly, the end of the dirty twine
still in her unsightly mouth. Zimena had withdrawn silently.

Dawson stood a moment longer, and then stepped into
the hall. These two ancient females were, he knew, the sole
occupants of the great house. A wild ambition fired him to
see all he could of this strange and forbidden place before he
left it. It was unlikely that he ever would have another oppor-

tunity. Only the senile ravings of the Señorita had permitted him to see as much as he already had.

Only two decrepit old women . . . Why not explore the whole place, being careful to keep out of sight, and leave when he had been the rounds? It could do no possible harm. Nothing would be disturbed in any way. What a story!

Just what was it they meant, this crazed old mulatto woman and the dreadful Señorita in her worse than second childhood, both babbling about men who had come as guests in other years—and who returned and never left again? What about the servant's reference to the buryings "out dar in de yawd nex' de wall"? Had he chanced on something far more sinister than just a crumbling mansion and two human relics of another age? Was the Señorita's drooling based on anything more than the mental decay of advanced years? Did not both women entertain themselves with mere childish fancies, driveling and pitiful?

Dawson heard a scraping sound at the foot of the stairs, and he turned hastily in the opposite direction. Two vast chambers he explored at his leisure, and musty enough they were. In one of them a rat scuttled across the floor, and an owl hooted at him from a damask tester. As he rounded a corner farther on, he met a young man whose clothes were distinctly of another period. Dawson stared, amazement overcoming his native politeness. The stranger was little more than a boy, and his eyes were blue as cornflowers. As he moved, the upper part of his body wabbled queerly, as though it were separate from the lower portion and not safely balanced.

The boy smiled radiantly and held out his hand to Dawson. When the latter grasped it, he found it icy cold and stiff as marble. He would have passed on, but suddenly the boy began to drag him up a flight of stairs. It was as though his hand were bound with steel to that other cold hand. Try as he would to stop, he must hurry after this strangely wobbling form. Up and up . . . and at the top, a man striding back and forth, his head mashed to red jelly. The terrible one paused, and took up his striding abreast of the two.

They reached another staircase, narrow and crumbling. The boy went around and peered under it, dragging forth a

*. . . they thought to remove the thick old wall . . .*

young man whose shirt-ruffles were drenched with blood. His face was white as chalk, his dark eyes stared incredulously, and his hair lay in damp ringlets on his high forehead. He rose slowly and uncertainly, as though he were drugged. A door opened, and a fifth young man came into the darkening corridor—a boy with a handful of rubies, like drops of cool blood.

Suddenly the five of them seemed to merge into a stewing, steaming, stinking mass. A sort of oily jelly oozed from them and trickled down the dusty stairs, like a long worm wriggling downward. Ribbons of flame rose here and there among them. A crackling of bones set up a deafening racket. Teeth fell in little white heaps at Dawson's feet. Something wet brushed his face and spattered down onto his white waistcoat—a sprinkling of icy blood, dark and horrible.

How he made his way to the front door, Dawson never remembered. Every way he turned he encountered strange youths wearing clothes in fashion decades before he was born. If he in his haste collided with them, they vanished instantly. And always that ghastly crackling sound in his ears, as of bones being crushed and ground to a powder in some hellish machine.

At the front door crouched old Zimena. She shook her knotted brown fists at him savagely, like some enraged witch.

"Yo' done let 'em in!" she shrieked. "Yo' say no, nuffin or nobody won't git in—but yo' done let 'em in! Dey's runnin' up an' down de stays lak wile-cats, an' dey ain't no stoppin' 'em now. Dis time dey gits de Señorita, an' pays her back—Ah knows, 'cayse dey's tole me 'fo' what dey wa' fixin' to do, ef dey gits de chance. Yo' done let 'em in! An' Ah's gwine to set 'em on yo', sho's Gawd! Ah libs eighty-one yeah, an' den de ghos'es dey comes back to choke me! Lawd Gawd, dis am sho' a jedgment day—an' it gwine ketch po' ole Zimena!"

The front door was opening slowly. With one bound Dawson was through it and racing down the steps. But the iron gate in the fence was locked, and Zimena had the key. He paused, out of breath, and set his foot upon the wrought iron. He would scale the high fence.

Then another strange thing happened. The blue-eyed youth whom he had first met in the upper corridor was standing beside him, still wobbling crazily. The boy laid his hand on the gate and smiled—and the gate swung open, creaking on rusty hinges. As Dawson passed into the street, he saw the youth topple . . . the upper part of his body rolled one way, and the lower part the other. Yet even as the reporter gazed, the gruesome spectacle disappeared.

The gate was closed and locked. The roses grew in a wild tangle over the ruined garden, covering the massive old mansion in a merciful blanket of crimson and yellow and pink. The January cold seemed not to have touched him. La Casa Rosa, indeed. . . .

Yet the next year, when Señorita Mercedes Antonia Angula died and the property passed to other owners, they thought to remove the thick old wall at the rear of the garden. Under it, workmen found the skeletons of more than fifty men, with scraps of old-fashioned clothing still clinging to the yellowed bones . . . the gay caballeros who had come to La Casa Rosa to gamble and to make love.

In the clenched hand of one of them was a heap of rubies . . . Miguel Blenco, without doubt, who had poisoned his own mother, that the demon-girl of La Casa Rosa might wear her jewels. . . .

# (*1878*)    *Walking Otto*

Old Otto Krane lived near the batture. He was old in 1878, but he always had been old. Middle-aged men remembered seeing him on the batture when they came home from the War Between the States. He had constructed a tiny shack near the water, and in this rude shelter he somehow existed.

In the summer he dug roots in the swamps and gathered the juicy, bulbous masses from which the vivid water flowers grew. He harvested certain leaves and stems and bark and buds and insects. Some of these he ate, and some he sold. Still others he utilized for mysteriously powerful potions which he doled out to the colored folk.

When the tattered gray soldiers came back, old Otto looked fully eighty. Twenty years earlier he had looked about the same age. Thirteen years later, he seemed no older.

"Yep," he would cackle, when twitted about his longevity. "I been here a long time. And I'm like to be here quite a spell longer. I'll see the hull of you laid away afore I goes, most likely. I don't come of a dyin' breed."

Questioned about his people or his youth, he would grin wisely, scratch his two wooden legs with his stout cane, and cackle prodigiously.

"Ain't no use you axin' questions," he would chuckle. "I don't never tell nothin'. Ain't got nothin' to tell, for one thing. My legs was cut off when I was five. I cut 'em off myself, of course—that's what I'd do, ain't it? What do I live on, down here by the ole river? Why, I lives on love! You'd expect I would, wouldn't you? A spruce young feller like me, rich and

94

handsome and overflowin' with words—o' course I lives on love!"

With that, he would spraddle off, his jaws busy with a fresh chew of tobacco. Where did he get his tobacco? He "growed it in the swamp," he said. He had a little patch hidden somewhere. Some said it wasn't tobacco at all—that it was a witch-weed whose juices nourished him and lent him his amazing vitality.

Faced with the "witch-weed" gossip, he beat his wooden legs impishly with his cane.

" 'Tain't no witch-weed what's keepin' me sound," he scowled, but his eyes twinkled under his bushy gray brows. "It's walkin', Why, I'll bet I walks a good hundred miles some weeks. I know I do. Got three legs—I ought to walk better'n you poor folks with only two, hadn't I? Walkin'— they ain't nothin' like it to improve the liver and rich up the blood."

Somehow the story got round that old Otto had money. Some said that he lived high once it got dark and the door of his shack was shut. Others opined that he starved himself from long habit, obtaining money in strange and unknown ways and hoarding it as all misers do, from sheer love of it. Lived on love, did he? Wasn't that what misers did—exist on the very worship of their gold? So the gossips, both black and white, gabbled on.

All along the batture, at that time, were great ponds of stagnant water. Small snakes wriggled therein, crayfish hitched hither and yon, and bullfrogs croaked in deep and masterful chorus. Nothing annoyed old Otto.

"The world was made for snakes and crayfish and frogs, jest the same as it was for me," he used to grin. "I reckon the little fellers got some right, same's us." Then he would hitch up his ancient trousers and flap his ancient coat tails and straddle off, chewing his juicy quid.

Occasionally he was absent for days. But prior to these trips, wherever they led, rumor had it that he called at the Post Office and was handed a fat envelope. It was even said that the envelope bore a German stamp.

"I don't see who he could be savin' it for—whatever 'tis

he's savin'," Aunt Betty Barnes remarked one day, as she saw him stump past her cottage. "He looks as though he was bound for Canady, he's that pert. It plum beats me—he must be ninety or so, and he's as spry as a cricket. S'pose it's because he ain't got no old legs to have rheumatiz in."

"He says he'd die if he didn't walk," put in Judy, a grandniece of Aunt Betty's. "I do like to talk to him, 'cause he can always think of a fairy story to tell. I'll bet he knows a hunderd of 'em."

"I didn't s'pose he ever got pinned down enough to tell fairy stories to the young 'uns," Aunt Betty sighed.

"He don't," declared the child. "Jest to me—that's all. He says he can't be bothered with a whole roft o' kids—they ask too many questions. You never can git no story at all out of old Otto, if you ask for it. I jest set down by the batture and sort o' hold my stomach. And he comes along and he sets down and he holds his stomach. And then when a bullfrog croaks, he starts tellin' me a story."

"Then what do you do?"

"I jest keep still and jest nod. He says I mind better'n anybody he ever run acrost."

Aunt Betty laughed.

"Next time you go along the batture I'll wrap up a piece of salt meat for you to give to Otto," she said. "I reckon he don't have much."

One day Otto sat on the batture in the sun. Judy squatted beside him, watching the crayfish and the gulls.

"How old be you, Judy?"

"Goin' on nine," Judy returned proudly.

"H'm . . . jest barely hatched," chuckled old Otto. "You won't never grow if you don't take to walkin'. It'll stretch your legs and make you tall. Ain't nothin' like walkin'. You know, they was once a hull grove o' willow trees, and every one of 'em walked a hunderd miles every day. Yes sirree. Trees used to be like that. That's why they knows everything what goes on.

"Don't fergit that, young lady—the trees is always a-starin' at you, findin' out what's goin' on. They knows everything— they's smart. But they only tells it at night, after everybody's gone to bed. I can hear 'em, though, right along—and I can understand 'em, too. That's why I knows so much. Can't fool old Otto, no sirree."

After that, Judy always listened to the murmur of the trees.

Once old Otto said, "If anything ever happens to me, young lady, I'm goin' to make you walk. You don't walk half enough, for a young 'un of your age. You mope around too much. You'll be sick as a bug before you know it. I'd die if I didn't walk."

But one morning Otto Krane's body was found floating in a batture pond between the wharf and Rousseau street. His belly had been ripped open from breast to groin. Judy Barnes saw the men fishing him out and lashing him to a piece of plank, the better to carry him somewhere or other, and she wept bitterly.

No more would the cracked old voice tell her fairy tales. No more would the stout cane beat upon the battered wooden legs. Old Otto was dead. It was more than Judy could bear.

Within the next few weeks a whispering began to go round. The whisperers said that old Otto Krane was walking the batture, holding his guts in his riven belly with his two hands. They said he straddled painfully on his wooden legs, wobbling this way and that, peering out over the river, looking for the tough roustabouts who had murdered him for the money they believed he kept hidden in his shack. And then, they added, he would turn and peer landward from the batture, over the little ponds to where the cottages of the poor whites huddled like chilled gray rabbits.

Judy Barnes lived in one of those gray cottages. She wondered if a ghost ever told fairy stories to small girls. She began to be sure that she never could be afraid of old Otto, even if he were a ghost. She knew he had not been a miser. No man with money would wear splintered old wooden legs like Otto's, even though he dreaded to spend his hoarded gold.

Judy could hear the footsteps of all the people who were hurrying to watch for old Otto Krane's ghost on the batture. They passed her house, and she could peer through the mismatched shutters and hear the meaningless things they said and the vapid jokes they cracked. It seemed a pity that the old man's ghost had to be pestered so. Judy wondered if he, being a ghost, would know her if he saw her.

One night the rain fell in torrents. Aunt Betty tucked the bedclothes tightly around Judy and set a tub on the floor where the roof leaked the worst. The child could not go to sleep. She kept thinking of old Otto's ghost out there in the cold rain.

"He ought to go into his shack," she thought.

And then she remembered that the men had torn down his shack when they were looking for the gold they thought he had. The Negroes had long since gathered up the scraps of splintered boards and uprights and toted them off for firewood.

The longer Judy thought of old Otto's ghost out in the chilly rain, the more she wanted to cry. Everybody was in bed now. It must be near midnight.

Noiselessly she arose and slipped on her clothing. She picked up a folded blanket from the foot of her bed. She would take something out to Otto's poor ghost, to keep him warm in the sharp wind and driving wet.

The door did not even creak as she stepped out onto the rickety gallery. My, but the rain was icy! Her thin arms grasped the blanket as she sped along the slippery path. She thought she saw a light on the batture, and she made for that.

Just where was it that old Otto's ghost walked? she wondered. And just what was a ghost, anyhow? The priest had said she was a wicked child to think of such things, when she had asked him about it. He had added ten extra *Ave Marias* to her penance, on account of the question, and told her to go home and be a good girl.

She was quite near the batture now. Yes, there was the light, right over there. It wasn't a fire, or the rain would have put it out long ago. When she got within a yard of it, she saw it was Otto Krane. He was sitting on the batture, holding his stomach as he used to do. He seemed to give out light, so that all around Judy could see the rivulets of rain flowing riverward.

Old Otto was rocking himself gently backwards and forwards, holding his belly tightly, gurgling and bubbling like rainwater when it pours along the gutters. And all at once he looked up at her, and began to croon instead of gurgle.

He got to his feet (or what served for feet), still holding onto his middle. And then Judy could see that his belly was ripped open and gaping bloodily. He was trying to hold in his intestines and his kidneys and his liver, and he was having a hard time doing it.

"Oh, Uncle Otto!" she exclaimed, using the name by which she always thought of him. "Wrap this blanket around you quick, so your innards won't fall out!"

She wasn't in the least frightened. It was so good to see old Otto again. She threw the blanket over his drooping shoulders, and he drew it tight around him. The rain was still pouring down, but somehow Judy's soaked clothing was drying out. She felt warm and comfortable, especially now that her companions "innards" were safely in place. She wished he would say something.

Now he was beckoning to her. She was to follow him, it seemed. He walked very fast, and she trotted obediently behind him. That was the beginning. She walked until dawn came, and then she was out in the wet country, knocking on somebody's kitchen door.

An old couple gave her breakfast there, making much of her and not seeming to notice her odd companion. Old Otto sat across the table from her, chewing his tobacco and shaking with contented mirth. She had a nap under a chinaball tree, and then they went on again.

It seemed to Judy that she traveled with old Otto Krane for days. Always there was a good meal, always a snug place to sleep. But nobody except herself ever seemed to see Otto, and he never spoke a word even to her—just smiled and chuckled and glided on ahead. She had no idea where they were going.

Then one day her guide turned into a narrow road that led to a cypress grove. The palmettos were thick and sharp, and she had to hurry to keep up with Otto. Pretty soon they struck off into a path. Finally they stopped, where a little circle of stones was sunk into the moist ground. And there old Otto stood, as though nothing in the world could ever move him.

"What is it, Uncle Otto?" Judy asked, becoming a bit frightened, it was all so queer and still.

But old Otto answered never a word. Judy put her hand on his arm—only there was no arm to touch. She could see the arm, just as she always had done—*but it wasn't there to touch!* A lump rose in her throat. Where was she? She wished she could see Aunt Betty or Daddy coming between the trees. . . .

But a man was coming along the path, swinging a spade over his shoulder. It was Judy's father who had lately gotten work in Grosse Tete. They were very near Grosse Tete now, he said . . . a hundred miles from New Orleans . . . How did Judy ever get here?

Old Otto was still standing by the little circle of stones, pointing downward with his stout cane. He beat his wooden shins with it, and it made a great rattling, although John Barnes did not seem to hear.

Then old Otto spoke. He stepped over beside the little girl and bent close to her ear.

"Dig, Judy!" he gurgled. And then he vanished.

John Barnes told it afterwards—how Judy took the spade and tried to drive it into the soft earth inside the circle of stones. How, after a few objections to so foolish a proceeding, he took the spade from her and himself began to dig. How they came upon a stout strongbox filled with gold pieces. And how they subsequently smoothed over the hole and pressed down the dirt, and cautioned each other to say nothing to anybody about the box. And how they wrapped it in the blanket which lay on the ground beside the stones. And how the blanket smelled like a rotting corpse, and nearly made John Barnes ill—although Judy could not smell it at all.

That was in 1878. When Judy was sixty-nine years old, she still had one of old Otto's gold pieces to show to her grandchildren. And she still had a lively tale to tell of how, when she was nine years old, she walked a hundred miles to Grosse Tete with the ghost of old Otto Krane . . . to find ten thousand dollars in a box under a circle of little stones. . . .

(*1873*)　　*Tears of Heaven*

Young Franz Hartzein saw Caroline Koehn coming along the path, and he hastened to greet her. The long, full skirt of checked blue calico which she wore swished about her small feet and caught on a twig.

"Ach," Franz laughed, as he stooped to disentangle the dress, "what would you do without your Franz when you get into difficulties!"

"I never could do at all—you know that quite well, don't you?" she rejoined, as he kissed her yielding lips lightly. "Mother would say we were terribly immodest to be kissing each other out here where everyone can see."

"Nobody has seen anything at all, sweetheart," the young man assured her fondly. "It is less than an hour after dinner, and you know the enormous dinners they eat. They can scarce see over their stomachs at this hour—if they are awake, which I doubt. Anyhow, every man is paying strict attention to his pipe, and every Hausfrau is finishing with the dish washing."

They both laughed merrily, and Caroline bent to pick a dandelion.

"Do you think every Hausfrau is stupid, Franz?" she asked, her slate-blue eyes serious, and her fingers fiddling with the prim row of buttons on her dress.

"No, indeed—they are the saviours of the world!" he declared. "Think of the excellent cheeses they make—the beer they brew, the bread they bake, the noble little pigs they roast! Ach, now, meine beliebte—don't twist my meanings.

You will be a Hausfrau yourself, you know, after we are married."

"And I should dread to think that I was just to grow thick and dull, knowing only the baking and the cleaning and the sawing and such things, Franz dear. I want to understand and enter into all your life, as a wife should."

"Should I then learn about the making of Kuchen and Wiener Schnitzel and the stitching of seams?" he laughed, patting her cheek. Nein, nein—we shall not quarrel over that. You shall always know everything there is to know about my doings."

"I was speaking to Father Apfel yesterday, Franz," Caroline observed shyly.

"Ja? Did you mention that we are planning to marry next year?"

"Yes, Franz—and I asked him which was the nicest month to be married in."

"Everybody always says June."

"But Father Apfel said May." She executed a gay hippety-hop. "He said, 'The month of Mary is the blessed month for young brides.' I like to think of being married in 'the blessed month,' Franz—don't you?"

"Yes," he returned tenderly. "And, besides, it is a month sooner than June. Let us set the date, then—we are to be married next May. In May, of 1872, you will be Frau Franz Hartzein—think of that!" He caught her round the waist and they danced a measure or two.

"Oh, Franz dear!" she cried, out of breath. "What *will* people be saying of us! They will think you have had a glass too much beer or something, and that I am a wild rattle-head. I hope Mother does not hear of it—she is so strict and proper, you know."

"She is a wise mother," the young man nodded. "You must bring up our girls exactly as she has brought you up."

"Oh, Franz!" Caroline's cheeks were pink and her eyes were lowered.

"It is not immodest nor vulgar to speak of the family we expect to have," he said gently. "To me it is very beautiful and sacred. Little children of one's own must be marvelous.

Do you know where we are standing at this moment, sweet-heart?"

"Why, yes, Franz. This ground is on Saint-Claude street, near Clouet—in the Third District of New Orleans. German settlement, substantial people, religious, well-to-do, law-abiding . . . I can think of more, probably." Her eyes were dancing saucily.

"But that is not the right answer, anyhow," he grinned. "This is a vacant lot with a live oak on it, ja. Also, it belongs to one Franz Hartzein, and he is going to build a house on it, for his wife and himself."

"Oh, Franz—really? You mean our house is to stand here?"

"Ja. It seems very wonderful to me, Caroline."

"It *is* wonderful. I shall make curtains for its windows and linen for its tables—and I shall keep everything in it as bright and shining as a new spoon. *Our* house, Franz—think of it!"

Caroline told her family that day.

"Ach, Franz is a good harness-maker," assented her father, weighing out coffee and sugar and salt meat to be delivered to Frau Garbrecht, around on Louisa street. "He is sober-minded and industrious, not running to dances all the time like that Philip Gurgin, who was after you last winter."

"Philip was not after me," Caroline blushed. "He is Franz's best friend, that is all."

"He was, too, after you!" the grocer declared. "I know what I see. He would have cut Franz out if he could, friend or no friend. I know what I see."

"Oh, Father, how silly!" the girl laughed. "Here comes Minnie Bollar—I must tell her the latest news."

A plump, brown-haired girl of twenty-one—three years older than Caroline—entered the store. She carried a large market basket, and perspiration beaded her smooth brow.

"Ach, it's hot today," she puffed, setting the basket on the spotless counter. "I'm sewing carpet-rags after dinner, Caroline. Come on over by us. *Mutter* has been making seedcakes, and I know you like them."

"Caroline has the fine news for you already," Johann Koehn beamed. "She and Franz—oh, you have dropped your pocketbook, Minnie."

"Ja, always I am clumsy and drop things," sighed the girl. She stooped to retrieve the stout purse, misery clouding her eyes and tearing at her heart. So, after all, Franz. . . .

"Franz and I are going to be married next May," Caroline's voice was rippling on. "He is going to build a house for us on a lot he owns. Kiss me, Minnie—I am so happy!"

Minnie kissed her, thinking of the lips that had kissed Caroline's mouth before hers had—worshiping those lips, longing for them, dreaming of them pressing upon her own. There was a roaring in her ears, like some devastating wind come to trample and destroy. Franz. . . .

"You will be sewing carpet-rags then, too, maybe," she said softly. "And you must learn to make the salt-rising bread and the Hassenpfeffer and the Schmerkäse—and so many things." Her hurt heart was crying, "For Franz—she will make them for Franz—and he will sit across the table from her—it will be their table and their house—and their life, so far away from mine—and I love him so—Franz, Franz!"

She made her purchases, talking as gayly with Caroline as she could. Anton, Caroline's older brother, came in and offered to carry the basket home for her.

"It is too heavy for a girl," he twinkled, picking it up easily. "Besides," he added, as they stepped out onto the banquette, "I want to speak to you about something right away. My sister . . . you know?"

"She told me," Minnie replied, fumbling with her Taschentuch. "They will be very happy, I should think. Franz is a nice boy."

"There was a time when I feared you thought him too nice," Anton smiled down at her. "But now I know better, of course. Minnie, I'm six years older than you are, and I've been to the war and all ,and maybe you think I am gruff and ugly sometimes. But if you'll marry me, I'll make you a good man. I'm not really ugly at all, and I've been fond of you for a long time now. . . ."

"I'll see, Anton," Minnie sighed. "It's such a hot day— and I have so many carpet-rags to sew—and I must be hoeing the beans, *Mutter* said—but I'll think about it, Anton. I hadn't planned on getting married yet awhile."

"Caroline's planning for next May—we could have a double wedding," he suggested hopefully.

"Nein, nein, Anton—in double weddings one couple gets all the luck. I don't want to give all my luck away—and I don't want to steal Caroline's luck, either."

"Well, we could make it at Christmas."

"But I haven't yet promised to marry you, Anton," Minnie laughed. "And here you are, setting the day already."

"Well, somebody has to set it," Anton persisted. "You'll marry me, I've made up my mind to that. I've a nice little nest egg for us to start on. I told Mother, and she was pleased and satisfied with my choice. She has a bolt of linen to give you."

"But Caroline—the linen should go to her."

"There is other linen. This bolt is for you, Minnie—for us. Let us set the day."

"Nein, nein, Anton—do not hurry me so! Such a time to speak of marriage—carrying home the groceries! I thought better of you than that!"

"Any time is a good time. You'll marry me, Minnie—promise!"

"I'll see—I'll see! Let go my hand, Anton—there is *Mutter* at the door already!"

"I think you have a fellow now," Frau Bollar smiled, when Anton had started home.

"Nein, he was only carrying the basket," Minnie denied.

"He was carrying your hand, some of the way—I have eyes," tittered the mother. "You needn't blush—I was young once myself, and courted, too, by more than one. Don't you make the mistake of letting the right one go by, Minnie. Anton Koehn is a fine young man, and any girl should be proud of him."

"Ja," agreed Minnie listlessly. Her heart was calling, "Franz, Franz. . . ."

In January of the next year—1872—Franz Hartzein went to New York. He was to lay in a stock of fine leathers and other harness materials, with whips, fly-nets, and so on, at the same time keeping his eyes open for the latest fashions in house furnishings. He would have volumes to tell Caroline, he promised.

Immediately upon his return, the building of the new house was to start. It would be ready by the twenty-second of May, which fell on a Wednesday and had been settled on as their wedding-day. At least the house would be far enough along so they could manage and be there to superintend the finishing.

Franz traveled by boat, and the voyage would take a number of days. But as soon as he reached New York, he would write. So Caroline hemmed tablecloths and napkins, and whipped long seams in muslin sheets, crocheted lace for pillow-cases, and embroidered pillow shams.

Frau Koehn was making white petticoats and chemises and drawers and nightgowns, all with the most delicate tucks and flounces and frills. She was schooling Caroline, too—how to make the lightest and whitest Brod, the tenderest Sauerbratten, the most toothsome Wurst, the most featherly Kuchen.

There were German stews and potato dumplings and complicated cabbage mixtures; the art of drying herbs, of rendering lard, of compounding tallow salve, of molding candles, of bleaching linens, of starching shirt-bosoms, of keeping household accounts. Don't peel the Kartofeln too thick—save onion skins for dye—save orange and lemon rinds for flavoring—use grape leaves for pickling—make soft soap in the spring—put up ketchup and preserves in the summer—smoke hams under a barrel—polish the lamp-chimneys with ammonia every morning—put bits of red flannel under the edges of carpets—save goose grease for colds.

The weeks sped by, and no word came from the absent Franz. Caroline began to worry and chafe, imagining all sorts of dire calamities. Herr and Frau Koehn themselves grew anxious, although they felt sure all must be well. The thoughtlessness of youth, they said.

One day Caroline met Philip Gurgin. Philip looked tired, and she was glad when he turned to walk with her.

"What do you hear from Franz?" he asked lightly. "Letters every few days, I suppose."

"No, Philip," the girl replied, a sob choking her. "I have had no word at all."

"What?—no word at all?" In his amazement, Philip stopped short. "You mean he never has written you all the time he has been away?"

"Not a single line," Caroline replied, tears trickling down her soft cheeks.

"I have had no letter myself," Philip went on, "But I took it for granted that Franz had not neglected you like that."

"I am so afraid . . ." began the girl.

"No, no—Franz is well and happy," the other hastened to assure her. "I have a friend who lives in New York—a young man named Hans Schmoekel. I had a letter from him last week, and he spoke of meeting Franz. He wrote that our Franz is something of a high-flyer—he saw him going into one of these theaters where the actresses wear . . . ah . . . tights."

"Oh no!" Caroline gasped. "Franz never would go to a place of that sort!"

"Ach, all the men in New York do so, I am told," Philip replied. "It is only here that they are so particular and strait-laced. But that is our way."

"Philip," begged Caroline, "do not tell anyone else about the terrible . . . ah . . . tights!"

"Certainly I shall not," he promised.

Caroline's heart was like lead in her young bosom. After all, Franz was not true! Still, perhaps he would tell her all about it when he returned. But why hadn't he written? Even her father and mother felt incensed about that.

The next week Philip showed her a letter he said he had just received from Franz. Caroline read the date first, to make sure, trembling so she could scarce read it at all. Franz spoke of the "charming ladies" he was meeting, more especially a girl names Frances Leigh. The letter went on to say, "I find I love Frances madly, yet I am here to prepare for my marriage with another. If only I did not have Caroline on my hands. . . ."

Poor Caroline could read no farther. She ran all the way home, tears blinding her.

"Mutter, Mutter!" she cried, flinging herself onto Frau Koehn's ample bosom. "Put away all the nehen and the clothes!

I am not going to be married at all! Franz wants to marry somebody else—and I never will marry him now!"

So, after much talk and vast excitement, all the clothes and the linens were laid away in a green chest in the garret. Herr Koehn swore and Frau Koehn wept.

"Wait till that donkey comes back again!" blustered Johann. "Just wait till he comes back!"

"Nein, nein—our girl would not have him now, Vater," his wife counseled. "And he could not have her."

"You are right," agreed the German. "He could not have her! Gott sei dank that we found out what he is before she got married to him!"

The next time Caroline saw Philip, he was very quiet.

"I have been thinking so much about you," he told her gently. "Poor little one, you have been hurt indeed. And I, who have loved you from the first moment I ever saw you—I am powerless to help you!"

"My heart is broken," Caroline sobbed. "I do not want to live, Philip! I would be so much happier dead—why can I not die?"

"You are young," Philip murmured softly, looking into her eyes. "Time will heal your heart. You will laugh again. And then I shall be waiting for you—I shall always be waiting for you, Caroline."

Philip worked in a chemist's shop. Sometime he would have his own store, he told her. It was a nice, dignified business, almost a profession. A chemist was somebody. Far superior to a harness-maker, he said to himself—but he was too wise to say it aloud.

With all the whisperings and the nods, only Minnie Bollar kept her faith in Franz.

"There must be some mistake," she argued to herself. "Franz is not like that. He never will be like that—light-minded and changeable and flighty. He will come back and make them all look like fools."

Anton was attentive to her. He had nice, gentle ways and she knew he was honest and fine. But how could she love him when Franz filled all her heart?

One day Caroline went into the shop where Philip worked,

There he was behind the counter, trim and neat and gentlemanly. There was a churchlike stillness about the place.

"Philip," she said, standing on tiptoe, "I will marry you if you want me."

"Today?" he asked eagerly.

"Yes," she answered. "If you like."

"Wait till I get my hat," he whispered.

When they stepped out into the April sunshine after Father Apfel had married them, Caroline felt stunned and a little sick. Philip took her to the house where he boarded, and left her in his room while he went back to the shop.

"Today is Monday, the twenty-second day of April," little Frau Gurgin murmured, looking dully out of the window. "A month from today I was to have married Franz. But if he comes back now, he never can marry me. That was my plan—to take myself away from him, so he never could come and tell me that he had made a mistake, and didn't want me!"

She wept until she had no more tears. If only she could have died—but people never die when they really want to, she reflected. This boardinghouse—it was horrible!

A week later, on April twenty-ninth, Franz Hartzein came back to New Orleans. He hurried to the Koehn store—he must see Caroline and tell her all the splendid things he knew he must have failed to tell her in the almost daily letters he had sent. Traveling by water was a slow and tedious business. When he and Caroline took a trip to New York, after they were past their first youth and their children were sufficiently grown, they would not go by boat.

He was met by a stormy-visaged Johann Koehn.

"Do not step into my store!" the grocer thundered. "You and your New York—and your whores in tights—and the girl you were running with! Have you married her yet! No—and you won't, either!"

"I don't know what you're talking about," Franz replied, blinking. "I am going to marry Caroline on the twenty-second of next month. I came to see her. Where is she?"

"Where is she, indeed! With her husband, Philip Gurgin, of course. You don't deserve any decent girl, to go away and leave her like that!"

The grocer pushed the young man outside and banged the door shut. Franz stood there dazed. Caroline had married Philip!

He made his way to the chemist's shop. Philip stood behind the counter, as he had done the day Caroline came in to say she was ready to marry him.

"I know why you have come," he said, before Franz had a chance to speak. "It is about Caroline. And I do not wonder. Let me tell you. Caroline did not miss you as much as one would expect. She was very gay after you went to New York. Then last Monday she came in here and stood right where you are standing now, and asked me if I would marry her. I asked her if it was because of you, and she said it was.

"I am your true friend, Franz, and I took up the burden that belonged to you. I married her, as she desired. No one ever heard from you after you went North. I had to save Caroline. It was your child, she said."

"You lie!" cried Franz. "You know you lie! Caroline— why, she is as pure as a flower, and you know it!"

"I know what I know," sneered Philip. "I repeat, I saved you and I saved Caroline and the child she will bear. No friend could do more."

Franz felt that he had been struck dead. He staggered home, numb and broken. As the days dragged on, he never saw Caroline. He sat in his small shop, cutting leather and sewing harness-straps. He seemed to have gone blank. Never once did he go near the lot on Clouet near Saint-Claude.

But very early in the morning, on Wednesday, the twenty-second of May, which was the day he was to have married Caroline, he took a new strap and went to the vacant lot. The grass was sweet and wet with dew. The great live oak seemed to open its eyes and reach out its gray arms in warm welcome. There was a light fog, and it seemed to clothe him in its wan folds.

He climbed the oak, and sat on one of its stout branches while he fastened one end of the strap securely around it. The other end he buckled closely about his neck. He had sewed the buckle on and punched the holes in just the right places. Then he slipped quietly off the limb. . . .

They found him hanging there, when it grew lighter and the fog lifted. The whisper ran round that the New York girl had jilted him, and that he had come back to take Caroline Koehn as next best. But Caroline had, of course, married Philip—like a sensible girl.

When Caroline heard of it, she fell in a faint. The next morning she lay cold and still beside Philip. Her heart had stopped in her sleep, the doctor said.

The neighborhood was hushed and sad. Philip Gurgin went about his duties in the shop white and quiet as a wraith. There was a fear in his eyes, people said, and a look as though he were listening for a voice.

One day he was on his way to his boardinghouse for dinner when he met Minnie Bollar. She did not speak.

"Minnie!" he cried desperately. "There is something I must tell you! You've *got* to listen! Somebody's got to know—I can't keep it any longer! You loved Franz—don't ask me how I know—so you're the one to hear it.

"Minnie, Franz *did* write to Caroline—almost every day while he was in New York. I wanted her so—and I went to the post office and asked for her mail, and got the letters and destroyed them all. I invented all those terrible stories about him—I wanted to turn her against him. And then I forged a letter, and told her it was from him, and let her read it—that one about another girl whom he wanted to marry.

"When Franz came back, I told him she had been wild and was going to have a baby—I said it must be his baby. Poor Caroline, she was so good and so chaste—but I had to get rid of him somehow.

"And now Franz has hanged himself, and Caroline is dead, and I have this weight on my soul! I have murdered them both, Minnie—what shall I do?"

"Go to Father Apfel," she advised him bitterly. "He can talk to you—I cannot."

It was just about this time that the neighborhood began to say Franz Hartzein's ghost was haunting the vacant lot. It walked from the banquette to the live oak, people said, and then strode back and forth beneath the tree all night. In the morning it walked to the banquette and vanished. Night after night this strange thing went on.

"Ach," Johann Koehn said to his wife, "it is not Christian. There is Franz Hartzein, dead and buried, yet he is walking already every night. How can a dead man get up out of his grave and walk around all night, and then squeeze himself back into his tomb again for the daytime? It makes not sense."

"But I have seen him, Vater," put in Anton quietly. "It is Franz, and he walks. His head bends to one side, and his eyes are very terrible, and his great purple tongue hangs out. He sways as he walks, like a tree sways in the wind. It was the most terrible thing I ever saw. Yet they say that the morning when he hung himself was still and sweet."

"Ach, you are crazy, Anton, and you make the creeps go up my back!" growled his father. "I do not remember what the weather was when he hung himself. I do not believe in ghosts. The people are all imbeciles."

But Frau Koehn said nothing. In her heart she whispered, "Poor Franz—God made a fool of him!" She would not have dared to say such a thing aloud. Of Caroline she never spoke.

People told other things about the ghost of Franz Hartzein. They said the flesh was brown and dry on his bones now. That he carried the strap in his hand, and knotted it to the limb from which he had hung. That a terrible stench clung about the tree, and that no animal would pass the lot after dark.

Once a tramp thought to sleep in the live oak, and the strap had been drawn tight around him, and had bound him where he was until dawn, when a long, bony claw came scratching at it and near tore his ragged clothes from his quaking body. The tramp's hair was snow-white, though it had been black when he climbed the tree.

When it rained, passers-by heard groans and sobs coming from the direction of the tree. They would hurry by, their teeth chattering. One reported that a white Shape had pursued him and seized his umbrella and tossed it to the top of the tree. There it was, sure enough, rent to ribbons.

When this had been going on for nearly two years, Frau Koehn one day called to Minnie Bollar. Minnie had come to buy butter and nutmegs, and the grocer looked startled when his wife beckoned to her. She shut the sitting room door and bade the girl be seated.

"Minnie," she said, "I'm going to talk about something. I've got to. Franz's ghost won't be still until I do. And out there nights and in the rain and all—it isn't Christian."

"I know it," Minnie nodded. "But what can any of us do?"

"I keep remembering. It was one day when we three sat and talked—him and Caroline and me. He told me how he loved her. And he said, 'Why, if ever I were to die and suffer torment, Caroline's tears would ease all my pain.' "

"Yes," Minnie answered, her own tears dripping down onto her dress. "But Caroline is dead, too. She has no tears to shed."

"But there might be a way, Minnie," the bereaved mother persisted. "When Caroline heard that story about Franz and the New York girl, she came home and cried for days. One of her wet handkerchiefs I wrapped in a rosary, and laid it at the foot of the Holy Mother on my bureau. It was soaked with her tears. I never have taken it away. I thought the Holy Mother would understand. Caroline's tears—they are dried in that handkerchief—nothing can take them away."

"What do you want me to do?" Minnie asked.

"Take it to the place where the boy killed himself. Maybe the tears will heal his hurt spirit. Wait—I will get it for you."

That night, Minnie Bollar stole out of her house. It was still and dark and near midnight. When she came to the vacant lot, her heart pounded so she could scarcely breathe. She turned and started towards the live oak.

A nauseating odor almost overpowered her. A fine rain began to fall, and she stumbled over a loose root. The weeds were waist-high and scratched her hands. She had nearly reached the tree when she saw a gaunt, dark Shape moving slowly back and forth under the oak. It seemed to sway and shiver, and she could hear terrible little moans, like someone whose heart is breaking.

Minnie drew very near. She knew that she must. Suddenly the Shape turned and faced her—the horrible staring eyes, the twisted head, the protruding tongue, the dry brown skin—all these made her ready to run shrieking from the place. But this was Franz, and this was what life had done to him— what love had done to him. This was Franz—this ghost, this Thing!

"Franz," she said, holding her voice as steady as she could, though it threatened to die in her throat, "I have brought Caroline's precious tears, shed for you—here in her handkerchief! They must heal you. . . . You said they would. Take them, Franz—from one who loved you truly!"

She had not meant to tell him that. But, after all, great love knows nothing of shame. The handkerchief lay in the palm of her hand. Would he take it? Must that awful hand touch her living one? She shrank and drew in her scant breath. She held out the handkerchief to this Thing which they said was Franz. . . .

A breath of wind shivered past her, lifting the scrap of cambric high in the air. Minnie gave a little cry of despair. The handkerchief was sailing high above the tree. Strange she could see it so distinctly, though the night was dark. It hung there like a white bird a moment, and then it began to glide downwards. Slowly it settled on the head of the Thing. The Thing lifted a claw and grasped the little white square. Minnie turned and ran blindly.

But in a moment she stopped. There was something she must wait for, if it ever happened.

The Shape stood still beneath the live oak, its hand pressed to its spectral heart. And now another Shape was gathering beside it—a slender Shape, like a young girl.

"Caroline!" whispered Minnie.

All her sodden grief seemed slipping away. Her heart was growing light again . . . happy, like it had been before this trouble came upon them all. The two Shapes stood silent a moment. Then they began to walk away together. They passed her, and never seemed to see her or be conscious of her presence. It was as though they were living people and she were the phantom. On they walked—on and on and on. But now Franz was not twisted and horrible. He was straight and joyous, and a soft light glowed around the two.

They were not on the ground, nor on the banquette. They

were walking down the sky to the horizon. It seemed as though they walked for hours—going, going, going, always down the tender night sky.

Then Minnie heard the branches of the live oak creaking. The moon suddenly came out, and she saw a cruel black strap hanging from a limb of the tree. She touched it, and a strange fire seemed to race through her blood. When she looked again, the strap was gone.

The moonlight was streaming down onto a house, in the middle of the lot. There were curtains at the windows, and pots of flowers on the galleries. There were lights in it, and she could hear children's voices, and a bird singing. Then suddenly it, too, was gone.

There was only a vacant lot full of weeds and rubbish, and a straggling live oak creaking in the wind. But there at her feet lay a small square of white cambric. She stooped to pick it up, and it vanished as the house had done.

"I have seen a lifetime," she told herself reverently.

No ghost ever haunted that vacant lot again. The live oak swayed in the wind, season after season. Three years later Minnie married Anton Koehn.

"It is not good to be too selfish," she told herself. "Anton's love is steadfast and beautiful, and love was not made to waste. It is strange, but I love him very much. Franz and Caroline will be happy about it. . . ."

# (1840-1925)    *The Devil's Mansion*

They say the Devil used to have a house in New Orleans. They say he kept his woman there, dressing her in silks and velvets and loading her with priceless jewels. They say, too, that he ruled the roost, as the Devil would, coming and going when and as he saw fit.

But he did not come and go by the front door. He passed through the front gable of the house, high up, and paused on a secret balcony up there, surveying the premises at his leisure, and then descending upon the woman of his choice like a monstrous evil bird of the night. They say, they say. . . .

But they used to, point to the house that stood at 1319 Saint-Charles avenue and tell you, with a shudder, that the Devil lived here. And that if you peered up to the point of the front gable, just at sunset, you could see him standing there, grinning and twisting his evil lips, his eyes keen as needles and his sharp little horns quite visible.

There are those who saw him often enough, truly. Though in later years they preferred the other side of the street, giving no valid reason.

The house itself, a tall, ornate structure, stood for more than a hundred years. It was built in the 1820's, though there seems to be but the vaguest record of this. There is a mention of the site being acquired, and then the house seems to have materialized, like a mushroom, overnight. Gossip has it that the Devil, needing a domicile, started the house with one room, entire and complete, set in one place one Monday night. He worked all the week, setting at least one room in place at a time—one room, finished and furnished.

But, because the woman was waiting, and he could not work on Sunday, he hurried his labors and made a botch of it. So miserable a botch, in fact, that no two rooms had the same floor level. All over the house, in place of every threshold, there were steps, up and down, up and down.

Servants used to groan at the prospect of another day's work in that bewildering house. But that was at a later day, after there were servants. For in the beginning, gossip says, Satan brought young Madeleine Frenau there, and called her his wife.

She was a coy, beautiful young woman, with a tripping step as light as a brook murmuring over pebbles. Her voice was like a cuckoo calling, and her hands were like the petals of peach blossoms. No servants were needed in that house, for nothing ever gathered dust or became disarranged. Gossip said that small red demons scoured and polished every inch of the place six nights a week, and feasted on offal the seventh night.

One day Madeleine Frenau disappeared. And for some time the house remained vacant. It stood, dour and forbidding, its three stories of dark green walls with their fantastic ornamentation gathering mold and grime. The windows on the ground floor were heavily barred, and the brick pillars on which the house rested were sodden with moss and slime. The fountain at the side was dry and grass-choked.

Then a family moved in—a family with a bevy of boys and girls, who grew up there, giving gay parties and entering joyously into the social life of that olden day. In 1920 an old, old lady who had attended parties there in 1840, spoke of the ghosts which then haunted the place. And they were the same ghosts that haunted it when it was demolished in 1930. They had grown so terrifying that not a tenant could be induced to live in the house. Though it was solid and sound as in its youth, it had grown to be such a menace to the community that it was torn down and a business building now takes its place.

The great dining room ran the whole width of the house. It was a dark and gloomy apartment, with steps leading into the central hall, the butler's pantry and the rear yard. It was here that every day at dusk the phantoms came.

No matter who occupied the house, nor what furniture they brought and used, every day at dusk an enormous dining table appeared in the center of the room, under the great crystal chandelier. If a table were already there, it made no difference—the phantom table materialized just the same. It was spread with snowy damask, and was rich with silver and crystal and delicate china. Two places were laid.

And presently came two ghostly Shapes—a man and a woman—and sat them down in carved, tall-backed chairs. The conversation would ripple on for a space, food would appear and disappear. Dishes were replaced by invisible servitors.

Then suddenly the woman was gazing fixedly at her companion, her eyes dilating with apprehension. With desperate strength she caught up one of the great satiny table napkins. Before the man could fight her off, she had it around his neck, pulling the knot tighter and tighter. His face grew livid, and the blood spurted in a crimson torrent from a severed artery. Still the woman pulled at the cruel knot, while her lover writhed and struggled.

But at length he lay limp and still in his chair. The woman gazed at him, shaking his inert shoulders to make sure life had departed.

"You are gone, Alcide!" she cried, shuddering a little. "And I am glad—glad! You had to go—I am glad I killed you!"

And then she noticed her hands, there on the white table-cloth—red with her lover's blood, the fingers dripping from that warm and sticky stream still trickling from the dead man's crushed and twisted throat.

She untied the napkin, but that was soaked with red, too. She threw it in the grate, but the candle which she held beneath it refused to ignite the wet linen. Only a great stench of rancid smoke arose to choke and blind her. She wiped her hands on her wisp of a handkerchief—on the tablecloth—on her gown—on her petticoat—on one of the heavy curtains. But the blood would not come off. She even dipped her fingers in one of the wine goblets, but the crimson stain was deeper and uglier than ever.

So she ran from the room, stumbling up steps and down steps, moaning and crying for some place to wash her hands, too blind in her terror to find a washbowl or a bucket of water.

So it went on, year after year. The later tenants could not endure it. Some stayed a week, a few remained a month or two. Only once did a family become permanent. That was when Laura Beauregard Larendon, daughter of General Pierre Gustave Toutant-Beauregard, and her husband, Charles B. Larendon, moved in.

Maybe it was because the Larendons had seen the gaunt ghosts of war stalk up and down the beloved southland, and maybe it was because Madame's French blood understood that other French girl of an earlier day. At any rate, they did not mind the ghosts. They were fond of the long halls and the countless deep window seats and the richly carved Italian fireplaces. The fountain gurgled and rippled, and mocking birds nested in the trees.

Then came the small daughter, and the death of Madame. Brokenhearted, Charles Larendon took the infant to Atlanta, and returned alone to the "Devil's Mansion." For years he lived there by himself, defying the ghosts and the prying neighbors. But through him and his notes and diaries we have at last the secret of the mysterious house.

The Devil, tradition says, hurrying with the building of the house, left his lady to her own devices for one week. And in that week Madeleine Frenau looked upon a certain young man with favor. When Satan brought her on swift wings to the Saint-Charles avenue mansion, the young man followed.

Though the Devil took his fill of the woman and her charms, still he must be abroad about his business. It was during one of these absences that the lover, Alcide Cancienne, ventured to enter the house. The lady's reception being so cordial, he returned again and again. Her boudoir became his headquarters.

Every day at dusk they dined sumptuously. But one day Alcide seemed moody and unresponsive. Even wine failed to restore his accustomed gay humor.

All this time Madeleine had been telling him she lived alone. Now he looked at her with speculative eyes. Had he discovered that she was the Devil's harlot? At dinner she plied him with judicious questions. Finally he told her of the thing that was on his mind.

"The other night," he said, "when I was on my way here, I met a man just outside. He stopped and asked me what street we were on, saying he was a stranger in the city. I told him, and he asked me if I knew a woman called Madeleine Frenau. I replied that I did, and he laughed loudly and asked me if I were in love with her. He was a tall, powerful man with piercing black eyes and expensive clothes. Do you know who he is, Madeleine?"

"No," the lady lied, her heart almost ceasing to beat, she was so frightened. "I cannot imagine who he would be. But what did you tell him, Alcide?"

"I told him the truth," young Cancienne spat at her defiantly. "I told him your body was ripe and warm and delicious, but that I did not love you. He laughed at that, a deep rumbling chuckle that put me in mind of the sea when it tears a great ship to bits.

"This man said he knew you—that you were his woman. But he said he would be more than glad to make me a present of your body. He did not mention your soul, if you have one. His offer was that I take you, and a million pounds of gold with you. But that for all time I must be called 'L,' and you must be called 'Madame L' and that only. He was not joking, for on my breast is a huge L, which burns like fire. And before my eyes there is constantly a flaming L, which comes between you and me, no matter how close I hold you. What can that L stand for, Madeleine?"

"I do not know," she shivered. But in her heart she knew that it stood for "Lucifer."

"And," her lover continued, "the man said that I could take you away tonight."

"I shall be glad to go," Madeleine replied warmly. "I shall make you love me very much indeed. You will be glad you took me."

"Oh," young Cancienne announced airily, his eyes cold and

hard, "I am not going to take you. I had no intention of doing so, at any time. There are other girls much younger than you. And besides, no mistress is fit to be a wife."

It was then that Madeleine strangled him with a napkin, and found her hands drenched with his blood.

After she had roamed the house half the night, the Devil came home. He slithered in through the wall of the front gable, as was his wont. And when he saw Madeleine wringing her bloody hands and searching for a place to wash them, he laughed like a lion roaring.

Then he bundled her under one long arm, and her dead lover under the other, and to the little secret balcony on the roof he bore them, still shaking with silent laugher. After him he locked the little door leading to the balcony, and set himself in the peak of the gable, where Madeleine could see his evil face grinning in the moonlight.

"I am hungry," he slobbered. "Hand me up your lover, that I may eat."

Somehow she hoisted the heavy body up. Sucking and crunching, the Devil devoured every portion of the youth except his skin. That he tossed back to Madeleine, and the wind caught it and filled it like a rubber man, and there it stood leaning against the wall, billowing and bulging and flapping its empty lips.

Then the Devil reached down and clutched at the terrified girl. She was too paralyzed even to cry out. Presently her empty skin floated down, limp as a pancake.

And the Devil stayed up there in the peak of the gable, while the cats came and fought over the sodden skins. When no trace of them was left, save a few gummy tufts of hair, the Devil withdrew, leaving only the mask of himself to grin and jeer and mock at mankind from the peak of the gable.

Charles Larendon finally went away. Then a Mrs. Jacques lived in the house. Every night the weird spectacle was re-enacted in the great dining room, so that the Jacques family sought another room in which to enjoy their meals.

Mrs. Jacques stated that upon numerous occasions she smelled a strong odor of smoke, bitter and choking, but no fire did she ever find. Often doors opened and closed, for no reason whatever, and unseen feet hurried up and down the medley of steps between the many rooms. The bathroom was the worst—its doorknob was forever turning, turning, but no human hands turned it. There never was anyone there—unless it was the wraith of Madeleine Frenau, looking for a place to wash her hands.

And when some, bolder than the rest, made their way to the secret balcony on the roof, there was the Devil watching them, turning and twisting his hideous head to catch a better glimpse, his black eyes glittering and his lips pulled back in a snarl over his long spiked teeth.

No, it wasn't a stone head nor a bronze head, they declared—it was the living head of the living Devil, set in the gable of the Devil's Mansion—bound there by the flesh of the man and the woman whose bodies he had consumed.

Why? Because the Devil was careless, and worked when the moon was full. The dark of the moon is his time, and the dark of the moon only. It was his punishment, they say, for his moment of folly.

*The Whispering Hands*

Tradition says that in 1852 there lived in Apollo street (now Carondelet), in the Fourth District, a French jeweler by the name of Antoine de Laurens.

His jewelry shop was located on the ground floor of a building on the woods side of the street. He and his daughter lived in the spacious apartments above the shop. This daughter, Claire, was twenty-four at the time—a tall brunette, pretty and well-educated, but so thoroughly domesticated that she preferred her sewing and embroidery and oher household arts to going about in society.

Her isolation worried her father to no small degree. He was a widower and she his only child, and he was beginning to look forward to the time when she would have a husband and family.

De Laurens' lifelong friend was a Spaniard, Ruiz de Acosta, who kept a piano shop in the next square. De Acosta's father had kept a fine furniture shop in Royal street, while beside it stood the jewelry shop of Paul Georges de Laurens, Antoine's father. The fathers being fast friends, the sons naturally followed suit.

It was common knowledge that the elder De Acosta and the elder De Laurens had courted the same young lady—Mademoiselle Geneviève Marie Dumont. Both men were then in their forties, while the girl was nineteen. She chose De Laurens, and later De Acosta married another. The fact of the courting seems to have engendered no jealousy nor bitterness between the two men, whose friendship remained as firm as ever.

Only the one son was born to Geneviève and Paul Georges; the De Acostas had two sons, of which Ruiz was the older. The three boys were as close friends as their fathers had been.

Strangely, when they had grown to be young men, Antoine de Laurens and Ruiz de Acosta both fell in love with Mademoiselle Suzanne Pujol, a laughing little French girl who lived on Orleans street. She married Antoine, and the next year Ruiz married Mademoiselle Martine Lamothe. To Antoine and Suzanne came the daughter, Claire. But no little ones ever blessed the hearth of Ruiz and Martine.

Then, in 1832, the scourge of cholera swept through the city. It claimed Ruiz de Acosta's parents and his brother, Juan. The same week death struck down the father and mother of Antoine, as well as his lovely wife. The two households clung together in their grief, visiting the twin tombs in Old Saint-Louis Cemetery almost daily.

"El bueno Dios has inflicted upon us most terrible punishment for our sins," mourned Ruiz. "It seems, Antoine, that life will now be desperately empty."

"Ah, mon ami," returned Antoine, his eyes red from weeping, "you still have your Martine. But oh, my Suzanne, my beautiful Suzanne!"

"But you have also the pequeña Claire and your dear mother," sobbed the Spaniard. "We shall all need one another more than ever now. I can scarce bear to enter my shop. Every chair, every sofa, every table, every armoire—they all cry out to me of family circles and lively talk. The very place tears my heart from my body!"

"Mais oui—I have me the same feelings," nodded Antoine. "I think we both need a change. I have been to look at a property beyond Carondelet street, on Apollo, and it appears to be of a suitableness."

"But to move away out there, Antonio!" Ruiz was scandalized. "It is a wilderness—un yermo! And those Americanos toscos all about—they have not enough manners even to know how to pray decently!"

"But they buy well," Antoine sighed, dabbing at his eyes

with his pocket handkerchief. "After all, we are merchants—
it is our business to sell and to make money. You are like my
own brother, so I will make the propose.

"Let us go out there to Apollo street, especially in the
new and more remote portion of the Fourth District, and buy
us a patch of land. You in one square, and I in the adjoining
square. When we have each built us a place in the middle of
the square then we can sell off the rest of the ground as we
choose, and for the good price.

"There is always a place for une joaillier, so it is well
that I move my stock to the new location. But you, Ruiz, are
sick at the heart. The romance of your furniture it gives you
the ache and the grief. So it will be wise if you sell it all, as
quickly as you can. Dismiss your cabinet-makers, and make no
more of the sofas and the tables and the warm family things.

"When the new place is built on your ground, you must
deal only in pianos. They are furniture of a kind, oui—but
they will not tear your heart, like the sofas and the chairs and
so on. Let us go tomorrow and look at that land, mon frère."

So now, twenty years later, they were both well-established
in the New Town. Antoine's mother had died five years before
—the second great grief the two families had borne. She had
brought up Claire, schooling her in every graceful and gentle
art. Antoine was now fifty-one, while Ruiz was fifty. And not
a day passed that they did not mention "chérie maman," as
they all lovingly called the late Madame Geneviève de Laurens.

One evening in August, Antoine was gathering his brooches
and bracelets and earrings and gold chains into a strong metal
case, preparatory for the night. He did this daily, before closing the heavy batten blinds and doors. The goblets and table
silver and the less costly things he left in the shop. But the
jewels he took upstairs to his own bedroom.

Antoine de Laurens had always cherished an intense fear
of robbers. So, when he built this place, he conceived a neat
trick in the way of a locker for his treasures. He had in his
chamber a great mahogany bed, which had been fashioned
in the old De Acosta shop on Royal street. This had a high
tester and curtains of brocaded silk. In the thick headboard
was set a wide, invisible door. This was known only to An-

toine himself, the old cabinet-maker who had executed the work being now dead.

So every night he toted the metal case to his chamber, bolted the door, and opened the door in the head of his vast bed. Just behind it an iron-lined cupboard was set deep into the wall, with a steel door to protect it. From one year's end to another, the bed never was moved.

This night, as soon as he had rearranged the bedcurtains, there came a faint tapping noise. He could feel the color leaving his face, and a sort of stiffness crept into his muscles. The tapping continued, and a light hissing sound accompanied it, as though someone quite close at hand were whispering.

Antoine strained his ears, but no word could he catch. He made a dive for the door in the headboard of his bed, and swung it open. Bringing a lamp, he peered in carefully, and into the locker as well. But he found nothing.

Then he almost dropped the lamp. There on one of his pillows lay a human finger! He set the lamp down and lifted the pillow from the bed, that he might better examine what lay upon it. A horrible stench filled the room, almost overpowering him. When he brought the pillow to the light, he could see that the finger was a woman's, small and white and tapering. And the base, where it had been severed, was an oozing jelly.

How could he ever again bring himself to lay his head on that pillow! But, even as he gazed, the finger shot upward and vanished. He could hear Claire coming along the hall outside his door. His heart gave a great thump, and he jammed the pillow back onto the bed and opened his bedroom door.

The whisperings had ceased by now, and the stench seemed to have gone away. But his gorge rose at the memory of that slimy finger lying on his pillow.

When he joined his daughter at dinner he fancied her face was paler than usual, and that she seemed preoccupied. He did not dare ask if anything bothered her. Never could he tell her about the whisperings and the finger. No girl's nerves could withstand a shock of that sort.

He ate but little, choking down the food as best he could. When dessert was served, there among the small iced cakes lay a human finger, dead and white and horrible. His nostrils caught a whiff of the same nauseating odor which had come pouring into his bedroom. At that moment a faint thumping started at the other end of the table, and a sound that was like frantic whispering.

Antoine turned to his daughter. Her face was like still wax, but her eyes were bright and quick.

"There must be a wind," she observed evenly. "I can hear it whistling down the chimney. Evy set poison for the mice— though I have told her before that they die in the walls. Please do not feel that I am a poor housekeeper, chéri. I shall forbid Evy to set any more of the poison."

"I suppose they come in from the fields back of us," her father returned. "It is nothing, ma petite. Indeed, this household is run like clockwork. Chérie maman herself could not manage more charmingly."

The finger had vanished from among the cakes.

The next morning, when he took the metal case out of the safe behind his bed, he stifled a scream. On top of the case lay, not a finger, but a whole hand! It was as wet and slimy as though it had just come out of pickle. When it disappeared, in a moment or two, Antoine could have sworn that the white marks of it still remained on the case.

Never before had that case seemed so heavy. And when he opened it, to take out the jewels, there was the ghastly dead hand clutching a diamond locket. He sold the locket that day, wondering if any sinister omen went with it. When he heard shortly that the society belle who wore it had died in a fainting spell, he wondered more than ever. What had he done to be so visited?

The tappings and the whisperings were almost constant now. Sometimes he would meet his daughter flying down the stairs, white-faced and breathless. But he did not dare put his quaking terror into words, nor did he question her.

Once he slipped ten gold pieces into the Cathedral poorbox. That night the thumpings in his bedroom were louder than ever, and the whisperings more insistent. When he lifted a glass of water to his lips, just before retiring, a white finger lay in the bottom of it. He dashed the glass to the floor with a cry—and spent a laborious hour picking up all the splinters, rather than face the questioning looks of even a slave. But, of course, he found no finger on the carpet.

The thing went on for months. Antoine was certain that Claire looked more haggard every day. But then, even Ruiz de Acosta looked worn and colorless to him. It was the fault of his own eyes, of course. The cursed fingers were sapping his vitality. Everything seemed drab and flat.

Perhaps, after all, it would be wiser to consult with Ruiz. He always had taken the warmhearted Spaniard into his confidence. Surely a few dead fingers could make no change in their friendship.

De Acosta happened into the shop at about six o'clock, when Antoine was making ready to gather his more costly jewels into the big metal case for the night.

"Ah, my dear Ruiz!" he exclaimed, hurrying to greet his friend. "I have not seen you for the whole week! You look malade à la mort—mon cher ami, what is the matter? Let me call a physician, Ruiz! Fevre shall ride on the new black horse—it will take no time at all. You are very ill—sit down at once!"

Ruiz was indeed in a bad way, but he would have no physician. His face was white as death, his lips were blue, and he shook like a leaf. He dropped weakly into the chair which Antoine hurried to place for him. Going to a little wall cupboard at the back, the jeweler poured a glass of old brandy and brought it to his friend.

"You look as though you had seen a ghost," he declared. "What has gone de côté? Martine is not ill, I trust?"

"No—not ill, in the sense that she is sick," Ruiz returned, sipping the brandy gratefully. "But I have terrible things which I must tell you, Antonio. You always have been like my own brother—and mi hermano you must still be, even though I seem to grow weak-minded and foolish. But Martine and I— ah, we cannot account for some things that have been taking place, Antonio!" He groaned miserably, and put his hands to his aching head.

"I know," Antoine replied, feeling suddenly quiet and composed and master of the situation. "You see dead fingers here and there. You smell a frightful smell. You hear tappings and thumpings. Oui, that is your trouble!"

He brought his teeth together with a little snap. What a choice fool he had been all this time not to confide in Ruiz, so they might fight this bewildering battle together!

"You know, then?" exclaimed Ruiz in amazement. "Then it must be—"

"Certainement," nodded Antoine. "I also am haunted by these horrors. That is the precise word for it—haunted. We are being haunted, Ruiz!"

"But who could be haunting us, Antonio?—and why?"

"Le bon Dieu only knows!" De Laurens sighed. "But it is wearing me to skin and bone, I know that. What have you seen, Ruiz, and when?"

"I have seen, smelled and heard—as it seems you have," returned the other. "And not only Martine and I. You recall young Francisco Almudez, who is my distant cousin? He was here the week before last, you remember, and so greatly admired your lovely Claire. The night before he left, he found a dead finger on his pillow—ah, mi amigo querido, you cannot imagine the state of mind that young man was in! He shook like an aspen tree and vomited like a camel and ran as though Satan himself were after him. In the end we did convince him that the cheese he had eaten an hour earlier had merely disagreed with him. It was the best we could do."

"Nom de Dieu—everyone will find out!" cried the jeweler. "Both our shops will be ruined! What are we to do, Ruiz?"

"I have been thinking. I would not have been so greatly discomposed when I came in here, had not one of those fearful hands appeared right against your street door as I was about to enter," rejoined Ruiz, with a shiver. "I was speaking yesterday with one of these 'spiritual mediums,' as they call themselves. Without referring to my own problem, I led him to reveal some of their methods.

"So I determined to place the matter before you. Is it not possible that this is some one of our loved ones struggling to send us some message?"

"Oh, Ruiz—a stinking dead finger! And hissing like a snake! It is une sacrilège! Impossible!"

"I was afraid you might think so. But consider: I asked this spiritual medium how departed souls contrived to express themselves to those still on earth, should they desire to do so. He said one way was by means of rappings. Now, we surely have heard rappings. We must count for letters, he said—one for a, two for b, three for c, and so on. And then put them together to form words, if that can be done. But, of course, first we ask questions."

"It might be," assented Antoine. "At least, we should make the try. Wait a moment, until I arrange these things in the case and bolt the battens, and we will go upstairs."

As soon as they had ascended to De Laurens' chamber, they heard faint tappings. Both shivered involuntarily.

"You make the first try," Antoine directed. "Ask something. I have my pen ready, and I will jot down the numbers of the raps."

De Acosta pondered.

"Where is my cousin, Francisco Almudez, at this moment?" he asked slowly.

The tappings began coming in little groups, with distinct pauses between each. When they stopped, Antoine counted his marks.

"Fourteen, twenty-one, five, one, twenty-five, fifteen, eighteen, eleven," he read. "N-u-e-v-a Y-o-r-k. They are real words, Ruiz! Nueva York—that is New York. Young Almudez is then in the city of New York."

"But he is not," De Acosta objected. "I had a letter from him when he arrived there, and he was embarking for England the next day, to be gone until October. Bah, this message is no message, after all!"

The next morning De Laurens summoned a plasterer and had the wall behind his bed virtually torn out. That was where the tappings had most frequently sounded. Perhaps some mechanism was hidden in the wall. But there was nothing—except a deplorable mess to clean up, after the plasterer had restored the hacked wall. Anyway, the man knew nothing about the door in the head of the bed.

As the day grew late, Ruiz burst into the jewelry shop.

"Look, Antonio!" he cried, waving a paper under his

friend's nose. "A telegraphic dispatch! It is from Francisco Almudez, and it is dated yesterday, so he *was* in New York!"

"Then it *was* a message," nodded Antoine, his eyes like saucers, "It must have been."

"Sin duda," replied Ruiz. "And I have more to tell you, mi amigo. There was so much excitement yesterday that I forgot. You remember that my father had our bedroom suite designed and made especially as a wedding gift to Martine. Well, every time she goes to the chamber where we now keep it, the things fly at her as though they were alive. The great dresser rose and nearly tipped over onto her. Only the other day the armoire pranced half-way across the room and hit her on the head. Everything is bewitched, I tell you.

"Another thing: I have one particularly beautiful piano which I intend to present to your Claire as a wedding gift when she marries. Old Manuel Campos, who, as you know, always has been my watchman and was my father's watchman, tells me that that piano is played every night as the clock strikes twelve. Not tunes, you understand, but a sort of beating time on the keys. More than once he has taken his lantern, lifted the piano top and looked in, thinking perhaps a rat or a mouse had slipped in and was running across the wires. But not a thing has he found."

"Tapping," Antoine ruminated. "Beating time. There are no two ways about it, Ruiz—somebody has a message for us."

"That is something we shall have to find out," said his friend. "We shall get to the bottom of it eventually."

Ruiz had been gone only a few minutes when Claire came down stairs.

"Ah, m'amie, you have been crying!" her father exclaimed folding her in his arms. "Tell me, what has hurt mon petit chou?"

At length she told him—dead fingers, smells, rappings, hissings. She could keep it to herself no longer.

For a month things went on much as usual. Then Ruiz brought alarming news.

"That Manuel, my watchman," he exploded, "he has eaten two of his own fingers!"

"Mon Dieu, non!" cried Antoine. "It is not possible! Mais non—why eat himself?"

"It is all the devilish rappings," wailed the Spaniard. "He counts the rappings in the piano—but, alas! he cannot spell. He fancies they spell e-a-t, eat! He sees the dead fingers, too. He says his stomach would not permit him to attempt swallowing them, so he cut off both his own little fingers and ate them!

"But that is not the worst, Antonio. Old Manuel reasoned that by the eating of the fingers he would be delivered from all this nuisance. And it followed that whoever else ate the fingers would likewise escape the annoyance. So he went to the kitchen, where black Bufa was preparing crab gumbo. While her back was turned, he popped his two severed fingers into the pot of gumbo. He ate, as well as we. But so it is that you look upon a cannibal, Antonio mío!"

"Sacrebleu—un cannibale! You cannot be serious, Ruiz!"

"De veras, sí! My stomach turns round and round like a wheel, in consequence. That Manuel he is a fool, sí, though well enough intentioned. But this thing cannot continue. What are we to do?"

"There is one thing left," Antoine replied. "Claire is young and receptive. I had thought to shield her safely away from all this bothersome mess, but our ghostly tormentor feels otherwise. Claire is also visited by this uneasy spirit. We might as well find out whether or not she really can help us. Something must be done, or we shall all be out of our minds.

"And I have some news for you. This morning came a letter from that young Francisco Almudez. He tells me that he could not bring himself to go to England, for one reason alone. It seems he is in love with my Claire. He craves my permission to propose marriage to her.

"Now, as you know, he is un lapidaire. Think of it— un lapidaire, who can become a partner in my business—your kinsman—and my dear daughter married, with half a dozen fine babies to gladden my heart!"

"A thousand thanks to elbueno Dios!" cried Ruiz, jumping up and down with joy. "Yo lo creo! My prayers have been answered! Martine and I will come over this very night, and we will all ask questions of that spirit until we receive a good message, if it takes until dawn!"·

"Do not go. I shall send Fevre with the carriage to fetch her," arranged Antoine. "We shall all have dinner first—and then to the message!"

It was near midnight before the rappings began at all.

"I wonder who it really is," Martine sighed.

"Who raps?" Claire de Laurens asked in a clear voice.

"Three, eight, five, eighteen, nine, five, thirteen, one, thirteen, one, fourteen," came the taps.

"C-h-e-r-i-e m-a-m-a-n—chérie maman," Antoine interpreted softly. Claire was sobbing.

After that came, *"We are crushed—help us!"* over and over again.

The night had resolved itself into a season of terror and grief. As the first streaks of dawn appeared, there came the one word, *"Tomb."*

As soon as offices were open, Ruiz and Antoine were applying for permission to open the De Laurens tomb. The Old Saint-Louis Cemetery, with its narrow grassy aisles, was still drowsy as they made their way to the twin white tombs. A strange silence, eerie and forbidding, seemed to attend them, urging them on, yet warning them of something startling.

When the marble slab was lifted away, two white hands clung to the inner surface of it. Almost on the instant, they vanished.

But inside the tomb was a huge metallic casket which never had been deposited there by any of the De Laurens family.

"It crushes chérie maman," wept Claire. "She said she was crushed—and she is!"

"There has been a terrible mistake," the sexton admitted. "An order came in late one day last August, to open two tombs for the reception of two caskets, which might arrive late at night. They were being shipped from a great distance.

"I remember it was quite dark, and we had only our lanterns. I instructed one of my helpers to remove the front slabs, giving him the location of the tombs. I recall now that, when the caskets came, it seemed too long a way to the tombs.

But it was raining, and it never occurred to me that my man might have made a mistake. But De Laurens was not the name—neither was De Acosta. Yet a casket went into each one of these tombs."

Both caskets were that day removed and placed in their proper tombs. Only once in a hundred lifetimes could such a mistake have occurred. . . .

Claire de Laurens married Francisco Almudez at Christmas time. In a year Ruiz was selecting a locket to give her when her first baby was born. He chose one especially fine and costly.

"Non, non," Antoine shook his head at his friend sagely, "not that one. I should not have displayed it at all. That is the one which was returned—you remember the awful hand? I am stupid—you must make another selection."

"Of course," Ruiz agreed. "But what if this locket brings death to some other wearer?"

"It shall not," the jeweler smiled. "This very day I am giving it to the Church. It shall be blest and broken up for use in the new sacred vessels. It shall look out upon the world with a new eye. . . ."

## (*1908*)     *The Magic of Aga Bab*

In 1908 a barber named Philip Dusa had a shop in Claiborne
avenue. His living quarters were above the shop, and his wife
did sewing to help out when business was slack.

When the weather was warm, Mrs. Dusa frequently took
her embroidery or hemming or quilt-piecing out onto the shady
front gallery. Sometimes, when there was a rush of customers,
the Dusas postponed supper until very late. On these occasions
Mrs. Dusa sewed until it grew dark, and then went inside and
lighted the gas.

One evening in May, when the barber was kept later than
usual, Mrs. Dusa laid her sewing aside and went out to sit on
the gallery. She sat very close to the south end, so she could
glance down through the railing and watch people passing. She
could see almost to Gravier street, and often she would lean
over and exchange a word of gossip with an acquaintance.

It seemed, this night, unusually dark. Mrs. Dusa sniffed
the light breeze, observing mentally that there would be rain
before morning. The street grew very still. Not a horse, not a
mule, not even a racing small boy. The darkness hung heavy
as a velvet curtain. Something seemed to freeze the barber's
wife and shut off her breath.

From up the street, near Gravier, came a queer scraping
sound, very faint, very distant. To her straining ears it was
like a giant turtle hitching itself across a rough stone, its shell
dragging with each clumsy step. And then, along the banquette,
she saw a white Shape. It cleaved the darkness like a great
wedge of moonlight, ploughing nearer and nearer the Dusa

135

barber shop. As it approached, it swayed from side to side, plunging heavily about. Mrs. Dusa could hear it breathing in great gusts, like some monster from its Mesozoic wallow.

When it came within a few yards of her, the half-light surrounding it showed what looked to be a white-sheeted man fully ten feet in height. As it swayed, she could see an enormous iron-gray head, with eyes shooting out on stalks like those of a snail. Four hairy arms waved like flails, with gigantic claws, yellow and scaly and dry, clutching the air. The legs were like stilts, with three knee-joints each, bending this way and that.

As the Thing came even with the gallery, it leaned over and leered at her, stretching its wide, evil mouth in a terrifying grin. The glittering eyes poked themselves in between the spindles of the railing like adders, following her in a weird and sinuous weaving.

A fluff of wind sent the white draperies of the Thing flapping over the gallery rail. The nauseating odor of fresh blood filled the air. With a bellow like that of a bull, the monster reached out a claw caked with filth. The claw tapped the gallery floor, like bones rattling against a tomb-side. Three more noisome claws followed, creeping like hungry crabs. The woman sat paralyzed, her hair rising stiffly from her cold scalp.

Swiftly the claws rose, like menacing jaws, and flung a shower of small objects into her lap. The great head, with its loose swathings of white, again came close to the gallery rail, peering over it, grinning widely, the hooked nose sharp as a hatchet, the horrible eyes creeping and wriggling nearer and nearer. And all the time, the sickening smell of fresh blood grew heavier and yet more heavy.

The claws touched the woman's ankles, stinging like bees, scorching like flames. They seemed to be stripping the flesh from her bones—tearing, scraping, ripping muscle and tendon, nerve and vein and ligament—clawing her to shreds, while she sat frozen and dumb and helpless.

She closed her eyes an instant, expecting death to blind her and destroy her. When she opened them, the Thing was gone. She sat on her cool gallery, the palm leaves in front of the house rustling like paper, a breeze mewing from the river, the faint stars peeping out of the night sky.

With a smothered cry she fled into the house, lighting the
gas with hands that shook so she could scarce get the match
to a flame. That frightful Thing she had seen out there on the
gallery—surely she must have fallen asleep and had a nightmare! Ah, that was it. But her heart still pounded and her
breath still came in convulsive jerks. What would Philip say,
if he knew how foolish and nervous she was! He would tell
her she sewed too steadily, and needed more exercise, and that
they were eating too much pork. Philip always laid seizures
to overindulgence in pork.

Mrs. Dusa sank wearily into an armchair. It was then
that she became conscious of an unusual heaviness about her
cotton skirt. She glanced down at her lap. What was all this?
One by one, with stiffening fingers, she picked up the strange
objects and laid them on the marble-topped table—nine black
candle-ends, burnt and battered, a handful of dry tuberoses,
and two small clay figures with a nail trust through each
heart. It was when blood began to flow from the wounded
hearts that Mrs. Dusa rushed to the door and reeled, shrieking,
down the stairs to her husband's shop. And, pursuing her, was
the hideous Thing.

Dusa was stropping a razor, his towel-swathed customer
lolling in the barber-chair beside him.

"It's a ghost!" his wife screamed, bursting into the shop
like a hurricane. "It's a ghost—as tall as a tree, with a mouth
like a wash-kettle and eyes like snakes and legs like step-
ladders! There it is, Philip! It clawed the flesh off my legs—
it'll burn us up or poison us or eat us alive! Oh, Philip, what
shall we do?"

"Hush, Louise—are you crazy?" the barber snapped, annoyed at this wild interruption. "If you must have hysterics,
go upstairs and have them. But shut the door."

"But, Philip," Mrs. Dusa panted, no longer seeing the
Thing at her heels, "that's where the terrible Thing is by this
time—it's gone back upstairs! I tell you, it came at me like a
devilfish—at least four arms, it's got—and eyes like eels—and
it bellowed—"

"What is it—a sure-enough ghost?" inquired the lathered
customer, sitting up like a corpse in its coffin. "Have you got

a ghost, Dusa? I've heard of a Spanish barber named Millon, who used to have his shop here where yours is—and a ghost murdered him and ate him up."

"Ate him up?" Mrs. Dusa's eyes almost popped from their sockets. "What did I tell you, Philip?"

"Well," continued the customer, "it was something like that. It happened twenty years ago, though. Queer things there have been in this house, they say—didn't you ever hear?"

"Don't tell her!" scowled Dusa. "She's got enough foolishness in her head, as it is. No sensible person believes in spooks —but then, no woman is sensible. Go and attend to the supper, Louise, and stop your nonsense."

Mrs. Dusa knew about how far she could go with Philip. So now she withdrew, still sobbing, closing the stair door behind her. But she did not ascend. Instead, she gulped back her sobs and seated herself on the dark stairs, with her ear as close to the door as she could conveniently get it.

Alexander Maunsell, reclining at ease in the barber-chair, began his story. Philip Dusa listened, his jaw dropping and the lather drying on his suspended razor. And Louise Dusa listened, crouched on the stairs like a tree toad hugging the lichened bole of an oak, shuddering and quaking and choking back her panic as best she could.

It seems that, about the year 1880, a Spanish barber by the name of Matías Bonaventura Millon bought the small building on Claiborne avenue. He had recently married Rose Ferrara, an Italian girl, of whom he was already beginning to tire. As he was thirty-two and his bride eighteen, perhaps this was not unnatural to one of his temperament. However, it piqued the lady to such a degree that finally, after they had been married some three years, she flew at him in a rage.

"So I am not good enough for you!" she screeched. "Me I bring you money, I bring you a property, I bring you a hundred customers—I can sing, I can cook, I can wear clothes! But no-no, all that is not enough! Bambino—that is what you want! I cannot give you a bambino in a day or a week. I think you are a horse, you! I think you are a—"

At that moment her husband struck her in the mouth.

"Remember," he glared, his upper lip drawn tight so that

his long teeth gleamed like fangs, "remember that I am Matías Bonaventura Millon, a Spaniard. También, remember that I have ancestors—and one of them worked with Torquemada four hundred years ago. I have a family tree—sí, and I am passing generous to have taken you for my wife at all—you, who do not at this moment know the maiden name of your own maternal grandmother! Your ancestors—quiénes, dondé? Nobody knows! All you know is that you are here—una joven, whom I deigned to marry. Now, be about your duties—see that la comida is not late again, or you shall taste el castigo along with la carne!"

He stamped off. He was on his way to meet the queer little man with whom he had spoken the day before. Dios, what a queer little man he was, de veras! Surely not more than four feet tall, but a Spaniard—and wise as the Holy Ghost. Strange tales he told . . . born in 1450, he said . . . the immortal, the never-dying one, the laugher-at-time.

"But how could anybody be four hundred and thirty-three years old!" Millon scoffed to himself. Then he thought of the Wandering Jew, and the sweat came out on his forehead in cold beads.

The little man was mounting the three steps to the shop as Millon came down the stairs. He dragged off his bizarre peaked cap and wiped his hooked nose on it.

"Buenas días," he squeaked, wagging his great head with its mat of grizzled curly hair. "Buenos días, and you are not like to forget me, señor."

"No, not likely," smiled the barber dryly. "Nor the story you tell, neither. I was on my way to meet you, as appointed."

"And it gave you the start to find me coming in at your door," tittered the other. "Well, ten seconds ago I was at our meeting-place. But I decided it would be far more comfortable here at your shop."

"How did you know where my shop was?"

"How did I get here in ten seconds?" wheezed the little man, screwing up his withered eyelids and shaking with mirth. "Ah, Aga Bab could tell you that. But Aga Bab never will tell you that. Aga Bab could talk from sun to sun and from moon to moon, and not tell a millionth part of what he knows."

"So that is your name—Aga Bab?" asked Millon.

"Sí, señor, that is my name—Aga Bab," chuckled the little man. "And you are fresh from a quarrel with la señora, I see."

The barber squirmed.

"How did you know that—cómo?" he demanded.

"How do I know everything?" giggled Aga Bab. "It would make pretty telling. But I have other matters to discuss today. If I bring you a hundred new customers, will you grant me a small favor? Una cortesía muy insignificante?"

"To be sure," agreed Millon, thinking wrathfully of Rose's one hundred customers who were not enjoying his services as regularly as they should be. "And what is la cortesía muy insignificante you crave?"

"Oh, it is a very trifle of a thing. It has to do with my health," the visitor sighed, puckering his face and seeming to shrink to even smaller proportions. "I need a panacea for my ills every now and then, and I find it convenient to depend on a younger man to obtain it for me. I am a very old man, you know, and it is well for the old to share themselves to some degree. You will do my little errand, sí?"

"Ciertamente," nodded the barber. "But I should like to see some of the hundred customers first."

"Aha, you mistrust me, even so early?" The little man arose to his feet. "We shall be fast friends. Only a fool would not mistrust me, señor. Yet I have made a thousand men rich—rich beyond dreams. Come, let us walk together. Let us go where there are trees. Trees are my friends."

So they started out. Millon found himself hoping he would meet none of his customers . . . This absurd dwarf in his shabby clothes and broken shoes and uncanny cap—what would they think? How could he explain the mite away? But on all the way to the first clump of sycamores, they met no one Millon ever had seen before.

They sat down on the fresh grass, and a mockingbird started to trill from a tree.

"I wish to talk," Aga Bab said, showing his yellow fangs in a smile and holding up a shriveled forefinger. Millon experienced a lightning-sharp pain through his body from head to foot, as though a white-hot needle had shot through him. The mockingbird had stopped singing. "I wish to be sentimental, and to talk about little children," the dwarf continued. "You have no little ones as yet, I recall."

"I never told you that!" Millon returned, wincing at the thought of Rose's barrenness.

"You have no need to tell me—any more than you need to tell me that la señora cut her finger this morning and the blood dripped into your coffee."

"It is no such thing!" denied the barber hotly.

"Ask her," the other advised sweetly. "La sangre en el café—ask her about that. La sangre, la sangre," he smacked his lips, "it is what we all live by, in one way or another. A drop or two will not hurt you, mi amigo. You look sickly enough at this moment—and then you quibble about a drop or two of fresh blood! Dios, how do these silly, weak men of today ever manage to get on their legs at all!" He spat at the spotted trunk of a sycamore, and started his wheezing laughter again.

Something within Millon revolted.

"I shall have no more to do with you!" he exclaimed, rising. "You are a mysterious person, and all mysterious persons son malos. I do not want your hundred new customers, and I shall do you no favors! I am going back to open my shop, and I must ask that you keep away."

"Oh, todo, todo!" the small one cried, laughing aloud and hopping to his feet. "Nada omite, señor! But I fancy you will presently be changing your mind. No man gives me his promise without keeping it. And you have promised me the little favor—do not forget that, amigo mío."

"I am not your friend . . ." began the barber, but he did not finish.

Suddenly Aga Bab straightened and began to stretch upward. When he was perhaps ten feet tall, Millon turned his gaze full upon his strange companion. There he saw a gigantic head on an ungainly neck. Even as he gaped, the eyes pushed themselves out on long stalks, like glittering dandelions on great stems. As the eyes sought his face, Millon strove to scream, but no sound came. They wove to and fro, among the lower leaves of the sycamore, like snakes with tiny lamps for heads.

Four hairy arms, with claws for hands, menaced him. He turned to run—but what chance would he have, when this monster possessed three knees to each leg?

The barber found himself sobbing like a child. What chance did he have, indeed? Here in the clump of sycamores, with a tree-tall monster leering down from the midst of a million waving leaves—why, the strangling claw-hands could squeeze the life out of him and the awful mouth suck him dry before anyone would be passing that way! What had he gotten himself into by swapping pleasantries with a pitiful little wretch who had dogged his heels and presented him with a cake of magic shaving-soap which grew larger and heavier every time he used it? That had been the bait—yes, bait was the correct word. Millon groaned and covered his face with his icy hands.

"I want," rumbled the monster, the awful eyes fixed on him, "A child. A small infant, but not too small, not too soft. You will bring it to me—the one which cries all day in the house next but one to your miserable shop. Bring it to me here—tonight, at eleven o'clock. You will be busy—your shop will be crowded with customers. But, mind—the infant must be alive. Do you agree?"

"Sí, sí." Millon shivered. He would have agreed to anything, at that moment.

He turned and started homeward. At the third step the little man was bobbing along at his side, grinning cheerfully up at him.

"I have known you, Señor Millon, for quite a long time," he babbled, saliva dribbling down from each dirty corner of his unwholesome mouth. "El señor likes them young, no es verdad? There is la Señorita Bermondez, for example, who considers him quite the fascinating dandy. The new embroidered waistcoat enchanted her. A chicken liver, placed in the left pocket, would have ensured her complete surrender. Try it, *señor*—try the fresh chicken liver if you would win at the game of hearts!"

"I do not know what you mean," the barber defended. "I have a wife. Why should I run after a light o' love?"

"Why, indeed?" wheezed Aga Bab. "Because you are a man.

One flower does not make a bouquet. No man who is a man is satisfied to sit sniffing at one blossom all his life. He decays. Man was made to create. It is youth that is the essence of all creation.

"So the wise man uses youth, and pours it lavishly into his plans and specifications. It does not matter where he gets it—it is youth that he must have. Take the advice of an old, old man, señor—do not economize on youth. Take it wherever you find it, whenever you want it—the oftener the better, the more the fuller. You can't store it up ahead of time—it sours. Gather it fresh, fresh—and warm and rich and red, like hot wine flowing down a mountain!"

The dwarf licked his lips, running his tongue round and round. His breath blew like a wind over the barber—a wind fetid and bitter and foul.

But when Millon reached his shop, Aga Bab was no longer with him. At which corner he had turned, into which door he had vanished, Millon did not know.

Crazed thoughts were swirling in the Spaniard's brain. He must get the crying infant. Otherwise those hell-eyes would lick the flesh from his bones. He must get it before he served his customers, six of whom were already waiting on the steps as he approached. He let them in, and set the water to heating on the little stove behind the screen.

He had been absent a long time, they complained. Yes, he replied, his wife was ill—she had broken her leg—she had asthma and rickets and chills—he did not know what besides. But, gentlemen, he must get a fresh supply of towels—only permit him to get a fresh supply of towels!

And all the time he was running down the street, back and forth, clutching an infant that cried, that must not be smothered, that represented youth, that . . . No, no—he was Matías Bonaventura Millon, thirty-five years old, a barber in good standing, and here were his customers, waiting to be shaven and shorn!

He went to the big closet under the stairs, at the rear of the shop, and dragged a sheet from the shelf, rolling it tight under his arm.

"A moment, gentlemen—I shall be back with the fresh towels—only have patience!" And he was out of the shop.

Where was it the baby cried? The next door but one. Ah, yes—nobody about, and the door ajar. What fortune! And there was the brat on the dirty bed, snarling and choking and mouthing, its full bottle of milk out of reach. Millon caught it up and wrapped it in the sheet, the bottle also.

He was back in the shop in no time. Back in the closet, too—chucking the baby into a hamper, the rubber nipple in its mouth, the bottle propped safely. He covered it securely, grabbed an armful of towels, came out and shut the door tightly. No one knew as well as he how thick and tight that door was. No sound would come through it.

Nobody had seen him take the child. Dios, it was good to have that much over with! When he had served all these customers his small moneybox would clink quite respectably. If this would only keep up . . . What was it Aga Bab had said about a hundred new customers? But there was that sniveling baby . . . Still, it was safe in the closet, and no one knew . . . The mother ought to be thankful to be rid of the wailing brat. If she came running down the street with a wild cry, he would know nothing, nothing. . . .

He had no time to eat supper, and sent Rose scuttling up the stairs when she came down to see why he was so late. The last customer left at fifteen minutes before eleven . . . No time for supper now. Afterward he recalled vaguely that he had lifted the sleeping infant from the hamper in the closet and wrapped it in a dark cape. He recalled, too, finding Aga Bab already at the clump of sycamores. His voice was thin and uncertain . . . truly, he was very old.

"I grow old," he croaked. "The fountain . . . it is at hand!"

He unwrapped the child. Now he raised a forefinger with its long, sharp, yellow nail, and made a clean slit in the infant's throat, just at the jugular vein. His lips were at the wound, sucking, sucking, his loathsome eyes closed in ecstasy. Slowly the baby grew white as chalk. When it was limp and lifeless, the monster flung it aside. He stood straight and strong, his skin smooth and firm, his eyes bright and clear in the moonlight.

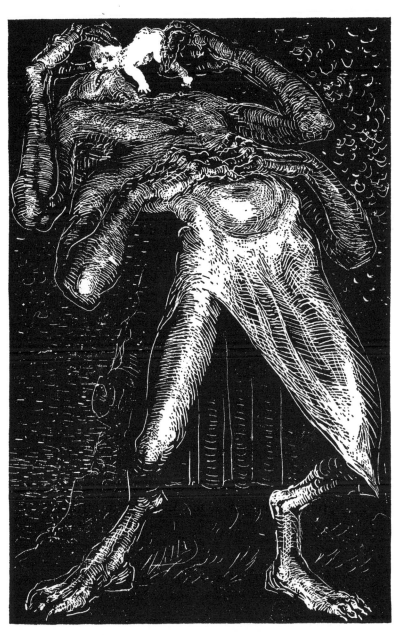

*"A drop or two will not hurt you, mi amigo."*

"They will find it!" Millon gasped in terror, as his foot nudged the child's body.

With a harsh laugh. Aga Bab drew a heavy curved knife from his bosom and gouged out a section from one of the sycamore trunks. A few more twists of the wicked knife, and the cavity was deep. Thrusting the soft little body in, he sliced enough from the outer section to make it fit snugly over the corpse. Then he spat upon the exposed wood and the severed piece, fitted the latter back and bound it to the tree with three circlings of hempen cord.

"Grow!" he commanded, and spat again upon the spotted bark which he had lately held in his twisted hand. "I, Aga Bab, have fertilized your heart, according to the ancient law of trees. Grow and be mighty, as I am mighty!"

Indeed, at that moment he did seem mighty.

"A hundred customers a day—indeed, you cannot serve them all, señor," Aga Bab boomed. "So I shall come and help you. Never was such a frenzy of business—never was the money-box so full! But once every month you are bound to procure me an infant and bring it to me here. It is a bargain, Matías. And it pays to keep bargains which one makes with Aga Bab."

The next day so many customers came that the barber had to go out for fresh supplies before noon. Aga Bab was busy shaving the child's father, at the moment. The man was giving the particulars of his despair and grief, until Aga Bab warned him gently that he was likely to slice his nose or snip an ear if he kept thus in motion.

Hurried though he was, Millon must on his way pass the clump of sycamores. Three tall tuberoses grew at the foot of the tree circled with hempen cord. No tuberoses ever had grown there before. *But the tuberoses smelled like fresh blood.* In a daze, the barber turned and ran the other way.

One night, in the arms of Juana Bermondez, whose shabby establishment he paid for, the Spaniard was cajoled into promising a more luxurious apartment and a new wardrobe. Money . . . what did he care about money? The box in the shop was always running over now. Rose did not need it—he provided well enough for her. Juana was younger, anyhow—barely eighteen. Her flesh was beautiful and soft and clear, like pearls and wine. And she was Spanish—his own breed. He could smell her very blood when he put his lips to her throat—young blood, hot and racing and alive! Something stirred in him. The room was very dark . . . hot blood . . . he, too, would drink of it! . . .

Juana Bermondez lay very still on her soiled couch. Millon arose and lighted the lamp. He felt like a giant. What did he care that Juana was dead? She had served her purpose. Besides, she was with child.

Came a faint scratching at the door, and Aga Bab crept within.

"You will not know how to be rid of that," he cackled, pointing to the figure on the bed. "Give me the heart, and I will show you the death charm."

"Take the heart," the barber heard himself saying.

But it was not the heart of Juana that Aga Bab took—it was the half-formed child within her. He sucked its baby blood greedily, and put the soft mass back into the girl's belly, folding the slit membranes over it neatly.

He took phials from the inner pockets of his greasy clothing, and set them in a row on the untidy bureau. Then he proceeded with the body of the girl. When he had finished the corpse was no more than two feet in length, dry and scaly and entirely unrecognizable. Only her long hair wrapped her from head to foot in a sable winding-sheet.

So, hair-shrouded as she was, Aga Bab thrust her under one arm like a stick of firewood. When they came to the sycamore clump, she was shrunken still more. He jammed her into a space in a tree-trunk, the size of a man's shoe. It seemed to Millon that the trees were twice as tall as they had been in the spring. The smell of fresh blood was everywhere now, but chiefly in Matías Millon's own nostrils.

Each month he contrived to obtain a young child for Aga Bab. He always stole crying babies. The mothers were terrified for fear they would be accused of making away with the squalling brats themselves, so they moved abruptly and said nothing.

In a little red book, Millon wrote down each name, with the date. Also he added the doings of each day. It might be well to have a finger which would one day point straight at Aga Bab. So, on the fly-leaf of the book he wrote Aga Bab's name.

After a time the sycamore boles would hold no more. They were growing prodigiously—the neighborhood was remarking about it, and about the hundreds of tuberoses which flowered beneath them. Some of the French people who came to visit from the Old Town referred to the spot as La Place du Lis. Better Nenes en el Bosque, the barber thought, smiling grimly.

Millon hated the clump of sycamores. Still more he hated those stormy nights when Aga Bab dragged him forth in the wet, to burn nine black candles in the midst of the mortuary trees. On these nights the dwarf swelled and blustered, expanding to his terrifying ten-foot height, his eyes leaping out on their glistering, snakelike stalks, and the stench of hot blood so overpowering that the barber vomited at the mere recollection.

Now the time had come for another repository. Even the tiniest shrunken corpse could not be left lying in the open. Its very condition would arouse the whole city. One word, and the whole matter of vanished infants would be let loose on the winds. There had been too many of them. It had been going on for four years now. The sycamores were fairly stuffed.

"Under the stairs," Aga Bab said.

A little plaster gouged out . . . a triangular trough under each stairtread. . . . Safe again.

So it went on. And tuberoses began to grow thick in the strip of grass between the banquette and the street, for all to see. Millon shuddered, but his custom was so great that he and the dwarf could scarce take time to breathe, from early morning until near midnight. Only on Sundays the shop was closed. And then, while Rose cooked and baked and mixed and iced and brewed upstairs. Aga Bab burned nine black candles in the closet, while the smell of tainted blood, sour and foul, filled the place.

There were no excuses which the barber could invent by which he could hope to escape. Church? This was his church. Company? Here was much company. Exercise? Here was sufficient exercise for man or devil. Aga Bab grinned and grimaced, wringing his taloned hands and mumbling his unintelligible chants and orisons. Sometimes he would stand in the stair door, and rise to his ten-foot size, peering into the apartment upstairs, leering and gaping, sending his fearful eyes here and there among the Millon belongings, leaving trails of slime wherever they touched.

The day came when Matías Bonaventura Millon, descendant of the helper of Torquemada the Terrible, could endure it no longer. He had killed, he had drunk blood, he had grown heavily rich—how rich, only he himself knew, for he hid it behind the plaster under the stairs, always a little above the last shrunken corpse. Aga Bab would not find that. Anyhow, Aga Bab never was interested in money.

So the barber sent Rose away to visit relatives in Baton Rouge. He heated two wash-kettles of water to boiling, and overturned one of them on Aga Bab. Immediately he trussed the scalded dwarf, and boiled him in the second kettle until both flesh and bones were jelly. Still, when he went to throw the mess into the sewer, the small shrunken body gathered itself together. It was dead enough, 'tis true, but he must go through the usual performance of drying and shrinking it, before sealing it behind the plaster under the stairs.

In the little red book, Millon made the mistake of adding Aga Bab's name at the end of the list. It belonged there, of course, and nobody ever would see the book, for he sealed it also behind the plaster.

Now he was rich and he was free. Rose was sent for, and life started anew. He dug out the tuberoses from in front of the shop—but the next morning they were there again, blossoming in greater profusion than ever, though it was late November.

One day the shop remained closed. The Millons and everything they possessed were gone. Nobody ever heard of them again. And nobody would occupy the building, which finally was sold for taxes.

"Well," finished Alexander Maunsell, rising from Dusa's barber-chair, "I have talked us to eleven o'clock. I must hurry home."

But the next day when he passed the shop, and Dusa

stopped him to ask about some detail of the story, he denied all knowledge of it.

"Told you a story about a devil-dwarf?" he snorted. "I never did. I haven't been near your shop for a week. Last night I was in Donaldsonville on business—I have just arrived home. Ask the other five men who accompanied me, if you doubt it."

Which rendered things exceedingly perplexing. Particularly as Mrs. Dusa also had seen and heard Mr. Maunsell. Now the question was: What was it that Mrs. Dusa saw coming down the street and peering over the gallery-rail? Dusa could not ridicule her story, because he had heard the story of Maunsell. . . . Or was it Maunsell? Also, there were the little objects which the Thing had flung into Mrs. Dusa's lap—the nine black candle-ends, the dry tuberoses, and the two clay figurines. The barber had chucked them into an old shoebox and thrust the box into the closet under the stairs. It was there now.

But when he opened the door of the closet, he was nearly overcome by the horrible odor which assailed his nostrils. It enveloped him like a noisome cloud. All he could think of was a slaughterhouse.

Then, all at once, the Thing stood beside him. He knew it was the Thing, for he had twice heard it described. It must be the Thing. . . . And his heart froze within him. Was that infernal creature set to destroy him, as the Millons had been destroyed? Or had they been destroyed?

Would the Thing pounce upon him and suck him dry, too? But, no. The Thing bent itself twice double and squeezed into the closet, to vanish as though it never had been.

Dusa groaned. Whatever was to become of him, if he had illusions like this? It must be the cabbage and cheese he had eaten at dinner. Mrs. Dusa also had eaten—and on the day before, too—cabbage and cheese; assuredly that accounted for everything. There was no ghost, no demon, no monster. Merely cabbage and cheese. Dusa cleared his throat with a sense of profound relief.

This closet, now. He would go in and feel of the walls himself. That preposterous story about shrunken corpses and a little red book and a fortune in coins behind the plaster! Why, there was not room under the stairtreads to hide a shaving-mug, let alone a corpse! As for that smell—why, did he not throw the soiled towels into the closet? Doubtless they had mildewed—they were always damp. A sad waste of towels, but preferable to corpses.

So he went into the closet. He had not noticed before how lumpy and uneven the walls were . . . and how spotted and moldy. And in one corner was a trickle of some thick, brownish liquid. . . .

After a week of terror, during which burnt black candle-ends and dried tuberoses and tiny clay figures confronted him at every turn, the barber decided to confer with his wife. She had sulked steadily since the night the Thing had first appeared. Often he had come upon her dissolved in tears. Now they consoled each other, exchanging suggestions.

Finally they began prying off the plaster in the closet. Behind it they discovered first a shrunken brown foot. Mrs. Dusa nearly fainted, but curiosity proved stronger than fear. Removing more plaster, they came upon a shallow niche. In it lay what looked to be the dried corpse of a small monkey. Beside it was a little book bound in moldy red leather—a book of daily notes, and an endless list of names and dates. On the flyleaf was written, in a fine, pointed hand, *Aga Bab*. But also, the last name at the very end of that interminable list was Aga Bab. It tallied with the story which Alexander Maunsell denied he ever had told.

Continuing to remove plaster, they found it packed with tiny skeletons. All human, but no larger than little dolls. In one corner, standing upright behind a thin layer of cement, were two dried figures—a man and a woman. The woman had a wedding ring slipped over her shrunken wrist. The man had a rusted razor thrust into his chest. Had Aga Bab returned to enjoy the last tortured shrieks of the Millons?

Layers of money they found, too. And then the Dusas devised a plan. They gathered every shred of the bones together and put them into a wooden chest. One day soon thereafter they drove out into the country. Beside a lonely bayou road they made a bonfire and burned the chest and its gruesome contents. The money they had already put safely away. It would mean comfort in old age.

So ended the magic of Aga Bab. Who he was or what he was, nobody to this day ever has learned. Some say he was Torquemada's helper come back. And some say he was Matías Millon's own evil self, grown bold and powerful for a season. . . .

(*1900*)     *The Return of Esposito*

"There's something been happening at the old rice mill down the street," young Irving Norton reported, when he went home to supper one day in January, 1900.

"Which old rice mill?" his sister Bernice wanted to know.

"Why, the only one we've got around here, of course— the one on Elysian Fields avenue, near Victory," he replied.

"What's been happening?" Mrs. Norton asked. "I hadn't heard."

"Ghosts," returned Irving. "You needn't laugh—plenty of folks have been seeing 'em. It ain't only one ghost, either— it's two, and sometimes it's three or four. Old man Walker saw two of 'em last night, and he was pretty much worked up over it."

"Did he tell you?"

"No, his boy Bud did. Said one of 'em had a red sash around his waist, and a big cutlass stuck in the sash."

"A ghost in a red sash! Does old man Walker drink?" Mrs. Norton sniffed.

"No, you know he doesn't. And he did really see something. He wasn't making it up, Ma."

"Red sash—very likely!" chuckled his mother.

But as time went on, others began to tell Mrs. Norton about the ghosts that were haunting the old rice mill.

"I don't believe it, in spite of 'em!" she sputtered, when Bernice came home with another report. "I'd have to see it to believe it, and I don't ever expect to see a ghost. There's no such thing—'tain't natural."

153

" 'Tain't supposed to be natural," Irving grinned. "It's queer as can be, and that's why folks talk about it. But they keep telling about those ghosts in the old rice mill, and by cricky, I'm going to see 'em if they're to be seen!"

"You'll do no such a thing. Catching your death o' cold in some drafty old shed or other—you stay home where you belong."

But the tales were too much for Irving.

"I'm not going to miss *all* the fun," he told himself.

So, on a night early in March, he and Bud Walker and Bud's father gained entrance to the rice mill through a rear window. Up the dusty old stairs they crept, to an unused room on the second floor. It was bright moonlight, and they could discern a number of tall packing cases stacked in one corner. This upper floor had at one time been used for living purposes, and a broad fireplace occupied part of one wall.

The trio crouched behind the packing cases, waiting for they knew not what.

"Maybe we're pretty silly," whispered Irving. "If the ghost knows we're here he'll stay away."

"Don't you worry," insisted Mr. Walker. "I seen him my-self once, ramblin' round like he was lookin' for something. I didn't see him very close-to—we was down on the street, but I saw the ghost, all right. And what I seen once I can see again."

They grew cramped and chilly. Then suddenly Bud plucked at Irving's sleeve.

"What's that?" he hissed.

"Mouse, I guess," Irving yawned. "It's getting pretty late and my knees ache like sixty—"

"S-sh!" warned Mr. Walker. "Something's at the window!"

They craned their necks hopefully. A light pecking sound reached their straining ears. Somebody was coming in at the window—a dark shape, like a squat man with a scarf wound round his great head. They could see the glitter of something thrust into the broad sash round his thick waist. But the strangest thing was the way he stepped through the window, as though it were level with the ground.

A soft glow began to fill the room. Behind the visitor came

another figure—a tall, gaunt man in a clerical collar and a flattish black hat. And then, slowly and apparently with great hesitation, two blue-coated forms trailed the first pair.

Not a sound did these four make. The leader strode away from the window, and made straight for the fireplace, where he knelt and began to loosen the bricks which served as a hearthstone. The light was very clear and steady now, and the watchers could see that his sash was crimson and his skin very coarse and swarthy. The tall man seemed to glide along the rough plank floor; his feet, which appeared to strike the floor clumsily, made not a sound. Nor did the blue-clad ones cause so much as a creak along the old boards as they followed.

Only the bricks, where the leader was digging, clattered and thudded as he threw them aside. The old mortar scattered and crumbled. Once the tall man, who seemed to stand as a sort of guard just behind the leader, half turned and removed his shovel-hat. Frozen with terror as they were, the three watchers saw that he had no ears—only bloody patches where they should have been, with the long hair matted and caked with mud. The two other figures seemed detached, somehow, as though they merely waited, a trifle bored but with plenty of time for whatever might occur. They, too, moved with noiseless steps, peering at their queer companions.

Presently the metal instrument with which the leader was digging struck a softer substance. He bent lower, his coarse black locks hanging like dank rags beneath the dirty scarf around his head. Faster he worked, and ever faster, as though the dawn must not find him here nor so engaged. His mighty shoulders heaved and struggled, and finally he reached down and grasped a stained wooden box, bringing it to the surface and depositing it on the floor with a bang.

And now all grew deathly still. With his cutlass, the strange digger pried up the thick lid of the old box. A heavy lock fell to the floor without a sound, and the great hands lifted the cover back on its rusty hinges.

He began to scoop out great handfuls of yellow coins—so yellow that they shone in the light and gave forth a luster of their own. He filled his pockets with them, he thrust them into his shirt until it bulged. The supply seemed inexhaustible.

Then he tore the scarf from his head and made a great bundle of the remaining coins.

The blue-clad figures seemed to sway and waver in the light, and the earless one slunk to one side. Only the masterful digger rose clear and vigorous, striding to the window and stepping out firmly—onto what? Just behind him trailed the other three, as though they obeyed some silent command which only their ears could catch.

The light was gone now. Even the moon had waned. The place was dark as a pocket, and still as a tomb is still.

"Let's get out of here!" came a shuddering boyish whisper from behind the packing cases. "Don't you let go of me, Pa! And don't you let them things come back and get me— Pa, don't go so fast—we'll fall down stairs!"

Somehow the three got out of the old rice mill. They never knew exactly how.

"We've got to look round under that there window," Mr. Walker said, pausing outside the door. "It didn't seem like they come in by a ladder, but we've got to make sure. If they just climbed in, it ain't so queer. Here we are—and there ain't nary ladder nor nothing. And there ain't been no ladder— the tall grass ain't even mashed by anybody walkin'. Didn't no-body walk through it, neither, by gum! They didn't come that way."

"But we don't dare to tell it," young Norton shivered, as they neared his gate. "Nobody'd believe us—we'd be a joke. They'd say we dug that box up and stole the money our own selves."

"I guess maybe they would," agreed Mr. Walker. "I sure thought I was going to die of heart failure most of the time. We'd all better get calmed down a bit before we go in—you boys are white as chalk and I don't reckon I'm much better. Je-ru-salem Joseph!—that was some sight!"

Irving could feel his hair still standing on end, and his tongue was dry as paper.

During the next few weeks, the three kept their own counsel rigidly. The empty box had been found the next day, of course, and all sorts of conjectures had gone the rounds. But

lately whenever anybody mentioned ghosts, people only snick-
ered. The spell was over.

One Sunday afternoon, Bud Walker joined Irving in the
Norton's back yard.

"Pa wants you should come over," he said hurriedly, cock-
ing a wary eye toward the Norton rear door. "We got something! He's up in our attic, digging in an old trunk that used
to belong to his Aunt Gertie. Hustle up—and don't let anybody know where we are!"

The two boys found Mr. Walker seated in a broken rocker
near an attic window, running a grimy finger down the yellowed pages of an old scrapbook. Several others lay on the floor
beside him.

"You boys come just in time," he rumbled, his thin hair
all awry. "These here scrapbooks of Aunt Gertie's tell all about
it. And what they don't tell, her diary does. You see, Aunt
Gertie was a cripple, but she always knew what was going on.
She took more newspapers than anybody you ever see, and she
cut out everything she thought was any account. If it wasn't
in the paper, somebody told it to her and she wrote it down
in her diary. Every day of her life she did that, and she didn't
do much else, 'cause she couldn't. She used to think I was a
good kid, and when she died she willed me all she had—and
part of it was this trunkful of scrapbooks and diaries. Now,
look here!"

He turned to clippings dated in 1880—fine, small, hand-
set type, with the lines very close together. Mr. Walker talked
as he read.

"Here's about Giuseppe Esposito, the Italian bandit," he
droned. "Up in the mountains of Italy, he was then. He kidnaped an English minister—Curate Rose, it calls him—and
wrote back to England for a big ransom. He didn't wait long
before he cut off one of the Reverend Rose's ears and shipped
it on to the family, as a reminder to rush. After a little, he cut
off the other ear and sent that. It created so much excitement, it says here, that the Italian government raided Esposito
and put him out of business. The minister got away, but so
did Esposito.

"Why the bandit chief picked on New Orleans as his place

of refuge, I don't know. But it seems he did. He came right here, that terrible cutthroat did, and set up a harmless-looking little fruit stand on Customhouse street, between Burgundy and Rampart. We'll go along there sometime, and see what we can see—but of course that was a long time ago. Esposito even married a nice Italian girl here, and they say she never knew what a ruffian he was.

"But after he'd been here a while, what with the stories of his outrages and all, Dave Hennessey got wind of who he was. Dave's dead now, of course, but he was only a detective then, instead of Chief of Police. It don't say how he found out about Esposito, but he did, and he told his brother Mike. The two of them arrested Esposito one morning at the old French Market, and they sent word to the Italian government. In spite of all the bandit could do—and he tried to do plenty—they got him onto a boat and took him to New York, and from there to Italy. His own country sent him to prison for life. Some say he escaped, but nobody really knows.

"Now, it seems Esposito had his own gang here in New Orleans, unbeknown to his wife, and they made their headquarters at this here old rice mill down the street. That's where they cooked up their schemes for robbery and murder and general devilment, and that's where the old rip buried his wealth—right under those fireplace bricks. I never did see a hearth in a second story go down so deep, but I guess it was built for safety.

"Some say that one of Esposito's old gang shot chief Hennessey. And some say another one of 'em shot his brother Mike in Houston, Texas. I don't know—but somebody sure did it.

"Now, there's that old rice mill, and there's the things us three saw in it. Esposito's dead these many years, and the Curate Rose is dead, and Dave Hennessey's dead, and so is his brother Mike. If those had been just thieves we saw, they'd have took other things besides that money—there's been thieves there before, and they've stole hundreds of dollars' worth of brass and such.

"But I know who we saw—only we've got to keep still about it, or folks would laugh theirselves to death. We saw old Esposito—that's the boy we saw. And the English minister, with his ears cut off, all smeared and bloody. And Chief Hennessey and his brother Mike—and I know it."

"You mean 'twas their spirits come back?" Irving shuddered, a weird prickling running up and down his spine.

"Sure, I mean 'twas their spirits come back. Don't you remember how they come in, and the queer light and all?"

"And how they never made any sound," put in Bud, his eyes bulging, "except the bricks."

"Yes—and how they stepped right out a second-story window, and kept walking away, just as though they were on a path. Well," finished Pa Walker, gathering up the dusty old books, "I guess likely 'twas a spirit path—back to the world they'd come from. But we was too smart for 'em—we seed 'em for sure, don't you boys ever forget that!"

Some weeks later, part of the story did find its way to the newspapers. But that was long after the gossips of Elysian Fields avenue had licked off the rich cream and smacked their lips over the incomparable flavor.

# (*1808*)   *The Ghost of the German Countess*

In the days when the uptown section of the city was known as the Faubourg Sainte-Marie, that portion was mostly swampland. During the régime of Jean and Pierre Lafitte, the Barataria pirates who flourished in the first quarter of the 19th century, one of the houses of the scattered few then available in the Upper Town was used as a rendezvous for their cutthroat band.

It was a vast and rambling structure, of the type known as a castellated plantation house. It had a flat roof, massive walls and many battlements. Precisely what went on behind those sturdily bolted doors, no tongue can say. But that there were crimes galore, murder and rape and torture and robbery and many foul deeds besides, there is not the slightest doubt. The very isolation of the house was an invitation to pirates to bring thither captives, with the hope of added entertainment and gain.

It is said that from one of their sea raids they brought in a German Captain and his tall daughter, Frieda. The girl was blonde and beautiful, with thick braids of silken yellow hair bound about her shapely head.

The Captain was known to be transporting a casket of fine sapphires, destined for the Spanish royal collection. The value of these gems was almost beyond calculation, many of them being personal gifts from noble houses. It had been the Captain's mission to land at this port and that, gathering the precious collection together.

The Fraulein, left a good deal to her own devices on board ship, and being deprived of any household tasks, did much exquisite embroidery. Her own dresses were heavy with it, in the most brilliant and effective colors. Not a gown did she possess that was not elaborately enriched by her own clever needle.

When the Lafitte band boarded the vessel commanded by the German Captain, their first demand was for the sapphires. News of the priceless stones had leaked out, and this was the principal reason for the capture of the ship.

The Captain, however, flatly refused to yield up the jewels. He even defied the pirates to discover their hiding-place. Furthermore, he forbade his daughter, on pain of his eternal wrath, to disclose her knowledge of the whereabouts of the sapphires. Threats and beatings availed the pirates nothing. So they brought the Captain and his daughter, in irons, ashore at New Orleans.

The girl wept and screamed, and her clothes were torn almost from her body in her struggles to evade the murderous ruffians. Finally, however, when she had bitten and scratched more than one burly outlaw, she settled down to a fairly tractable frame of mind. Unable to speak any tongue except her own, she eventually made the pirates understand that she would accompany them quietly if they only would permit her to take her beautifully embroidered dresses with her. She was allowed to do this, and tied them into a fat bundle which she insisted on carrying in her own arms.

The two captives were hustled to the great plantation house in the Faubourg Sainte-Marie. Here the Captain was put to torture and died in agony, without, however, having disclosed the hiding-place of his treasure. Meanwhile, Fraulein Frieda had been taken to a chamber on an upper floor of the house, and treated to all manner of luxury. Whenever she asked for her father, she was told that he was teaching German to Pierre Lafitte, and could not come to her until the pirate had mastered enough of the language to converse with her.

Finally the young woman became so alarmed and suspicious that she began to demand that she be taken to her father. When she grew too insistent, the pirates sewed her lips together, had her eyes gouged out, and then strangled her.

A new ship had come up the river that very day, bringing news of the lost sapphires and the missing sea captain. So furious were the royal ones over the loss, that great sums of money were offered for the return of the jewels.

Now, bold as the pirates were, they knew that conviction for piracy meant death. Many victims they had forced to walk the plank to a watery grave. But walking the plank was a more comfortable end than swinging by the neck until one choked to death. There was no way of claiming the reward, even if they found the sapphires, without its being known that they had plundered the ship and kidnaped and murdered the Captain and his daughter. Anyhow, they had failed to find the jewels.

They held a secret conference, and decided to remove all traces of their two victims. One Trudeau, a member of the pirate band, was chosen to secrete the two bodies. He was instructed to do this alone, and never to tell any living person, even his mates, where he had buried them.

That night the pirates left Trudeau alone in the plantation house. It was raining hard, and the wind blew a furious blast. Every rafter of the great house creaked and shivered. And Trudeau had two dead bodies to dispose of. The Captain had been buried in a shallow trench in the cellar, but he'd have to come out of that. Poor Frieda still lay in the upper chamber, bloated and disfigured and horrible. Trudeau dragged her down the stairs by the feet, her head bumping on every stair. The Captain, in a bad state of decomposition, was rolled in a piece of sailcloth and hauled up the ladder to the ground floor.

So the two rotting bodies lay huddled in the broad hall, while Trudeau hacked at the thick masonry under the stairs. After a while he had a cavity sufficiently large to hold them. His lantern flickered and sputtered, and the rain drove in torrents against the batten blinds. A small snake wriggled from a crevice and brought a cry of disgust from the pirate.

He took the Captain first. The corpse swayed and slithered, and he had difficulty in getting it hoisted up to the cavity. Then, when it refused to arrange itself suitably, Trudeau gave vent to a savage growl and drove a great spike through the chest and deep into the masonry which backed it. The bones crunched, and a terrible stench filled the place. Trudeau bent to his bucket of mortar and began to plaster the Captain thickly over. When the body was covered, he heaved a deep breath of relief and wiped the salty sweat from his face and head.

But Frieda still remained. Now why, reasoned Trudeau, should he bury the embroidered gown? He knew a wench who could wear just that sort of a garment, and look upon him with a favoring eye because of it. So he stripped off the dress, being careful not to tear it nor to snag off any of the bottoms. Nom de Dieu, but the dress was heavy! And the embroidery was lumpy. Too lumpy, although the fancywork looked well. He fingered the lumps . . . how hard they were!

With a sudden fierce light in his greedy eyes, Trudeau drew the edge of his knife across one of the lumps of embroidery. Something fell into his waiting palm—a flash of blue fire. He bent close to his lantern, examining the glassy lump in his hand. A sapphire, by all that was holy! Soon he was slitting other embroidered lumps. The heap of sapphires on the cypress bench was growing.

When he had extracted every sapphire which the gown contained, he drew a leather pouch from his bosom and tied them tightly in it. A creak on the stairs made him grow cold with fear, but he kept doggedly on. His little eyes gleamed with utter satisfaction at his find. Trudeau was not faring so badly, even though they had left him to a night with two corpses as rotten as jelly.

Of a sudden, the pirate bent to his further labors. He hustled Frieda and her tattered dress into the other half of the cavity, and spiked her to the masonry with three spikes. Then the mortar in great blobs. Then a layer of bricks, even and straight, to make a new facing. More mortar, and then a rough dusting of soil and mold from the cellar, so that the work ceased to look fresh. A day—two days—and nobody could notice the difference. He swept the floor carefully, removing every evidence of the new-made tomb. Then he dragged three or four old chests back to their habitual place against the wall under the staircase. The job was done.

But might not there be more for Trudeau? The storm outside was still raging, and the night was but half gone. Upstairs he went with his lantern, the yellow light feeble enough in the wide, still spaces. He caught himself shivering foolishly when a white face glimmered at him over the bannister rail. He was not going to believe in ghosts, even here and on a night like this. So he hurried on to Fraulein Frieda's chamber.

Ah, yes, here were her dresses, all hung neatly on the closet pegs. More embroidery, more lumps. Trudeau's knife flashed busily, and the blue stones fell into his hand. The pouch in his bosom was full. But here was the Fraulein's reticule. Trudeau was a huge man, and a bulge here and there would not be noticed.

But the telltale dresses must be made way with. Again Trudeau busied himself with bricks and mortar, under another stairway. A rat dislodged a brick somewhere, and Trudeau sweated anew. After all, this job was simple. One could stuff clothing into a cavity so much more easily than stinking human flesh.

Now that Trudeau had finished his night's work, he was anxious to go. He knew the swampland was unsafe in such a storm. If he were to lose his way, he might meet a miserable death. But he would not lose his way—a grown man, and dawn so near!

He was a bit startled when he found the front door unfastened. He was so sure he had brought the great hasp down close and neat, and shot the bolt home. However . . . he slammed the door after him sharply and secured it from the outside. Then he started down the path.

He felt someone touch his hand, and stopped still in his tracks. A faint bright Shape danced along the path, just ahead of him. Its hair was pale as spun gold, and its step was light as thistledown. It beckoned to him, smiling and alluring. What girl was here, away off by herself so, and no house in sight except the plantation house of the pirates? His heart beat hard for a minute, but the girl smiled and waited. And suddenly, Trudeau, with a great laugh in his throat, plunged after her.

He left the path, and the mud and slime of the swamp began to drag him down. Still the girl danced ahead, beckoning and smiling. He sank to his waist and could not extricate himself. And it was then he knew he had been following Fraulein

Frieda—a ghostly Fraulein Frieda, who had but one gift to give—death!

No one ever saw or heard of Trudeau again. But one, whose curiosity had been greater than his terror of corpses, had remained behind to see where Trudeau hid them. His footstep it was that had sent the stair creaking—his white face peering over the banister rail. And he it was who glimpsed the ghostly Fraulein beckoning to Trudeau along the path. Both Trudeau and the sapphires were a mile under the swamp by the time the watcher dared to search for the spot where they went down.

And in the plantation house the Fraulein's spirit moaned and wandered, seeking her lost father and the jewels she had helped him to keep hidden. As the years went on, she became bolder and bolder. Two cats were her familiars—a mammoth black cat and an equally large white one. They roamed the bleak flat roof, but never a sound did they make. In the 1860's, the ghost had become such a constant visitor that the neighbors called her the Countess. Some even went so far as to report that she was a real woman, and that she rented the place.

The city had grown all around the old mansion by this time, so it was no longer isolated and lonely. The Countess, as the wraith continued to be known, wore gorgeous embroideries. Being unique, she was tolerated. She walked up and down the broad galleries, up and down the front path, up and down the steps. Always just at nightfall. And the few rash tenants who defied ghostly manifestation, moved away with more haste than ceremony. The Countess, they declared, walked up and down the stairs, and up and down the halls. And when she got to the back of the staircase, she covered her empty eyesockets with her ghostly hands and screamed, and pointed to the wall.

Now why, the neighbors whispered, should the Countess point to the wall, unless there was something hidden behind or within the wall which so worried her? Along in 1863, people grew bold and curious. When one, a trifle braver than the rest, elected to spend a night in the "Old Haunted House," as it had come to be known, he emerged with tales of a voice, praying and calling all through the night, and always in German.

He had seen the cats, yes, but they had made no sound.

The Countess he had heard only. More than once he had searched the place from end to end, to hear her still, to see her never. Yet that very morning she walked on the gallery in her gay embroidered draperies, her pale gold hair circling her head in smooth braids. That was the strangest part of it—the neighbors grew old and their joints grew stiffened; but the Countess remained always young and nimble.

Finally, in August of 1863, the house was condemned as unsafe. When workmen came to tear down the masonry behind the staircase, they found two skeletons sealed within it—two skeletons spiked to the wall behind, and bits of embroidered cloth thrust in with the bones. Other embroidery they found, in another wall, cut and hacked and slashed and raveled. The earthen pots of gold, which tradition said were buried somewhere about, never came to light.

But after that, the Countess never was seen again. The bones of Frieda and the Captain were laid in a decent grave, and she walked the earth no more.

## (1900)  *The Witch of the French Opera*

Madame Marguerite Sauvé stood behind her glistening counter of delectable French pastries. Her shop was in Bourbon street, a square or two from the Old French Opera House, where Madame had been a chorus girl for more years than she ever acknowledged.

Madame's head was held high, as usual. The liquid poudre blanche, which she used lavishly, made her features into a sort of mask from which her dark eyes flashed pleasantly like discs of jet. Her black hair, well-brushed with dye, was piled high on her head after the mode of that period. Her eyebrows also were brushed with the dye, and made an imposing setting for her quick eyes.

As a matter of fact, Madame had been born Marguerite O'Donnell in the year 1842. Her mother was French, but Michael O'Donnell was only three years from Ireland. She was Maggie O'Donnell in those days, with five husky Irish brothers and seven buxom Irish sisters. She was the baby, was Maggie— and the only French-looking one in the lot.

She married Octave Sauvé when she was eighteen. The War Between the States took all of her brothers and four of her brothers-in-law. But Octave came home without a scratch. He grew sour and crabbed enough, as the years went on and no babies were in prospect. What was life without little ones to frolic with and plan for? He berated poor Maggie until she was sad and resentful indeed.

"Sure," she wept, "it isn't as if I could find a baby in the rainbarrel!"

"You do not care for me as you should," scolded Octave. "So le bon Dieu looks into your selfish heart and punishes you by sending no little ones. But me I am punish' also, and I do not deserve!"

There was an eternal wrangle in the house. At length Madame could endure it no longer. So she applied at the French Opera House for a place as chorus girl. She was thirty-three at the time, but she said she was twenty-four. She could sing, oui; and she could dance, with a little training. Octave worked at night, and he never knew. She was very particular about that.

During the yellow fever epidemic of 1878, she lost every member of her family. Octave sickened, and went last of all. So, down the years, she lived in one shabby room, applied the liquid poudre blanche and the hair dye a little more heavily, and cut a year or so from her age every time she had occasion to refer to it.

In 1900, old Monsieur de Boisblanc took a fancy to her. Heaven only knows why. Perhaps because he was half-blind and could not see how brown and withered her skin was under the poudre blanche, and how unsteady her fingers were as she poured his champagne. Maybe it was desperation, on her part, for Maggie O'Donnell had been a virtuous girl and Marguerite Sauvé had been a virtuous woman. But old Monsieur de Boisblanc, who had no end of money, took her to his house and to his bed. He dressed her in silks and gave her diamonds and a lady's maid. And when he died, three months later, he left her ten thousand dollars.

Madame Sauvé was a bit bewildered. She had moved out of the De Boisblanc mansion within an hour after its master's demise. With part of the money she opened the pastry shop. Les Camélias, she called it. She acknowledged forty summers, dressed in severe and intensely fetching black, and managed her pastry business like a veteran.

Everybody who went to the French Opera House flocked to Les Camélias. Its orange sherbet was famous. Its delicate puff tartes, its heavenly gateaux, the frostings and the icings and the glacés, the chocolatière that was always full and steaming hot, the dragées, and méringues, the darioles, the pâtes brisées, the crème au vin—oh la la la, they were every one divine! Expensive, oui—taste heaven and die bankrupt. There was nothing so fine in all New Orleans.

So Madame stood behind her counter. A faint smile hovered about her firm lips. Septime, the pastry chef, was not doing as well as formerly. But she had an ad inserted in various newspapers, as was her method—Baltimore, Charleston, Savannah, Tampa, Mobile, Galveston.

This morning she had received a reply from one Carlos Alfaro, now in Tampa. He was twenty-one years old, he wrote, had been in this country un año, understood la Inglés sufficiently, and was a master hand at making fine pastries. He added that he was related to that illustrious General Elroy Alfaro, President of Ecuador. All of which Madame took with a grain of salt, except the pastry-making. He wrote variously of that, in a manner to convince the most exacting.

Very well, she would send for this relative of the illustrious General. He could not be worse than Septime, who was at this moment wasting almonds and messing in the tin of best French chocolat. She hated that Septime, who was always tilting his head and asking impertinent questions. This Carlos, now— he was young—alarmingly young. But she could manage him. She would keep him well under her thumb. He might even be interesting.

Most of the small tables in Les Camélias were filled. Madame smiled and nodded graciously. Only a few years ago she had been bowing and smiling to these same people from the great stage of the French Opera House. They were too young to know that she had joined the chorus in 1875.

"Oui, Madame, the ices are delicious—the pastries are delicious," they chattered. "Les Camélias is enchanting. We shall come again tomorrow, of course."

No wonder Madame beamed and purred. Everything she touched seemed to turn to gold. Everything was going like clockwork—except that Septime. Today he had twitted her openly about the poudre blanche. Well, she would soon be rid of him and his foolish tricks . . . telling her that she should have a husband to run Les Camélias. A husband, indeed! Every woman knew that a husband was a hindrance and a nuisance.

That Septime wanted his hand in the cash-drawer—a pretty plan!

So Carlos arrived, and Septime departed. Carlos was slender and dark, with gentle ways and eyes as fathomless as those of a fawn. His fingers were nimble and he knew something about the making of fine pastries. But, had his eyes not been so beautiful, Madame would have sent him packing before the day was out. Pastry chef, pah! Pastry helper, oui. But amid all those marvelous creations which Septime had been wont to produce, this Spanish boy was lost.

Madame was in despair. She would teach him herself! True, he was eager to learn. So she poured forth the secrets she had absorbed from Septime, and from François before him, and from Victor before him, and from Eugéne who was the first in Les Camélias. Carlos listened attentively, and daily grew more proficient.

Madame Sauvé was a trifle at a loss. She was conscious that her first waking thought was of Carlos. That her heart leaped when she saw him entering the door of Les Camélias, ready for the day's work. That all day, as she flitted back and forth, she lived only when she paused beside the slim Spanish youth in the spotless apron and the tall starched cap. When he turned his dark eyes upon her, she trembled and panted. When he spoke, she stood rooted to the spot. When he sent in some special triumph for her approval, she all but expired with ecstasy.

It puzzled Madame exceedingly.

"Ah, I know!" she told herself one Sunday, suddenly discovering. "It is because I never have had a child! Carlos takes the place of the child I should have had. He fills my heart, my day, my life—he is like my son! So it is not strange nor terrible any more—all is correct and natural!"

When Carlos pressed his young body against hers and suddenly showered kisses upon her mouth and eyes, it was just as natural, though scarcely so correct. She was hungry for kisses, starving for caresses, dying for love. Carlos gave her all three, in generous measure.

"Ah, Carlos darling," she told him one night, lying in his arms after her apartment door had been safely bolted, "at first

I tried to make myself believe I loved you as a son! It was stupid of me—although of course I am a few years older than you are. But a son—that was silly. It is better to adore each other honestly, as lovers should."

"But," he murmured gently, caressing her round breasts, "I think you should pay me more salary, Marguerite. I have the feeling of poverty, and that is discouraging to my art."

"I shall double your salary from tomorrow," Madame responded. "You are my angel, my life! Come and live here with me, Carlos!"

"No, Madame, it is better if I do not live here. It would occasion the large scandal, and that would be bad for business."

"You break my heart when you call me Madame. Call me that other name which means 'summer' in your language."

"You mean 'El Verano'? But that would be a man's name. Better that I name you 'Spring'—'La Primavera,' dear Madame."

She nestled closer to him. He called her Spring! He did not know of the wrinkles behind her ears, then! She would be careful to smear the poudre blanche on especially thick . . . perhaps a touch of rouge on her lips . . . if one moistened it with glycerine it did not come off. . . .

Her weary lids closed over her aching eyes. Carlos laughed and sneered when he saw her old face lying on the pillow at dawn. But Madame was asleep, and knew nothing of the laugh and the sneer.

Presently Carlos began to whine a little. He was overworked. He had no time for amusements of any sort. He was young—Madame was making a slave of him. One night when they reached the door of her apartment he refused to come in.

"Oh, but my dove, my precious one!" Madame exclaimed in horror and amazement. "I have brought my arms full of the choicest pastries—there is wine, there is tobacco, there is an incomparable bed—and there is me myself! Ah, you must not say you will not come in, Carlos!"

"I am here too much," he replied petulantly. "I think people are beginning to notice. You should let me out more from the pastry shop—I come too early and I leave too late. It is killing me!"

"But Septime worked longer hours than you—and so did François and Eugéne and Victor!"

"But you did not love Septime and François and Eugéne and Victor. Or did you?"

"Mon Dieu, non! What are you saying, Carlos? Me—love those crapauds, those poux? Surely you are fooling, Carlos!"

"But they were your pastry chefs. I am only your pastry chef. How do I know?"

"But you are the only one, the jewel of my heart, my life's adorable one, I keep telling you! Those others—I could not have endured their touch. I would have sent them to jail if they had so much as hinted at romance!"

"Yet with all your love for me, you work me as hard as you did them. It is not fair. I do not believe you love me at all!"

"Oh, Carlos, Carlos—what it is you want?" Madame was in tears.

"I want to work three hours a day only. I am high class— I bake the Spanish delicacies which no other chef can create."

"You bake what I taught you, and very little else—and you are lazy, too. I pay you too much now!" It was Maggie O'Donnell who spoke. But it was Marguerite Sauvé who burst into a storm of weeping, and begged only that Carlos forgive her for being a hardhearted fool. She would permit that he work but three hours a day, of course.

"And I will not work on Sundays—and I need ten dollars more a week for clothes, mia Primavera," he said, putting his arm around her and helping her to unlock the door. "Si, of course I will come in—I was only playing before. But I need clothes—you know that, querida mia."

"Of course you shall have clothes, my precious! Go to the store where I have an account—buy anything you wish. What is mine is yours. Ah, Carlos, why can we not be married? We could manage the shop so beautifully—it is a divine idea!"

"Not yet, Marguerite. I should have more experience—it will mean a great following for us. We must not get into the rut. Later we will talk of marriage. No man of sense marries before he is thirty."

"Very wise," Madame assented joyously. Marriage—marriage with Carlos! What did it matter that she would be sixty-

seven when Carlos was thirty? He would not know. There were
many things which could be done to aging skin . . . warm tallow . . . hot olive oil. . . . She could say she was thirty-eight
or so.

She spread the pastries on her marble-topped table. Carlos drank too much wine and grew painfully unpleasant.

"I think I shall call you Lisette," he babbled sleepily.
"Lisette is a nishe name and a nishe girl."

"What are you talking about?" Madame demanded in
alarm.

"I'm talking about Lisette. Lisette. Nishe gal, Lisette. Not
old hag with bags under eyes, like you. Lisette—nishe young
gal. Bangle on her arm—says 'oui' when I ask her—always 'oui.'
Nishe Lisette. . . ."

Madame took off his clothes and put him to bed. Then
she crept in beside him, shaking with terrible sobs. How much
of this Lisette babble was true? Was there a girl, then?

She had made her will, leaving everything to Carlos. On
the morrow she changed it, leaving him nothing at all. That
Lisette. . . . Later, hearing no mention of the girl, she grew
contrite. But she did not change the will back again.

She engaged a chef to assist Carlos, who now worked only
three hours a day and not at all on Sundays. She paid Carlos
an enormous salry. He had purchased marvelous clothes. How
she adored him! He was charming to her now.

When he came into Les Camélias, during his off-hours, he
was most stunning. Madame introduced him to two or three of
the older customers as Señor Carlos Alfaro, of Ecuador. They
did not know that he had built the puff tartes they were consuming. They invited him to their homes and introduced him
to dozens of their own friends. His name began to appear in
the society columns. He had a room at the best hotel . . . such
a good address. He was quite the rage, with his emerald ring
and his walking stick and his slight, delicious accent. The girls
loved his manners, the ladies loved his delicate compliments.

But Madame Sauvé—she was forgotten. They had merely
met him in her pastry shop. She was desolate and discouraged.
What was life for, anyhow? She should have known he did not
care. . . .

So things went on for half a year. Then, one summer night, Madame was returning to her apartment earlier than usual, she saw Carlos walking in front of her—Carlos and a girl. He appeared to be fond of the girl, who was as blonde and blue-eyed as Madame was brunette. They laughed and chatted, leaning together like lovers. And the girl wore a bangled brace-let.

Madame passed her apartment and followed them. They turned at Sainte-Ann, walking a few doors riverward. Madame's heart was in her throat. Carlos was going inside with this hussy!

"No, no, Lisette," came Carlos' voice, laughing. "You won't lock the door on me tonight, will you?"

So it *was* Lisette! Madame reeled against the wall, faint with misery and rage. Life, which had opened for her a golden door into Paradise, had banged it in her face. Carlos was hers no longer. Carlos belonged to Lisette. The dark enveloped her.

During the days which followed, she learned that the girl's name was Lisette Leboeuf—a common streetwalker who lived on Sainte-Ann, near Royal.

So that was Carlos Alfaro's taste! That was the meaning of the lingerie and other perplexing articles listed on her last bill from the department store, where she had given the Span-ish boy carte blanche to buy and charge to her account. Twelve pairs of silk hose, a silk lounging robe, a fur rug, five bottles of imported perfume, yards and yards of expensive lace, a satin coverlet. She had meant to investigate at the time, but there were so many things to attend to . . . so much aggravation and worry. . . . So her money was buying luxuries for Lisette Le-boeuf, the prostitute favorite of her own young lover! It was a degrading picture. . . .

One day Carlos did not come to work. Madame put on her small chic hat and went to Sainte-Ann street. She did not ring. The door opened at her touch. She ascended the stairs and opened the first door she came to, quite at random. But she opened it noiselessly.

The room was in disorder and not very clean. The dresser was a mess of cosmetics and brushes and bottles and soiled linen. An open letter lay on the table. Madame bent over it. "Darling Lisette . . . your Carlos. . . ." It was too much.

On the bed two people slept soundly—Carlos and Lisette Leboeuf. A great rage seized Madame Sauvé. To claw, to tear, to kill—to strangle, to torture, to crush! A fiend shrieked at her, bidding her to strike as they slept. Then Carlos snored. Madame drew back. Not now, not here. There would be another way.

Silently she circled about the apartment. In one corner, behind a cheap, red-flowered screen, stood a table holding a gas plate and a few unwashed dishes. A mouse was nibbling at a bit of brioche, a cockroach was examining a scrap of cold meat. A sugar bowl was black with ants. Madame turned away in disgust. Not now . . . not now. . . .

Life was over for Marguerite Sauvé. She was sixty years old, and she had made a prize fool of herself. Nothing mattered now. It was the end. Monsieur de Boisblanc's money had brought her nothing but agony and defeat.

She went back to her own apartment and locked the door. How still the rooms were!—as though someone had died. . . .

"Well," she thought bitterly, "I have died. My life has gone for nothing. No children, no husband, no lover. No place, in all the world. My shop is only a shop, where people come to buy dainties for their stomachs. I stand behind the counter and bow and smile and serve them. I am nothing to them.

"Carlos does not love me—he never did love me. I was a good thing—how he must have laughed! A hundred and fifty dollars a week, three hours' work a day, clothes, a charge account—what a fool I have been! I shall always be a fool. There is no use living, if one must always be a fool!"

She sat down at length, and wrote a letter to the police. She was committing suicide, she told them, and no one was to blame. But, she added, she would be coming back. She had work to do, and her ghost would be coming back—and they couldn't stop her.

And then she shot herself through the head.

There was the usual three-day hubbub. Madame Sauvé was dead. Les Camélias was closed. The help were all sent away. Carlos Alfaro shook his dark head and wondered where he could find another job. Then he went to tell Lisette Leboeuf. Lisette was not overly pleased. Carlos had made a bungle of things. But they spent the day together, and retired early.

About midnight, some late wayfarer saw a white Shape coming out of the Old French Opera House. It went down Bourbon to Toulouse, then to Royal, and turned the corner of Sainte-Ann. It glided silently along the banquette, its snow-white hair wreathing a dead-white face. The eyes were like flaming torches, and the mouth was tight-set. It paused at a door, a little distance from Royal, and went in.

A girl roomer in the place saw the Shape coming up the staircase. Being an artist and curious, she neither screamed nor moved. The Shape passed her, and went on to Lisette Leboeuf's door.

"I saw her plainly," the girl declared afterward. "It was Madame Sauvé, who kept Les Camélias, the pastry shop."

"But," she was reminded, "that is impossible. Madame Sauvé is dead."

"Nevertheless," she contended, "it was Madame Sauvé who came upstairs and went into Miss Leboeuf's room."

The Shape glided into the room where Lisette Leboeuf and Carlos Alfaro were sleeping. The place was very dark, but the Shape knew the way. It walked to the red-flowered screen. The ghostly fingers fumbled at the gas plate and turned on the gas. The white Shape closed the windows tightly, and went out and locked the door. Then it trailed wearily down the stairs and out onto the banquette, where a startled passer-by saw it peering in at a shopwindow. When he spoke to it, it vanished.

They found Carlos and Lisette in the morning. The Coroner called it suicide. But the little artist said a ghost had murdered them. She was laughed at, of course, but she stuck to her story.

From that time on, whenever a new tenant took possession of the room where Carlos and Lisette had died, a white Shape came from the Old French Opera House, went down Bourbon to Toulouse, and thence to Royal. It turned the corner at Sainte-Ann, and glided up the stairs. For years this went on. The neighborhood took to calling the Shape the "Witch of the French Opera."

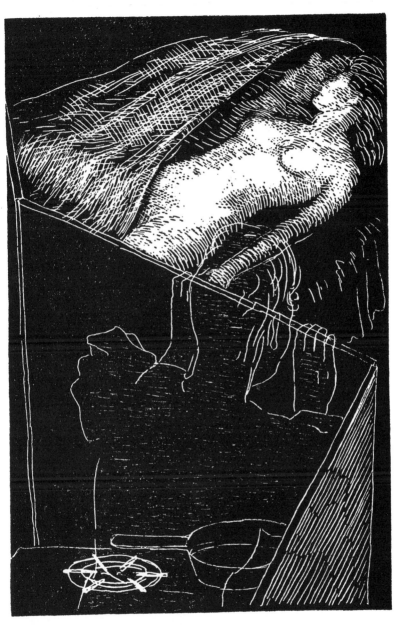

*The Shape glided into the room . . .*

Finally a new tenant of the Sainte-Ann street room found a letter written in a fine, pointed hand in faded ink, crammed between the mantelpiece and the chimney. The words were blurred. "Darling Lisette. . . ." And down at the end, "Your Carlos." The tenant tossed it into the fire.

Suddenly a white Shape stood beside the fireplace, uttering little moans and mewings, and reached a desperate ghostly hand into the flames. But the paper was gone—its feather-ash flitted up the chimney in the draft. The white Shape seemed to shrink and shrivel, and then it disappeared. The tenant remembered only the eyes, like torches. . . .

The Witch of the French Opera never walked again.

# (*1898-99*)  *The Ghosts of Carrollton Jail*

Perhaps the most startling of all the inexplicable tales told about the ghosts of this old city is that series of recitals by members of the police force concerning the manifestations which occurred in 1898 or so in the Ninth Precinct Jail.

This old structure was built about 1850 and was, when Carrollton belonged in Jefferson parish, the old Jefferson Parish Prison. It stood at the corner of Hampson and Short streets, fronting on Hampson. It was used continuously until the summer of 1937, when, along with three other precinct jails, it was condemned and demolished.

It was a brick building of two stories, with great doorways and heavily barred windows. Despite the flowers and shrubbery which flanked its approach and strove to lend it a semblance of grace and beauty, it was a bleak and hideous place. No blaze of light ever could have made it cheerful or acceptable to those unfortunate ones whose fate it was to be detained there.

In a square central courtyard was reared a gibbet. Many there were who shudderingly climbed those pitiless steps. Many there were who swung there at a rope's end until oblivion swallowed them up for all eternity. The thieves, the felons, the murderers, and those who had plotted and carried out crimes still more horrible and vile—all had languished in the narrow, airless cells of the old prison. A most unlovely and unhallowed spot, which for a season housed two men who had raped and murdered a small girl, and afterwards butchered her poor little body. These monsters were lynched in the yard of the jail itself by enraged citizens.

179

That was a long time ago. And it required the driving rains of many a year to tone down the hues of fresher masonry which replaced that chiseled away by a party of escaping prisoners.

Not a cell but had its ugly history. Every inch of wall space was covered with penciled inscriptions which only so tainted an aggregation of humanity could have fathered. There were ribald rhymes, obscene outpourings of filth and degeneracy, a line to a ladylove from one too gross to realize the insult of its very location, threats and coarse jokes and base riddles and nasty drawings, with here and there a roaring paraphrase of Holy Writ.

They came and they went, these poor damned human creatures whose feet never could walk the straight way, whose itching fingers must forever clutch at the forbidden. They huddled in the noisome cells while their skins bleached a sickly gray and the vermin ate them and the noose waited. They cursed and rotted and went forth with hopeless feet. They flew into mighty rages, and bit themselves, and hung themselves, each in his own fetid corner. Then there were those who hugged the slender string of days they had left on earth, dreaming dreams and seeing visions, and promising over and over again to come back when the spirit should be freed. To come back. . . . How? Why?

That they did come back is a matter of record. They came peering in, pausing here and there, causing strange things to happen, peopling the somber old prison anew, startling and perplexing those astute and hardened arms of the law who doggedly refused to believe in apparitions but who could find no other answer to the astounding riddle which unwound itself in their midst, day after day and week after week.

As long as the old walls stood, it seemed that every ancient brick had its ghostly tenant. Even as the wreckers tore at it, there were those who declared they saw human shapes writhing in the clouds of dust when the bricks came hurtling down. The shapes hovered and grinned and grimaced, some of them with wry necks and bulging eyeballs, others with twisted backs and knotted legs and bloody holes gaping where the worms had fed, their hideous mouths leering and drooling, and their matted hair falling in foul handfuls among the rubbish.

The rafters had their ghosts, and the brown old sleepers had their ghosts, and every board in the cypress flooring had its ghost. But the bricks that came from the terrible cells were fairly feathered with them, as the workmen tell it. It seemed that every prisoner who ever had suffered incarceration there, and every victim that the greedy gallows in the courtyard had strangled, returned to witness the last act of the desolate and degrading play in which he once had had so tortured a part.

Half a century after the building was erected, the ghostly visitants became so numerous and so persistent that the situation came to the attention of the newspapers of that day. During October of 1899, detailed accounts of various unexplainable things which took place in the "Old Ninth" appeared in the public prints.

At that time, Sergeant William Clifton was Police Commander of the District, and in charge of the jail. He had for years served with distinction in the New Orleans Police Department, and had succeeded Sergeant Shoemaker, who died in July, 1898, as head of this particular jail. Sergeant Clifton's force consisted of a clerk, a deputy, two doormen, and eight patrolmen.

The great front entrance gave onto a broad hall, on the left of which was the door opening into Sergeant Clifton's office. This room was meagerly furnished with a desk, a washstand, a sofa, and a number of chairs. Behind the Sergeant's office, with a narrow passage between, was the clerk's office. Here were desks and chairs, and a railing dividing the room.

Sergeant Clifton, with half a lifetime of police experience behind him, was a staunch admirer of General Beauregard. The General's portrait adorned his office, being hung from a stout nail driven into the wall above the washstand. One night Corporal Perez was in the office, and the two men spoke of Beauregard.

"As fine a man as ever drew breath," Sergeant Clifton remarked. "A wizened little Frenchman who never knew fear and never accepted defeat!" And he saluted the portrait with a flourish.

With a crash, the great picture fell to the floor. At the same moment the washstand, with its bowl and pitcher, lunged forward and fell also. Strangely, nothing was broken or even chipped. But, stranger still, the heavy cord by which the portrait was hung, was found to be in perfect condition, unbroken and unfrayed. The nail in the wall was solid, and slanted slightly upward. No possible reason could be found for the picture's falling.

The next night, while Sergeant Clifton and the Corporal were telling of the incident, the Sergeant again saluted the portrait, illustrating his action of the night before. Without warning, the mirror which hung just below the General's picture, plunged down from the wall, and the washstand and its china were again thrown from their place. This time the washbowl was smashed, but the other things were intact. The nail from which the mirror hung was strong, and was firmly driven into the wall. The mirror cord was nowhere worn or broken.

"It seemed," said Sergeant Clifton, "as though invisible ears had been listening, and that unseen hands pushed the things from the wall. I had a distinct feeling that the attitude of agreement with my remarks was so strong that it compelled action of some sort, and this was the peculiar form it took. I know that the portrait and the mirror could not have fallen unaided."

Upon another night three friends—two gentlemen and a lady—dropped in to chat a moment with the Sergeant. They were old friends, and the call was very welcome. During the conversation, Mrs. G. leaned casually against the north wall. It was a bare brick wall plastered over, with not so much as a calendar upon it. Suddenly the lady reeled away from it, barely retaining her balance.

"Something pushed me!" she cried, her eyes wide with alarm. "Something pushed against my shoulder! It was big as a mountain, and it pushed me right away from the wall!"

The gentlemen laughed at her, joking her about getting old and feeble-minded. Being neither old nor stupid, it piqued her a bit, and she again leaned against the wall, to prove that she wasn't a weak-minded ninny. But in a moment she was reeling into the center of the room again, bumping into the group of men and clutching at them to keep on her feet. This time she was white with terror.

"I don't care what you say—something's in that wall, and it pushed me away!" she cried. "I could feel its breath, and its hand brushed my face! It took me by the shoulders, just as either of you might do, and sent me spinning out into the room! Somebody's there, I tell you—somebody *must* be there!"

But nobody was there.

Yet, at that moment, something drifted back to Sergeant Clifton's mind—a picture seen years before. A murderer, who had boiled his wife's corpse in lye and made soft soap of her, had been brought into that office from his cabin out in the parish. He had leaned against that wall, cowering there just before the mob roared in and tore him well-nigh to pieces. His blood and brains had spattered that wall, and the clubs, as they battered his life out, had dented it.

"Yo' shan't git me!" he had screamed as they reached him. "I'll go t'rough dis wall—an' by Gawd, I'll come back t'rough it agin after I'm daid, an' mash yo'-all to a pulp!"

Had he come back, "pore white trash" that he was, with his heaving shoulders and his tempest of rage and fear, to push away any who might lean against that wall by which he had met blinding death? Mrs. G. never had heard of the man—had not heard even of ghostly happenings in the jail. Yet here was the grim " Old Ninth," unpacking its heart like a whore to any stranger who might happen in! The Sergeant felt a bit out of patience with his jail.

Several nights later, Sergeant Clifton was sitting at his desk reading. Suddenly he was grasped by the shoulders and his swivel chair was whirled completely round. Breathless, he demanded what his assailant meant by such actions. But no assailant was there. The lights were on full, but no one was in the room nor in the hall. The doorman said that no one had come in. Yet Something had taken the Sergeant by the shoulders and spun his chair round. He shivered in spite of himself, and set his mouth in a tight line. This sort of tomfoolery had got to stop!

But it didn't stop.

The sofa in his office was frequently used by the men to

catch a much needed nap at night. Officer Dell, who drove the patrol wagon, came in one night and stretched himself out on the sofa. Suddenly the sofa slid along the floor as though the building were tipped on its foundations—a full yard it traveled, then gathered itself and rolled back to its accustomed place. Driver Dell sprang up and blinked.

"My God!" he exclaimed. "What's got me? I'd swear this here sofa was riding round with me! I must be loony or something. Didn't you see nothing, Sergeant?"

"Yes," Clifton nodded, "I saw something. I saw your sofa riding you round, just as you say and it rode you back, too. Go to sleep."

"Not for mine!" whooped Driver Dell. "I sleeps somewheres else from now on—not on that there thing what rides round by its own self—no-siree bob!" And out he ducked.

But it was the same wall against which the wife-killer had been beaten to death. The Sergeant had ordered the sofa moved around there, after the episode with Mrs. G.

Not long after that, another officer thought to grab a half-hour's rest on the sofa. The thing not only slid out into the room, but bounced the occupant off so violently that he sprawled on the floor, striking his head on the corner of the desk and injuring himself badly. Sergeant Clifton rushed to his assistance, and saw the sofa rolling itself smugly back against the wall.

It happened again and again, until the men began to shun it as they would the plague. Then somebody moved it to another part of the room and rested upon it undisturbed—until an ambitious Negro, sent to brush down the cobwebs from the walls, brushed the haunted wall vigorously and laid his broom on the sofa. From that time, the sofa seemed linked inseparably with the ghost-ridden wall, and gave its occupants no peace.

At eleven o'clock one Wednesday night in October of 1899, Mounted Officer Jules Aucoin stepped into Sergeant Clifton's office to make a report. The Sergeant was out at the moment, and Officer Aucoin stood waiting. A large lithograph-portrait of Admiral Dewey adorned one wall—the force had taken pains to glue it securely to the plaster. Suddenly it began to revolve like a wheel. Aucoin straightened and rubbed his eyes, wondering if he could be addled. But no—the portrait was whirling serenely round and round, as though a spike had been driven through its center and someone had set it spinning.

Aucoin dashed into the hall and shouted to his brother officers, several of whom came on the run.

"It's the picture!" he squeaked, unable to control his voice. "It's Dewey—he's whirling round!"

But the picture wasn't whirling round when they returned to the Sergeant's office. The Admiral's substantial countenance, with its ample white mustache and its cool eyes, gazed down upon the excited blue-coats in calm patience.

"It's old Jones again!" snorted Officer Aucoin. "We ought to have known better than paste Dewey on that wall. Old Jones'll never let it alone." They all knew he referred to the wife-killer, who had not been old and whose name had not been Jones.

Strange and unacountable noises, furniture tumbling about by itself, things falling—these and numerous other uncanny happenings kept the Old Ninth policemen on edge.

One night Corporal Harry Hyatt heard heavy footsteps in the hall—so heavy that they seemed to shake the place. He stepped to the door of the Sergeant's office, wondering what giant was abroad. Although he still could hear the heavy footfalls, from the spot where he stood to the front door and then back again, he could see no one. Back and forth they went, one shoe scraping a little, back and forth. Corporal Hyatt could even feel a movement of the air when the footsteps passed near him, and smell a faint scent of cigar smoke. But not a thing could he see. We went along the hall and asked Doorman Foster if anyone had come in. Foster said that no one had come in nor gone out for fully half an hour.

"Guess it's Harvey," grinned the doorman.

Harvey had been a racetrack tout—a gigantic fellow who had wrung the necks of two jockeys and cut the tongues out of their horses. He had been brought into the Old Ninth, and had stood there in the hall with the cold stump of a good cigar between his fingers. He wouldn't have smoked, handcuffed, even if they had let him. He killed two guards there in the hall with his bare hands, and handcuffed. And then he got away, nobody ever knew how, and they never found him.

"Naw, it wasn't Harvey," returned Hyatt. "That kind don't come back."

But later that night he picked up an evening paper. A gigantic man known as Robert Brewer had been found dead in a small town in Pennsylvania. He was blind and his leg had been broken, but he had made a precarious living selling newspapers. After his death they had found an old notebook and a bundle of scribbled papers among his poor effects. He was Harvey, the racetrack tout, wanted in New Orleans for four murders, and elsewhere for other crimes.

"Well, I guess he came back, game leg and all," grunted Corporal Hyatt. "And he wasn't brought, neither."

The next night at the same hour, out in the hall, the heavy footsteps began again—back and forth, back and forth. Corporal Hyatt stepped to the door.

"Quit your kiddin', Harvey," he said briskly, to empty space. "You can smoke your cigar now, can't you?"

As suddenly as they had begun, the footsteps ceased. A great cloud of tobacco smoke gathered within a yard of him, thinned, and slowly rose to the stained ceiling. A cold shiver ran along the Corporal's spine and he stepped hastily back into the Sergeant's room.

One night after the clerk had finished up some extra work, several of the patrolmen drifted in. In the corner, on a small ledge, a few books lay piled under two heavy iron weights, such as are used with grocery scales. Suddenly the weights were flung with great force at the men, who sprang aside just in time to dodge them. The metal discs struck the floor at their feet and rolled to the baseboard.

"They didn't just fall off the ledge," one of the policemen maintained, when he told about it. "They were thrown, and they were thrown hard. Who could have done it, nobody knows. That ledge isn't anywhere near a window—and besides, a window would have been too high, and they're all barred. There's only one door to the room, and we were facing it. The lights were all on bright, and the clerk and three of our men were there, besides myself. We haven't got a practical joker in the place, and we were all busy talking. The doorman said nobody'd come in or gone out. There wasn't anybody in that room, or in the passage, or in the Sergeant's room, or in the front hall. Ghosts—that's the only answer. But I'd like to know who they figgered on hitting."

Time and again there was "a walking" along the hall, along the office floors, and up and down the stairs. They got to calling it that—"a walking."

On the second floor there had been formerly a row of four dark and moldy cells, known as "condemned cells." Here were kept those prisoners whose days were numbered. In a little while they would be hustled out to the square courtyard, where the gallows cast its gaunt and menacing shadow. Here they sweated and prayed and cursed, taking their own lives when they could, warring with an unjust destiny and that malevolent thing called The Law.

These stinking cells had later been remodeled into a courtroom. One night, very late, the footsteps being unusually frequent and heavy, several officers followed them upstairs and into the courtroom. The place was eerie enough, with its hollow stillness and its empty seats. The footsteps circled the room, the policemen tiptoeing along cautiously. Then the steps stopped, and the men stopped, too. Suddenly the great docket —a thick book weighing many pounds—flew from the Judge's desk, crashing onto the floor with a noise which brought Sergeant Clifton up the stairs three at a time. Nobody had touched the docket—in fact, nobody had been near it at the time. But the footsteps had stopped just beside the desk.

"I wish the damned Thing would laugh or something," muttered the Sergeant. "This walking business is going too far."

That night, seated at his desk, he happened to glance at the clock. The hands stood at three A.M. Suddenly a pair of strong hands closed round his neck, crushing the muscles and choking off his breath. He threw out his arms to ward off whomsoever was attacking him, and instantly the murderous grasp was loosened. He whirled round, but no one was there— no one had been there. Yet the marks of a great hand were still on his throat, and the bruises were visible for some days.

"I guess I won't ask 'em again to laugh," he mused rue-fully, telling of it.

Head Doorman C. W. Foster told of an afternoon in July, 1899. He was in the clerk's office alone at the time. Chancing to glance into Sergeant Clifton's office—the doors were on a line across the narrow passage—he saw two women standing by the desk. As the Sergeant was out, Officer Foster stepped over to the office to see what the women wanted. Evidently they were quadroons, being very light in color, and they were dressed in thin silk with a small figure or flower in it. One was in yellow and the other in a greenish-blue. Both were young. They stood there as stiff as posts—unnaturally stiff, Foster declared—staring straight ahead of them.

"What can I do for you—" the doorman started to ask, when the women disappeared.

"They didn't go anywhere," he declared. "They were just there, and the next instant they weren't there. It was like lightning. And I kept thinking of those two wenches we hung out there in the courtyard—they cut the guts out of a couple of other wenches that were after their men—and made the men eat the livers, or something like that. I recall that when they were first brought in they had on green and yellow clothes —very gaudy, what was left of 'em."

Officer Foster, by the way, was a quiet, middle-aged man, intelligent and well-educated, and not one given to fooling or imagining things. What he saw, he saw. On a night not long after the ghostly visitation of the two quadroon women, Door-man Foster was sitting in Sergeant Clifton's office. Several of the men were about, and the lights were on bright. Looking up suddenly, he saw Sergeant Shoemaker standing by the desk. The Sergeant having been dead for more than a year, Foster was astounded at seeing him there. In a moment Sergeant Shoemaker started over toward the sofa, his head bent and his step slow. Then, when he got to within a foot of the sofa, he vanished.

"He disappeared, just like the two Negresses disappeared," Officer Foster reported, shaking his head in bafflement. "And I sure knew Sergeant Shoemaker if anybody ever did. I'd known him like a brother for years—knew his ways, his walk, his clothes. And it was Sergeant Shoemaker I saw. He'd come back to his old office, I reckon, to see how it was getting along."

The members of the department weren't the only ones whom the ghosts visited, according to these old accounts. Cell Number Three was notorious for its tragedies.

One night Charles Marquez, Negro, was brought in on a charge of contempt of court. He was an intelligent colored man with no criminal tendencies, having been arrested on a capias issued by Judge Duggan. The other cells being full, Marquez was shunted into Number Three. They found him on the cell floor in the morning, unable to stand, scarcely able to speak, beaten and bruised and wounded in a hundred places. Questioned, his eyes rolled in terror, and his breath came in frightened gasps. They had his wounds dressed, and then he told his story.

"Yo'-all hadn't mo'n got out in de corridor when dey started comin' at me," he shuddered. "Ah means de ghosts—'cayse dat's what dey wa'—ghosts. Dey wa' gigglin' an' chucklin' an' bubblin' lak fish in de mud, an' Ah could feel 'em clammy as frogs. Dey come tru de baws—jes' oozin' tru lak gray gravy in t'ick gobs. An' dey 'gins to claw mah clothes off an' dey digs at mah eyeballs an' yanks at mah lips an' twists mah elbows. Dey chase me in de cawnah an' dey kicks me an' pummels me till Ah fink ev'y bone in mah carcass be done busted, An' dey rams hot pokahs in mah ears an' squeeze mah belly into mah backbone an' bends me double, an' den dey cracks me ovah de haid wid a beam an' dey drags me round lak a ole rag—an' Ah *is* 'bout a ole rag by dat time. Dat cell it am a debbil-cell—it ain't human, dat cell ain't!"

The appearance of the poor creature was said to bear out his statements. Not one of the personnel of the jail force had been near Cell Number Three from the time Marquez was locked into it until he was taken out of it.

But Cell Number Three had a reputation. Every prisoner they put into it for a night told the same tale and bore the same evidences of mistreatment. Nobody outside the cell ever heard a thing. Yet the occupant was always removed half-dead the next morning, gibbering about ghosts and devils and terrible beatings.

They say that once long ago, when the prison was very crowded, three murderers were locked in there together. One was a prisoner, one had hacked his old father and mother to death, and the third had drowned four babies in a sack. They fought all night, according to the old story, kicking and biting and tearing and pounding. In the morning two of them were dead, and the other died before a priest could reach him. Not a cry had any of them uttered—only the horrible grunts and thuds of battle betrayed them through the darkness.

Perhaps the most subtly gruesome apparition of the whole bloodcurdling array was the phantom which Night Clerk Joseph Crowley saw in September of 1899. He was sitting at his desk in the clerk's office one night, writing. Looking up suddenly, he saw standing there just outside the railing a tall, thin man. The light was very bright, and he noticed that the man wore a dark beard and was dressed all in black. He wore no hat, and his skin was so colorless that Crowley thought he must be ill.

The clerk opened his mouth to ask what the stranger wanted, but his throat felt paralyzed. The man stood there, silent and stiff, and then turned toward the door. Crowley said he had no sense of the man walking—he just glided until he had nearly reached the door, and then he vanished. The clerk rushed into the hall, but there was no one in sight. Officers about the place had seen no one—the doorman had seen no one.

A few nights after that, while Crowley was still feeling squeamish on the subject of ghosts, he was in his office talking with two of the patrolmen—Edward Harrison and George Shage. They were all facing the door into the passage, when suddenly the tall, pale man appeared in the doorway. His black clothes, his black beard, his hatless head, his stiff pose, his silence—all were the same as formerly.

The clerk pointed to him in alarm, and all three of the policemen started toward him. When they had nearly reached the door, he suddenly disappeared. Recalling Crowley's account, the three policemen searched every foot of the building, and took lights out into the grounds. But not a trace of anybody did they find.

Officer Harrison, a stern, practical man then in his fifties, declared there could be no doubt about the apparition.

"I don't believe in ghosts," he told reporters emphatically. "A policeman doesn't deal with supernatural things. But I know I saw that man, and I know I saw him disappear. It was the quickest thing I ever saw happen, and we all saw the same thing. His face was queer—like a dead face. Maybe it *was* a dead face. But if I see that face again in a thousand years, I'll recognize it."

So much for the Old Ninth. But though it swarmed with phantoms and rocked with the weight of an unseen eerie host, they never spoke. They appeared and they vanished, they walked and they accomplished weird feats. But through it all they preserved a silence worthy of more than a word in passing.

The Old Ninth is no more. It remains to be seen whether its ghosts have followed its bricks and its wreckage . . . old wine in new bottles.

$(1907\text{-}27)$     *The Flaming Tomb*

They say that heart responds to heart. And there is a tomb in
Metairie Cemetery which responded to its mother-tomb in
faraway Germany. Even now 'tis said that it pulses and glows
like a living thing, although it is only an empty shell with grass
growing thick and rank around it. Visitors to the cemetery
circle close, having heard of the woman who guards it, and of
the methods she employs in order to attain the greatest possible
degree of efficiency.

In 1911, Josie Deubler built the tomb of pink granite,
and it cost her seventeen thousand dollars. The beautiful
pink granite came from a Connecticut quarry which is now
abandoned.

The tomb itself is tall and stately, being set upon a grassy
mound which elevates it considerably above its fellows. Mrs.
Deubler built it for herself, cherishing a fancy that it sym-
bolized the entrance to a heavenly home—the generous bronze
doors, each with its friendly knocker, and the whole sur-
mounted by two pink marble urns with carved pink marble
flames rising from them, the broad threshold, and the shrubbery clustered about it.

But there was more than this: it was a perfect replica of
the family tomb in Germany. There are those who say that
Mrs. Deubler selected the lot in the midst of Metairie with
almost fanatical care; that she supervised the plans to the
last minute detail; and that she stood so close to the workmen
while they were erecting it that more than once they had to
ask her to move aside.

Constantly she carried in her mind a picture of the tomb in Germany. She compared every block, every angle, and found it good. She watched the two great pink urns set into place high above her head. "They will light my way," she said. The two heavy bronze doors with their knockers—"The gates that will let me into Paradise," she smiled.

And then came the bronze statue of a woman, life size, which was to stand before the entrance. The bronze woman was taller than Mrs. Deubler—her arms outstretched as though to open the door. Did she symbolize to Mrs. Deubler, in some unutterable way, the mystic *ka, ba* and *khaibit* of ancient Egypt? Or did she take unto herself those strange and mystic qualities afterwards, reveling in her half-world, her quasi existence? For certain it is that through this inexplicable figure flowed the current which brought puzzlement alike to private individuals and the public which came to gape and gasp and flee away in unreasoning terror.

When the tomb was first finished, its beauty and its unusual design attracted a steady stream of sight-seers. Mrs. Deubler wrote to her relatives in Germany that it was completed and appeared to be perfect. Perhaps that established the strange bond, for immediately rumors began to circulate that the tomb, aside from its architecture, was different from the rest of those in Metairie.

One of the sextons noticed it first. It glowed, he reported, like heavy rose-colored glass with a light inside. Then another sexton, waiting until darkness fell, witnessed a curious phenomenon: the pink carved flames rising from the surmounting marble urns were joined by flaring tongues of bright fire, which mingled and rose like watch-fires in the evening air.

And not this alone, although it would have been startling enough. The bronze woman, the second sexton declared, leaned over and grasped the handle of one of the knockers, wielding it until the whole place resounded with the clamor. He turned and ran, the awful din ringing in his ears until he had outdistanced it. Even then, his imagination still caught the echoes creeping through the graveyard greenery after him.

"She moved!" he shuddered to his companion at the outer gate. "That bronze woman moved, I tell you! She had holt of the knocker, plain as day, and she was bangin' away like Billy-hell!"

But these reports failed to disturb Mrs. Deubler's peace of mind. She smiled complacently, and planted more shrubbery and rosebushes around the pink tomb. She patted the bronze woman knowingly, smoothing her hard draperies and nodding understandingly.

"Ich liebe dich!" she whispered to the bronze doors. "You will keep me safe where I shall be going one day."

So she died, and her body was deposited in the tomb. And the bronze woman—the *ka, ba* and *khaibit* of ancient Egypt—stood guard faithfully. The tomb in Germany held hands with the tomb in Metairie—their pink marble urns blazing with unearthly fire, and their twin sentinels standing grim and watchful by the gate.

Curious observers claimed that the figure moved about the tomb. That sometimes she tapped upon the doors with her metallic knuckles. The sextons became irritable on the subject, because the crowd which sometimes gathered beat down the grass and broke the rosebushes in their eagerness to see. More often, gossip said, the figure hammered with the knocker— beating as though an army were pressing at her back, and the gate were her only loophole of escape.

The place became so notorious that relatives had Mrs. Deubler's body removed and sent back to Germany. So the tomb stood deserted.

One day in August, 1914, just at dusk, a sexton by the name of Judkins beheld so strange and astounding a sight that he forbore to tell about it until forced to do so. He was walking through the cemetery, he said, and he came opposite the empty pink tomb. The unaccountable flames were rising high as bonfires from the marble urns, and an odor pungent as incense filled the air.

He paused a moment, thinking that the bronze woman looked taller than usual. And then, while the man's eyes fairly started from their sockets, *she turned and walked down the cemetery path between the tombs!*

Judkins, scarce able to believe his senses, started after her. He could see her moving just ahead of him, her bronze feet clattering on the gravel and little shells, her dark arms swinging slightly as she went. In and out she picked her way until she reached the street gate. He watched her until she turned the corner, and then he sat down on a whitewashed stone to collect his wits and regain his breath.

The next day Anthony, a newer sexton, whispered to him, "That statue to the 'burning tomb' is gone—did you notice? Who took it away—do you know?"

But Judkins knew nothing. He was afraid to know anything, for fear he might be accused of stealing the statue and selling it for its metal. Judkins was an honest man, and he couldn't afford to lose his job.

A few days later, Anthony came to work with a white face.

"Judkins," he said, "I'm tellin' you we're in for trouble about that there pink tomb. The statue went and disappeared, and didn't none of us see who carted it off. That looks bad, because we're responsible for this here cemetery. When folks pays good money for marble and such, they think it's our job to keep it settin' where it's been set. Now, this here iron angel—"

"Woman. It ain't no angel," corrected Judkins.

"Well, woman, then. This here iron woman's gone. But do you know what I heard last night, up at the drugstore? I heard that somebody seen a iron woman trampin' along a road, out in the country. They stopped and got out of the car and touched her, and she was sure 'nough hard and cold—real iron, I tell you, with green streaks up and down in the folds of her clothes. And the minute they touched her, she disappeared—and the grass had caught fire where she stood, and they tromped it out."

"You mean it was our bronze woman?"

"Sure. But who stole her out of here?"

"Nobody stole her," replied Judkins, a queer twist to his mouth. "She walked out. I seen her myself." And he told his story.

The first World War was raging, and time went on. Nobody paid any attention to the absence of the bronze woman. And then, on November eleventh, 1918, late in the day, she came striding back. Judkins saw her turn in at the gate.

"She looks beat out," he thought, but he stood quite still in the gathering dusk.

Her draperies were weather-beaten and muddy, and her face lined with dust and ashes. There was a grim set to her jaw, and her sightless eyes stared straight ahead.

With Judkins following on silent feet, she made her way through Metairie. Slowly she walked, and still more slowly. When she came to the pink tomb, the whole place grew gray and somber and deathly, as she turned to face the empty vault. Then her feet found their old position. She seemed to shift herself, and sort of balance and settle; and then she stood straight and stiff, as she was when the tomb builders first placed her as a part of that weird mortuary group. Again she was only a cemetery piece—something to be gazed at, to shed the rains and withstand the tempest.

The bronze woman walked no more. But a wild red light played all about the tomb when night came on. There was no reason for it. No pink granite could, unaided, give forth a brilliance like that.

Some thought it might be the reflection from a red traffic light which hung some distance away in the street; but when the light was removed, the tomb was still the center of that unearthly glow of rose and ruby. Someone else suggested that perhaps the lights from a certain large signboard illuminated the pink tomb. But the signboard lights could not reach that far, and no other tomb in the vicinity received so much as a beam from them.

When the tomb was offered for sale it was bought by a New Orleans attorney. The bronze woman remained motionless until his daughter died. When her body was sealed in the vault, the flames from the pink urns reared and belched. The statue leaned forward, it is said, and grasped the knocker, nightly clanging forth her challenge to Death. Finally the body within was removed, and the ugly commotion ceased.

The rains drench both tomb and statue, the winds sweep them, the sun parches them, the stars peer down and find the roses dead and the grass grown coarse and unruly. No soft ferns bless the hard pink house of death, no early violets lift dewy eyes to the grim black figure beside it. The sextons leave it alone.

Is it some deep bond of hatred existing between the old tomb in the now devastated Fatherland and this costly one here in the garish but victorious New World, that nightly stirs mystic fires to a red and awful glow? Do souls dwell in fury still, waging some eternal war of frightfulness and lust and greed?

So the sextons of Metairie reason it out among themselves, each relating his own weird experience with the mysterious "flaming tomb" and its still more mysterious bronze sentinel. And the inquisitive watchers still trail in by two's and three's, stepping lightly and lingering long—hoping against hope that the bronze woman will again be up and away before their astonished eyes.

# (1900)    *The Ghosts of Shiloh*

The most beautiful house in the Vieux Carré stands on the woods side of Chartres street, directly opposite the ancient Convent of the Ursulines. Fifty-seven feet wide by seventy feet deep, not including the broad galleries along the front and rear, it stands intensely solid, mute, brooding and inscrutable.

A bronze placque on its stately front announces to the passer-by that it was once the home of General Beauregard— Pierre Gustave Toutant-Beauregard, descended from Tider the Young, who in 1290 led a party of Welsh against England's first Edward. So today it is called Beauregard House.

Granite staircases curve in sweet grace from each end of its high front gallery. There is wrought-iron lacework railing both gallery and stairs. There are massive supporting columns, smooth and staunch, and tall iron gates like twin sentinels on guard. And there is the great entrance in the center of the gallery.

Tradition says it was built in 1812 by Joseph le Carpentier, grandfather of Paul Charles Morphy, the world's greatest chess player. Paul Morphy was born in the second room to the left of the hall, in June, 1837.

Precisely when General Beauregard moved into the great house does not seem to be recorded. Tradition says that he was at the time Major Beauregard, fresh from the Mexican War.

We do know that on an April day in 1866, he stood on the stately granite steps of the Chartres street mansion, and spoke to a gathering of men clad in tattered gray uniforms. They had been his men on the bloody battlefields of a war but a year ended. They cheered again the slight figure with its serious dark face and eager eyes, harking back to Manassas and the hell of Shiloh, again for the moment part and parcel of that beautiful Cause which still blazed like a cross of fire deep within each unforgetting heart. The "Great Créole" was speaking to his own. And we do know that he lived in the Chartres street house until 1869.

Then came Giacona, the Italian wine merchant—the odor of garlic and strong perfumes; noisy music, troops of dark-skinned children and overdressed swarthy women; the clatter of dishes and the din of scolding mothers; interminable clothes-lines hung with a motley array of vivid garments all over the spacious courtyard, right back to the two-story slave quarters at the extreme rear.

The Giaconas, it appears, had need to barricade themselves. They added a great double-hook of iron—an ugly claw six feet long and more than an inch through—reaching from the front doors to the left sidewall, clamping the front entrance shut like some medieval castle gate.

The Mafia had its eye on the Giaconas. And it was here, on the rear gallery, that Corrado Giacona shot three Italians to death in 1909. They had come to inquire about this and that—snarling, beady-eyed men—but their real mission was to extort five thousand dollars from Corrado Giacona. He gave them his answer in cold lead hotly fired. You may still see the bullet holes through the fan-windows of the dining room. There are bullet holes, too, in the heavy front doors and the gallery columns.

And there the intruders lay like cordwood, stiff and stark and horribly still, on the rear gallery. Even today, if you are lucky enough to ever get into it, you may dig about in the moldy corners of the old garret and find bundles of letters and records of the Giacona transactions, all written in spidery longhand, in careful Italian.

Three cycles—Morphy, Beauregard, Giacona. Beauregard House is now restored and preserved. The four vast cisterns, set two by two in the courtyard, one topping the other, are long gone. The ancient flower garden, reaching to Ursuline street, is gone. But the bees and the mosquito hawks, the pigeons and the mockingbirds are still there—even the chameleons, blowing rose-colored bubbles and snaring luscious insects for an early luncheon.

"Yesterday is a wind gone down." But when the night grows still and eerie, there are those who will tell you of strange goings-on in Beauregard House. The whole square is peopled with Italians, and they all hurry when they pass the brooding mansion where Beauregard slept and dined and planned and came back to remember.

Spend a night in Beauregard House, with the candles unlit and the doors barred fast. There are those who have done so, before World War II, laughing bravely at the start, and hurrying away at dawn with white faces and tales which would chill any normal blood.

The colder the night, the more weird the performance. And this is the tale they invariably tell:

The night closes down tightly until about two o'clock. Then the great folding doors of the ballroom, to the right of the central hall, glide apart. True, they stand open all day long; but at night they mysteriously close, apparently to commence the drama properly.

The strangest thing of all is that the furnishings of the whole place seem to dissolve like fog, and every room becomes filled with things of another century—carved rosewood and mahogany, hangings of stiff velvet and brocade and heavy foreign laces, crystal chandeliers holding dozens of small kerosene lamps, thick carpets and high-backed sofas, ornaments of bronze and marble, vast gilt-bordered mirrors, Dresden figurines and handwoven coverlets.

Even the courtyard is different then. No matter what time of year it may happen to be, there are suddenly blooming peach trees and persimmons and pomegranates, banana palms and magnolias, roses and flowering orange and lemon, crêpe myrtles and altheas and cape jasmines and bay and hibiscus. Black servants move here and there over the old paving-bricks, or pass up and down the white staircases into the dining room.

From the ballroom comes the General in his shabby gray uniform, and he pauses in the still drawing room a moment, the mirrors reflecting his sad, quiet face. Then he goes on into the broad hall, his eyes full of old dreams. He peeps into the second room on the left, where a slim shadow of a man sits at a misty chessboard—and the General smiles faintly and passes on.

To the very end of the hall he strides—and the hall is fifty-four feet long. Into the dining room, which smells of garlic and wine, and out onto the rear gallery. All at once there are shapes there—a heap of three dead men, very messy, their blood oozing in thick red rivulets and dripping down through the gallery floor onto the courtyard bricks. There is a smoking revolver hanging in mid-air—the Italians of the neighborhood will tell you, crossing themselves and running across to Saint Mary's Italian church to dip their fingers in the holy water stoop, that this is because Corrado Giacono has not been dead long enough to join the rest.

Then Beauregard turns and goes back through the long dining room and into the hall. Figures spring up on every side —figures in ragged gray uniforms, some with their faces shot away, some with no legs, some with shattered arms, some with guns, some with swords, some breathless, some running, some kneeling, some fighting through a cloud of acrid smoke, a horse now and then appearing in the terrible midst. Sometimes there is the pale outline of a little country church—cornfields lush in the sun, a scared darky with a packet of letters or a brace of chickens.

You see a moving panorama, as though you looked through the General's eyes, away back to April of 1862. You hear one groaning word from his lips—"*Shiloh.*" And that must be what you see, as he sees it every night—the battlefield of Shiloh! What a hell it is—death, like a rain of fire blasting dry stubble —death, with every agony known to man, coming onward in a living tide—shrieking, cursing, vomiting—stamping out twenty-four thousand brave men, cracking their bones, trampling them to jelly, crushing them like worms—and the General watching it over and over again—damn Buell!—and Johnston killed on the first day!

Golden banners drooping over green fields—drums struggling with defeat—the old house responding with every beat of its fiery old heart, pounding back to the General its cry of love and loyalty and honor! Can such things be, across so many moldering years? They say so.

And then the General straightens. He is a little man, but the majesty of command sits upon him like a cloth-of-gold mantle. The fury and the stench and the pestilence and the horror seem to subside. Yet there seem to be thousands of men, living and dying and dead, all around. Even the three stark corpses on the rear gallery get to their feet and come in at the door. There is Paul Morphy, in immaculate old-fashioned clothes, standing at attention. As with one movement, the multitudes salute the General, and then they begin to fade slowly away.

As they grow dimmer and yet more dim, and the blood-soaked cornfields disappear, General Beauregard still stands. And suddenly you see the weirdest moment of all, although you do not see a thing. But it is there—every fiber of you knows it and feels it and responds: the spirit of the old house straightens its brick features into a grim, hard line, wrings the darling General's lean hand in a grip of iron, steps back a pace . . . and salutes. And the General understands.

Things settle back to dull reality. The house is its drab self again, old and stained and very tired. The General is no more. Paul Morphy is no more. Giacona is no more. Shiloh has faded into morning mists.

Would you climb to the garret of the old house? Where, then, are the garret stairs? Nobody knows. Nobody remembers them. Nobody ever took them away. The dormered garret is boarded up—it is now a matter of ladders and limber legs and agile feet.

But, after that one astounding night, you see but one thing in Beauregard House, and you hear but one thing and remember but one thing—the phantom battlefield of Shiloh, seen through the phantom eyes of the General, whose name the old house bears with a pride beyond anything that is earthly.

But you must have the "seeing eye". . . .

# (*1869*)     *The Lady of the Door*

Charles Duffield, one of a firm of private detectives who flourished in New Orleans during the latter part of the 19th century,
has left a record of a strangely baffling case. News of it became
so widely circulated that it finally found a place in the newspapers of the day.

There came one day to the detectives' offices, it appears,
a gentleman who represented a Spanish family by the name of
Lanzos. To Duffield and his associate, Gerome Martinez, the
Spaniard told his story.

This man, Señor Santiago Delmas, speaking in choice
Castilian, stated that in the Faubourg Marigny stood a house
which had belonged to the Lanzos family for generations. On
account of ebbing financial resources, the property had been
sold late in 1865, to a merchant by the name of Gabriel
Clemente Angué.

The last Spanish owner had been Balderio Lanzos, younger
son of old Pedro Lanzos. Balderio was a rake and a spend-
thrift, and had gone through the family fortune within a few
years after his father's death. He cared nothing for the ancient
mansion, and sold it to Monsieur Angué with all its furnishings
and heirlooms. The merchant, recognizing the beauty and
worth of the old things, left them as they were, retaining the
old Lanzos servants as well.

"But, you see," Señor Delmas continued, "that is not all.
Señor Pedro Lanzos made a will. He had had an elder son,
Esteban, of whom he was intensely fond. The old gentleman
had married late in life, which meant a wide discrepancy be-

tween the ages of himself and his sons. The younger son, Balderio, was always at odds with his father. But the elder son was possessed of tact and judgment, as well as an amiable disposition, and was always smoothing out family disputes.

"One day, however, a general quarrel was hatched by Balderio, during which he accused Esteban of stealing family jewels which he himself had purloined and lost in gaming. He was so clever in his statements that the father suddenly turned on his favorite son. Esteban, stiff with true Spanish pride, refused even to defend himself, but left the house and the country within the hour. Old Pedro, himself too proud to apologize to anybody, never attempted to trace his elder son nor communicate with him.

"Then, after years, news came to him that Esteban had died in Spain. That was all—merely the bare item of his death. But the father's old heart, yearning silently all the years of Esteban's absence, melted completely at last. And when he made his will, he revealed that he did not believe Esteban to be really dead—that he felt too near him for death to be possible. He said, in that weird document, that every day he had expected to see Esteban come walking in at the door of the old house, as though nothing ever had come between them. But Esteban never came.

"So, in this sure belief that his dear son still lived, he willed the house and all his property to Esteban. Only in case that the elder son's death without heirs could be proved beyond the shadow of a doubt, was the property to revert to the profligate Balderio. As neither Esteban nor any of his possible children could be discovered, Balderio did come into possession of the house and the fortune, and did lose the one and waste the other.

"But now comes a curious dilemma. With both house and fortune gone from the family, here now appear two claimants—the son and daughter of Esteban who, it seems, married in Spain an aristocratic lady who bore him these children, Jaime and Anita.

"It appears that when Esteban set out for Spain he determined to leave the name of Lanzos behind. Calling himself Esteban Garcia, the name of his maternal grandmother's people, he entered Spain and quickly found a place in commercial circles. Knowing the New World, he soon became a member of a large firm of exporters. In a few years he was well-to-do, and at his death was the owner of a substantial fortune.

"To only one person had he revealed his true name and the place of his birth—the priest of the small church which he had attended since his arrival in Valencia. Shortly after Esteban's death, this aged priest imparted his secret to Jaime and Anita. It was because of their desire to mingle with their father's family that they started the investigation which resulted in their being identified as the rightful heirs of old Don Pedro.

"Yet, here is the paradox: they stand forth as the undisputed children of Esteban Garcia, who declared to his priest that he was Esteban Lanzos, son of Pedro Lanzos of New Orleans. But there was only his word for it. Any man could have made a like statement.

"I said 'only his word for it,' but there was something else. He carried with him, when he left this city, an ancient seal ring which had been in the Lanzos family for centuries. It was a strange seal—a stag's antlers on a man's head, with a pair of eagle's wings outspread at the base of the neck, and a javelin horizontal just below."

"But a moment," interrupted Gerome Martinez. "I should like to ask whether or not it could be proved that this seal was the genuine Lanzos seal. Is it not possible that a man clever as Esteban Garcia undoubtedly was, could discover in Spain the ancient seal of the Lanzos family and have it copied into a ring?"

"Certainly it would be possible," agreed Señor Delmas. "And that is part of my mission—to establish the fact that the ring was genuine. The old priest's story was most precise. He said that Esteban told him that in the New Orleans mansion was a closed room—a 'haunted room,' he called it. It seems that upon a single occasion Esteban did enter that forbidden room, and there he found and read certain documents, and made some sort of seal with the old Lanzos ring. As we can seem to come upon no other impression of this ring, I am hoping against hope that it may be possible to locate the one of which he spoke, or some others from that mysterious room."

"You would like to visit the old Lanzos mansion, Señor?" Charles Duffield asked.

"That is what I came to this city with the intention of doing," nodded the Spaniard. "Can you gentlemen interview the present owner, and arrange such an expedition, and also accompany me?"

"I shall call upon Monsieur Angué at once," bowed Duffield. "There is little doubt but what the visit can be arranged."

That same afternoon, at about two o'clock, the three men were driven in a carriage through the quiet shaded streets of the Faubourg Marigny, which is the French Quarter of today. Royal street was fronted by houses whose occupants were wealthy and influential. Aristocratic names were thick on the rue Royale in those days.

They turned at Esplanade and presently came upon a vast stone mansion with spacious grounds. A wrought-iron fence separated it from the banquette, and Martinez rang the bell set into the fence beside the gate.

The front door opened slowly, after a time, and an aged colored man peered forth to see what was wanted. When he glimpsed the three callers, he hastened down the broad steps and unlocked the gate, bidding them enter.

"Yo'-all is de gemmen what Mass' Angué done say be comin', Ah 'specks," he quavered, ushering them into the wide hall. "Mass' he done telled me to show yo'-all anywhar yo' wants, an' ansuh all yo' questions to mah bes' cability. Mass' he am sorry he got to be at de sto', but he cain't he'p hisseff 'bout dat. He say yo'-all be aftah sumpin' mighty impawtant lak, an' Ah sho' hopes ole Abel kin he'p yo'."

His cracked old voice trailed off into a wistful monotone as he closed the heavy door. The visitors caught glimpses of old, old hangings of ruby damask and cloth-of-gold, faded velvets of peacock and royal blue, frayed embroideries and gold fringes, bronze statuettes and marble urns and alabaster cups and tall crystal ornaments. Everywhere was a sort of cathedral stillness—great arches leading from room to room, mirrors spotted with the mold of years, festoons of yellowed lace streaked with mildew. The Turkish carpet underfoot was worn almost through in places.

"Show us the rooms, Abel," said Duffield. "Slowly, because we are looking for something which may mean a great deal to the family you used to serve."

"Yo' means ole Mass' Lanzos?" The withered old black hands were clasped tightly together. "Laws sakes, suh, dat fambly am all daid an' gone, Ah reckons. Baldy he fell in de rivah. Ain't none ob 'em lef' 'ceptin' ole black Mincy an' Abel, no suh."

"That's what we want to find out," Martinez said gently.

And then they began their explorations.

"Every stone in these walls brought from Spain," Martinez remarked. "And Angué has had the unparalleled good taste to leave everything exactly as it stood when he bought it. Just now his wife is away for a few months, but she shares his views. He says he is going to have the broken fountains and statuary in the yard restored, but otherwise the place is to remain unchanged."

They went over every room carefully, taking notes for future reference. At the end of one of the long corridors was a closed door which they passed by. Duffield hung back a little, examining the carved panels and the beautiful arch of the casement.

"Aren't you showing us this room, Abel?" he asked.

"Oh, no suh—ain't nobody nevah goes in *dat* room," the old Negro replied. "Dat am *de* room, suh."

"You mean the haunted room? I've heard there is one."

"Yassuh—dey calls it ha'nted. Dey finks it am ha'nted, an' Ah *knows* it am. Don't nevah go near dat room if Ah kin he'p it, no suh. Ain't nobody been in dat dar room sence anybody kin 'membah—sence de house wa' spick an' span new, Ah reckons."

"Why not?" Señor Delmas inquired. "All one need do is just to walk in. Or is the door kept locked?"

"Ain't no need to keep *dat* do' locked," Abel mumbled, his eyes rolling. "Anybody what tries to git in dat do' ain't lookin' fo' what he gwine see. No suh, don't nobody nevah go in *dar*."

"But, Abel, why not?" Duffield asked.

Slowly the old darky pointed. They turned and faced the door, the hall seeming suddenly to grow pitch dark. There, standing erect against the dark old cypress panels, was a tall, slim girl. Her hair hung about her like a raven cloud, one great sapphire blazing just above her forehead. A gauzy white garment wrapped her from head to foot, and the toe of a satin slipper showed under the filmy hem.

One arm was raised high above her head, and the upraised hand held a lighted black candle, flickering feebly through the gloom. But all around her glowed a cloudy light which flamed and dulled, moment by moment. The eyes of the young woman blazed as Duffield advanced a step, and the cluster of brilliants on one of her fingers flashed like lightning.

"Who is she?" Martinez asked in an awed tone.

"De leddy ob' de do'," Abel muttered. "Ain't nobody gwine pass in. Ain't nobody nevah done pass in—'ceptin' once."

"What do you mean—about that once, Abel?" Martinez said softly.

"Jes' once," nodded the old servant, his eyes on the tall white figure at the end of the hall. "Jes' once. 'Twa' fawty year back, Ah 'specks. Li'l Mass' Es'ban, he wa' mebbe 'bout twelve year ole. An' one day he say, 'Abel, Ah's gwine in de ole room, an' ain't nobody gwine hurt me. Ah is de Lanzos ob' de line, an' Ah b'longs whar Ah goes.' An' when de leddy ob' de do' she come an' h'ist up her hand wid de black candle an' all, li'l Mass' Es'ban he smile an' pass right fru her—an' her still standin' right in de do'!"

"And did you go in, too, Abel?" the Señor wanted to know.

"No suh, not dis yere niggah," Abel shivered. "Ah stan's right yere, an' waits fo' de li'l Mass' to come out. An' when he comes out, he walks right fru de leddy ob de do' again, an' he say, 'Ah done ben in a grave, Abel—an' Ah done lef' mah mawk in dar, 'cayse de white leddy she say Ah kin.'

" 'No, Mass' Es'ban,' Ah say, 'de white leddy she stan' outside de do' all de time yo' ben in dar—'cayse Ah seed her.' 'No, Abel,' li'l Mass' he say, 'de white leddy she done ben inside wid me all de time,' An' he meaned it so plain dat Ah wa'n't gwine argufy 'bout it. Ah done seed her, an' li'l Mass' he done seed her. Mebbe she kin be seed in bofe places to once."

"What was that the boy said about leaving his mark in the room?" Duffield asked.

"Jes' dat—when he come out he say he done lef' his mawk."

"Well, that's what we want to find, Abel," Señor Delmas said, striving to speak naturally in spite of the strange white figure glistening against the dark door. "If we can find that mark, it may mean that this house will again come into the possession of the Lanzos family. Esteban had a son and a daughter—and that mark may be all that is needed to prove that they are indeed Esteban Lanzo's children."

Suddenly the men were aware that a strange thing was happening. The figure was standing aside, and the door of the haunted room was opening slightly. Gathering their courage, the three passed inside.

What they beheld was weird enough. The place, almost dark, was like some cavern which has gathered the damp dust of ages. Tall bookcases lined every wall, the volumes falling out and littering shelves and floor with their crumbling leaves.

"Bring a lamp, Abel!" called Duffield. "Let us stand where we are, gentlemen, until we can see where we step."

When Abel brought the lamp in shaking hands, he turned and fled. And suddenly the three who remained found themselves gazing on the floor at their feet, their eyes half-starting from their heads. For there lay a human skeleton, a few shreds of lace and gold thread still clinging to the brown ribs. The long black hair lay in a thick cloud under the dry bones— a sapphire flashing like a blue star among the dull tresses.

Clusters of diamonds clasped one fleshless arm, and a glittering necklace lay within the collarbones and shoulder blades. Ghastly enough, without the long knife which was still thrust deep between the ribs, where once the heart beat warmly. In the clawlike fingers hung a wisp of paper, brown and fragile as mist. Duffield held the lamp close, to read a faded signature and a date—*Bernadine Lanzos, 14 abril, 1767*—the rest of the writing was obliterated by time and moisture.

Martinez had opened a metal box which stood on the worm-eaten table. From it he drew a sheet of paper, stained and discolored and fragile—the fly-leaf of some book, it appeared to be. In the center of it was a heavy blob of dark wax, with a seal stamped deeply in it. And scratched on the paper in a boyish scrawl, as though done with some pointed bit of metal, he read, *Esteban Lanzos, el martes, dudécimo agosto, 1827*—Esteban Lanzos, Tuesday, twelfth August, 1827.

The two others gathered round him, reading as he read. It was a ghastly setting—chairs and sofa fallen to decay, hangings rotted and green with mold, cobwebs swirling in corners like glowering thunderclouds, the crumbling carpet, the terrible disarray of moth-eaten books and disintegrated bindings, the desolate cerements of a room closed for a century, green lichen encrusting the carved marble fireplace, the little lizards which eyed intruders from the high writing desk, the cockroaches that swarmed in every crevice, moisture smearing the filthy windows like demon fingers—above all, the dried and musty skeleton sprawling its hideous length on the foul floor, a loathsome crimson toadstool rising from one twisted kneejoint.

"Let us make the wise little experiment," suggested Señor Delmas, drawing his breath carefully in that place of evil decay. "But, above all, let us make it elswhere. There is another paper in this bronze box—we shall take the whole concern into another room and examine everything with great care."

Shuddering in spite of themselves, they again passed through that awful door with its spectral guardian—only now there was no phantom.

"Ah done heerd yo' speak up," old Abel was saying, his white head wagging from side to side as though keeping time to some ghostly chant. "Ah done heerd yo', an' *she* done heerd yo'. An' she done fade herseff away—herseff an' dat dar black candle an' dem lightnin' eyes. An' she ain't come back. Mah ole bones done be tellin' me she ain't gwine come back no mo'. She ain't nevah let nobody pass befo', on'y once. An' dis wa' fo' de same chile o' de Lanzos line. Come in de dinin' room, whar de table done be big."

So to the dining room they went. Señor Delmas produced

a bit of sealing wax, and held it near a candle flame. When it had dripped sufficiently onto a sheet of note paper, he stamped it with an ancient seal ring which he produced from an inner pocket. And there were the two, as alike as two peas—the one from the haunted room, and the one he had just made—a stag's antlers on a man's head, with a pair of eagle's wings outspread at the base of the neck, and a javelin horizontal just below.

"You will notice," el señor continued, "that there are three flaws, or chips, in each seal—a round one on the upper prong of the right antler, an irregular one on the face's left cheek, and an almost imperceptible one in the middle of the javelin. Use this glass—it brings them up clearly. Such flaws could not be duplicated.

"This is the Lanzos signet ring, which Esteban used in making the wax seal on the twelfth of August, 1827—and which he entrusted to the old priest in Valencia, who entrusted it to me, and with which I have just now made this new imprint. Let us see now what the other old paper is in this box, gentlemen."

They unfolded it with infinite care—the original grant of the ground upon which the Lanzos house stood, to Don José Vicente Lanzos, dated in 1699, and bearing two signatures— Carlos II, King of Spain, and Souvolle de la Villentry, Spanish Governor of Louisiana. From his pocketbook Señor Delmas drew another document—being later notations and a confirmation of the first document, dated 1766, and signed by Carlos III, King of Spain, and Don Antonio de Ulloa, Spanish Governor of Louisiana. In the bronze box, under the folded paper, lay something like two quarts of magnificent unset diamonds and sapphires.

"The two papers tally perfectly," el señor announced. "There is now no question regarding the clear title. My young people have a great deal of money, and they long to possess the Lanzos family home. They will reimburse Monsieur Angué handsomely for this property and whatever expenditures he may have made upon it. He has agreed to let them have it, and a true gentleman he is. These Lanzos jewels, of course, belong to the two young heirs by right of inheritance."

Because they knew how much it would mean to old Abel, they called him and explained carefully.

"Praise de Lawd!" he exclaimed fervently. "Ah knowed de leddy ob de do' wa' sho' gawdin' sumpin'—keepin' sumpin' in an' ev'ybody out. She kep' Baldy out, time an' agin—Ah seed it mahseff. She jes' kep' a-standin' an' a-standin', he jes' couldn't nevah git by 'er. He done use' to swear an 'cuss, but she jes' blazed him out an' off."

"We'll close the door in good order," suggested Duffield.

And back they went, with hushed footsteps, to the open door at the end of the dark hall. But a strange sight met their gaze. As they approached they saw again the tall, slim, white-robed woman. She was bending over the skeleton on the library floor. Slowly the bones arose—one by one, in proper position, until the whole skeleton stood erect, clothed only in its cloud of dusky hair. Then, like an ear of pale corn sliding into its sheating husk, the skeleton and the "lady of the door" merged—merged, glided along the hall, down the stairs, through the street door, and down the steps. When the eerie white figure came to the red rosebush by the gate, it reached out and plucked a rose . . . and vanished like a wreath of fog.

And who was Bernadine Lanzos, who died on April fourteenth, 1767? Old records said that she was the granddaughter of Don José Vicente Lanzos—the lady who would have been his heir. Tradition says that she fell in love with a youth of whom Don José disapproved, so he locked her in the great library and left her to starve to death. But she died, instead, by her own hand, rather than cry out for deliverance to an unforgiving grandparent whom she could neither love nor honor.

# ( *1903* )   *The Swirling Specter*

When Joseph Horn went back to his cell in the Parish Prison, after being convicted of stealing a certain lady's purse containing a sum of money, he devoted his time to examining his dirty fingernails, shuffling a pack of greasy cards, and wiggling two toes which had a soft corn between them. He never was quite sure whether the corn was on the second or on the third toe, and it took a deal of speculating and a vast amount of toe-wiggling to arrive at any sort of conclusion.

He reflected that, if they hadn't caught him with that infernal purse in his pocket, he would have had money enough to get the corn removed, and buy a pair of sporty new shoes into the bargain. He thought again mournfully of the suit of flashy clothes he had seen in a shop window on South Rampart, and which could have been his with the money in that fat woman's purse. Also some peacock-blue socks, with a necktie to match. The fat woman was a fool—just going to pay her taxes, she told the Judge tearfully. What good were taxes, anyhow? If he'd only ducked in under that gallery when he saw the cop coming. . . . And here he was, in a pair of old cotton pants and a faded shirt.

Blonde Elsie'd got another man by this time, sure. Gladys wouldn't have him mooching around now, after he'd done time —not for a while, anyhow, nor unless he could get hold of some dough. Trixie would go back to Frank—he'd had Trixie really going for a week or so there. Young Jumbo Finnegan would steer clear of him, of course. Well, you couldn't blame Jumbo—nobody likes to have the busies snooping round on account of your pal being a jailbird. To hell with the whole pack of 'em—he'd go to Birmingham or Memphis or some place when he got out, Horn decided. Change his name, too. "John Harris" would do just as well as "Joe Horn" any day.

He saw Deputy Dillon coming along the corridor with one of the turnkeys.

"Joe Horn," the Deputy was droning. "Joe Horn wanted."

"Yes sir—right here. I'm Joe Horn." And Joe Horn stood close to the bars of his cell, peering out with red-rimmed eyes.

"Want you to mop," grunted the Deputy. "You been a good boy since you been here. Can you mop?"

"Yes sir," replied Joe Horn. To himself he groaned, "Hell —what a life for a white man—mopping!"

"Well, come on out o' there, then, and mop. Get two days for one, when you mop." And the turnkey unlocked the cell door.

From then on it was mop, mop, mop. Water, ammonia, soap, disinfectant—water, ammonia, soap, disinfectant. Slop, slosh, wring, sop up. Dig into the corners when somebody was watching. Be careful not to edge too near the door. Don't spit in the bucket. Rinse the damn floor good, so nobody'll slip on it—one slip, and you'll be in solitary. God, how a soft corn can ache when it feels like it!

Wonder who Elsie's roped in by this time. Wonder if Shep Johnson would stick by a pal out o' luck. Damn it, the soap's in the bucket again—hope old Dillon didn't see that. They see everything, even when it ain't there. What a yap he'd been to think he could get away with that God damned woman's pocketbook! There was old Dillon ambling down the corridor now. The soap was safely out on the floor, and not too wet. The Deputy paused, eyeing the prisoner up and down.

"Pretty soft," he observed. "Real ladylike job. Say, Horn, can you nurse?"

"Can I what? Yes sir." Horn bit his tongue.

"Give a guy his medicine, and watch him so he keeps covered up. Report if he acts like he's dying or something. Night shift. Come on—get goin'. You can sleep until supper. On twelve hours, off twelve. Two days for one, same as mopping."

"Yes sir," said Joe Horn, and left his mop and bucket where they were.

After supper Deputy Dillon took him to the hospital suite on the Gravier street side. This, by the way, was in the Saratoga street Parish Prison, in September of 1903, when the horrible old red brick bastille was considered quite grand and adequate, being then only ten years old.

"This guy you're settin' up with is Lewis Lyons," the Deputy grunted. "Killed the District Attorney, you know— J. Ward Gurley. Pretty sick. Give him his beef broth and stuff, according to the schedule. You'll see. And stay awake. I'll come for you in the morning. Here's the bell, if you need any help."

The lean form on the cot turned a pallid face toward the two newcomers.

"Got a new nurse for you nights, Lew," the Deputy said. "You look pretty peaked. Time for his broth, I reckon, Joe. It's up to you to keep the ghosts chased away until morning."

The sick man sucked in the broth weakly, and Horn straightened the sheets and shook up the pillow.

"What you got, pard?" he asked gently. "They didn't tell me."

"I don't know—just sick, I guess," responded the patient listlessly. "They'd better let me die—my eyes are so bad I can't see what's going on, anyway. What you in for?" ·

"Swiped an old slut's purse. I'll help you turn over if you want to, and maybe you can go to sleep."

So this was Lewis Lyons, one of the most brutal murderers of his time! He didn't look as though he could kill a chicken now. He'd swing—if he lived that long. Mercy if he didn't. That gallows they put up out there in the corner of the Negro yard every now and then was pretty tough. "Marryin' the widow," they called it. More than once had Joe Horn heard the crash of the trap, as the "spectre on the pale horse" rode by. He recalled hearing, as a boy, about the killing of Jere Duggan in this very building—how the giant Schneider had fairly hacked the head from the little man—and was hung in the corner of the Negro yard.

Plenty of poor devils had paid for their crimes in the corner of the Negro yard. And more and more would pay. They had a fine new gallows up in the tower that they'd use one of these days, when the old one wore out—if it ever did. And when it got dark in the filthy old yard. . . . No, Joe Horn didn't believe in ghosts. Only women and niggers believed in ghosts.

Horn could hear the rhythmical footsteps of the guard out in the corridor. Were they afraid he'd make a run for it, up here behind the barred windows, locked in with a man so sick he couldn't turn over in bed without help? Pad—pad—pad, came the soft shuffle of the guard's feet. Joe Horn smiled. No place to run to, except into the chapel, anyhow. Foolish to stick a guard up here.

The sick man moved wearily and Horn gave him a drink of water, noted it on the chart and sat down again by the window. They sure meant to keep folks in here. The bars looked wide as barrel-staves against the faintly lighted night.

Lewis Lyons . . . the murderer. Horn wondered what Lyons thought about, when he was well enough to think. Was he ever afraid of meeting the soul of Gurley, whom he had killed? It must be queer to meet the spirit of a man you had killed. He wondered if the spirit of Gurley would be a trace afraid of the spirit of Lyons. But spirits would be different. Spirits were all saps, if there were such things as spirits.

Lyons groaned softly in his uneasy sleep. A distant clock chimed eleven. That corner of the Negro yard must be mighty dark and mean at this time of night. Eleven o'clock. In fifteen minutes he must give Lyons a tablet and another cup of broth. Pad—pad—pad. . . . The guard in the corridor was like a machine. The tablet, the cup of broth.

"Close in here," Lyons sighed as Horn eased him down onto the pillow again.

"Window's as high as it'll go, pal," Joe told him. "Keep covered, though. There ain't much of you to stand a chill."

"What do you care?" the patient whispered, sneering a little. "Want to keep me alive so you can see the fun when my turn comes, I s'pose, like the rest of 'em."

"Forget it," Horn replied. "Better sleep if you can."

Somehow it grated on him, this man who had killed another so foully, so uselessly and so bloodily, pitying himself when it should come his turn to die. Oh well, nobody wants to die. He'd gone to sleep again, anyhow. Poor devil, sick as a poisoned rat. . . .

Where was Gurley now? What was he doing, what was he thinking, how was it with him? Was there anything in this Hereafter business the preachers had so much to say about? Thank God, he wasn't such a fat-head as to run to church. Must be nearly midnight. Suppose Lew Lyons died on him, here in the night? Oh well, the guard was just outside. Some use for a guard, after all.

Joe Horn sat hunched in his chair by the barred window. The place was very still. Even the light seemed to grow dimmer. A sort of vague smokiness crept through the air, and a silence that was cold and sickish. Joe could hear his heart thumping lightly against his ribs, as though he had been running.

Then over near the narrow cot, he saw Something— a filmy shape, wavering and swaying and weaving from side to side. He sat up suddenly straight, his jaw dropping and his very blood freezing with fright. The Shape was growing plainer and more real, and it approached the cot and stood there at the foot of it, leaning over to peer at Lew Lyons.

Horn could see clearly now, and it was as though he himself were free of his body. All he knew was that awful Shape at the foot of the prison cot—the shape of a man, chalk white, his head leaning far to one side as though half-severed, blood gushing from him here and there, soaking his winding-sheet, running in rivulets onto the concrete floor and dripping from his hands. Then the flesh seemed to fall away from his face, leaving only a gaping skull, with the wild eyes still rolling and bulging, gazing at the form of Lew Lyons covered with the coarse prison sheet.

Then the figure raised its bloody arms above its horrid head, and from empty air it plucked a skull, a rib, an arm bone, a shoulder blade, a thigh bone, a tuft of greasy hair, more ribs, a withered hand, a jawbone, and a cluster of ribs like a basket. At once the bones assembled themselves and attracted more, a few chunks of dried flesh still clinging here and there, and a choking stench filling the place with steamy horror.

They were circling round the cot now, grinning and jibbering, smeared with gore from the streaming hands of that first bloody Shape. They reached up over Lew Lyons, gripping hands, and began turning like some ghastly whirlwind with its funnel at the ceiling. Round and round they went, faster and even faster. Horn could not see the cot now, but he knew who the first Shape was—it was J. Ward Gurley! Horn had seen enough pictures of him—he ought to know.

The whole room seemed whirling and swirling, with stinking blood spattering walls and floor. His heart pounded like a tilt hammer, his whole body thumped like an aching tooth— if only he could get away, away! The guard in the corridor— well, he'd rather be shot like a dog than stay here an instant longer. The spirit of Gurley turned to leer at him, its long arm reached out—and Joe Horn, with a bloodcurdling shriek, plunged out into the corridor, screaming as he fled.

One way only was open to him, and into the dark chapel he dashed, stumbling and staggering and voicing his terror like a maniac. His outflung arm hooked about something cold and hard—ah yes, the statue of St. Joseph—one of those things the fool Catholics prayed to! Well, Joe needed to pray now, if ever a man did!

"St. Joseph!" he screeched. "St. Joseph! I ain't no Catholic, I'm a Baptist—but you got to do something for me, and do it quick! St. Joseph, you listen to me, man! Don't you let that Gurley thing get me! You're a saint, and you got to do something—*you got to do something!*"

He fell beside the statue, his arms hugging it tightly, his head jammed against its hard, painted knees.

"St. Joseph!" he blubbered, "I ain't no Baptist no more! I'll go to Mass tomorrow morning, if you say so! 'Tain't true about Gladys and that bunch of whores—and the old bitch got her money back what I stole—and I ain't never killed nobody —I never even seen that Gurley, 'cept his picture in the paper —I tell you, Saint—"

They found him later, wedged in between the saint and the pulpit. Captain Rennyson shook him savagely.

"What in the name of God do you think you're up to?" the Captain demanded. "Didn't you know you couldn't get away? Or did somebody smuggle in dope to you? Answer me that!"

"I wasn't trying to git out," Horn shuddered, as six deputies dragged him out of the chapel, "and I ain't never took no dope, sir. I just saw *him*, that's all. That Gurley, whirling round Lyons' cot in a sheet, and all that blood and stuff! Captain, don't you never put me in there to nurse Lew Lyons again! Put me to work in the yard, sir—in the daytime—or any place, 'cepting in with that Lyons!"

Captain Rennyson gave him a long, queer look, his eyes steady and hard. But Joe Horn's eyes were steady, too, though his teeth still chattered.

"They all tell the same thing," the Captain sneered. "They all say they see Gurley and a stinking lot of bones and stuff whirling round like a churn. I think you're all damn liars, that's what I think. From now on, you keep your fool mouth shut, hear me? And from now on, *you mop!*"

# (*1874*)     *The Ghost of the Treme Street Bridge*

In April of 1874, a vast furor was created in this city by a ghost which nightly appeared near the Treme Street Bridge, at the Old Basin. Thousands of people congregated there to witness the phenomenon. Some even discharged firearms at the spectre, without effect.

Each night for nearly a month, as the clock of Saint-Louis Cathedral chimed the hour of midnight, a vague, luminous Shape rose out of the black waters of the Old Basin. As it rose it glowed brighter and brighter, until the breathless watchers beheld it as a woman. It walked to and fro, to and fro—a young and lovely phantom in white draperies, a small flag clasped to its bosom, and an expression of intense longing on its sweet face.

What was her quest? the silent crowd asked themselves. Then they would notice that her garments dripped with slime and the writhing roots of underwater weeds, and a great fat worm coiled itself at her throat. Slowly she faded into dimness, and finally sank into the waters.

Another night she appeared at the midnight chiming of the Cathedral clock, but this time she was old and haggard and worn. Her eyes burned with brilliant green fire, and she clasped a lighted candle to her heart. Its fitful flame did not scorch her, nor was the light extinguished though her fumbling fingers often grasped the burning wick. It served to show all the more hideously her gaping mouth with its toothless gums and drooling ooze. The nose was flattened and sunken, and in the hair were lodged knots of shrimp and small dead fishes. Her draperies were sodden and partially rotted away, so that at every movement her limbs came into view, the bones glistening where the gray flesh had sloughed off or been eaten by sea creatures. This ghost, also, walked to and fro for a time, and then sank into the watery depths.

The same phantom appeared in still a third form. When midnight chimed she rose from the waters, again clad in white. But the grief of ages was in her eyes, and her hair was drawn back tight over her skull until her forehead shone. Clasped closely to her breast was a sleeping infant. But the ugly fat worm had wound itself about the little one and there was horror in the woman's eyes, along with the terrible grief. Green slime clung about her, and a sickening odor pervaded the still air. Back and forth the phantom walked, longer this time, as though she dreaded to return to whatever cavern it was that served as her horrid prison. But finally she sank, suddenly this time.

Who was she? Why did she change from young to old? What of the child? . . .

An old, old man later explained the mystery which had baffled even the newspapers of the period.

"I saw the ghost," he said, sitting beneath an althea tree in his courtyard. "I saw it frequently during that April in 1874. I was twenty-five years old at the time, and I know it was a genuine ghost. I know it, because I know whose ghost it was. But I never said a word, because there are things you don't always want to stir up.

"It was the ghost of Helen Rockworth—my family all knew her. She was a lovely girl, engaged to be married to a young man by the name of Jerome Gail—my elder brother's particular friend. Both my brother and Jerome went to war in '61. I remember with what agony of heart Jerome left his fiancée —but the Cause needed him and he was glad to fight for it.

"When our boys came home in '65, ragged and done for, something happened to the engagement between Jerome and Helen. There was a whisper of scandal—even of loose living, on her part. Later Jerome married another, and Helen became a woman of the streets.

"It seems that on a night in early April, 1870, he saw her on Old Levee street, coming out of one of the dives there, where seamen and riffraff and the lowest of the low congregate to drink and fight and hatch all manner of evil. She looked old and starved and wild, and she had a baby at her breast—but she appealed to Jerome, in her drunken madness declaring that his jilting her had made her what she was. He shook her off, loathing her touch—and that night she drowned herself in the Old Basin.

"Jerome never said a word. Her family wouldn't even claim the body, and she was buried in Potter's Field.

"But after a time he and his wife became very unhappy. There were no children, and they wanted children. They patched it up by adopting a little one—a girl she was, fragile and delicate as a wild flower. Jerome's wife was the chief factor in the adoption—he signed the necessary papers without reading them over.

"The baby grew and he became passionately fond of her. There was something about her eyes that haunted him, and little ways she had with her hands, and the ringlets of soft hair on her forehead. It worried him. And one day early in 1874, he got out the adoption papers and read them through. The little one was the child of Helen Rockworth!

"Jerome was frantic between love for the baby and the fact that her mother had been the girl of his heart. The next day the child fell from a high window and was killed. After the funeral, Jerome went to the Old Basin. They found his body there, after a watchman reported having seen him throw himself into the water.

"It was only a few nights after this that the ghost began to be seen from the Treme Street bridge. I knew who it was. It was Helen Rockworth. Sometimes she came without her baby—young and sweet and lovely as she used to be, before Jerome went away to war. Then she would bring the baby—hideous and old, as she grew to be in the degraded life to which she sank. She wanted to get away from whatever torment the Hereafter meant to her—she wanted to get to Jerome, only she never could, because the child came between them.

"She was there for all to see—parading her ugly sin and

her bitter defeat before all those hundreds of eyes that never would know nor understand. Maybe it was part of her punishment and her expiation, I don't know.

"Then she ceased to appear. I have always thought that she met Jerome's spirit, somewhere there on the terrible black waters, and that he forgave her, fully and willingly. So the baby whom he loved, but who never had had a father, must have served as a sort of divine tie between the two harried spirits. The Hereafter must be kinder than the world we know. . . ."

# (*1880*)    *The Beautiful Lost Children*

The passion for gold is stronger than death, it appears.

Across from the cemetery at Saratoga street and Jackson avenue stands a double house, set on a line with the banquette.

In other years Pierre Lefevre lived there, working like mad for the gold which he hoarded year after year. Never was there enough to satisfy him. He denied himself everything, living on scraps of stale food which he contrived to collect after working-hours, and allowing himself to burn but one inch of tallow candle each night.

The neat stacks of gold coins grew slowly but steadily. They were his god, his complete existence. He hid them in the chimney by day, in a niche which he had cunningly constructed. But the thought of their being stolen tormented him during every waking hour, and brought him hideous dreams when he slept.

"Some day I shall spend it and live like a king," he used to assure himself feverishly.

But the years crept on and Pierre never could bear to part with even one beautiful shining coin.

"They are my little children," he would mutter, sitting in the sunshine on Sunday. "Their hair is yellow in the sun—how could I part with my beautiful little children? Who would love them and take care of them as I do?"

But when he was very old he grew frightened. His joints were stiff with rheumatism and his back was bent almost double. His fingers were knotted and his teeth were gone. And one day old Pierre knew the end was near.

"My ears are too deaf to hear thieves," he whimpered, fondling the pretty coins. "And my sight is so poor I scarce can see you, my beautiful ones. There is no joy left to living—I am lame and sick and very tired. I must put you to bed and tuck you in tight, where you will be safe and snug."

So that night he stumbled out into the rear yard and dug a deep, deep hole. It must be deep enough so that the little golden children would be warm in their new bed. He laid them all into it, carefully, tenderly, and tamped the earth down solidly above them. Then he piled on a great heap of trash and refuse and broken wood.

That night old Pierre died.

But old Pierre comes back. Tired and bent and in sore trouble, he hobbles across from the cemetery and moves painfully about the yard at night, muttering and shaking his gnarled old fists at whomsoever dares to set foot along the path. They are there somewhere, his little golden children—somewhere beneath the roots of the four o'clocks and the petunias and the night jasmines. But he cannot find them. He pokes and pries on painfully bent old knees, groaning and twisting in agony as he digs his ghostly nails into the dewy soil. Why don't they answer when he calls? He croons to them in his ghostly old voice, saying over soft, endearing names. But they never answer a word.

Sometimes, the neighbors will tell you, he brings others to help him—the ghost of an old woman, and two or three masculine shapes, all troubled and anxious. When they appear in their weird graveclothes, every leaf and flower stands still as death. The air in the yard grows cold as death, too, and a trifle stale and strange and altogether terrible. When old Pierre reaches a certain spot in the yard, he stamps his ghostly feet upon the ground and utters a dreadful, despairing cry. Then suddenly he vanishes, and the flowers sway again in the night breeze.

Numberless persons have dug in that yard. They have watched old Pierre from a safe distance, and have gone to the very spot and dug as deep as a well. But they have found nothing. Yet old Pierre comes back and back. Neighbors admonish unruly children, "If you're not good, old Pierre Lefevre will catch you and put you into a hole tonight, along with his other children."

Poor old Pierre, with his clawing ghostly hands and his broken ghostly heart! . . .

(*1776-1863*)     *The Golden Witch*

In October of 1863 a young priest stood at the ruined gate of
an ancient house in Washington avenue. A small boy overtook
him and paused uncertainly beside him. The priest had a
foreign look, and the boy wondered momentarily who he
might be.

"Don't go in there, Father," the youngster cautioned,
brave in his very timidity. "That house is haunted—I thought
maybe you didn't know. There's a witch upstairs—a gold witch
that folks have to keep giving things to, so she won't throw
spite-spells on us. And there's a roomful of bones in that house
—a man got in there once and saw them, and he came out and
he died the next day. He said the witch breathed death on him
—my father heard him say it. Don't go in there, sir—the
witch'll get you, even if you are a priest!"

The stranger was French but his mother had been an Eng-
lishwoman, so he understood the boy's speech perfectly.

"I am not afraid of witches, my son," he replied, smiling.
"If there is any old lady in the house, I shall try to be polite
and pay her compliments, you may be sure."

The boy did not answer, but eyed the visitor curiously and
sidled away. The young man turned again to the great dark
pile which rose above the tangle of undergrowth and Spanish
moss which wove a barrier between the live oaks and the
ground.

The building itself—which had been, in other years, almost a palace—intrigued him. It was a great rambling brick
structure containing more than seventy rooms, with porches

and galleries and what had once been beautiful balconies. The finest home in New Orleans, they said at the time of its building.

The priest sighed lightly, and stepped carefully over the heap of stone and rusted iron which had been a sturdy fence and a gate of intricate pattern. Slowly he made his way through the thicket, his feet catching now and then in tough tendrils and dry roots. Finally he stood opposite the front entrance. This had been, a century before, a splendid and imposing spot. Now the visitor stood on fragments of ancient flagstones, rotting wood and crumbling bricks and ruined marble on every hand.

He sighed again and began a careful ascent of the fallen steps leading to the great door. Sometimes the foothold quivered, and he had to step quickly to avoid losing his balance. When he gained the threshold, he found the front doors closed and solid enough, with heavy wrought-iron gates protecting them.

He stood a moment, breathing in the sweet still air which sifted through the massed greenery of the place. The house had been built in the midst of a double square of ground. Now it was stained and blackened by time and neglect. The "Black House" it was called by passers-by. Warped and broken, its casements seemed to shrink and shiver in the shadows of the gnarled old oaks which kept faithful vigil. For many decades it had been drenched by driving rains, gnawed and defaced by small wild animals, until now it huddled there like some prehistoric mammoth, dull and dark in death, pitiful in dissolution.

The avocat had smiled a little when he made his careful explanations to young Father Souvard.

"You must understand, Père Souvard," he had said in polished French, "that for generations we have had a difficult duty to perform as regards the great house—we must keep the taxes paid, oui, and the money was always in our hands before it was due. But we were not permitted either to repair or to rent—no one must enter the house, no footstep must disturb its silence, no hand must so much as touch it. Strangers were desecration. We were helpless, for this was made an iron rule, and we were pledged to keep it to the letter. Orders will not keep vandals out. The law will not do it. So we had perforce to find other and simpler means.

"The front doors we have kept fastened, 'tis true. But for the inside of the house I cannot answer. We did the best we could in our own fashion. The only manner in which we could protect it was to permit the report to be circulated that the place was haunted. The method was crude enough, but I beg that you will not take it amiss. It has been effective, and it has saved your inheritance from being carried away piecemeal by thieves or burned by vagabonds."

"I understand," Father Souvard had replied. "It was your grandfather who first undertook the administration of the property?"

"Oui. He was a young man at the time, too. Your great-grandfather, the Marquis de Souvard, left everything in his hands. We have done the best we could. It was once a magnificent property. You have come all the way from France to see it—the first Souvard to do so since the Marquis left New Orleans in 1766."

"I have, of course, just recently inherited it," the priest had replied. "My father, the grandson of the Marquis, has just passed away, as you know. I cannot, as a priest of the Church, retain possession of anything in the nature of a personal fortune. My intention is to sell the property as soon as possible. Being the last of the Souvards, the money derived from this sale will at once be turned over to my Order. Doubtless the old Marquis would have found such a course to his taste."

"Oui," the avocat had returned, a little thoughtfully. "It is fitting. You wish to visit the old house today?"

"At once," young Père Souvard had nodded. "But I must go unattended. My great-grandfather would have wished it so. Give me the keys, s'il vous plait, Monsieur."

So now he stood viewing his inheritance at close range, the thick bronze keys in his hand. They were like the keys of a cathedral. The lock was stubborn, but presently one of the twin iron gates lurched open, a hinge giving way wearily. The door itself presented far more of a difficulty. The priest shook it repeatedly, pushing against it with all his weight. When the lock finally did turn, the door fell inward with a mighty crash. It lay in great splintered sections, sending up a cloud of choking dust and filling the wide hall with débris. The whole structure seemed for the moment to rock and tremble. Was it safe? Would the floors hold?

Father Souvard smiled at his own momentary fears. Cypress floors were well-nigh imperishable. A moldy stench came belching heavily out at him. As he looked in, a dark and discolored drapery dropped in a noisome heap from an archway, and lay like a dead thing. In spite of himself he shivered, crossing himself from old habit. Picking his way step by step around the rubbish made by the fallen door, he entered the first of the great rooms.

Slowly he explored, trying to store each phase in his memory, taking note of the moldy portraits, eaten and torn; the marble statuary wound in the gray veils of spiderwebs; the carved furniture of ebony and mahogany and rosewood, which fell to pieces as he touched it; the peeling walls, the crumbling plaster, the disintegrated carpets, the ruined tapestries; the magnificent chandeliers under which he did not dare to stand; the books which lay in heaps where they had tumbled from the shelves, like crumpled sheets of dusty ivory; the cloudy glass and the blackened silver and the soot-smeared china; the fireplace which leaned dangerously, the doors which sagged, the bits of shattered glass which had once been windowpanes, the sodden masses which had once been snowy damasks. All these Père Souvard saw, as though he had entered into a strange dead world.

Then he ascended the grand staircase which circled upwards from the lofty entrance hall. Its marble steps were green with slime, and small lizards darted noiselessly from the corners. It was a long flight of stairs, and the air at the top was musty and bitter, in spite of the broken windows. The young man crossed himself again involuntarily, blinking in the dim light. A broad corridor confronted him, so long that he could not see to the end of it. Well, he would take this first, then.

But when he did come to the end of the corridor, he wished he had left it alone. The sight was a hideous one, beyond reason or explanation. For, piled from floor to ceiling were human bones, bleached white and picked clean, as though some monster had feasted well and flung the refuse into a corner. The skulls grinned, leaning crazily on thigh bones and among rib-clusters, many upside down; here a jawbone and there a shoulder blade. A horrible odor of human decay pervaded the whole place. It seemed as though tongues of flame darted here and there among the bones, but Père Souvard told himself that was due only to his excited fancy.

This mountain of human bones in an ancient house constituted an almost stupefying complexity. How had they come to be deposited here? Was this the secret dumping ground of some murder syndicate which had found safety in the sinister reputation of the old Souvard mansion? Had the bitter sorrow and sentimental memory of one man long dead provided protection for criminals, instead of holding a shrine sacred to great love?

Forcing down a terrible revulsion, Père Souvard turned away from the nauseous bones. There were numerous suites still to be viewed. For this he had vowed to do—to examine with his eyes every inch of the house which had held at once so boundless a happiness and so vast a grief for its builder, the Marquis de Souvard. It was proving to be a desperately depressing and gruesome undertaking, to be sure. There was still one more chamber on this floor. Well, he would see the third floor, with its fallen-in roof and staggering walls, and come back for that last room.

He felt that that room would take more courage and fortitude than all the rest of the place put together. It was the chamber which had belonged to Henri Joseph Louis, Marquis de Souvard, who came to New Orleans from France in 1753, at the age of twenty with his mother, the old Marquise, and his two sisters, Adèle and Clarisse. The young nobleman had fallen out of favor with his sovereign, Louis XV. With his vast wealth he came to America, purchasing land which later comprised the city of Lafayette and the town of Jefferson. It made a splendid plantation, stretching out on every hand, arpent after arpent, the soil rich and fine, the crops abundant and profitable.

At once he had built this house for a family mansion. And

here the young Marquis brought his bride, who had been Mademoiselle Yvonne Marie Françoise Préval, a New Orleans belle. So they came to call her la jeune Marquise, and his mother la vieille Marquise.

And now the young priest, his eyes filled with horror, made his slow way to the ancestral chamber. His hand was cold as it rested on the clammy doorknob of the room. Then he opened the door and went in. The picture which met his gaze was desolate indeed.

In one corner stood the immense carved rosewood bed, so high that four steps led up to its side. Its brocade canopy hung in shreds, and its curtains were mere rags, speaking all too eloquently of moths and time. At the far end of the chamber yawned a tremendous fireplace as high as a man's head, its carved marble dislodged and green with mold and lichen, the ancient ornaments still standing on its uneven shelf—Sèvres and crystal and filagree, inches deep in soot and grime.

Above the mantel was fastened something which had once been a portrait, black and ragged now, its frame fallen away. A mirror, cracked and clouded, hung on another wall like a great eye which age has thickened and blinded but which still strains to see Life's little procession. Chairs and sofas, tables and dressing-stands, bits of china and porcelain and glass and tarnished metal—what a sad and dismal ruin it was! This . . . and the mountain of white bones at the end of that interminable corridor! What a riddle—and what a heritage! Still, Père Souvard reflected, there was One who could solve all puzzles. Sometime, somehow.

Presently he became conscious of a subtle change. He stood still as a wooden man, his heart scarcely beating—as though his spirit watched while his body remained aloof and quiescent. A great chair in the center of the room had seemed to gather itself and take on polish and perfection; its rosy damask upholstery shone lustrous and clean. And suddenly, seated within its deep cushions, appeared a skeleton, fleshless and grinning. Yet the bony hands were moving, plying a golden needle threaded with bright silk—embroidering a rose on a square of creamy satin.

As the priest stood motionless, he sensed a great change

taking place all about him. There was glass in the diamond-paned windows now—clean glass through which the delicate greenery of wisteria leaves glimmered, with a ray of golden sunshine slanting in onto a thick carpet of lovely, subdued colors. There was a little gilt cabinet of velvet-bound books; the fireplace was a magnificent thing, polished and fine, with a soft fire glowing in the grate; the bed was dignified and splendid, with gold cords and tassels among its silken curtains and lace draperies; a crystal dish of fruit stood on a small table, and a vase of gardenias graced a dressing-stand; the vast mirror glittered like a lake, reflecting gilt and rosewood and crystal and silver.

But in the mirror was another reflection also—a woman seated in a deep chair of rose damask—a woman dressed in lace and brocade and taffeta, with dainty beribboned elbow sleeves and powdered white hair, the points of tiny satin slippers peeping from under the edge of her gold-colored, panniered skirt. She was not a young woman—indeed, she seemed very old, but her fingers were nimble as she plied her golden needle and its bright silks. A word rose in François Souvard's throat—a questing word out of another life and another world. He did not recognize his own voice when he spoke.

"Madame," he said in French, "what do you here?"

The woman leveled her glance upon him, the jeweled bracelets on her arms tinkling musically and a faint rustle slithering through the stiff folds of her silk gown.

"Ah," she murmured, a light smile curving her mouth, "you have been a long time in coming, mon fils. I have waited nigh onto a century for you to come to your senses. The girl is dead, of course—the twins are dead, your sisters are dead. But we two, we are here. You were always my own, my whole life, Henri—the others only came between us. You thought I died, too—but I never could die while you lived, mon fils!

"You fair lived at the tomb-side of that insipid Yvonne, whom you worshiped—and forgot me. Doubtless she was a good girl and a good wife—but, Henri, I was your mother, who had held you from the first moment you drew breath! There could be no love in the world like my love—it followed you every instant of your life, caring for you, hoping and planning for you, teaching you beauty and delight and grace, praying for you, building you!

"And yet, when death struck, it was the girl you worshiped —the girl and her children! You laid one wreath on my casket, oui, with respectful tenderness—but you wrapped her in roses and wreathed her with incense and clothed her with impassioned prayers, while your tears grew for her a new Tree of Life—she and her children. Me you took for granted, to be loved somewhat and revered suitably—but she was the one you adored! It was *her* death that broke your heart. I could have died a thousand deaths and you would have wept and said, 'Pauvre Maman!' But if Yvonne were ill an hour, it destroyed you!

"And then, when the Yellow Scourge took us, you forgot me altogether—you forgot life, you forgot reason, you forgot pity. You left us all in a cold tomb which the winds and the rains did their best to devour—but you took Yvonne away in your heart. You went away—left the house of love to crumble as it would, the roses to die, the trees to perish.

"So I have waited, mon Henri . . . and now you come back to me, with a barren heart and a false tongue. 'Madame, what do you here?' A pretty speech, indeed! Your portrait over there could do as well as that."

How terrible she was, in that strange quiet rage! How harsh her high-bred voice had grown, as her bitter words poured forth! The priest's eyes glanced back of her, and paused in amazement. The portrait which had hung in tatters a few moments earlier, now gleamed forth richly from its frame of dull gold leaf.

It was the portrait of a young man in court dress—powdered wig, grave face, coat of canary brocade, breeches of ivory satin, cascades of priceless lace at throat and wrists, the jeweled hilt of a sword showing at one side, the eyes dark and tender, the mouth firm and well-shaped, the nose straight and fine, the tilt of the head proud yet sweet. An unusual picture—Henri Joseph Louis, Marquis de Souvard, painted in 1753, when he was twenty years of age.

"Oui, I have waited a long time," the hard old voice went on in precise French, the embroidery laid in her lap now. "I want you to have one last glimpse of the old life—all those friends whom you loved—all the ones who came a little before me in your heart. I was only Maman, whom you took for granted. . . . You did not think I saw. . . . Why should you know I suffered? Stand where you are, Henri. They will obey me, every one."

Somehow the young man could find no words. His tongue seemed shriveled in his mouth. What was this, anyway?—some mad dream from which he would presently awaken and which he would forget? Or did his soul inhabit some former body, living in that long-dead day for a brief season? . . .

The old dowager sat quiet. The door at the opposite end of the room was opening, inch by inch. . . . Then through it a skeleton came walking, stiff and white, its bony feet clicking like castanets against the wood of the doorsill. Behind it stalked another—and another and another—the procession appeared endless. The great chamber was filling with them, the lights from the high chandelier glinting on smooth skulls and empty ribs.

They ranged themselves about the apartment like the trunks of dead trees rising in some devastated orchard. And still they came clanking in from that awful corridor. When the last one had taken its place, five little rabbits crept in and snuggled themselves at the old woman's slippered feet. La vieille Marquise—whose spirit had waited almost a century for this abundant hour!

Then another change came over the stately old chamber. The skeletons became blurred and cloudy for a moment, as though a merciful fog had clothed them. But after the blur cleared, there stood an assemblage of young men and women attired in clothes fashionable in another age—fashionable before the heads of the sixteenth Louis and his Marie Antoinette had rolled into the brutal, bloody basket.

There was a rustle of rich silks, the faint snap of tabatière lids, the soft slither of painted fans, a breath of delicate perfume, the flip of a lace handkerchief, the suggestion of a smile on that sea of aristocratic countenances. And the little rabbits rose and changed—changed to two sweet young women, a boy and a girl, and a slender, violet-eyed young matron who stood apart as though someone held her at arm's length and refused to allow her to come nearer.

Père Souvard remembered the old family story—how in one short week the mother, the two sisters, the wife, and the twin son and daughter of the young Marquis de Souvard had died of yellow fever in 1766—in this very chamber, perhaps—stripping him of all he held dear. How he had lingered here in agony, visiting their tomb daily, striving to live down his bereavement and his loneliness. And how he had at last returned to France, leaving the place in the hands of his avocats, at once a tomb and a memorial of his short years of love and delight. True, late in life he had married again—a Parisian girl, Mademoiselle Deuzan, who became the mother of Paul Louis, who became the father of Armand Placide, who became the father of François Antoine, Père Souvard.

Was he seeing aright, or were his fancies running riot? Was this really the social circle in which his great-grandfather had moved, and which the Yellow Scourge had ravaged so terribly? Were they all here for this last ghastly parade, a company of dry bones in the midst of crumbling splendor and departed magnificence? Was it possible that they could so return, summoned by one ghostly old woman's jealousy and deadly hurt?—one old woman whose very spirit could not distinguish between her son, who would now be one hundred and thirty years old, and that son's great-grandson?

Again the portrait over the mantel drew his eyes . . . and he ceased to marvel at the old woman's blunder. But for the difference in costume, he and the Marquis were one and the same—point for point, feature for feature. The likeness was amazing in its perfection.

The old voice took up its weary refrain again.

"We shall all go out of here—we have stayed overlong. This time we need never come back. Our tombs are worn and old . . . we shall sleep or we shall wander, as each may choose. But le jeune Marquise—she shall go first! Out—out—out! No longer to breathe the air she breathes—never again to hear her voice like fountains bubbling—never again to stand at one side while she claims the caresses that should be mine! And before any you shall go, Monsieur le Marquis—you whom I have loved with undying love, and hated with undying hate!"

The last words were a mere cracked high note, as the wind screams through a dead forest in winter. A bitter breeze touched the young priest's lips, like a devil's kiss. He felt himself pushed out of the room, along the broad hall, down the old marble staircase, out of the fallen door. Something hurried his unwilling footsteps.

He could hear a horrible rattling roar behind him, like a million dry staves clattering and pounding. He ran down the overgrown path and paused breathless at the gate. An army of skeletons rushed past him, driven by an ancient crone who dropped her flesh and her old-world clothing at the broken gate. And so they herded down the road, to vanish in the gathering twilight. A sickening odor settled all about, like a current of foul air from a mortuary chamber.

As Père Souvard stood there wondering if he were indeed in his right mind, the small boy who had at first accosted him came trotting by.

"Oh," the child said, bowing politely before the man of God, "you've been inside—I know you have, because you look so white and scared. I told you the old Black House was haunted, Father—don't you remember? My uncle and I went past it as dusk one day, and I heard the ghosts crying and the bones rattling. My uncle said it was only the wind in the trees."

"I am sure it was, my son," Père Souvard agreed quietly.

"No," the boy continued, full of his theme, winding a bit of string around one thumb, "grown folks always say things like that. But the niggers tell the truth about them—and they say it's ghosts and bones. The man that died said it was ghosts and bones, too. And I believe it. Anyhow, everybody believes about the witch upstairs. Did you see her? Was she very golden and very frightful?"

"You should say your prayers more diligently, my child," the priest advised, forcing a smile to his frozen lips. "And try to think of wiser things than witches." It was the best he could do. . . .

"I have a buyer for your property—he has been after it for ten years or more," the avocat told Père Souvard the next day. "A good price, too. He offers more each year. You will sell at once, I think you said?"

"Oui, at once," Père Souvard answered. "But on one condition only—that the house be pulled down immediately, and all the wreckage given to the poor."

"This is a time of war and help is not plentiful," the avocat returned. "Still . . . if they who receive are willing to do the pulling down . . . I shall arrange, Monsieur le Marquis."

A week later Père Souvard was on board ship, bound for France and his lifework. He was thinking of the last sight he had had of the haunted Black House . . . A multitude of humans, black and white, chopping and heaving and prying and dragging . . . marble, glass, brick, wood . . . posts, columns, rafters, joists, planks, doors, carved marble, inlaid satinwood . . . The house was then already half gone.

"I wonder," his thoughts ran on, "if every brick bears a ghost with it. They say so, these strange Créole blacks. I wonder . . . have I done well or ill? . . . Oui, oui, I have now to do only with my own future . . . '*Ave, Maria, gratia plena; Dominus tecum: benedicta tu in mulieribus, et benedictus fructus. . . .*' "

(*1909*)  *Up the Garret Stairs*

In May of 1909, certain mysterious manifestations in this city drew the attention of the newspapers. Spiritualistic mediums awoke to the fact that the times were opportune, and arranged séances whenever and wherever possible.

To some of these, newspaper reporters were admitted. Reporters not being particularly sympathetic towards things occult, however, it was deemed expedient to pick and choose among those who presented themselves in this capacity.

A medium widely known at the time, living in Lee Circle, consented to permit a single reporter to attend one of her séances, stipulating that he must be "by nature quiet and serious-minded, and endowed with an unerring sense of justice." Feeling that this was a large order, the city editor summoned one Ursin Beauvais and gave him the assignment.

"Spread yourself a little," he instructed. "Might be well to speak with authority—from experience, that is."

Young Beauvais leered pleasantly.

"Spiritually speaking, as it were," he remarked, "when do I get my day off?"

"Might ask that at the séance," grinned the man on the desk. "If you bring in a rotten story like you did last time, you can count on a year instead of a day."

"Humph!" snorted the reporter, and was on his way. He hated these fool spiritualistic bouts he was always being sent out to cover.

The room in the house in Lee Circle was dimly lighted

when the reporter was ushered in. A small group of people sat waiting for what young Beauvais called "the show."

Finally the medium appeared and, after some preliminaries, went into her trance. Speaking in a halting, infantile voice, she mentioned this name and that—members of the "circle"—and gave them messages "from the beyond," as she expressed it.

The spirit of an infant which had died when a few hours old conversed freely with its mother, describing in adult phrases its present surroundings and condition.

The reporter was yawning discreetly when the medium said, "A spirit is here who says his name on earth was Hypolite LeMaitre. He says he was an old man when he passed on. A grandfather, I think. Yes, and he says his grandson is one Ursin Beauvais. That is right. Is there anyone here by the name of Ursin Beauvais?"

"That is my name," replied the reporter, feeling a trifle embarrassed.

"Thank you. This Hypolite LeMaitre, your grandfather, has a message for you. He says to tell you that if he had not died intestate he would have left you a large fortune. He repeats, had he *not* died intestate, you would *not* have failed to be his heir. But, he says, though he did *not* make a will, he did *not* forget you. And he says you are *not* to lose faith in his good intentions. He tells me you occupy at the present time a room in the garret of the house in which he was born. Is that true?"

"Why, yes," assented Beauvais. "It is. I do."

"Thank you. Your grandfather says he wants particularly to warn you *not* to part with anything whatsoever that is in your room at the present time. He says to tell you he will meet you on the garret stairs."

The voice paused and then began on a message to somebody else. Ursin Beauvais could feel a strange prickling up and down his spine. How could this medium know where he lived, and how, and who his grandfather had been? Of course, he always had understood that these professionals had ways and means of finding out all sorts of things about people who had died, as well as about the living relatives. It was an old game, played by priests and high priests of this and that, from time immemorial. Still, it was a bit strange. . . .

About midnight, after he had turned in his stuff for the day, he started home. He stopped in to chat a few minutes with Elise Pettingill who lived on Royal between Ursuline and Hospital streets. Elise, being the girl of his heart, knew the queer late hours his work compelled him to keep. She lived alone with her father in a small apartment, working as a typist in a wholesale drug concern during the day. The father was twisted and stiffened with rheumatism, and unable to do regular work, so he attended to whatever household duties he could.

"I won't marry a girl and have her work, and my salary couldn't keep the three of us." This summed up the reasons why Ursin had not yet married Elise. His own mother had died two years ago, and his father had gone down with his ship when Ursin was sixteen. Both his father and his grandfather had been sea captains.

"I've been to another of those fool séances," he told Elise, laughing. "This one really was funny. My grandfather Le-Maitre, it seems, had a message for me. But it was all about what *not* to do."

"Was he going to meet you on a windy bridge or something?" the girl smiled. "That's what they usually do."

"No," Ursin returned, feeling suddenly cold. "On the garret stairs."

He left after a few minutes. The old streets were dark and still. He could smell wisteria and peach blossoms and yellow jasmine. He was in no hurry, and he made his way at a leisurely pace to the big old brown house on Frenchman street, between Royal and Dauphine.

The house had been built in 1830 by his mother's grandfather. It was crumbling now, but it no longer was owned by the family. Things had been a bit strange and baffling. His mother had been Clarisse LeMaitre, an only child, and born in this same house. There always had been enough money to live comfortably. When she married Alcide Beauvais they had continued to live in the old house.

After his father's death, Ursin and his mother and his

grandfather had lived there. He remembered his mother questioning "Grandpa" one day about how money matters stood.
Grandpa had smiled whimsically and said he guessed there was
no need for worry. Once in a long time he would spend a day
uptown. There always was money in the bank. But one had to
ask Grandpa for it. It was given instantly, but Mrs. Beauvais
disliked the asking.

Grandpa LeMaitre died early in 1905. He left no will. It
was then that the terrible shock came. Taxes had not been
paid on the LeMaitre property for so long that it was about to
be sold at sheriff's auction. When an investigation was made,
it was found that the aged sea captain's bank balance was
seventeen dollars and thirty-five cents. He had no life insurance
and no other investments.

Ursin got a job at reporting, and he and his mother moved
to two rooms in the garret of the old house. The family which
bought it occupied the remainder of the place, taking several
other roomers. It was spacious and had, in its day, been fine.
But that day was long gone.

Mrs. Beauvais died three months after her father's death.
She had been climbing the steep garret stairs, and she had
fallen. The doctor said it was a paralytic stroke. She managed
to mumble a few words to Ursin before she lapsed into un-
consciousness.

"I saw Grandpa," she whispered, her mouth drawn out of
quiet. As he turned at the top of the first staircase, an icy
draft made him shiver. The day had been hot—so hot that he
all semblance of its natural shape. "I saw him . . . on the
garret stairs. He said 'not—not' "

She never got any farther. Ursin tried to forget the torment in her eyes. She had been such a nice mother, and she
was only forty-three.

This night he let himself in quietly. Ursin always was
was carrying his linen coat. Still shivering, he started up the
stairs leading to the garret. He felt something brush against
his hand, and he smelled an odor which reminded him of
cellars and damp moss and moldy leaves.

Suddenly he heard soft footsteps, and something passed
him. The staircase had been pitch dark but now the whole

place seemed to glow, like a sort of luminous fog. The fog gathered density and made a Shape just ahead of him. It was the Shape of a man, bent and old. He could hear the slithering footsteps and the tapping of a cane. There was something familiar about the Shape. It turned its face ·presently, and the jovial blue eyes twinkled at him as they used to do when he was a youngster.

"Grandpa!" he exclaimed. "I thought—why, I thought—"

The old man shook his grizzled head and seemed to chuckle. His lips moved soundlessly. Then one word came drifting, as though from a great distance.

"Not—not—not—" the pleasant old voice quavered, and sank into nothingness.

The radiant fog thinned and died away, and darkness again shrouded the staircase. Ursin was at the top now, wondering if his nerves were playing tricks on him. It had been a night of queer happenings. What did it mean?—the misty Shape, the knowing smile . . . "Not—not—not—" Who had passed him on the stairs?

Now again he saw the perplexing Shape. It was over there where the roof slanted down. That was where the old green sea chest stood—Grandpa's sea chest. He could see the Shape raising the lid and rummaging through the crusty old rags which lay within. Ursin could remember his mother's rummaging through them in the same way—old shirts, old socks, old underwear, scraps of sailcloth, an old carpet slipper or two.

"They've all been wet as sop," she had sighed in disgust. "They're dry and stiff and hard as chips. Sea water—that's it. They're all salt this minute, or they'd rot. Ugh!—what a mess! But they used to be Pa's, and somehow I hate to throw them away."

She had shut the lid down with a bang and snapped the padlock on. Ursin had the key to that padlock in his pocket at this moment, on his keychain. Now . . . how could the lid be raised, when the chest was padlocked and he had the key? Even as he questioned, the Shape disappeared.

The house itself was still as death at this hour. Faintly he could hear horses' hoofs down in the street . . . carriage wheels . . . the faraway sighing of a railway switch-engine . . . a

Negro whistling . . . palms rustling like starched petticoats . . .
Ursin shivered again, without knowing why.

He was glad to close his room door and light his lamp.
Mrs. Timmons, the landlady, had been house-cleaning and his
curtains were down to be washed. She had moved the sofa
and the armoire to different locations, and he had to look for
the washstand. The room was a queer jumble of things, anyway—whatever he felt like keeping, after his mother went.
Sometimes he wished he had left the house altogether, and
gone elsewhere to live.

The next day Mrs. Timmons told him she had had the
green chest moved into his room.

"I'm going to have a third room finished off in the garret,"
she said, "and rent them all. I've got the house pretty well
filled up now, but summer is always right dull."

So the sea chest hadn't been there under the slanting roof
last night. Yet the old man had stood over it and raised its
lid . . . Again Ursin could hear the queer, cracked old voice . . .
*"Not—not—not—"* . . . Strange. . . .

He told Elise about it a few nights later. She was a bit
frightened.

"Maybe the house is haunted, Ursin," she said, her eyes
wide. "Why don't you move somewhere else? Such things
scare me."

"Maybe if they scare me I'll get a better job," he laughed.
"Ever since I've done reporting I've wanted to own a paper.
Not a big paper—just a little one, at first. I'd have to begin
that way—small. If I made a go of it I could go in heavier the
next time. Would you be willing to marry a country newspaper,
Elise?"

"Yes—if I liked the editor well enough," she sniffed, while
he kissed her. "I was born in Gai, you know, half across the
state. You might buy the *Gai Gazette*. I expect it may have as
many as fifteen subscribers."

"I like the name," he grinned. "Well, maybe we'll buy
the *Gai Gazette*—some day."

That night he was met again by the misty semblance of
Grandpa LeMaitre. The next night also. He began rather to
dread the stairs. Were there such things as ghosts and wander-

ing spirits? Might there be some message his grandfather desired
to give him? Then why didn't he give it? Only *"Not—not—
not"* . . . That was no message. That was mere babble.

Still, hadn't his mother seen the misty Shape, too? He
recalled this with a start. And all the Shape had said to her
was, *"Not—not—"*

He began to think. What did he possess that had actually
been his grandfather's? The sea chest, of course. The Shape had
gone to the spot where the chest had stood for years. How
could a ghost know the chest had been moved? Or was it a
ghost? What was in the chest, anyway?

He unlocked it and threw back the lid. A musty, bitter
odor poured from the depths, like damp caves long sealed.
The space within was crowded with old, dried things, like salt
fish. That was the one thing Ursin could think of—salt fish.
He picked up a stiff gray rag and dropped it back again. It was
like handling ancient bones. Why in the world had Grandpa
LeMaitre ever kept them? Forgot about them, undoubtedly.

All the next day those "salt fish" kept coming to his mind.
He remembered a pair of gray socks tied tightly together.
When he thought about it, a good many of the "salt fish"
looked tied together. He'd better dump the whole lot of rubbish in the garbage can and use the chest for some of his own
clothes.

"God knows I'm disorderly enough," he sighed ruefully.
"If I put my stuff in that chest I'll *never* be able to find what
I want, when I want it."

That night the misty Shape walked beside him all the way
up the garret stairs. He could hear the cane tapping, tapping,
across the uneven garret floor. The workmen were coming the
next day to finish off the third room, Mrs. Timmons said.

The ghostly old Captain LeMaitre went into Ursin's room
with him—he would not be shut out. His blue eyes twinkled
like stars and he shook with silent mirth. He hobbled over to
the green sea chest where it stood by the window, and he raised
the lid without bothering to ask Ursin for the key. The padlock held perfectly—but the lid of the chest opened, just the
same. Was it a ghost-chest, Ursin wondered, that the ghost-
captain opened?

And as Grandpa LeMaitre stood there leaning over the open chest, his old hands running lovingly through the "salt fish," his old voice boomed out, as it must have boomed out across the decks of his good ship *Mercedes* in the old days—"*Not—not—not—*"

Then it stopped, as though a plug had been rammed into a trumpet. Something seemed to push Ursin towards the chest. Standing there close to the baffling, misty Shape, he stooped down and lifted one of the "salt fish" from the chest. It had three tight, hard knots in it.

"*Not—not—not*" boomed the old sea-voice, like distant thunder, the bright blue eyes dazzling Ursin like twin sapphires.

He looked at the rag in his hand. Suddenly he knew. *Knots!* Not *not,* but *knot!*

He tore at the gray, salty rag. It was so stiff and hard it broke his nails. But finally it loosened. Inside the first knot was a splendid sparkling green stone. It seemed to have a thousand brilliant facets. The second knot yielded another stone, and the third knot still another.

"*Knot—knot—knot!*" muttered Ursin, sucking a bruised thumb. "How dull and stupid I've been!"

He turned to tell of his find to the ghostly old visitor. But Grandpa LeMaitre had vanished.

The next day Ursin had in his possession a sack of green stones. He remembered the jeweler where his mother had bought her trinkets and he went there, showing the man one stone.

"Where did you get this?" the jeweler asked. "I have known of only one man, in all my experience, who ever brought me an emerald as fine as this one. He was an old sea captain named LeMaitre, and he must either have had an emerald mine or been a pirate. He's dead now, I think."

"He was my grandfather," Ursin answered. "Will you buy this stone?"

"Instantly." And the jeweler named a price which almost cut off Ursin Beauvais' breath.

He sold but one. The rest went into a bank's safety deposit box. Elise Pettingill didn't see him for a week.

"I've bought the *Gai Gazette,*" he announced to her when

he came back. "I've bought us a house in Gai, too. You and your dad'll both like it. I've bought us a dog and a cow and a canary bird, and I've hired us a cook and a yardman. I've bought two suits of clothes and a lawn mower. And now we're going to buy a marriage license."

"But how—"

"*Knot—knot—knot,*" he laughed. "I'll tell you all about it on the way back. I think we must have pirates or something on one limb of our family tree!"

# (*1835 on*)     *The Haunted House of the Rue Royale*

The most widely known of all the haunted houses in this city is the old Lalaurie house, which stands on the uptown corner of Royal street and Governor Nicholls, formerly Hospital street.

It has been known as "The Haunted House" for more than a century, and is the only one so listed in the guide books. Tourists never miss an expedition which includes it, and they explore its great rooms and balconies, its halls and galleries and winding stairs with wide eyes and an appreciative shiver.

Tradition says that the house was built in 1773 on a royal grant of land given to Jean and Henri de Remairie in 1770. That later, Louis Bartholmey de Macarty bought it for a town house; and that from him this forty-room mansion passed to his daughter Delphine—who first married Don Ramon Lopez y Angulo, then Jean Blanque, then Doctor Leonard Louis Nicolas Lalaurie. Certain court records set forth that the site was bought by Madame Lalaurie on September twelfth, 1831; that the house was "built and ready for occupancy in the spring of 1832." Other records (in the City Hall) show that the house and its grounds were purchased by Louis Lalaurie and "Delphine Lalaurie, née Macarty," from Edmond Soniat du Fossat, before Octave de Armas, the Macartys' lawyer, on August thirtieth, 1831.

Be these things as they may, the house remains still a gem of stately proportions and rich effects, as to the interior; although the exterior is, like all the Vieux Carré houses, plain to the point of severity. But there is the beautiful lace ironwork around the balcony, handsome arched windows all about, and a noble entrance. Dignity is the keynote of the whole structure—one of the largest and most impressive houses in the French Quarter.

Here it was that Marie Delphine de Macarty, as Madame Lalaurie, entertained lavishly and delightfully, her beauty and wealth and position drawing about her the cream of that day's choice society. There is no question about her popularity and her charm. We do know that she married Doctor Lalaurie on June twelfth, 1825.

For the next nine years, brilliant season followed brilliant season. The house swarmed with guests—balls, soirées, masques, receptions, musicales, family gatherings, house parties, dinners.

Every imaginable luxury abounded. There were slaves by the dozens—polishing the magnificent hand-carved doors (the doors are still there), the thousand-prism chandeliers, the great mirrors, the massive black fireplaces, the princely armoires of rosewood and mahogany, the heavy gold and silver plate, and the tall windows with their myriad small glittering panes.

Satins and velvets, and brocades that would stand alone—laces and linens and jewels and gold fringe—perfumes and filigree and priceless china—they filled the house and made it what it was.

The high-ceiled rooms rang with gay voices chattering in French and Spanish, light feet pattered on the stately mahogany staircases, high heels tapped along the marble floor of the wide hall, dainty hands rested on the slender baluster rail. The great came to dine, the rich came to loll, the clever came to dance, and a few came because they were fond of Madame and her pleasant family.

Once in a while a strange little phrase drifted round the circle of Madame Lalaurie's closest friends. A light hint fell upon ears attuned to hear. Where was Mélanie this morning?—Mélanie, whose black hands were so quick with buttons and buckles, and who had the knack of inserting hairpins with surpassing deftness. Where was Carlo this morning?—Carlo, whose swift black feet ran so many miles for thread and scissors and fruit and tea and beads and laque and flower seeds and what not. What detained Sarah, the small coffee-colored maid who handed about cups of café noir and seed cookies, and dusted the stairs and washed Madame's poodle? What ailed the head of Barnabé, that he kept it wrapped in swathings like an East Indian?—black Barnabé, who knew just the right temperature for wines and exactly the proper thickness to slice gâteau d'amandes. What was the secret muttering between old Deborah and lean young Octave, over the washtubs in a corner of the courtyard? Why were yellow Jacquot's eyes rolling yesterday, as though he had spied some dread phantom stalking the rear galleries? Why? . . . Why?

Madame ordered more linens, more French corsets, another Turkish rug. She sang on the stairway, she wore roses and pearls in her hair, she learned a little fetching poetry. She had black Berta take young Lia and school her in the arts of dressing hair and laying out skirts and selecting handkerchiefs. Lia was slim and chocolate-colored, swift and keen and quiet. She was to be Madame's own personal maid, with Berta to order and supervise and take the responsibility.

But one morning Lia's slim body came hurtling down from the roof, smashing onto the banquette with a sickening thud, and narrowly missing Monsieur Montreuil, who lived next door and who was a distant relative of Madame Lalaurie's. It was unfortunate, for the young slave was useful and clever. But Madame could afford to lose her—she had an army of slaves and could buy more any time she felt like it. Lia had been a fool to go up onto the roof, anyway.

Then came that never-to-be-forgotten day, April tenth, 1834. The newspapers of the time tell a tale which, for multitude of horror and revolting detail, has never been rivaled in New Orleans newspaperdom.

As the years went on, the house began more and more to stand out as a weird and sinister menace to the community. Passers-by ran, or crossed over to the opposite banquette. Negroes hurrying home after dark shunned the entire neighborhood, going riverward as far as Decatur, and woodsward to Dauphine or Burgundy. No power on earth could have forced them to pass the Lalaurie house. The very name had become a word with which to frighten recalcitrant black youngsters—and many not so young.

Madame Lalaurie was in France by this time. It became impossible to find tenants for the mansion. Those who did rent it told of being constantly awakened from sleep at night by hollow voices whispering in the corners and down the chimneys; by horrible noises of heavy bodies being dragged across floors; of chandeliers falling with a crash of glass and metal; of terrified Negro chatter from the dark and deserted kitchens; of shrieks from the courtyard; of wails and prayers and poundings under the floors; of mad jibberings from the empty garret; of a murderous whip flailing the air in awful rhythm, cutting human flesh to ribbons while a Negro throat shrieked agonized supplications; of jeers and taunts and threats and unprintable filth screamed in a clear, cultivated soprano; of the rustle of silks and the scent of exquisite perfume and the touch of soft, frenzied fingers, clutching and clawing in demoniacal fury.

A colored servant, having been induced to sleep in a room above the old stable at the rear of the courtyard, awoke one night to find firm hands throttling him, and a woman's voice babbling curses in rapid French. For a moment he saw her face bending over him—a pale face with black eyes and a white forehead, the hair done in old-fashioned bands, and a snarl of mad rage on the twisted lips. Then black hands tore the white fingers away, forcing the assailant back and back. Then the two vanished through the wall, as though it had been smoke instead of solid brick. The horses below him plunged about in their stalls; and a dog which had been sleeping in the stable came whimpering up the stairs with his scruff stiff as spikes and his whole body shaking as though with ague. In the morning a long gash at one side of the Negro's neck gaped bloody and burning with fever.

The house, standing empty for months at a time, became overrun with rats and other vermin. Great cats roamed through the majestic old rooms, adding to its accumulated filth, strewing it with bloody feathers and gnawed bones and the rotting carcasses of half-devoured rats. A black snake coiled its slimy length in one of the third floor powder rooms, adjoining the chamber in which the Marquis de Lafayette is said to have slept in 1825.

Much of the old Lalaurie furniture still remained—rosewood armoires in which generation after generation of mice made their nests and raised their young. Cockroaches swarmed in every crack and crevice, waving their repulsive feelers and scurrying down into depths beyond human ingenuity to explore.

And into all this, a stage perfectly set for supernatural manifestations, came the horde of black wraiths, to writhe and screech and rehearse over and over again some ghastly drama which had shunted them out of mortal existence and into whatever realm they seemed to be herded.

At the close of the War Between the States, when money was desperately scarce and conveniences few, the mansion was scrubbed and scoured and used as the Lower Girl's School. In 1874, black children who had been taught along with the white girls, were excluded. During the 1880's a conservatory of music was housed there. It seemed that the ghosts were laid at last.

Then came another period of vacancy. The place was bought and sold as an investment only, and tenants could not be tempted into it. Again the cats and rats and roaches reigned supreme. Then one night a gentleman, somewhat tipsy, passed on the opposite side of the street. As he came abreast of La Maison Lalaurie he chanced to look upwards. There, poised on the very edge of the roof, was a small dark figure. Over into space it plunged shrieking, all but striking another passing pedestrian.

The slightly inebriated one crossed over. In the moon's bright light the two men paused beside the still form of a young Negress, crushed and broken. The newcomer bent to touch her, but she vanished as his hand descended.

"You shee 'at?" he inquired of the other archly. "Dish-'peared, she did. You shee shame shing?"

Yes, the other had seen the same thing. So together, addled and sober, they hurried away. But they met the next day, and the sober one still declared he had seen the ghost of a black girl leap from the roof of the Haunted House and crash down onto the banquette at his very feet.

Others began to see this grisly sight. Every moonlight night the young Negress came shrieking down through the still air, to vanish the moment anyone ventured to touch her crumpled body. Was it Lia, of the old Lalaurie household? Madame was long dead. Her son and her four daughters were dead. There was no one to ask, and no one to answer.

When the Italians began to seep into the Old Quarter, they needed housing space. One house of thirty rooms on Chartres street held thirty families. The forty rooms of La Maison Lalaurie meant shelter for dozens. So they swarmed into it, painting its stately carved front door red, its delicate terra cotta friezes red, and its mahogany stairs and marble floors red. They wrecked the remains of the crystal chandeliers, they smashed the carved marble firepieces in the lower lounge and the billiard room, they filled the beautiful courtyard with junk and rags and garbage and broken wood. And then they began to complain to the landlord.

Ghosts were besieging them, they declared. Black ghosts and white ghosts. A fruit peddler was going upstairs one night, and he met a giant Negro on the landing. The darky was naked and his limbs were bound with chains which rattled and clanked as he descended the staircase. While the Italian gazed after him he melted into a skeleton, the chains still hanging from his dry white leg bones, and a smell of scorched flesh trailing in his wake. When he reached the bottom of the stairs he vanished. No red wine could have been responsible for that awful sight, the Italian opined, and moved the next day.

Another Italian family, with twin babies, lived in a room on the third floor. The mother one day heard a twin screaming and choking, and turned to see a white figure bent over the cot where the babies lay. She rushed to her child, to find its mouth stuffed with hard breadcrusts. She removed them; but as fast as she laid them on the coverlet, they vanished. She glanced up and saw the white-swathed woman still standing there, but she vanished as the bread had done. The next day the white-robed figure picked up the other infant, carried it to the door and tossed it down the stairs. When the mother followed, screaming hysterically, no baby was there, and no woman. Back in her own room again, she found both of the twins sleeping on the bed as though nothing had happened. In abject terror, she moved.

Other Italian women claimed a sheeted figure stood in

their doorways, stole their children's food and switched them until great welts showed on their backs. Some said the ghost tore their clothes and hid their rosaries and broke their dishes and sifted bitter powder in their spaghetti.

Continually from the dark garret, groans and wails and thumps and a terrible rasping noise kept the tenants awake nights. Those who had the temerity to open the narrow garret door at the turn of the stairs on the third floor, said they beheld horrors beyond description which faded into nothingness when approached and touched. The whole garret space would be fairly booming with this hellish confusion; and then, all in an instant, nothing would be there to see nor to hear nor to touch—their lanterns would throw mild yellow beams into empty corners under the slanting roof. The door out onto the parapet suggested additional horrors which they were of no mind to discover.

There were tappings on windows and distorted black faces peering in—but nobody was there when they stepped out onto the gallery, and nobody could have gotten there without their knowledge.

Mules in the stable were killed before their very eyes, the killer always a white-robed woman who vanished at a touch. Dogs were strangled, cats were torn in two, the bodies of dead bats were found in beds. Always there were strange comings and goings, slitherings on the stairs, gulpings and vomitings and groans on the galleries—and yet no one ever was there. Even the Italian who kept a saloon on the ground floor began to say the place was haunted . . . So the Italians moved out.

A furniture store occupied a corner for a few months. But the furniture was spattered with filth, its upholstering torn and spoiled, and the merchant moved hurriedly before any more of his stock fell prey to the ghostly vandals.

The black girl still plunged from the roof when the moon was bright. Workmen employed to repair the old cypress floors began digging up human skeletons from under the house. The owner of the property, in an attempt to down the mansion's gruesome reputation, announced that the house had been built over an ancient Spanish burying-ground, and that over an Indian graveyard. Which was quite true, only—the bones were

*. . . groans and wails and thumps . . .*

too recent to have been deposited there before 1803, and they were too near the surface to have been at any time buried in graves. They were found in all sorts of positions, helter-skelter, some barely covered with soil, shreds of fabric still adhering to some of the bones; and whenever hair was found near a skull, it was Negro hair. Some of the skulls had great holes in them. The authorities said that at least some scraps of wood or metal would have been found with or among the bones, had they been interred in coffins. As they were not in a trench, their burial could not have been in consequence of an epidemic. So it all simmered down to one conclusion—they were bodies of Lalaurie slaves, buried thus in order that their manner of death should not become known.

So now we go back to the great mass of astounding facts which were disclosed to the public on April tenth, 1834. On that day a fire started in La Maison Lalaurie. Some say it was kindled by an old Negress, in very desperation. At any rate, during the excitement caused by the blaze, a fireman made his way to the garret door. Tradition says that he was directed there by the terrified old Negress who had set fire to the house. The fire itself amounted to very little.

The fireman smashed down the garret door and climbed the narrow dark stairway. There he saw a sickening, horrible sight.

It seems that Madame Lalaurie, under her soft and beautiful exterior, possessed a demon's soul. Laughing and lovely to her friends and family, she would suddenly fly into rages which none but her slaves ever saw. On these occasions (which were by no means rare) her sadistic appetite seemed never appeased until she had inflicted on one or more of her black servitors some hideous form of torture. As her word was law in that house, and as she had the power to punish in ways far more excruciating than mere death, she could command and receive assistance in her diabolical drama.

Freed of their terror of Madame, and protected in the guard house (where they were taken for safety, instead of to the hospital), the Lalaurie slaves told their terrible tales.

The man who smashed the garret door saw powerful male slaves, stark naked, chained to the wall, their eyes gouged out, their fingernails pulled off by the roots; others had their joints skinned and festering, great holes in their buttocks where the flesh had been sliced away, their ears hanging by shreds, their lips sewed together, their tongues drawn out and sewed to their chins, severed hands stitched to bellies, legs pulled joint from joint. Female slaves there were, their mouths and ears crammed with ashes and chicken offal and bound tightly; others had been smeared with honey and were a mass of black ants. Intestines were pulled out and knotted around naked waists. There were holes in skulls, where a rough stick had been inserted to stir the brains. Some of the poor creatures were dead, some were unconscious; and a few were still breathing, suffering agonies beyond any power to describe.

Newspapers of the time give a most appalling view of these garret discoveries. Livid fear flamed in the eye of every Lalaurie slave.

Quoting the *Bee* of April eleventh, 1834: "Seven slaves, more or less horribly mutilated, were seen suspended by the neck, with their limbs apparently stretched and torn from one extremity to the other . . . These slaves . . . had been confined by the woman Lalaurie for several months in the situation from which they had thus providentially been rescued, and had been merely kept in existence to prolong their sufferings, and to make them taste all that the most refined cruelty could inflict . . ." They compared her to a Diocletian, a Nero, a Caligula. Statements were sworn to by Judge Jean François Canonge, Felix LeFebre, Monsieur Montreuil, Monsieur Fernandez, and Messieurs Gockhatt and Fauche.

Then came the story of the young Negro maid, Lia. She had, the other servants said, pulled Madame's hair while dressing it. The mistress, infuriated, seized a heavy whip which stood behind her bureau, and beat the slave unmercifully. Her pain and terror blinding her to consequences, Lia rushed out of the room and up the stairs, Madame still lashing her with the cruel whip. Up and up, through the garret door, past the tortured slaves, up and out onto the roof, and beyond the parapet. Madame now had a double reason to lash her—she had had a glimpse of the Lalaurie punishment! One backward glance showed her that her mistress pursued her even here—so over the edge of the roof she threw herself.

Later, some said the Negress fell down the stairwell and crashed on the marble floor of the hall. Excusers of modern date have figured that it might have been a Negro child who fell while attempting to slide down the bannisters in play. But the first story stands.

While the fire was still unextinguished, Monsieur and Madame Lalaurie escaped from the mob by driving in a carriage to Mandeville, whence presently they started on their voyage to France.

Some say Madame died in a French forest, killed by a wild boar which she was hunting. Others say she died quietly in her bed. Still others say she returned to New Orleans after some years, taking up her residence in what was, in the 1850's, the Faubourg Treme, on the Bayou Road—calling herself merely "the Widow Blanque." There is a record of a Mrs. N. L. Lalaurie emancipating a slave, Orestes, on April twentieth, 1849, in Municipality Number One, which included the Faubourg Treme.

The old mansion was renovated in 1921, and has since been slightly remodeled. However, to passers-by the very bricks cry out the story of tortures which they cannot hold in leash. The old roof rises like a towering mausoleum, or like broad wings spread to cover its awful past and its unspeakable tragedies. People pass in and out of its great front door—but the tragedies always remain, deathless and sinister as an avenging deity.

## (*1885*)     *The Ghost of Love*

It was in 1870 that John Pelham brought his bride to live in the little house on the corner of Eighth and Chippewa streets. The house was set by itself in the midst of a garden space, and young Pelham had visions of fresh vegetables and tall flowering shrubs and many rose bushes. Already there were two fig trees and a magnolia, Japanese plums at one side of the house and a 'simmon tree on the other.

His bride had been Caroline Andrews of Mobile—a slight, pretty girl with chestnut hair and a creamy complexion. They began housekeeping by planting a wisteria vine on the south side of the house, where it would run up over the galleries and form a leafy curtain when the weather was hot.

John was over thirty and Caroline was twenty-two. And because of the eight years' difference, Caroline took extra care that the silver should be beautifully polished and the food served exactly right and that everything about the little house should be kept spick-and-span.

John grew more charmed with his bride each day. He loved her canary, he frolicked with her big white cat, he enjoyed the fragrance of the verbenas and mignonette which she planted along the garden borders. He liked to see her sitting on the cool gallery with her sewing or knitting, or perhaps directing the Negro maid about the making of some special kind of cookies or preserves.

Then suddenly Caroline decided to do without a maid. It would mean so much to the nest egg they were saving. Maids broke china and lost silverware and wasted food and stole things, she said. Besides which, she would dearly love to attend to everything herself. But the washing and ironing and scrubbing, these John objected to her doing—such tasks never should be performed by white hands. Caroline stood firm, however, and at the end of the month she let black Bessie go.

From that day on, Caroline Pelham entered another existence. In the morning, shortly after John left for his work, a ring had come at the doorbell. Caroline answered it, her cheeks a little flushed, her step a trifle nervous. Her fingers trembled as she opened the door.

"Well," smiled the tall young man who stood on the porch, "I kept my word—here I am."

"Yes," Caroline replied breathlessly, as he stepped in and she closed and bolted the door. "And I'm so frightened, Joe! Suppose someone saw you and told John!"

"Can't a book agent call to interest you in a set of art folios?" he laughed, catching her to him and kissing her hungrily. "Nobody in Mobile used to find out about us, and nobody here ever will. What's the use of being a pretty girl if you can't be loved? You know and I know that John Pelham couldn't love anybody as I love you. Am I to blame because I've got a rich wife whom I can't possibly divorce? I'd have married you myself if there'd been the ghost of a chance. But I can use Laura's money—and so can you, for that matter. You got rid of the nigger, I hope."

"Yes, although I had a time convincing John I didn't need her. We couldn't have her here, I know that. Help always talk. At that, I'm terribly afraid the neighbors will make remarks if you come often."

She laid her head on his shoulder and he smothered her face with kisses.

"The neighbors won't see me," he said, and winked at her knowingly. "I'm going to stay here all day—every day—and leave the house after dark. Your John never will know I'm here. There's plenty of room upstairs for me, if he comes home early."

"Oh!" gasped Caroline. "You never could stay here—not like that! John would find you and he might kill us both. You mustn't think of such a thing!"

"Very well, my dear." And Joe Curtis drew away from her coldly. "Just as you wish. But either I'll stay here, as I propose, or I'll find speedy means of letting your John know that you were my mistress for more than two years. The story won't hurt *me* any. Laura knows how well I like the ladies—that's why she's such a devil about refusing a divorce. Pure spite work. Come, come, little one—don't be a fool. Think of the cozy times we'll have here by ourselves.

"And there are so many pretty trinkets I can give you. I promise you never to let myself be seen. I can always slip out after nightfall and return before daybreak. I hope you haven't forgotten the fortnight we spent while your people were in Atlanta."

No, Caroline had not forgotten. She shivered a little whenever she recalled it. And yet, it had been quite a delirious experience. Possibly the utter secrecy of it had added half the zest and delight.

"Come, little Caroline Curtis," he mocked, locking her again in his arms.

"You know that isn't my name!" she cried.

"Never mind—it ought to be," he laughed.

She wished, during the strange weeks which followed, that John were as handsome and as winning as Joe Curtis was. She wished his caresses were as sweet and his phrases as graceful and his arms as fond. But she was thankful John was the quiet kind—content to sit reading a paper or book between supper and bedtime. Or, if they went out together, they returned fairly early.

As for Joe Curtis, he kept his belongings at a hotel. Sometimes Caroline was sure she heard the gate click while she and John ate supper. And often she knew she heard it click just before dawn.

She never heard a foot fall nor the creaking of a door, nor any sound at all in the house. But she knew that as soon as John had gone for the day, the door at the back of the little upstairs hall would open, and there would be Joe coming down the stairs, tall and straight and immaculate, his linen crisp and snowy and his shoes shining like mirrors. Maybe if

John were as dashing as that . . . But no, there was no way out now.

One day she sat down quietly beside Joe Curtis on the high-backed sofa.

"I am going to have a baby, Joe," she said primly.

"No!" he returned, blinking at her oddly. "Is it mine?"

"I don't know," she replied a bit uneasily. "I really have no means of knowing."

"It is mine, of course," the man laughed, "although John will get the credit for it. We'll make a bargain: if it's a boy, it's mine; if it's a girl, it's John's."

"Yes," Caroline nodded. "And you will have to go away then."

"For a short time," Joe agreed. "I'll go and get a few more thousands from Laura. I can always do that. She thinks I'm in Paris—but I'm only in love, little Caroline Curtis!"

So, rather gaily than otherwise, they spent the next few months. Then one morning the house seemed still and empty and deserted. No one opened the door of the upper passage, no one came down the stairs, no one called her "little Caroline Curtis." John came home at the end of the day, and after supper she hemmed flounces for the long baby dresses she was making.

The days crept on. Sometimes she was glad and relieved to have the house and her life to herself. But more often she was frightened. Would Joe Curtis come back, after the baby was born? The future looked difficult and perplexing enough. John said she looked strained and worried, but laid it to her condition.

When the baby came it was a boy. Caroline named him Louis. She wondered which man he was going to look like— her huband or her lover. If he were John's son, he was safe. But if he were Joe's son . . . She remembered the gay dark eyes and the handsome head and the jaunty manner and the glib lies. It seemed an outrage to foist Joe's son on John Pelham. But he might be John's son, after all. Would she ever know?

The years went on. She never dared hire a maid, for fear one day the bell would ring and Joe Curtis would be standing there in the door, mocking her with a musical laugh and calling her "little Caroline Curtis." It made her shiver—Louis would tell his father. She could not forbid it—she would not dare to do so. She could not deny it—her own son would have seen and heard!

Lines came in her forehead and crow's-feet at the corners of her eyes. There were a few silver strands in her hair—and she was not yet thirty-five. John said the housework was too hard for her. She had told him shortly after Louis came that she had hired a maid to do the laundry work, and she still kept up that fiction.

Then one day she heard a sound which froze her blood as she listened. It was Saturday and Louis was in the kitchen, whittling a dog from a piece of wood. It was a nice dog, although it looked more like a rooster, and Louis was whistling. Yes, some one was coming down the stairs. Caroline held onto her broom tightly and raised her eyes.

The man she saw was tall and straight and distinguished-looking, his eyes dark and limpid and his hair snow-white. His tapering fingers slid gracefully along the baluster rail, and a faint smile hovered about his mouth.

"Still playing at housekeeping," he said, standing there at the foot of the stairs. "I hear the child was a boy. Let me see him Caroline."

"No, no!" she panted, her hands at her heart. "No, no—I can't! My life would be at an end—everything would be at an end! How can you come back like this, to blot out my future and spoil my boy's life?"

She began to sob. Louis, busy at his whittling, heard voices. He liked the neighbors—he would go and listen while Mamma and somebody chatted. Maybe it was some agent—although Mamma never let agents in. What was that? Surely not Mamma crying? He ran to the front hall. Who was the tall, white-haired man, and why was he laughing in that queer way while Mamma cried?

"So," the stranger said, looking at Louis, "here is my boy. I should know him in a thousand, Caroline Curtis. And did you name him after me, as was proper?"

John Pelham, returning that night, found the house empty.

He searched every inch of it, even going into the garden and the little shed where tools were kept. Why had Caroline left no word if she were staying at some friend's house for supper? But she never did this. . . . Why tonight? Yet her hat and cloak and gloves were here. Louis' hat and coat were on the peg behind the bedroom door, too. And there were fresh shavings in the kitchen, where Louis had been at his everlasting whittling. Where could the two have gone?

John did not make inquiries until the next day, for he thought Caroline and the boy would be returning at any moment. No one had seen them go away, no one had met them as they went. No trace of them could be found. They had vanished completely.

There was nothing to do except wait. So John Pelham went back to his deserted house every night, and locked the door behind himself every morning. The rooms grew dusty and disordered. Brambles began to choke the garden. A blind-hinge gave way and was not repaired.

And then one night John Pelham came running out of his house shrieking like a madman. He plunged through the gate and down the street, still uttering those awful cries. Finally Henry Cardinal, one of the neighbors, caught up with him.

"It's them!" he shuddered, as his friend led him into the Cardinal house. "It's her and it's him—Caroline and the boy! I was sitting there in front of the fireplace, and she walked right out of it! The fire spluttered and went out, and then she came standing there in front of me! And then he came—Louis, just as he used to be!"

"You mean the ghosts of them?" asked Mrs. Cardinal, her eyes wide and frightened.

"Yes, the ghosts of them!" John Pelham declared. "She leered and snarled at me like a she-wolf, her teeth long and yellow and her eyes like balls of fire! I thought she was going to claw me—and the boy was right back of her. It was dreadful . . . but I've got to go back. It's my house and she can't drive me out of it!"

But, as the years slipped by, many and many a night Pelham came screaming out of his house, just as he had done that first time. Sometimes he was shamefaced afterwards.

"I ought to get used to it," he said to Henry Cardinal one Sunday, "She always comes out of the fireplace in the same way, after the fire has been smothered. She gnashes her teeth and glares and growls like some savage animal, and reaches out to claw at me. And just as she starts for me, I find myself screeching and running out. I can't help it, she's so frightful. She looks like Caroline, and the boy looks like Louis, and they're always the same. But maybe it's somebody else. Caroline never could hate me like that. She never did, and she never had reason to. She grew moody and nervous after the boy came, but she was a good woman."

"He's alone too much," the neighbors agreed among themselves. "He broods over his loss and thinks he sees Caroline. He sits there every night in that shell of a house, and he imagines all sorts of things. His wife ran off, of course, and took the child with her. There was probably a man mixed up in it somehow, although we never saw anything to indicate that. Poor Mr. Pelham!"

After years, John Pelham died.

"Maybe he did see ghosts, after all," the gossips whispered. "But why were they so vindictive? Is it possible that he went home that night and killed her and his boy? But of course she must have been gone all day—we never saw a sign of anybody round the house all that Saturday, and the child was home from school, too."

The place was sold shortly after Pelham's death. The new owners cleared the brush from the garden, repaired the broken steps, put new glass in the windows, and painted the house.

The first family that rented it moved out in three weeks. They had recently come from Texas, and never had heard about the house being haunted. But they told precisely the same story that John Pelham had told—a horrible ghost-woman walking out of the fireplace, after putting out the fire, snarling and snapping like a she-wolf and reaching out to claw the nearest person; and just behind her a boy, acting in the same manner.

A long series of tenants followed. Some stayed a day, some a week, none ever longer than two months. And they all saw the same terrible apparitions. One man stood his ground and had the flesh of his face clawed to ribbons.

After that, the house remained vacant for years. Rats gnawed holes in the floors and wainscoting, owls nested in the garret, and rabbits burrowed under it and brought forth huge and frequent families, unmolested ever by neighborhood dogs. Lightning struck the magnolia tree; and presently it stood, gaunt and riven, like a corpse laid open to the elements.

Finally a group of German-Americans got together and formulated a plan for a school where both German and English should be taught. They proposed to rent the little house set in the midst of a ruined garden, renovate it and use it as a school building. They reasoned that, as the ghosts were reputed to appear only at night, and as the school would be in session only during the day, the place would serve their purpose admirably.

So again the house was cleaned and put in order, desks and benches were moved in, and the school opened. It had been going a week when the ghosts of the madwoman and her son emerged from the fireplace. The children shrieked and rushed out of the building, to be told by their hardheaded German teachers how foolish and feeble-minded they were. But every morning at ten o'clock the same thing occurred. Even the teachers themselves had to acknowledge that they saw the fearful spectres.

"Ach, Gott!" the headmaster raged. "Is is sheep that I have hired for teachers already, that they must run every time the wind blows? If they their prayers said and their Bible read, as they shòuld, the ghosts they would not see! For this I should dock their wages, ja!"

Cold weather came on, and one morning a roaring fire was built in the main fireplace. The children gathered round for warmth. Suddenly there was a great hissing and steaming of the wood, as though water had been thrown upon it. Smoke and ashes belched from the grate. And from the cloud of it walked the ghost-woman, twisting and writhing and snarling and snapping, a veritable fury, her bony arms outstretched to claw at the children, and her hair streaming about her like muddy rags. The boy followed her, his face livid with rage, his empty eyesockets streaming forth little jets of yellow flame.

Nothing could induce either children or teachers to enter the house again, so the school had to be moved to other quarters.

For some years thereafter the place remained utterly abandoned. The fence sagged and fell, but no one was bold enough to enter. No dog would set foot even in the yard. Cats did, indeed, nap in the deserted rooms and sun themselves on the broken porches.

Then a little man came up from Cuba. He had been in prison there, he said, for some political offence. His cell-mate had been a tall American by the name of Joseph Curtis. This Curtis had died in prison, but before his death he had handed a wedding ring to the little man, whose name was Miguel Alvarez. He also gave Alvarez quite a sum of money, begging him to go to New Orleans and restore the ring to one John Pelham. to whose wife it had belonged.

"He confessed to a foul crime," the Spaniard told the man who then owned the haunted house. "It seems he had been this Mrs. Pelham's lover, and he believed himself to be the father of her son. The day he visited her he saw the son for the first time, and it sent him into a frenzy of hatred for the man she had married.

"Suddenly he wanted to marry her himself. His own unloved wife had died, and he was free. He urged Mrs. Pelham to flee with him, telling her that her own husband was maintaining a mistress. But she cut his words short, pushing him away from her and refusing his propositions and his arguments.

"Filled with mad fury against her husband and remembering the years of fear and misery occasioned by her lover, she was like a maniac. He seized her by the throat and bent her backward over his knees until he heard her spine snap. Then, half-insane himself, and with the boy fighting him off, he pulled back her head and rammed a broomstick down her throat and into her body with one frightful thrust. Laughing, he grasped the boy, flung him over the newel post and broke his back. He said it seemed as though a tide of blood were rushing at him, smothering him and drowning him in its crimson horror.

"Still, loving her as he did, he felt no remorse for what he had done. It was as though the Devil drove him. The dead woman and her boy now seemed impersonal—objects of which he must dispose, but which did not really corncern him and of which he had no understanding.

"He pried up one of the hearthstones and found a convenient cavity beneath it. Digging down into the soft earth, he buried the two bodies, covering them well.

"Then he cleaned up every trace of the deed, waited until dusk, and left the house and the city. I wish now to buy the place with the money which he gave me. I shall set it in order and occupy it with my family."

The transaction was completed in a few days. The first thing Alvarez did was to have workmen remove the great hearthstone and dig under it. There they found the bones of a woman and a boy, wrapped in an old carpet. The skeletons were removed and buried beside John Pelham.

From that time on, no ghosts ever appeared in the little house where Caroline had known love and pain and terror and remorse and death.

# (1902)    *The Fountain Woman*

On a certain street stands an old house of many rooms. It is in the old part of town—that portion once designated as the Faubourg Marigny, during Bernard de Marigny's régime. Bernard was born in 1785 and died early in 1868. But the house in question is said to be a part of the great residence erected by Bernard's illustrious father, Pierre Philippe de Marigny, who was born in 1751 and died in 1800, and who lies today buried under the floor of the old Saint-Louis Cathedral.

We are told that this is the mansion referred to in certain old documents as being located "somewhere between the Esplanade and the Champs Élysées," and where in 1798 Pierre Philippe and his family entertained for several months the three royal princes—le Duc d'Orléans, le Duc de Montpensier, and le Comte de Beaujolais, the first of whom later became Louis Philippe, King of the French.

In April of 1902 this house had been divided into apartments and was occupied by a number of poorish families. The spacious chambers which once had listened to royal laughter and court conversation were now frequently filled with the smoke of frying bacon and the soapy steam of Monday's washing. Cheap wallpaper now covered the great expanses where once had hung priceless tapestries and old masters.

For years there had been whisperings now and then about the ghost of a woman who walked the corridors, moaning softly to herself and crooning old French songs. She was gowned in diaphanous white silk which slithered softly as she walked, like the wings of butterflies against glass. Sometimes she made as though to cradle a child in her arms; and sometimes, they said, she peered hungrily in at the doors of rooms where infants slept.

If a girl were in love, other tenants would see this wraith hovering near her door, or even following her at a discreet distance down the long shadowy halls. Sometimes she paced the green galleries; sometimes she paused in the courtyard, no doubt seeing it as it had been in its heyday—a place of roses and fountains and birds and blossoming trees, instead of littered with old wagon-wheels and broken crockery and discarded newspapers.

No one minded the white ghost-woman. She was harmless and utterly impersonal, like a mist or a fog, or a cloud drifting before the sun. Apparently she had no mission, no motive, no quest whatever. She belonged with the house, like the roof and the chimneys.

During the early part of 1902 she seemed to disappear altogether. The neighborhood and the tenants of the house heaved an involuntary sigh of relief. At the best, a ghost is not the most ideal of companions.

Then a strange phenomenon began to take place. It occurred always at night, and occasioned frightened whisperings in the morning. No one seemed to know precisely how to describe it. Certainly no one could discover anything reasonable about it. Was it a ghost, or wasn't it a ghost, or what was it, anyhow? They called it "that thing." Some of them prayed and some of them cried, and some of them just wondered.

"Oh, but I sure saw that thing last night," the Widow Daily told Mrs. Joseph, who lived on the first floor. She spoke in a harsh whisper and her eyes were round and scared. "I was layin' corner-to-corner, like I has ever since poor Danny got himself kilt by a train. Me bein' a tall woman, 'tis comfortabler, and I can see all ways of the room like. An' if I can't lay like that, I allus dream a train's comin' bustin' right into the headboard of me bed."

"What did you see?" Mrs. Joseph wanted to know, chewing her gum expectantly.

"What I seen was queer as you please," the widow nodded. " 'Twas a founting, set right there in the middle of me bedroom. The moonlight was comin' in bright at the windy, and it shined right through the sprayin' water. 'Twas a white marble founting, and the water was blue-white and clear as glass.

"I laid right there, corner-to-corner in me bed, and I seen the water a-sprayin' and I heerd it gurgle an' fuss as pleasant as a bird's nest. And it run over the sides of the founting and dripped on me new carpet, and I thinks to meself, 'Tis no use me gittin' up, me carpet's spiled by this time, anyhow.' So I didn't git up. And me mind was that dull I never even begun to wonder where all the water come from, when there's not a tap higher nor the first floor in the hull house."

"Didn't nobody come by the founting, Mis' Daily?"

"No. Not nobody. Nobody come and nobody said nothin' nor done nothin', thank the good Lord. But 'tain't a sight for no lone widdy-woman, a founting settin' up in the middle of her bedroom floor, for no reason at all. I'm shiverin' yet, I am."

"And how did it go away, Mis' Daily?" The gum was shifted to the other cheek.

"It jest went, that's all. 'Twas there, a-sprayin' high an' wet. And then 'twasn't there at all."

"It was a shame to spoil your new carpet like that."

" 'Twasn't spoilt. 'Twasn't even wet—not a drop. Nothin' to show for the founting what I seen, and what caused me all that discomfort and anxiety. But I sure didn't dream it. I told ole man Hipple, on the third floor."

"And what did he say, Mis' Daily?"

"What *would* he say? Jest grinned, like he allus does. Said Mis' Hipple had to carry water up two flights to wash, and he guessed he'd ketch enough from the founting for one washin', anyhow, if that thing come spoutin' up in their room. He was jest pokin' fun. But mebbe he wouldn't poke so much fun if he was to see it. 'Tain't funny—it's awful. It's nothin' but a ghost-founting, and ghosts is allus bad luck."

The gossips went their ways, one shivering and the other chewing her gum industriously.

The next day Mrs. Dupas, living on the second floor, encountered Mrs. Monget, who occupied quarters on the first floor, next to those of Mrs. Joseph.

"Angie Daily seen that thing the other night," Mrs. Dupas

said hoarsely. "Me I thought she was makin' out some. But Clara Williams upstairs says it was in her place last night, and she's scairt as a owl. I hope to Gawd it don't come spoutin' in *my* bedroom, wakin' me up and scarin' me out of my mind."

"Me I got a flask of holy water," returned Mrs. Monget. "If I see that thing I'll shet my eyes tight an' throw the holy water at it. And I bet it'll be gone when I opens 'em."

"Mebbe it will an' mebbe it won't," the first speaker warned. "You cain't tell about them things. Clara Williams she got real brave an' sassy, an' she up an' out of her bed an' stuck her hand in the founting. An' now her hand looks like it'd been scalded, an' she says it pains her something awful. Me I think her hand's got a curse on it, and if it drops off or sumpin' 'twon't surprise me none. You cain't go foolin' with suppernatural things without gittin' hurt."

"Old man Hipple says it's all lies an' flimflam," sniffed the Monget woman. "But I don't believe Angie Daily'd make a humbug like that. Me I believe everybody gits scairt too easy, but I don't say they're lyin' about what they seen."

"Old man Hipple's got his turn comin'," Mrs. Dupas scowled. "He can laugh at suppernatural things all he wants. but they *gits* you, jest the same."

The next day old man Hipple was sick.

The doctor called—which was a great distinction and would not soon be forgotten. Every female in the decrepit old building held her head a trifle higher and her spine a little straighter because the doctor's span of bays had stopped in front, and the man of medicine himself had mounted the stairs to the third floor, leaving a faint aroma of drugs behind him as he climbed. He had come down again, quite matter-of-fact, and his colored driver had trotted the bays down the street at a brisk pace. The doctor had called. Nothing could take that away. It was almost as good as a funeral.

After a suitable time had elapsed, the Widow Daily crept up to the third story and rapped on the Hipple door. Little Mrs. Hipple opened it, and a whispered conference ensued.

"Well, I guess it won't hurt John none if you come in," Mrs. Hipple finally decided. "He's achin' to tell somebody what happened last night, and I'm plum wore out, what with the doctor an' all. I declare, havin' sickness in the house keeps a-body scramblin' night an' day."

So to the bedside of the invalid the Widow Daily was ushered. Almost at once John Hipple plunged into his recital.

"It's jedgment on me for sneerin' at spooks," he sighed, sitting up in bed and tucking the hem of the sheet into the collar of his nightshirt. "I though the wimmin-folks was jest makin' out about that founting thing. But I knows better now." He groaned softly and clutched at his middle.

"Did the ghost pitch at you?" Mrs. Daily inquired in an awed tone.

"It's jest his stummick," Mrs. Hipple assured her. "He et cucumbers yestiddy, and they always give him the grannies. You know how men-folks is, Mis' Daily. I told him not to, but he would have 'em."

"This here 'thing' you-all been gabblin' about," went on old man Hipple, blinking sagely, "ain't so funny. I thought I'd fool you-all, so I got the washtub up here and shoved it under the bed. I says to Annie, says I, 'If any old founting comes clear up here to this floor, I'm goin' to make good use of it.' But I laughed to myself jest to think what saps the rest of you was, takin' any stock in spooks an' sech.

"Well, last night after I et them cucumbers, I felt some distressed and I was layin' here awake, thinkin' I ought to git up an' take me some bakin' sody. We'd left the blinds open, an' all of a sudden I heard water runnin'—gurglin' an' spatterin', like it was in a reg'lar froth.

"I opened my eyes an' there 'twas—a white marble founting, right there in the middle of this room, spurtin' up nigh to the ceilin'! The light from the windy come shinin' through it like a rainbow. Why, I could see the very drops fallin' round the aidge of that there marble bowl. I never seen anything plainer in my life. The water was flowin' over in a flood, an' I knowed the carpet would be soaked an' leakin' downstairs on Mrs. Dupas, most likely.

"I felt queer, but I thought 'twas them cucumbers. So I up an' grabbed the tub and pulled it over to that there founting. It didn't seem near so funny as it had before, an' Annie here had stuck her head under the bedclothes, she was that scairt.

"Well, that there tub filled full up with water. An' when I went to pull it away, the water riz right up like a sea an' hugged me. I thought I'd fell in the river—walked in my sleep or sumpin'—an' my whole body felt like it was stuck full of blazin' hot needles. I tell you I was near drownded.

"Then Annie she pulled me out into the hallway an' we stayed there till it got light. We came back in here then, and the founting was gone an' the tub was gone, an' there wasn't no drop of water nowhere—not even a spot of damp. It beats me. But if that thing comes in here again, I'm goin' to stick my head under the bedclothes an' let 'er rip."

"But that wa'n't the whole story, John," reproved his wife.

"I know it—but I didn't know as you wanted I should tell the rest of it," grinned Hipple. " 'Twas like this, Mis' Daily: when that mess o' water riz up an' grabbed me, it turned into a woman—not a real woman, you understand, but a ghost! It was this here woman they say glides round the halls and galleries, only she was tall as a house an' strong as a ox.

"There wasn't no gittin' away from her, an' she like' to choke me to death. I got to die some day, same as everybody else, but I don't want to die any sech way as that. She must have been made o' needles, too, an' she glared into my eyes like she was lookin' with a pair o' headlights. I told that doctor about it, and he looked like he thought I was batty, until Annie told him she seen it too—an' the hull house had had the founting, off an' on."

The story began presently to leak out, and somebody dug up the fact that, while the de Marigny family had occupied the house, a young relative had come to live with them—Mademoiselle Claudine Tureau. When the Princes of France came to visit, Mademoiselle Claudine fell desperately in love with the dashing young Duc d'Orléans. She was eighteen and His Royal Highness was five-and-twenty. She was lovely, but there was not a drop of royal blood in her veins and she had not so much as a title. So, although stolen kisses and secret meetings were enchanting, le Duc sailed away after three months of lavish entertainment, and Mademoiselle Claudine never saw him again.

The girl's heart was broken. Also, there was to be a child. So, one night as she stood on the brink of a great sunken fountain, she leaned too far over the brim. Tradition says the fountain rose and took her to its bosom like a lover. Old records set forth that she fell in and drowned. They buried her in a tomb in old Saint-Louis Cemetery Number One. . . . *Ici reposent—Claudine Celeste Tureau—décédée le 20 Déc. 1788—à l'age de 18 ans.*

But, though the tomb was sealed tight as a drum, Mademoiselle Claudine could not rest. She must up and away, hither, thither, whither. Searching for her royal lover, no doubt, and returning to that disc of tumbling water which had so mercifully received her. Decades passed. Fortunes toppled, great ones died, the fountain became a dry and unsightly ruin. Year by year the ground sank and the dust settled; rubbish accumulated.

"Love is not love that alters when it alteration finds." So the spirit of Mademoiselle Claudine, clad in spectral white, came back to commune with the fountain. But she found it only, like herself, a spirit—the fountain itself was lying deep under the refuse of a cheaper and more tawdry day.

So those who had delved thus far into history, obtained permission from the owners of the property to dig in the yard. Almost on the modern property-line they came upon the remains of the great marble bowl of the fountain. Searching carefully, they one day sifted out a small bronze box, so tightly closed that a jeweler had finally to break it in order to get it open. There, wrapped in a square of white velvet, was a slender chain and a heart-shaped locket set with sapphires. Inside the locket was a ringlet of hair and a bit of melon-colored brocade. A tiny slip of paper bore the faded words, in a masculine hand, *De tout mon coeur*—With all my heart. There was no signature.

The story goes that the marble slab and the old bricks sealing the front of Mademoiselle Claudine's tomb were, with due permission, loosened. The little bronze box, tightly sealed once more, was laid inside and the tomb again securely sealed. Mademoiselle Claudine had recovered her pitiful little keepsake.

The fountain-ghost never appeared thereafter.

# (*1890*)     *Warring Wraiths*

What is anger like when it is engendered in a mind without form, a heart without being, a spirit without the familiar armor of flesh? Bootless and futile it must be . . . yet they tell us it flames and rages, driving the poor wraith to utter madness and to acts of unthinkable fury.

We have this exemplified in the case of a haunted spot in Cherokee street. It is an old tale, but still bitter with hatred and revenge. It began years ago and lasted for months.

Suddenly one day a shower of bricks, stones, iron and bits of wood descended into the rear yard of this house. The occupants laid it to small boys, or somebody who wished to even up an old grudge. However, when they ventured out to chase the hoodlums away, there was no one to be found. But the rain of missiles continued. The family found it difficult to dodge them. A trip into the yard became dangerous—not only dangerous but terrifying.

Where could this bombardment come from? Watched closely by the family, by neighbors, even by members of the police force, no one ever could spy out the source of them. They just came, seeming to materialize out of thin air. But always they fell in the back yard of that particular house— heaps of them, heavy and substantial, apparently of the earth earthy. They did not come from the back nor from either side nor from the house itself. Direction they took, certainly, but it was as though they were hurled by unseen hands.

"And that," avers one of the old neighbors, "is exactly what it was—a ghost war. I know who was fighting, too—an old man and a little girl. Sounds unlikely? But the things ghosts do are most often unlikely. They're always up to something queer and unreasonable.

"I'll tell you now. There was old Abner White who used to live a piece down the street. He hated children—girl children especially. He claimed they made fun of him and called him names, although nobody ever believed that they did, for in that day little girls were mighty modest and shy. More likely they were afraid of him, he was so dour and stern.

"Well, one day old Abner met a group of small girls on the banquette. They were bunched together, in a way they have, whispering and giggling and winking and making funny faces.

"When Abner passed them they jostled him, not meaning to, of course. They started to laugh, but he turned on them like a madman, cursing them at the top of his voice. One of them, little Ollie Voss, he seized by the arm. In a panic, she screamed —and they all began to scream, thinking Ollie was going to be killed. Old Abner shook her until her teeth rattled and then flung her away from him and stamped off down the street.

"Nothing was done about it, because everybody was afraid of starting a feud. Then one morning  word went round that Abner White had been found dead in his bed. The neighborhood heaved a deep sigh of relief when he was safely buried.

"One night soon after, Ollie Voss was standing in her cotton nightgown in front of an open grate. Suddenly a red-hot brick came hurtling out of the fireplace. It set fire to the child's nightdress and she was burned to death. Only one name did she shriek as her mother fought to save her—'It's old Abner White! He's there in the fireplace grinning at me! It's old Abner White!'

"They buried her in the old family tomb. The years went by and the tomb began to crack and crumble. So the family bought a new tomb in another cemetery and moved all the ancient bones. And that is when the bricks and stones and iron and wood began to rain down in the back yard where little Ollie had lived.

"A few of us knew what it was. The new tomb stood next to the one where Abner White was buried. He couldn't stand it. Even in the Other World he hated Ollie Voss, and he didn't intend to have her bones lying near his forever and forever. So he rushed across the Still River, whether or no, grabbing all the trash he could as he came, and dashed it down into the yard where the child used to play.

"But Ollie sensed it in her quiet tomb. And, with the courage and spite which she never possessed on earth, she hurried back to her yard and joined in the fray. So it was a battle between old Abner and little Ollie. Nobody ever won, and the yard was filled with rubbish which nobody dared to clear away. They said whoever touched it would die. Once a falling stone did strike a child, and she began to vomit and died in an hour. Some said she vomited lizards and spiders and bits of brains and splintered bone, but I don't know.

"Finally an old lady spoke to the family about the tomb being so close to Abner White's. They bought still another tomb in still another cemetery. The day they moved Ollie's bones, the horrible shower of missiles stopped. The next morning every scrap of the stones and bricks and stuff was gone— clean as though it had been swept, and the grass growing thick and fine, as though nothing ever had happened. And nothing queer ever happened there again, that I know of."

# (*1860*)    *The Haunted Spanish Barracks*

On the downtown woods corner of Burgundy and Barracks streets stands a great granite-faced structure which is designated in ancient historical records as being able to accommodate fifteen hundred men—soldiers, that was, of the Spanish Crown. It was built with two stories and a garret, plain and solid and austere, sometime about the year 1760. The granite was brought in slow sailing ships from Europe, and some of the walls are four feet through.

It is here that ghosts cluster in companies. Sometimes, the neighbors say, double files of them march up and down the narrow old galleries, their sabers clinking and their feet thudding in regular rhythm. Sometimes the moonlight glints on the bright metal of their equipment, and sometimes a voice issues a sharp order, to be drowned by a bedlam of shrieks and groans and curses. Then the ghostly troops vanish and only the terrible groans remain, resounding like the horror of a battlefield after the carnage has subsided.

But this was no battlefield. It has been, alternately, a barracks, a storehouse for Spanish gold, a jail, a bank, and living quarters for civilians. But the last-named use has proved a difficult problem for private owners and real estate concerns alike. There are too many tales, too many weird happenings, too many things unexplained and unexplainable, to permit of any sort of calm existence in the old place.

To begin with, the soldiers of two Spanish kings were quartered there. Tales of military roistering—the lawless excesses of hastily recruited troops shipped overseas to a far corner of the globe—are still extant. Personal jealousies, abuse of authority and opportunities for revenge were only a few of the reasons for the outrages which were perpetrated under the guise of colonial control and discipline.

One scandal there was, about which not a word leaked out for more than three generations. Then a young man, a bit too exuberant over a successful business deal, divulged his ancestral secret to a circle of his associates. The story spread like wildfire, to the dismay of numerous astute families. But it held like fingers of steel. Consequently, we of today understand many things which were still baffling keen minds in the 1860's.

In this modern age of cold fact and materialistic judgment, it is difficult to build up any real belief in phantoms and specters and ghostly voices. Cool reason scorns such fantastic notions, and assures us that these are merely products of an inflamed imagination and an evidence of most deplorable ignorance.

But spend a night in the old Spanish Barracks, with its gaping windows and creaking stairs, its dust-strewn floors and cracked walls and wind-swept galleries. Very likely you will see what three young Orleanians saw late in 1932, when they spent an interminable nine months there, rent free.

There is a winding stairway in one portion of the building, and above it, near the upper landing, is a small window set in the wall. Every night there is a light in that window, although it now possesses neither glass nor blind. Across the lighted window-space the outline of a man's head is cast—a man who sits nodding and mumbling, his head slightly bent as though he were counting coins on a table.

You can see the movements of his thin shoulders as his hands busy themselves with the silent counting. Sometimes he grins cunningly, and glances furtively over his shoulder as though fearing interruption. Sometimes a wisp of stringy hair droops over one eye, and he brushes it back with a gesture of impatience. Only one thing is of importance—the incessant counting of his unseen gold.

One of the young men who occupied the house crept up the winding stair one night, intent upon surprising the coin counter. But when he came to explore that portion of the building, he could find no door, no room—and no window where that window should be. There was the wall, to be sure, and there were the stairs. They took a tape-line and made minute measurements. But when they came to the place inside, there was only a wide corridor without window or niche. Certainly no old man, no table, no gold.

Yet did he continue his nightly performance. Even when one of them watched while the other searched, he sat there in the window undisturbed. But in the daytime there was not so much as a shadow in that strange window above the stairway.

The young men told the same things that others have told over and over again—others who have attempted to live there for a season. There were, when the moon shone brightly, a company of mammoth rats that danced a mystic round to silent music. Fat and sleek they were, those rats, with long, wise noses and thick necks and little tufts of white fur tucked under each bulging jowl. They rose on their hind legs, with their front feet clasped gracefully together, and danced as nimbly as bright drops of spring rain. They bowed and whirled in a veritable maze of intricate steps—backward, forward, left and right. And then, big as overgrown tomcats, they melted into the shadows and were no more.

The three youths strove in vain to trap them, setting out cheese and bread and bacon and cake and various other delectable morsels. But not a crumb would the fat rats touch. They seemed almost to laugh at the bait—as though, being immortal, they could afford to jeer at mortal delicacies. For immortal they are.

One of the youths, hiding behind an empty barrel in the courtyard, watching the ghostly dance, cautiously thrust forth an arm, thinking to grasp one of the rats. Instead, one of them trod on a finger—and it was as though a man had stepped on it, shod in heavy boots. The finger was crushed and bleeding and was put into splints and bandages for some days thereafter.

Then there is a narrow gallery running along a blank wall at one side of the house. It merges with a sort of passageway, which connects with a stair leading to the garret. This garret itself is a kind of labyrinth, where thick walls prove to be narrow tunnels running in mysterious and perplexing directions which never were on any builder's plan. The chance crumbling of softened mortar, the dislodgment of a loose brick—and there is a place unaccounted for and unrecorded.

Along the above-mentioned gallery, when the moonlight strikes the wall, heads appear—faces twisted in agony, eyes bulging, tongues protruding, lips drawn back in an animal snarl, noses slit from tip to forehead. They are dark faces, sinister and horrible—faces of men who suffer the torments of the damned. All in a row they stand, as they have stood for generations, snarling and leering and grimacing at whomsoever has the temerity to peer at them there in the waking night. When it storms they shriek and wail and curse, groaning and twisting and tearing madly at the wind and at the frightful wall.

Tradition says that, during the Spanish régime, the gold of the Colony was brought to New Orleans and stored in the Spanish Barracks. The place teemed with soldiery—some of them well-born, some of them habitués of Spanish prisons, some of them gutter-scum, some of them wily adventurers.

They knew the gold streamed in, they knew the strong room where it was stored under heavy guard. And the gold glowed rich and alluring. In some cunning manner it was spirited from the strong room—enough for a dozen substantial fortunes. Of where it was hidden, no record remains. But somewhere within those walls it lay. The ones who were chiefly accountable for the Spanish king's revenues from the Colony were deepest in the plot.

There was trouble in the Floridas, and troops were dispatched from the Barracks, leaving perhaps a hundred men in the building. A conclave was held, some dissenting and some agreeing to a bold plan. The ones who agreed vastly outnumbered the ones who protested. So the unruly ones were put in irons and secreted until a certain auspicious night.

On that dread night the captives were brought forth, chained more securely than before. Along a certain gallery wall were affixed heavy iron hooks, and each cruel hook pierced a man's raw back—pierced it deeply, so that that man was hung upon it like a quarter of beef, still living and writhing in agony. Some of the victims' mouths were sewed together with shoemaker's thread. And then, when the captors had spiked the poor wretches' feet to the wall, they plastered their entire bodies in with heavy cement, a prop of bricks laid evenly between them.

Only the faces they left out, so they might witness and enjoy the rare sight of their enemies' supreme torture. They had added to the horror of slow starvation by tying live rats to each man's belly, so the animal would gnaw out his vitals before it, too, starved. And then, when the poor devils were finally done for, the faces also were cemented smoothly over.

Remained only the division of the spoils, after which certain of the Spanish military gentlemen became suddenly interested in land grants and agriculture and the founding of families. That they did found families, with substantial plantations and slaves to operate them, is a matter of record. What would have been a bagatelle to the Spanish Crown served as the foundation for many a cleverly amassed fortune in the new Colony of Louisiana.

But to this day, along that awful wall with its brutal thickness, a row of knotted faces appears in the moonlight, hideous and ghastly beyond words.

And the great rats that dance, so sleek and fat and terrible—what of them? Tradition says they are the ghosts of the rat ghouls which fed on human livers and kidneys until their bellies bulged well-nigh to bursting—and then perished miserably, without air or water, in the midst of a man's rotting carcass, pinned in by the hard cement which even their sharp teeth could not gnaw away.

And the lean man in the high window, who counts and counts his coins night after night? Tradition says he was the keeper of the treasure, in a narrow room constructed between four upper walls—and that he, too, breathed his last under a layer of stiffening cement. But he comes back and back, true to his calling, his obliterated window revealed only by the knowing moon—his gold long gone, and even his name forgotten.

# (1880)  The Red-Headed Ghost of Parish
## Prison

Back in the last quarter of the 19th century tradition says that a red-headed woman stole the heart of the warden of the old Parish Prison.

The first time he saw her was on a street corner. She smiled at him, openly and without shame or reserve. In that day no woman smiled at a strange man unless she were either an adventuress or a streetwalker.

The Captain was in uniform, and this woman with the copper-colored hair was neither brazen nor cunning. Her brow was smooth and white, and her eyes a frank brown. Her wide mouth was firm and beautifully chiseled, and her teeth were small and perfect. Yet she smiled at the Captain, and turned to smile again.

It puzzled him, for he was a confirmed bachelor and hardened to the ways of wily females. The next time he paused on that corner, he saw her coming and he waited. With a grace born of experience, she smiled again and nodded. But she did not stop. It had been such a friendly nod that the Captain was disarmed for the moment.

But when it happened a third time he felt that it would be best to call a halt. Who the lady was he did not know. But he had his eye on a higher place in his profession, and scandals didn't help a man. She might have a husband, for all he knew.

The next time he saw her she was going down the steps of the prison just as he started up. She was wearing a white gown of some thin stuff, and the tail of her scarf brushed the

Captain's ruddy cheek. He felt a pleasant warmth all through him, and doffed his cap to her quite gallantly. Her smile was radiant, and he caught a word or two spoken in a rich, soft contralto. He was really chipper as he entered the grim old building.

"Who's the redhead?" he inquired of the doorman.

"Redhead, sir?" the man responded dully.

"Yes—the woman I just met on the way out. Whom did she come here to see?"

"There wasn't no redhead come in or go out, sir," the doorman replied. "No woman at all, sir, since I come on at eight o'clock, and it's now eleven, sir."

"Funny," the Captain ruminated. "Maybe she got as far as the steps and didn't have the courage to come in. Funny."

But the next day he came upon her in his own office. As he stepped in she was standing by his desk, toying with a Police Manual which lay there. The Captain noticed how white and tapering her fingers were, and how the light made a nimbus of glory round her shining head.

"Madame," he said, "whom have I the honor of addressing?"

"One who wishes you the best," the woman replied in that voice which had so thrilled him before. "Call me Charlotte, if you care to. I could not feel your presence here when I first came. Yet I thought you would be here presently to greet me. You have been among the bakers, oui?"

This was quite true, for the bakers of the city had asked for an interpretation of the ordinance having to do with the importation of certain flavorings and seeds, and a number of police officers had been present.

"How could you tell that, Madame?" he inquired.

"You smell of brioches and pain d'épices and bouchées and massepains and méringues and tartes de flan. Yesterday when I passed you on the steps you smelled of old books and leather."

"Your nose is useful, I take it, Madame," he bowed.

But he recalled that yesterday he had been to see a dealer in antique books on Royal street, and had also stopped at a harness shop on Chartres.

"What can I do for you today? You wish to see someone?" he asked smoothly.

"Oui, of a certainty I do—and I am seeing him," she laughed. "There is only one man in the world for whom I would mount prison steps. Tell me of yourself—I am eager to hear!"

A vague uneasiness assailed the Captain. After all, he was only a policeman, and he did not care to be ragged by his fellow officers about this red-headed woman who came to smile at him and offer such bold flattery.

"There is nothing to tell," he replied, wishing she would go. "I am very busy this morning—I beg that you will excuse. . . ."

Then suddenly he found himself seated at his desk, the woman bending over him caressing his cheek with her seductive fingers, smiling into his eyes, her copper-crowned head moving nearer and nearer his own. She laid her face against his, and he started away at the icy coldness of it. What was that she held in her right hand?—His bunch of keys!

In agony he saw one of the patrolmen approaching the desk—and this woman snuggling close to him, fondling his face, mouthing sweet names! What would the man think? What excuse could he possibly offer for such conduct?

"I came to report, sir—" the officer began.

"Yes, yes—but take this woman away first—she has no business here!" the Captain blurted.

"Yes sir," the patrolman responded. "But what woman were you meaning, sir? We haven't brought in any fresh ones this morning that I know of, sir."

The red-headed one laughed provokingly into the Captain's eyes.

"This woman here—the one in my lap!" roared the Captain. "I swear I don't know who she is, and I don't care! Take her away—lock her up—I don't care what you do with her, but keep her away from my office!"

"Yes sir," the officer answered respectfully. "Only, sir, there ain't no woman here."

That was how it began . . . the second time.

Although "Charlotte" did not again visit the Captain, the

prison itself began to receive her attention. Though time went on and the prison officials changed, the woman continued to haunt the place. Papers of 1882 take note of her activities.

Cell Number Seventeen was so haunted by her, and the inmates so terrified by her mysterious comings and goings, her inexplicable appearances and disappearances, that at least fourteen of them attempted to commit suicide there. Many of them succeeded.

Every time a hurry call came from that cell, whether the officers found a corpse or a prisoner half-dead from fright, they found the cell door unlocked and unbolted. This the occupant did not suspect. But the red-headed ghost-woman had been there and she had unlocked the door and drawn back the bolts.

So many gruesome tragedies occurred in Cell Number Seventeen that it was finally decided to discontinue its use. For long its door hung upon rusting hinges and dust gathered in its moldy corners. After a long time, when the old prison absorbed the Fourth Precinct Station, the haunted cell was scrubbed and scoured and treated to a heavy coat of paint and whitewash. The iron door was oiled, and the ghost no longer troubled to unfasten it.

However, the red-headed apparition was not to be discouraged so easily. She immediately transferred her attentions to the first cell from the corner of Orleans and Marais streets, in the third story of the City Prison portion of the building.

During the latter part of 1881, six women tried to kill themselves in that cell. Each jibbered of a red-headed woman who glided through the door, whispering unspeakably foul threats, laughing all the while deep in her throat and finally gliding straight through the outer wall. Yet in each instance the turnkey found the cell unlocked and unbolted. Sometimes the door would be partly open—a fact which the shivering, half-crazed prisoner did not appear to notice nor care about.

A number of times some group of bewildered prisoners wandered into Captain Bachemin's office, inquiring if it would be all right to go home. They all told the same tale—that a smiling, red-haired woman came to the cell door and opened it with a key which she carried in her hand, telling them they were free to go home and urging them to hurry. She even led them down the corridor, giving them detailed directions as to how to reach the stairway. But when they turned to thank her, she had vanished.

"Most like she's Irish," Turnkey Glennon would grin. "With her rid hid an' all, she's a rare 'un. Sure an' she's got me beat, for 'tis mesilf what locks 'em all in tight as the bark on a tree. An' yit, there they be, yellin' an' hollerin' at the top o' their lungs that they're bein' kilt dead—an' the fool door lollin' open like a fish's mouth, in spite o' me! 'Tain't like it ought to be, a-tall, a-tall."

But one of the very old turnkeys could have told them, if he had taken the notion. He could have told them of the time, when the prison was first used, that the "Countess Charlotte" was lodged in Cell Number Seventeen. Her real name he could not have recalled, for she was always the "Countess Charlotte." She was red-headed and handsome, and Lord! she had a way with her. French she was, and bold as the devil, but her manners were exquisite.

'Twas a captain in the police force whom she picked out for her advances. The turnkey was too crabbed and wary. But the Captain got to wandering past her cell every day or so. One day she called to him, and he found her so fascinating that before long he was taking her out for a stroll of an evening, now and then—handcuffed to his own wrist, of course.

Then came the night on which she left him in a Rampart street room, bleeding and unconscious. In her pocket were his keys and his gun, and the handcuffs she had worn. She slipped into the prison unobserved. How her accomplice had contrived to drug the doorman will never be learned. But a little later, when the turnkey had been bludgeoned to death on the stairs, the whole crew who had been brought in with the "Countess Charlotte" swung blithely out and away.

They found her and brought her back in less than a week. Smiling still, she heard the heavy door close on her as she was pushed into her old cell.

But she had one more play. In a crack in the wall, near the floor, she had secreted the prong of a long pin, like a hatpin. In the dead of night she fished this out and wrapped a bit of cloth around the blunt end to serve as a head. Facing the solid brick wall, she placed the point of the prong against her left breast where her heart beat, feeling for a depression between ribs. Then she steadied herself and lunged straight against the wall. Thy found her on the floor of her cell in the morning, stiff and cold, the prong driven through her heart.

More suicides occurred in this prison than in any other jail in New Orleans. Was it the red-headed phantom heaping death on death? The policemen laughed, even while they shuddered at the weird accounts and crossed themselves to ward off the evil influence of possible supernatural visitants.

One Saturday in January, 1882, Ella Scott, a colored woman, was toted in bodily between two towering patrolmen. Ella was too drunk to know or care where she was or what was to be done with her.

"Dump her in the haunted cell," somebody ordered. "She's too soaked to pay any attention to ghosts."

When Turnkey Glennon went to the third floor to light the lights at six o'clock, he noticed a white rag knotted about the bars of the cell door. The light was too feeble for him to see into the cell, so he thrust his hand through the bars. He touched a motionless fat body, suspended by the neck by means of the rag.

Glennon rushed downstairs for a knife, meeting Doorman Sheridan on the way. Together they hurried back to Ella'a cell and Sheridan cut through the knotted rag, letting the body fall to the floor.

"I'll have to be gittin' me keys," grumbled Glennon. "Wait a jiffy while I leg it downstairs."

But Sheridan's hand was on the door and it opened at his touch. The fallen Negress was helped to her feet, little the worse for her throttling.

"Whativer be ye up to, Ella, a-hangin' of yersilf like a good-fer-nothin' sausage?" the angry turnkey asked. "Were the ridhid after a-chasin' of ye, now?"

" 'Twa'n't no redhaid, neither," Ella glared at him, her swollen eyelids still quivering. " 'Twa' a *man*, an' he had a big white sheet wound round him, an' a black mask tied on his face, an' a peaked black cap down ovah his eyeballs, dat's what! An' he come runnin' in an' jab me in de face wid his fumb, an 'he yells Ah's gwine to git kilt sho', 'cayse de red witch she am comin' an' comin' fast!

"Ah runs as faw as Ah kin, an' bangs into de ole wall an' raps mah tin cup on de windy fo' help. But don't no help come. An' all de time dar's dat man, a-standin' an' a-starin' at me lak he had bullets fo' eyes.

"An' sumpin' it come rushin' an' racin' 'long in de hall, an Ah gits skeert an' tears at dar rag off mah drawers, an' gits ovah dar an' starts a-hangin' mahseff. One ghost am sho' bad 'nough—Ah wa'n't gwine stand fo' no two of 'em! Let me git out o' yere—quick!"

They took her downstairs for the remaider of the night, and no more phantoms molested her.

But they did say that the red-headed woman came tripping down the stairs after them, and that she touched Captain Bachemin on the shoulder, and that he felt her fingers like flames through his coat.

And she said, smiling that wide, frank smile that she had smiled to another Captain years before, "Tell me of yourself. . . . I am eager to hear. . . ."

# (*1874*)   *The White Skiff*

Helvar Nolt sat at the door of his tavern near the Old Basin. The April sun was hot and it shone in Helvar's eyes and blinded him. His mongrel dog, Snack, sprawled on the gallery beside him, snoring contentedly. A parrot screamed from a neighboring gallery, and Helvar groaned.

"Always it is the damned parrots!" he mumbled to himself. "Parrots in the daytime and parrots at night, screaming and squalling and driving my customers away already! If this it keeps up, me I go crazy. Sixteen years it is now—and sixteen years it is too much, oui!" He spat at a large blue fly and scraped his feet in the dust at the foot of the steps where he sat. The fly buzzed noisily and lit on Snack's ear, which jerked lazily until the insect found other quarters.

"Me I dread when night comes," the man went on to himself, his lips barely moving, his slits of pale blue eyes traveling upwards to the cloudless sky. "I get so I cannot eat, I cannot think, I cannot be a man. It is not right so. Every man has a right to say when he shall come, when he shall go, what he shall do, how he shall act. Me I might as well be black —ach, black, the devil! I am not black, by the grace of God— but I am crazy for sure! That woman will drag me to hell yet! Sixteen years me I have kept still—and worn my legs off—and worried myself out of my mind because I won't air family troubles. Troubles—oui, ja—me I should say troubles! The Wicket going to pot and my brain to jelly—damnation! Where is that wench now? Edna—Edna! You should be about the supper already!"

This in April, 1874. The Wicket set a regular table for three—Helvar Nolt and his two friends, Johann Gast and Pierre Dulac. A strange trio they were—the burly German Gast, the lean French Dulac; and the proprietor himself, whose father, old Gorm Nolt, had been of German and Norwegian stock, and whose mother was known all along the waterfront as Bingo Belle, in the days following the Battle of New Orleans. Bingo Belle, whose surname was Hollins, had claimed that her father was a Baratarian and her mother a mixture of Dutch, Créole and Choctaw Indian. Old Gorm had bellowed with laughter and said she was the spawn of an Irish washerwoman and God-knows-who.

But when evil days fell upon the old Wicket, and Gorm lay in a drunken stupor for a month because his place had fallen out of favor, it was Bingo Belle who came from the dives on the levee and built the tavern's trade up again.

Nobody ever quite knew why. Belle was tough as a goat, but she was twenty-five and she had sense. Her skin was like leather, her hair was a red mat, she had a hooked nose and big black eyes. Also she had six fingers on each hand, and wore rings on every one of them. Her feet were the quickest feet in New Orleans.

When she settled in the Wicket for good, she brought with her twenty-seven parrots and a yellow mongrel dog. Old Marie Pitard, the mulatto woman who did the cooking, looked askance at the pets. Whereupon Bingo Belle pounced upon her with tooth and claw.

"You feed my leetle birds and my chien, you yellow bitch, or I keel you!" she screamed, her hands blistering Marie's head and shoulders. "Oui, I keel you two time—peeg, feesh, hell-devil!"

Gorm Nolt was thirty-seven, and he took her to Père Antoine, at the Cathedral, where she was made an honest woman via the bonds of holy wedlock. She shrieked with laughter at the whole performance, and gave birth to a son the next year . . . *Helvar Nolt, born in New Orleans 22 August, 1816.* So the Cathedral record read. Helvar had been to see it for himself.

The Wicket had begun to prosper again. Old Marie took

over the care of the infant. She and her French jibberings were the first things Helvar remembered. His mother was always a fury from whom he shrank.

Then had come Jake, the slave, a coal-black giant bought quietly from the Lafittes at a dollar a pound—two hundred and seventy-seven dollars in gold, Gorm had paid for him. Jake could have picked up the Wicket in one hand and tossed it into the bayou. Instead of which he was meek as a lamb, receiving Belle's tirades in timid silence and her blows as though they had been drops of spring rain.

The mongrel died, and a white kitten took its place. "Mon chaton—mon cher petit chat," Bingo Belle called it, cuddling it fiercely and parading it before the parrots until they were hoarse with rage and jealousy. When it grew to be an enormous feline she called it "Mon matou, mon brave!"—snuggling it against her hard cheek and licking its nose with her quick red tongue.

Gorm would growl at that, and she would fling the cat in his face. Usually it scratched him frightfully, and he grew to detest the sight of it. But he kept still about that. Blustering and rough with everybody else, he kept his hands off from Bingo Belle, as she was still called.

By the time Helvar had turned two-and-twenty, he was alone in the world. Marie stuck to him until he was eighteen, but she was old and sick and done with living. Gorm died in a fit when he was sixty. For years he had muttered and mumbled, stuffing his ears with cotton and squeezing his fat eyelids shut as soon as night came. But every night, hot or cold, rain or shine, sick or well, he went out. Once Helvar had followed him—to be beaten and cursed and driven back to the Wicket like a disobedient child.

For eight years old Gorm had been at it. And now Helvar had been at the same thing for sixteen. Gorm had always gone alone and been alone. Helvar was less fortunate. Frequently he was followed. Of late there had been several watchers, among them an inquisitive newspaper reporter. That very week one of the daily papers had printed a highly humorous account of what was supposed to take place at midnight on the black waters of the Old Basin.

The Old Basin has been gone for many years. Old Saint-Louis Cemetery Number One remains, being one of this city's historic jewels. But the thoroughfare which it faces is now called North Saratoga street, instead of Basin street. It was on old Basin street that the Wicket flourished. Every time Helvar went to Canal street he passed the old cemetery. And every time he passed the cemetery he shuddered and remembered the muddy waters of the Old Basin, which he could see from the windows of the Wicket.

"Me I will tell them!" he declared, bringing his big fist down on the step where he sat. The yellow mongrel jumped, shook his ear, blinked, and dropped flat again with a prodigious sigh. "Oui, it is time I did tell them, and maybe ask their help. They should help, too—they are my good friends, oui. What are good friends for already, if they will not first help when a man he is in a perplexity? Tonight me I will tell them!" He got to his feet, sighing more heavily than the dog had done. "Edna, Edna—you should once hurry with the supper, ja!" He patted Snack and scratched him under the ears.

"Guten tag," beamed Johann Gast, as he came in to supper an hour later.

"Bonjour," bowed Pierre Dulac, seating himself and drawing his napkin from its ring.

"Good-day, gentlemen," nodded Helvar, from his place at the platter. "Will you have veal or mutton?"

"Pork," replied Johann, shutting his eyes. "And cabbage."

"Poulet rôti," sighed Pierre in rapture. "Aux champignons et artichauts et oignons farcis."

"Sí, sí," agreed Helvar. "It is well that we have beef pot-roast. Pass your plate, Johann—and yours, Pierre. Mind the gravy—it drips."

Then they all broke into a great laugh. Always they began supper in this way.

"But," thought Helvar, "after supper I must tell them. What are friends for, hein!"

So after supper he asked them up to his sitting room on the second floor, and lighted a tall candle on the center-table.

"My friends," he said, and sighed, "my *dear* friends, I have something terrible to tell you."

"Ah," groaned Johann, "that Snack has been poisoned! I told you those Gypsies across the bayou were no good. That is the trouble with having a dog—they always die. Mein Gott, it is tough already to lose a dog."

"Non," moaned Pierre, "it is that Edna! I knew she would not stay—no cook as good as that ever does stay! Mon Dieu!— do you think a large bottle of cologne—a very large bottle— would induce her to make in her mind the fresh decision? Ah, when I remember her gombo aux crabes—her vol-au-vent de veau—her lapin en gibelotte—her sauce veloutée! Ah, ah, what have you done, Helvar, that you make the lose of such a treasure?"

"You are both of you wrong," returned Helvar, rubbing his stomach. "It is that I have seen a ghost—that is my trouble. Ach, two ghosts—maybe three—and a flock of them also."

"What is all this talk of 'two ghosts, three ghosts, a flock of them also'?" snapped Johann, lighting his pipe at the candle. "The dog is not poisoned, nein. The cook has not left, nein. Then what, what? Out with it, Helvar! Are we not all of us the three friends already?"

"I will tell you, oui," Helvar nodded. "Only it is that you must wait till twelve of the clock. That is my trouble. After you have seen, I will first tell you the story. Is it the terrible strain I ask of you, the terrible sacrifice, to stay up in ease until midnight, when I have been saddled with my trouble like the mule for sixteen years already, ja?" His voice broke and he cupped his face in both hands as though he would shut out some horrid vision.

"Now, now, be assured!" they both cried, their friendly hands slapping his shoulders. "To be asked is to remain—you should know that. Oui, of a certainty we remain, if it be a week! Ja, a year!"

At a quarter to twelve a strained look came over the features of Helvar Nolt.

"It is the pull!" he exclaimed. "The pull that pulls me to that horrible place—the Old Basin!"

"But the Old Basin is not horrible, Helvar—except, of course, a dead cat now and then," comforted Johann.

.

"Do not say the dead cat!" begged Helvar, with a stifled scream. "Not the dead cat!"

"Jawohl—not the dead cat then already. I merely referred to the smell," Gast conceded amiably.

"Do not refer to the smell!" Helvar's face was haggard and drawn. "I am sick enough, as it is. I am pulled—always I am pulled. Come, my dear friends—and help me if you can!"

"He is pulled," whispered Pierre to the German, as they followed the keeper of the Wicket out into the soft April night. "What would you make of it, this pull, mon vieux?"

"Something that rhymes with it," Gast replied guardedly. "How much does he drink, I wonder, during the day? He walks straight enough, ja—and damnably fast, too!"

Indeed, they could scarce keep up with him. They were at the water's edge presently, and the night was black enough. But the moon was rising. In a few minutes they could see Helvar pausing just ahead of them, his eyes straining out over the dark waters. A bell rang faintly in the distance.

"It's twelve o'clock," the German said in a low tone. "Mein Gott, what is that?"

From the far side of the Basin a white skiff was moving. Nearer it came, shooting swiftly through the water. A strong wind sprang from nowhere, blowing so icy a blast that Johann and Pierre turned up their coat-collars and hugged themselves. All around the skiff played a cold white light, like the reflection from some great ice-bank.

In the skiff sat a woman, white as marble, rowing swiftly. Her body and head were sheathed in thin white draperies, and the white oars shone like paddles of ivory. In the stern of the craft stood a giant Negro, naked to the waist, so black that he shone gray. He carried a great string of fish, white as snow, their fins and tails feathered like birds.

As the boat came opposite the three watchers, it stopped. And they saw that the hands of the woman, as they rested on the motionless oars, bore six fingers each. They spread like fins, white as chalk, and glistening as though they had just come out of the water. A white cat peered from its perch on her knees.

Suddenly the boat started again. The light flared more

brightly than before, and a sickening smell of sulphur and Negro sweat floated in from the Basin. The black raised his string of fish and they turned into white parrots, circling and shrieking, dashing ashore at Helvar and pecking savagely at his face and eyes. He fought them off frantically, screaming and sobbing, but never turning away.

The boat was past by now. But on the churning waters stood the great white cat, braced like a lynx, its eyes like balls of fire, spitting and snarling and lashing out with its ugly claws. Once it made a rush at Helvar, scratching his cheeks and forehead and tearing his clothes. It exuded a scent like all the carrion in creation. Still Helvar made no move to escape.

Then, all in an instant, the cat was gone. A black fog gathered about the boat, enveloping the parrots and blotting out the icy light. The din ceased as suddenly as it had begun. Only the murky waters of the Old Basin, the rising moon, and three bewildered men gazing at one another remained. Without a word the three made their way back to the Wicket. Up in the sitting room again, Helvar Nolt relighted the candle.

"Did you hear what the ghost with the six fingers said?" he asked hoarsely.

"She said nothing," his friends protested.

"Then she must have spoken the thing just for me," Helvar returned, wagging his head wearily from side to side. "Always she says the same thing. Every night I am pulled down there to that horrible stinking place. Always she says, 'He threw me under the house, like a dead bitch, and I cannot rest! I'll pull you down here every night until you walk into the water and drown. You're his son, and I'll drown you as he drowned me. But you'll wait till I'm ready!' That's what it is she says. She pulled my father down there every night for eight years. She's pulled me down there every night since I turned forty—sixteen years, that's been. She was forty herself when she died."

"But, mein Gott, who is she?" exploded the German.

"They called her Bingo Belle," Helvar sighed. "And she was my mother."

"Mon Dieu!" gulped the Frenchman. "One's mother out

*From the far side of the Basin . . .*

on the Basin in a boat like that! Extraordinaire—incroyable! The whole thing it is so of a—a muchness!"

"You are right, Pierre," assembled Helvar. "It is altogether the too much of a muchness. Me I feel I cannot stand it any longer. And I ask you, my two friends, what am I to do—what am I to do?"

"Incroyable!" Dulac was muttering, scrutinizing Helvar closely. "It is of an utterness, mon vieux—all that fury, all that scratching and clawing—and not a mark on you—not a thread of your clothing disarranged! I am at the nothing point—I have not the explanation!"

"Gott in Himmel, how can you expect to have it?" glared Johann. "It is Helvar that has the explanation, of course. Tell us, Helvar!"

"Sit, my dear friends," Helvar returned. "Me I will go and draw the beer for us." He latched the door carefully when he came back.

"It was my father told me," he continued, as the three drank their cool beer. "He said he stood the woman as long as he could. He had fifteen years of her, you must understand. Then, when she took the Negro for her lover, my father he made him a plan. One night he took her out on the Basin in a boat. He hit her on the head, and then he held her under the water until she drowned. He brought her in and buried her under the barroom floor.

"The next night he took the slave out to fish, and shot him. He dragged the body into the swamp and left it. Nobody should care about a nigger. Then my father he drowned the cat—but he left the cat in the Basin. He starved the parrots to death—there were nearly fifty of them then, and they all belonged to *her*. Ach, it was a ghastly business already! And it was my father that did all that—he told me himself. And then he fell in a fit, and he died."

Helvar's eyes were glassy with terror, and he clasped and unclasped his great hands.

"And," he continued, in a voice of mystery and bafflement, "what is it I can do now? Some night when I am pulled down there I shall walk into the water. And all people will say is that Helvar Nolt lost his customers and went and drowned

himself. Damnation, what is a man for, that he must be drowned
by the ghost of an old whore!"

"Hush!" cautioned Johann, scandalized. "She was your
mother."

"She was an old whore, just the same. There's no getting
round that. Her blood it is in me, and old Gorm's blood it is
in me—and what am I to do?"

"Permit that we think, Helvar," suggested Pierre.

"Ja, we will think already," seconded Johann.

After a time the German moved in his chair, filling his
squat pipe and relighting it.

"Johann, he has the leetle bright thought," murmured the
Frenchman. "Permit that we hear it, mon vieux, before dawn."

So Gast unfolded his plan.

"But," wailed Helvar, "it will require weeks! And if I do
not go down to the water when I am pulled, those hellish
ghosts will come up here after me. Me I do not want ghosts
in the Wicket—things are bad enough as they are already!"

"We can strap you to a post somewhere, and we can keep
the watch," observed Pierre stoutly. "Of a certainty you are not
to blame for staying away if it is that you are strapped."

"They would come and get me!" shuddered Helvar. "They
would tear me to shreds. There is no help for me!"

"Do not be a child," put in Johann testily. "See—there is
but the one thing left to do, but we will help you. Go to the
Basin every night as usual. Always we two will be with you
there. The ghosts cannot pull you in, for we would yell. I will
take a pistol. A pistol makes a great noise. It will be only for
two or three nights. Then you will be rid of them for good
already. Come now, finish your Schnapps and we start about
things at once, ja?"

Finally it was settled. It was really a fine plan.

That night they took up part of the barroom floor and
began to dig. The next day everybody was curious . . . Ah,
mais oui—they were digging a cellar . . . to keep the beer
cold. Also, Helvar would lay in a noble stock of wines a little
later . . . and wines acquire the best flavor in a good cellar. . . .

They obtained a permit—all was in order. The few customers who stopped by in the daytime were excited and hopeful

—maybe Helvar Nolt was digging for gold pieces! Maybe he would find them . . . maybe he had an old map or something.

When the diggers came upon human bones, Helvar told the little audience calmly that the ground was once an Indian burial place. Only he and Johann and Pierre knew that the skeleton had six fingers on each hand, the dry phalanges still jingling with dozens of rings.

Helvar duly notified the authorities about the bones.

"These bones under my place," he said, looking a little bored, "they are bones of people already. No matter if they have been Indians, it is wicked to throw them out. I can put them all in a small box, and they can go in the tomb with my father. There is plenty of room, and my father he was used to the Indians. Only I am left to go in, after a while."

So he was granted permission to open the Nolt tomb and place the wooden box of bones therein.

"Now," he said to Johann and Pierre, "I hope that whore she is satisfied. I have done all I can."

To them his voice had the quality of a volcano just escaping eruption. They sighed in immense relief. They had been afraid he would erupt.

When midnight of that day neared, they were still with him, as usual.

"I feel the pull," he said, rising. "But it is not the same pull. It is a little pull—a stinging and burning here in my head, like small bees in a tree. Before, it was like a tornado, a fury—it scratched and clawed and tore, like the lynx-cat from the water. Come, we will go over to the Old Basin already. And me I will see what the little pull it means."

So presently Helvar Nolt stood on the Basin's murky edge. The icy wind sprang up, but it whistled past without the old fury. And when the white skiff and its multifingered ghost and its phantom slave and its fish and its parrots paused, the parrots remained afar off. Then Helvar spoke.

"Me I gathered your damned bones and put them in the Nolt tomb!" he cried out over the waters, his voice hoarse with rage. "But your blasted nigger and your cursed cat they can stay in limbo, for all of me! I'm through with the whole pack of you. And don't you dare come pulling at me any more!

Here's my last word to you—may you burn in hell torment as long as the world stands!"

With that, he spat into the water; and he fired his pistol at the boat, and smashed a bottle of holy water into the filthy Basin. In the twinkling of an eye the whole visitation had vanished as though it never had been.

"But why didn't you wait until the boat appeared?" Johann asked, nearly having fallen into the Basin at the report of the pistol.

"Why didn't you wait until they came, oui?" inquired Pierre, blinking in astonishment and catching his breath.

"Why . . . didn't you see them at all?" exclaimed Helvar, his mouth falling open in amazement. "I spoke to them—to *her*—and they disappeared on the instant. Me I think they were scared already."

"You are not making the leetle joke, mon vieux?" Pierre ventured gently.

"Joke—mein Gott, it is not the joke!" roared Johann. "We save for him Helvar's life—you with the holy water you give him, me with the pistol I lend him—both of us sweating like swine in that hole of a cellar—and you speak of the joke—mein Gott in Himmel, what do we come to already!"

"Me I saw them," Helvar said mildly. "Also, it was my spit. I thought you saw them also, like you have before. Now it means they came only for me, this one time already. So now I have killed them off. I am a man again. We have saved my life, oui.

"Come now, my good friends. The rest of our lives we spend together as one life. Tomorrow you move into my two best chambers. The cellar it will go on and be a real cellar. The Wicket shall be enlarged many times, ja. We shall have our share of the fine custom. We shall all three own the business. When one of us dies already, the other two shall have it."

"Ah, you make the too much of us, mon vieux!" Pierre replied, tears streaming down his lean face. "That money I have will help to build both the cellar and the new additions. I shall arrange to get it as soon as the bank is open this day!"

"Ach, it is the good heart you have already, Helvar!" Johann cried huskily. "All I have shall go into the Wicket

also. We shall be the three great hosts. I can attend to the
guests, and Helvar can see to the accounts. Pork every day, and
cabbage also."

"Poulet rôti, too, oui," ruminated the Frenchman, his
black eyes sparkling. "And a morsel of artichauts."

"And the veal and the mutton," chimed in Helvar, chuckling a little, as he used to do when first he took over the
Wicket at two-and-twenty.

Presently the three were back in the sitting room.

"Oui, of a certainty," finished Pierre Lulac, from the
midst of a rosy vision. "That Edna she makes me only to dream
of perfection. She does not know the trick. Ah—me I can prepare the sauces and the delicate dishes. Edna she will do to
wash the china and the silver. I shall take charge of our
kitchens, mes vieux amis. The guests they will travel to us from
the miles around, morning, noon and night. Consider, you
two—ris de veau aux truffes, beignets d'huîtres, crabes farcis,
chapons, papabotte grille, demi-glacé. . . ."

"Come," Helvar broke in hastily, kindly comfort flowing
from every syllable, "let us now have the cheese sandwich and
the beer already. . . ."

# (*1813*)     *The Mansion That Ghosts*
### *Carried Away*

A ways out, in the downtown portion of this city, there is a
road which forks. One fork leads to Bayou Saint-Jean. The
other ranges along to Gentilly Road, and so at length to Chef
Menteur.

It was at the fork of these roads that Daniel Clark built
his splendid rambling mansion in 1800. Daniel Clark himself
was a historical figure here. He was, at the time he built his
great house, an enormously wealthy merchant, middle-aged
and a bachelor. Later he was to represent Louisiana in Congress and gain the appellation, "the Irishman who became a
Créole."

After his death on August sixteenth, 1813, the mansion
was closed. The slaves went to other masters, and dust gathered
on the wide galleries and dainty balconies. Lawsuits began
over the Clark property and continued for decades. The windows were fastened, the doors were bolted, the batten blinds
were shut. No tenant ever came to disturb the silence and
desolation of the place.

But one night a workman, passing the house, witnessed a
strange sight. Pausing by the vine-covered gate, he saw the
front door standing wide open. Being curious, he made his way
up the grass-grown path, mounted the curving flight of steps
and peered in. From inside he could hear music—an eerie,
tinkling music—and the sound of dancing feet and merry
laughter.

Tiptoeing in, he saw a circle of Gypsies dancing round a

fire which they had built in the middle of the great second drawing room floor. The flare of the flames glinted on the gold leaf ornamenting the walls and the ceiling—caught the prisms of the chandeliers and shimmered away into a thousand rainbows—picked out a miniature of the Empress Josephine, another of Marie Antoinette, and another of La Pompadour—flashed across the diamond panes of a half-dozen windows. And in the midst the Gypsies, with their olive skins and their white teeth, their high red heels and their fringed scarfs, their clicking castanets, and the pot bubbling over the fire.

One slender dark woman there was who cried and screamed and writhed and pointed, her limpid eyes streaming with tears, her hair clothing her like a raven cloud. The Gypsy men embraced her and coaxed her to dance and forget. The old women mothered her, laying her head in their shriveled bosoms and smoothing her silken tresses. The young women and the girls held more aloof, timidly offering her roses and beads and bits of scarlet silk, and honey and little seedcakes.

Then she stepped into the heart of the fire, while the unseen watcher shuddered. Her tears dried, and she swirled in a wild and frantic dance. Faster and faster, until the whole room seemed whirling with her, the house rocking drunkenly on its foundations.

All at once the insane revel ceased, and each Gypsy laid hold of a piece of furniture. It was as though the massive things were toys, so easily were they picked up in the slim brown hands and borne out into the hall and onto the front porch.

Then the watcher stepped boldly forth—this was rank thievery and must be stopped. A moment the scene held. Then all in an instant, the Gypsies were gone, together with the things they had removed from the drawing room. They did not run away, he reported—they simply vanished as though they never had been. A horrible odor of scorching flesh assailed the man, heavy and sickening. And when he turned to re-enter the house to make sure the fire had done no damage, the front doors were closed and locked. A sprig of bay was caught in the latch. The moonlight shone in a silver flood on the cracked and uneven floor of the porch, and there in the heavy dust were his own footprints—his own, and none beside.

When the laborer told his story, his family laughed at him. The neighbors laughed, too. But some of them stole to the Clark mansion late one night to see what they could see. They reported the same mysterious experience, and they did not laugh any more. Gypsies who could vanish like that must be Gypsies from Some Other World. And that other world was something to be feared and respected—not molested nor inquired into too closely.

Came the day when one of the lawyers connected with the estate drove out for a call of inspection. To his utter stupefaction, he discovered that the entire upper two stories of the great house had disappeared bodily. It was as though some giant had lifted them off in one piece and thrown them into the sea, like snapping off the cap of a toadstool.

The lawyer forthwith stationed guards about the place. But the house continued to disappear under their very noses. Sometimes they beheld the phantom Gypsies, and sometimes they did not. In no instance did they attempt to break up the visitors' frenzied dance. But always there was less of the house in the morning than there had been the night before. Four massive stories in all . . . Where were they going?

"It's Zuleme, come for what belongs to her," the old crones of the bayou whispered when they passed one another. "A *Gitana* may take her own. Aye, aye, it's Zuleme—even her baby was taken away from her. Anyhow, the place belongs to Zuleme instead of to the daughter. Zuleme should have it—and Zuleme's going to have it—it is the *Leis Prala*.

"That Clark he was not of the *Calo* people. But Zuleme— was she not cut into ten pieces? And was not each of the pieces cut into another ten? No wonder they say a hundred Gypsies are carrying the old mansion away! Zuleme is carrying her own house off. There was no shadow-burying when that house was built, so now it is easy to carry off. Nothing sticks nor refuses. It is the *Leis Prala*."

When the lawsuits ended in 1885, not a trace of the house was visible. The ground had for years been picked clean and smooth. Not a brick, not a stone, not a timber, not a nail, not a shred of mortar remained. Yet no one had actually seen it go. Zuleme . . . and her hundred Gypsies . . . Was it one ghost or a tribe of them?

Only at night, late passers-by claimed they heard a woman wailing among the dead fig trees. On spring nights they could see her dancing between the overgrown rows of crêpe myrtles, bracelets tinkling on her ghostly arms, and her empty eye-sockets blazing with unearthly fire. When she came to the great live oak at the corner of the tangled yard, the Spanish moss reached down and enveloped her tenderly like smoke, and they saw her no more that night.

"The ghosts stole Clark's Mansion," the neighborhood said, and gave it a wide berth, dubbing it at length "Clark's Horror."

We may hark back a bit to Daniel Clark and some of his philanderings. Always tremendously popular with the fair sex, he had contrived to evade matrimony and kept the ladies, figuratively and literally, begging for his attentions.

A fortune of thirty million dollars was enough to insure a sigh of longing from every mother who had an unmarried daughter anywhere between the ages of fourteen and forty. Damsels by the score set their caps for him, widows became coy at his approach, and many a flirtatious matron would have sold her husband to the Devil if she could have been certain of becoming Mrs. Daniel Clark.

But alas for eyes of blue, gray, and brown! There was a confectioner who kept a high-class shop where the lower Pontabla Building now stands. His name was Jerome de Grange. His sweets were popular and of an extravagantly high price. The aristocratic ladies of New Orleans came to buy, to see and to be seen.

But De Grange had more than sweets—he had a Gypsy wife, and her name was Zuleme. She was petite and sparkling, her sloe-black eyes were languorous and alluring, her lips were rich and ripe, and her passionate response awaited only a suitable mate. A confectioner, no matter how dainty and delicious might be the creations of his art, was no fit mate for a ravishing Gypsy girl.

So when Daniel Clark came within range of those melting

Gypsy eyes, his feet left earth for a season. His world, his fortune, his dreams, his whole existence, revolved around one scintillating star—Zuleme de Grange. Obtain her he must.

With what variety of reasoning he impressed Jerome into his services as a species of legal ambassador, we cannot fathom. But that he did so is a matter of record. Jerome was dispatched to Europe with Godspeed and a large pocketful of cash. Immediately Zuleme packed a dozen red silk dresses and an amazing array of jewelry into a well-worn trunk, and eloped with Daniel Clark to Philadelphia.

It required but a day or so for Clark's lawyers to unearth the fact that De Grange had had an undivorced wife living at the time he married Zuleme. Not that it would have mattered to Zuleme, even if she had known. But this fact rendered the marriage void, so it was a simple matter for Daniel Clark to present himself and Zuleme to a Catholic priest in Philadelphia, and get her properly and legally married to himself.

As might be expected, once he was her lawful lord and master, her flashing beauty presently began to seem less desirable to him. The coquettish Gypsy idiom which she employed became an old story. Her tempers, her lack of education and polish, her overweening desire for loud clothes and enormous pieces of jewelry, the curses and endearments she shrieked at him whenever and wherever the whim seized her—these palled upon him so terribly that, by the time Zuleme's baby daughter was about to be born, in 1803, Daniel Clark wished devoutly he never had heard of either the confectioner nor the confectioner's lady.

Clark's fortunes continued to prosper. But he himself was like a fowl on a spit—turn which way he might, the blaze of Zuleme's wrath scorched him. He had long ago banished her from the great house. His money provided for her still, however. The child was born in New Orleans but was almost immediately sent to Philadelphia. The news of her birth was suppressed. Zuleme was suppressed also, chiefly by the statement made by Clark himself that she was not really married to him. She died some years after the birth of her child, disillusioned and bitter, cheated of the wild and delirious years of uncurbed delight which she had dreamed would be hers when she married thirty million dollars.

For the space of one little month she had lived in the Clark mansion as its mistress. Her red shoes had danced up its stately staircases, her birdlike olive face had peered out of its diamond-paned windows, her bright silks had swished in and out of its spacious drawing rooms, her be-ringed fingers had poked unceremoniously into the preserve dishes on its snowy tables, her dark eyes had sent glints of forked lightning in the direction of its master, and her shrill laughter had sent shivers of acute distaste racing up and down its sophisticated spine.

The smoothly running domestic machinery of the whole house was becoming demoralized. This slave must be sent away, that one must be whipped, the other must be ducked in the cistern. The place was too dark—all the curtains must be tied tightly back. The garden was too cluttered—she didn't like mignonette and she had seen a snake by the fence—pick all the hateful flowers and pull up the rest. Why would people fool with herbs! A priceless crystal dish had hurt her finger— smash it—throw it into the ash-heap! This dress was no good— that jewel was not right—the food was abominable—her maid was a black fool—this perfume was dishwater, fit only to be flung against the ivory satin wall of her boudoir. So it went on.

"I can stand only so much," Clark said one day to his friend, the Chevalier de la Croix. "One of these times I shall reach my limit."

"Hélas, mon vieux," the Chevalier sympathized, shaking his white head, "you will presently learn that all wives are not women. Some of them are vixens."

"Too true!" nodded the merchant. "Too true, indeed."

And suddenly one morning Daniel Clark packed Zuleme off, bag and baggage. Not a trace of her remained—clothes, jewelry, perfume, all were gone. The household breathed a sigh of infinite relief and settled back into its former efficient orderliness. Madame Salaun returned to take her place at the head of the establishment—tall, capable, wise old Madame Salaun, who had been saying her beads industriously ever since "the vixen" ensnared the man who should have known better.

Only once did Zuleme venture back. She came storming

at the great front door demanding that she be let in, that she was great with child—the child that should be born in its father's house. But Madame Salaun was occupied with the mending of a precious bit of table damask. No one had orders to open the door. The house closed itself like an oyster. And after a little, Zuleme the Gypsy went away, weeping bitterly.

The child was Myra Clark Gaines, who fought forty-nine years in the courts of the land after the death of Daniel Clark, and finally proved that she was his legitimate daughter.

No wonder Zuleme the Gypsy came back to carry off, piece by piece, the great house of the man who married her for an afternoon's pastime; and then, seeing her only as raw and unschooled, forgot that she might also be lonely and bewildered and deathly hurt. As the crones along the bayou said, it was the *Leis Prala*—the Gypsy "law of the brotherhood."

(*1916*)    *The Twin Green Spirits*

Juan Morales sat under the cherry trees with Marta Gonzales and the Three Wise Men. Marta was only ten, but the Three Wise Men were all over seventy. Juan was in between, being fifty-five and Corral Master at Jackson Barracks. He and Marta called the three the Wise Men because they were so very old and patient and comfortable, and had had more experience than all the armies in Europe. The Third District knew them as Armando Sagasta, Emilio Cardenas and Rafael Avegno—substantial citizens and lifelong cronies. Each had sons who had taken over the cares and responsibilities of business.

"I see you've got a new horse in the lot," Sagasta observed, lighting his pipe.

"Yes," nodded Juan. "That's Letty, the cream. She's Captain Geary's new mount. A nice girl, too—light-footed and pleasant and sensible, like a mare ought to be. She's a good pal for Dapple."

"You're of my mind," remarked Avegno, who was the oldest. "Horses are mighty like people."

"More'n you'd s'pose," agreed the Corral Master.

"I think they've got souls." Marta spoke slowly, in the low voice which had first induced the four to let her join their intimate circle.

"Maybe, maybe," assented Cardenas. "There could be worse things in Paradise than horses."

"Nonsense, Emilio!" snapped Sagasta. "It's worse than foolish to mix horses and religion."

"Saint John did it," grinned Avegno. "He saw a white horse in Heaven."

"I'd like to have a white horse when I go to Heaven," said Marta, making a nest for herself in the grass.

"Black Prince has got 'em all beat," bragged Juan. "He's got the style and the dash, that horse."

"I think Charley and Bos'n and Maude are pretty nice, too," defended the little girl.

"They're just boys—old steadies. Don't know a cherry tree from a cypress," muttered the Corral Master.

"Does Prince know these cherry trees?" Marta sparkled.

"Sure he does—always poking his black nose over this way."

"Maybe he talks with the tree spirits."

"With the what?" Sagasta wanted to know, raising his bushy white eyebrows.

"With Juan's cherry-tree spirits," Marta replied bravely, skinning a spear of grass down the middle vein.

"You got tree spirits, Juan?" quizzed old Avegno.

"Green ones," nodded Morales. "When the leaves come. They're green now, but I used to know 'em when they were about like Marta here."

"I expect your heart disease has gone to your head," chuckled Cardenas. "Although it would be diverting to believe in green tree spirits. The old Greeks used to."

"Heart getting any better, Juan?" inquired Sagasta. "You want to tend to it."

"Not so good," sighed the Corral Master. "But it'll last me quite a spell yet, I reckon. They used to say a weak heart makes a long life. I'll be as old as you boys in a few years."

Marta giggled. "Then you'll be Grandpa," she added.

The Three Wise Men smoked on, talking complacently of this and that. Marta went to sleep with her head against Juan's rough-clad knee. When she awoke she was alone, with her head on Juan's blue handkerchief.

"Humph!" she sniffed. "They all ran off and left me!"

She hunted up Morales and gave him back his handkerchief.

"I don't think the Three Wise Men would understand our tree spirits," she confided. "I guess I'll keep still after this."

"I guess I would," agreed the Corral Master, measuring out oats. "I've got an apple for Letty—want to feed it to her?"

"Um—um!" Marta was dancing, her dark eyes bright.

After his work was done Juan always sat for a half-hour beneath the little cherry trees. They were his trees, Barracks or no Barracks. Where did they come from? Nobody could ever answer that—not even the Corral Master. Cardenas, the dreamer, might take the story on trust. Old Avegno, the philosopher, might try to explain it away. But Armando Sagasta, the matter-of-fact one—he would laugh outright, enjoying the tale as a huge joke from first to last.

Sitting under the cherry trees, Morales smiled a little. This heart of his was tricky. It was good to sit quietly at twilight, when the heat of the day was letting up a bit.

H remembered when he was small and had typhoid. That had been in 1869. A long way back, it seemed. Still, here in the soft light of the dying day, it came back as clear as yesterday. Again he was a little boy, weak and listless and emaciated. Again he lived out in Saint-Bernard parish, fishing in the bayou, watching the crayfish, drawing queer pictures in the soft mud, making up stories about this and that to take up time until he was strong and well.

One June day he had gone a long way down the road. Madre had cautioned him not to go too far, and had had things to say about watching out for snakes. He came upon two small, dark-eyed girls perched on a stump. He eyed them a moment, and one of them spoke.

"You're the sick boy," she said.

"I'm not sick, either!" he flared.

"Yes, you are," she repeated sagely. "Everybody's sick until they're well, and you aren't well yet. I'm sorry you're sick."

"I'm not sick," Juan scowled again.

"Me, too—I'm sorry," chimed in the other small girl. They both wriggled off the stump and came over to the road.

"I'm Dolores Verde," the first one volunteered. "She's Mercedes Verde. We moved here after you came down with the fever. We're twins, and we're Spanish, too."

"Her name means Green Sorrow and mine means Green Mercy," Mercedes put in. "We'll grow like little plants, Madre says—Sorrow and mercy. Do you like that?"

"I don't know," the boy replied, blinking. "I hadn't thought. They're nice names, though."

They sat down under a tree and played a fanciful little game with twigs stuck into the ground. It was a gentle game, full of mystery and whimsical twists. Juan was to know later that everything these small girls did or said was whimsical as fairy lore.

All through that summer they played. The twins were a year younger than the boy, so he always pretended to protect them. Their chief delight was to play they were the souls of trees.

"The souls always have to live in the trees," announced Dolores, who usually took the lead. "Madre says sorrow lives longer than mercy, so I'll climb a tree that's taller than Mercedes' tree."

"But Father Prieto says mercy is kinder than sorrow," the other spoke up. "I ought to be kinder to my tree than you are to yours, then. Which tree will you have, Juan?"

"I'll call on you both. I'll be the Tree King. You can pick off buds and things for me, and I'll eat them when I come to call in my golden chariot."

"A Tree King would have a green chariot, I should think," Dolores objected.

"Leaves and flowers," supplemented Mercedes.

"Drawn by rabbits."

"Foxes. Rabbits would hop."

"Maybe tigers," suggested Juan.

They settled on tigers. It was a triumphal tour through a vast forest, where every living thing bowed respectfully as the King rode by.

"How do you do, Your Majesty," Dolores greeted, as Juan squirmed and clawed his way up into her magnolia mansion.

"I'm sorry to be late," King Juan apologized.

"A king isn't ever sorry," Mercedes sang out from the next tree. "Tell her her chairs aren't dusted—make her feel mean and small—that's the way kings do."

"I don't like that kind of kings—leave him alone, he's doing all right!" scolded the hostess. "I have some delicious food for Your Majesty—boy, bring on the supper!" She beckoned to an imaginary servitor, and gracefully handed the visiting sovereign a few small brown cones. The royal teeth bit into one.

"Gee, they're bitter!" The royal countenance puckered. "We'd better save cookies and stuff."

"Come over to my tree, King," called Mercedes. "I've got a fried-cake left."

"S-sh—call him 'Your Majesty!' " hissed the other. "Look out, Juan—I mean Your Majesty—there's a caterpillar on your neck!"

It was great fun. The other boys would have hooted at Juan for playing with girls—but the other boys didn't know. Autumn came, and they all went to school. But one Saturday, early the next spring, the three of them found a cherry tree in full bloom.

"Oh, oh!" Dolores cried. "It's a new tree—un cerezo! It'll be our tree today! I'll be its green spirit!"

"Me, too!" echoed Mercedes. "I'll have this side and you have that side—we'll play it's two trees."

"You're browner than we are," Dolores said to Juan. "You must be the Earth Prince around us."

The little girls shinned up the tree, while Juan humped himself up like a toad and hopped all round.

"I'm loosening up the soil so your roots can grow," he shouted.

A shower of white petals descended upon him.

"Now you're snowed under," Dolores called. "We'll play it's fearfully cold weather—so you're to huggle up close and keep our feet warm."

Juan obligingly wrapped his small body round the trunk of the cherry tree. He was remembering how cold his own feet had been when he had typhoid . . . and how once he had dreamed that he was dead and his feet hung out of the hearse.

"You must water us with your tears, if you're the Earth Prince," Mercedes directed. "You cry!"

"I can't cry whenever I want to, just to keep you watered," the boy reasoned.

"But if we aren't watered we won't ever blossom," mourned Dolores. "You can think of lots of things that'll make you cry. Think of how it would be if we got killed—all cut up and broken to pieces and mashed."

"That would only be when they chopped you down and made you into sticks, so the fire would be hot to bake cakes and things," Juan figured.

"Oh," Dolores shook her head, "nobody would chop down a real cerezo for firewood or anything else. They're too scarce."

"Yes, they would," the Earth Prince replied. "Mi madre has a table made of cherry wood. I talk to it sometimes, and ask it about the cerezas it had when it was a growing tree. It gets red as red when I talk, as though it were coming to life when it remembers the cherries. Then when la Madre comes in and I stop talking to it, it is just a table again—sort of a faded old reddish-brown."

"Does it talk to you, too?"

"Oh yes—lots of times."

"What does it say?"

"I can't remember just now."

"If I should die," asked Dolores, "would you plant a cherry tree for me?"

"And me, too?" Mercedes begged, wide-eyed.

"They're awful scarce," demurred Juan wisely. "Only a witch could find a real cerezo."

"We're witches," chorused the little girls. "You know we are. If we die, we'll find you dos cerezos to plant."

"You won't die," scoffed Juan. "Anyway, you won't be here if you die. Dead kids can't go round hunting up cherry trees."

"We'd come back," Dolores declared stoutly. "We're witches. And, anyhow, Father Prieto says there's everything nice in Heaven, so there must be cherry trees. I'll pull one up and bring it to you and make you plant it."

"Me, too," added Mercedes.

"That would be two cherry trees, then."

"Sí, dos. You could plant two just as easy as you could plant one. Maybe we'd stay and help you," Dolores offered.

"We aren't even dead yet," Mercedes giggled.

"Humph!" grunted Dolores. "Let's shake down more snow on the Earth Prince."

"It might spoil the cherries," Juan cautioned.

"Oh, witches won't spoil the cherries," laughed Mercedes.

"I like lilies better than cherry blossoms, anyhow," decided the boy. "Mi abuela has lilies—big white ones that she brought clear from Spain. They're long, like trumpets, and they smell like almonds and honey. I like them better."

"But they don't grow 'way up in the air on a tree, like cherry blossoms."

"But they've got a lot of big leaves, and I like them."

"If they came clear from Spain," argued Dolores, "and something happened to their roots, then you wouldn't have anything at all."

"Lilies are nicer for graves than cerezos are," Juan mused.

"Who said graves?"

"You said you'd be dead, didn't you?"

"Well, *we* could bring you lilies from Spain, then. Witches can fly round anywhere."

"You couldn't bring whole plants." Juan was digging his finger into the grass-root.

"Seeds, then," the little girls assured him.

"You'd lose them, they'd be so small." Juan wrinkled his nose upward at the two in the tree.

"We could put 'em in gum-balls," suggested Dolores.

"And the gum-balls in a bottle," added Mercedes.

"They don't have bottles in Heaven," Juan grunted.

"Of course they do," Dolores insisted. "Father Prieto says the saints have everything in Heaven, because most of 'em went without everything here on earth."

"But bottles!"

"Why not bottles?"

"You might as well say they have kerosene lamps and plows."

"No," Dolores was very sure. "God is light. Plows would mean work. Nobody has to work in Heaven."

"Um. . . ."

"Come up here with us and live in the cherry tree."

"No."

"You're afraid!"

"I ain't afraid; either."

"You are, too, afraid!"

"The tree isn't big enough for three. It'll break, and then we'll all fall."

"You shouldn't be a fraidy-cat," Dolores counselled. "Father Prieto says all fears are like skinned cats—very horrible, and always following you and yelling. And, after all, they're foolish, because they aren't real, anyway."

Juan's imagination being unusually vivid, he shivered. All that day the horrible skinned cats stuck in his childish mind—the skinned cats, which would be fears, always following him. . . .

On Friday, the twenty-third day of June of that year—1871—Dolores and Mercedes Verde were run over by a train and killed. Their poor little bodies were mangled and torn. Juan saw the man taking them from the bloody tracks. Their little heads rolled and sagged. Somebody picked up a small shoe, dripping with sticky ooze. It was too ghastly to remember. Yet Juan remembered it as long as he lived.

That week he wandered solitary down the road until he came to the cherry tree. The blossoms were gone and the breeze purred idly through the shiny green leaves. Where were the witches? Gone. . . .

When Juan Morales was in his late twenties, he married Josephine Molera. She was a sweet, pretty girl, level-headed and clear-eyed. They called him John now, and he had forgotten the witches. He was tall and strong and he worked hard. Sometime after 1900 he became Corral Master at Jackson Barracks. He and Josephine lived on Dauphine, near Jourdan avenue.

He liked the horses, and after some years he began to hobnob with the Three Wise Men. It was in 1915 that he made friends with little Marta Gonzales. She loved the horses and watched them by the hour.

"But," Juan would say resentfully to himself, "if it wasn't

for my leaky heart I'd be doing bigger work than tending to horses."

On Friday, the twenty-third of June, 1911, he came to the Barracks corral and paused by the-stable door. He had opened it to go in, but just where he would have stepped lay two cherry seedlings, less than a foot in length. Something seemed to pound at his brain, and a killing pain shot through his heart as he bent to pick them up. They were fresh and fine, the soil still moist on their young roots. Nobody owned up to having put them there.

Juan had not seen a cherry tree in years. Suddenly he saw two small girls, and heard them calling him the Earth Prince . . . "If we die, we'll find you dos cerezos to plant. . . ."

A rivulet of cold sweat trickled down the track of Juan Morales' spine. He wrapped the baby cherry trees in a bit of moist paper and laid them on a beam. He planted them at sunset-time, perhaps two hundred feet from a certain telephone pole. And he named the seedlings—one Dolores and the other Mercedes. In his heart he wondered if the witches might some day return to play with him as they did long ago. But no man says these things aloud.

The Corral Master was very choice of the two cherry trees. He watered them diligently and built a protecting fence around each. They grew astonishingly. He always talked to them, picking off persistent green-and-bronze worms and such insects as appeared hopeful of establishing a residence among the glistening green leaves. The soldiers at the Barracks laughed and called them "John's twins." He called them his twins, too, but his laugh was soft and wistful. For some reason he did mention the cerezos to Josephine, who had rheumatism now and was somewhat deaf.

One night he went back to the Barracks for something he had forgotten. It was dark, but when he reached the little cherry trees there was a vaporous green haze around them, as though each held a dim light. A still voice seemed to be speaking, but he could not understand.

One Monday, when the cherry trees were two years old—it was on the twenty-third of June, 1913—he worked later than usual. It was sunset-time when he reached the cherry trees on his way home. The green haze was very distinct this time, and it grew greener and brighter as he approached. Then he was conscious that there were two of them—slim green Shapes, with faces like cherry blossoms.

Juan stopped still. He seemed drifting into a world of dreams. He sat down between the little trees and the slim green Shapes swayed and nodded, each from its tree.

"I know you," he said to them joyously. "You're Dolores and Mercedes—and you're witches. You said you'd come back and bring me cherry trees."

"But," came a voice like a distant bell, "you said you liked lilies better. . . ."

"The lilies are gone," he sighed, remembering that la abuela was dead and her house torn down and her garden a thicket. "I haven't seen lilies like them for forty years. I wish . . . I wish I were little again, playing along the roads in Saint-Bernard . . . I wish we were playing witches and Earth Prince in the cherry trees. . . ."

He was very tired when he awoke. Josephine was a bit cross because he was so late.

"No sense in working so," she grumbled. "They don't pay you any more for it."

The next night he stayed late on purpose. It didn't matter about Josephine. He sat between the cherry trees, and the slim green Shapes with cherry-blossom faces came and talked to him. They smiled with great assurance and put a bottle into his hand—a round bottle of queer, shining crystal, like a miniature moon, with tiny brown pellets in it.

"Lily seeds," they said. "We brought them for you because we promised we would. There *are* bottles in Heaven— only you can't see them except with the eyes of the spirit. . . ."

So that was what it was . . . the eyes of the spirit. Juan found it quite marvelous. His playmates belonged to him again. He hid the crystal bottle in the earth, midway between the cherry trees, patting the sod down flat and even. The witches laughed like chiming bells when he did it.

"Graves," they whispered. "The seeds are for your grave, Earth Prince . . . Don't forget. . . ."

His heart bothered him quite a bit that week. Later, he

began wisely to slow up, saying nothing. He never had made many friends—Josephine always had complained about that.

"I want to be buried here between the two cherry trees, when my time comes," he told the Three Wise Men in 1915. "I know what I want, and it's my right to rest easy. This is my place. Josephine will want to send me out to Saint-Bernard. But here's where I belong, and here's where I'm going to be."

Sometimes in a spare hour he played whimsical games with Marta Gonzales. He even told her about Dolores and Mercedes Verde, with a sweet and mellow warmth which his diseased heart had missed for more than four decades. He spoke ruminatively to the Three Wise Men about the skinned cats, which were the fears that beset mankind. For some reason they did not laugh, discussing it with friendly seriousness.

Juan Morales died on Friday, the twenty-third of June, 1916, at three o'clock in the afternoon. Two slim green Shapes, with flower faces, slipped in through the blinds and laughed and joked with the still-faced man who breathed with such difficulty over on the bed.

"Don't you mind, Earth Prince," one of them said, as Josephine gave him a spoonful of medicine. "There's a cherry tree waiting for the three of us—blossoms and leaves and ripe cherries, all at once. It's a wonderful tree, like they have in Heaven. We're witches, so we know where it is. Don't forget the lily seeds in the bottle—they're for your grave, you know. . . ."

The medicine was intensely bitter, and Juan seemed drifting on a pale green cloud with cherry blossoms along the edges.

"Your grave," came a voice like a bell. "Don't forget to have the lily seeds planted there. Your grave—you're not going to mind it, you know. You can be the Earth Prince all the time if you like, and we'll serve cookies instead of cones. I'll bring cookies from Heaven. . . ."

"Me, too," chimed in another soft voice.

And then, while the clock in the sitting room was striking three, the slim green Shapes lifted him between them, light and willing. And down a green road they fared, laughing a little, in search of ageless cherry blossoms. . . .

Josephine buried him in the Saint-Bernard cemetery, in

spite of all his pleadings and instructions. Who ever heard of burying a husband between two cherry trees near an Army barracks!

In about three weeks, rumors began to float round the Third District. Juan Morales' ghost was haunting the cherry trees at Jackson Barracks! With tears and head-shakings, Marta and the Three Wise Men talked it over.

"It's the two little girls," she said, "that he used to play with when he was small. Their spirits came back to the cherry trees, and they're there now. That's why he comes back—he never can rest out there in Saint-Bernard."

The Three Wise Men sighed and meditated. Death was a strange and unanswerable problem. Who came back and who did not? The rumors grew more persistent.

"He wanted so to be buried between the cherry trees. It would be well to see for ourselves," advised Armando Sagasta, leaning on his cane. "Let us meet here near the Barracks tonight, and wait until the ghost arrives."

"Very well," agreed Cardenas. "My son is going to a meeting—I can get away easily. Will your son interfere, Armando?"

"He says he is going to a meeting, too," Sagasta replied. "But your son, Rafael—will he let you out?"

"He also goes to a meeting tonight," answered old Avegno, wiping his spectacles. "I think it is a lodge or something."

"They all run to some lodge these days," sniffed Sagasta.

"It may be that we shall be able to speak to Juan," Cardenas remarked hopefully. "He would speak to us, I should think."

That night, near twelve o'clock, the Three Wise Men waited. Presently small Marta came tripping lightly over the grass to them.

"Oh, so late for the little one to venture alone!" exclaimed Sagasta. "We must keep her close with us."

Others arrived, drawn by eerie reports, and huddled about, waiting for the apparition. Suddenly an electric quiet hushed the air, as though a storm were about to break. Then a sheet of vapor swirled and swung for a moment near the Barracks telephone pole. It settled and folded and hovered, and took on the semblance of a sheeted man. Its head was bent low, and it began walking toward one of the cherry trees.

A horrible stench swept over, as though all the filth in the world were breathing forth pestilence. And a squalling, hissing sound, as of a thousand cats battling for food and deliverance. Then the watchers saw in the glow given out by the pacing Shape, a horde of clawing, struggling things, red and bloody and unspeakable—skinned cats they were, shrieking their misery to the night and this wraith which walked between the cherry trees!

"It's his fears following him!" whispered Marta in terror. "He told me they were like skinned cats! Oh, oh—how they cry!"

"Why did they put him in el cementerio!" wailed old Avegno under his breath. "He wanted to be laid here—it would have been so easy."

"Wives are ever contrary," explained Sagasta, wiping the cold moisture from his face. "We could do nothing with her, you remember."

The Shape was walking from one cherry tree to the other, back and forth, the horrible skinned cats swarming after him, climbing his ghostly back, tearing at his ghostly wrappings.

"Juan, Juan!" Marta cried shrilly, wringing her small hands in despair. "Shall we chase them off? We are here with you—can't we help?"

The crowd gathered a little closer, terrified but curious. Back and forth moved the Shape. Once it turned a terrible countenance toward the four—the soft flesh falling from its jowls. With one bony hand the wraith scooped away the skin and stinking mush, wiping the facial bones clean. Small Marta closed her eyes and doubled up on the grass.

"One moment . . . pardon . . . I am sick!" gasped Cardenas.

The other two turned away.

When they looked again, the ghost of Juan Morales stood midway between the two cherry trees. A slim green slip of vapor moved from each tree toward him, and the ghastly cats slunk away. The green mists gathered on either side of the phantom, and together the three moved to the telephone pole and vanished.

The crowd melted away.

"I ought to have told you about the bottle before," Marta said, weeping softly.

"What about la botella? Tell us, little one," urged old Avegno gently.

So she told them about the crystal bottle, like a miniature moon, and the gum-balls in it.

"He buried it here between the trees, and told me not to tell," Marta said. "He thought when they dug his grave here they would find it and plant the seeds—the seeds of the lilies from Spain."

"Las rosas de pasión desde españa!" whispered Cardenas reverently.

"Could you show us the precise spot, niña?" Sagasta asked.

Marta walked a little way, pausing midway between the cherry trees. The moon had come out and the world seemed soundless and at peace. Marta pointed at her feet.

"Here," she said.

"Where los gatos fought the most savagely!" muttered Cardenas, shaking his grizzled head.

"We shall dig, señores," announced Sagasta. "It is fortunate that somebody left a spade leaning against the tree."

"Por Dios, the spade was not there a moment ago!" exclaimed Avegno.

"Nevertheless, it is here now—and a very good implement it appears to be."

After a few spadefuls, something shone bright in the moonlight. Sagasta bent his old back and picked it up.

"It makes my hand prickle," he said.

"It is the bottle from Heaven!" whispered the child. "The seeds are inside—for Juan's grave."

"And there they shall be planted!" declared Avegno. "I am older than any of you. It is now nearly two o'clock and we are very tired. Give me the strange bottle. This day we shall all go to Juan's grave and plant the lily seeds for him."

They slept little that night. Before noon they reached the Saint-Bernard cemetery and sought out Juan's grave. Marta dug two holes with a trowel—one at the head and one at the foot. The queer, luminous bottle was uncapped, and she peeled the gum from the tiny seeds. She laid the gum and the bottle in old Avegno's hand, and dropped the seeds into the moist earth. But the bottle and the gum vanished even as the four looked.

"It is a queer business, all of it," Avegno declared, wiping his watery eyes and shaking unsteadily on his old legs. "I hope Juan's lilies will grow."

"We must come back tomorrow and water the seeds again," said Cardenas wearily.

But when they returned on the morrow they found two great plants, full of perfect white lilies.

"I cannot understand it," reasoned Sagasta. "Yesterday we plant the seeds, and it should take a whole season—maybe two —for them to make plants of this size. Yet here they are—here they are."

"They smell like almonds and honey," Marta ventured, sniffing hard.

The lilies seemed to lean toward the four, as though they smiled and invited.

"It is not permitted to pick flowers from graves," said Cardenas the dreamer. "Nevertheless, these are the lilies of peace. Juan has his desire. Marta, pick a flower for each of us. Juan would have had it so."

It is said that when the Three Wise Men died, one by one, Marta Gonzales found an additional flower beside her own. And when she put the stems in the ground, they rooted and blossomed anew. Marta died when she was eighteen, and the lilies died with her.

But Juan Morales slept peacefully, nor ever again visited the cherry trees with their twin green spirits.

# (*1874*)     *The Lost Pearl*

Late in January of 1874, two Orleanians, Hubert Grahame and Numa Pitot, went on a hunting trip. Returning with well-filled gamebags, they thought to save time by taking a shorter route home.

They were near Lake Pontchartrain, and turned to cross what was then known as the "cut-off," in Bayou Saint-Jean. It was nearly dark, and the white shell road underfoot was only a gray ribbon blending with the dusk.

"We'll both have fine dinners tomorrow," remarked Grahame as they crossed the little bridge. "I promised my brother-in-law a brace of rabbits, but I'll do much better than that by him."

"It was bécasse I was after," returned his friend, "and I got twenty or more, besides a dozen bécassine. My wife stuffs them with truffes—which is hard on my pocketbook, but worth the expenditure."

"Ah," rejoined the other, "you make my mouth water. It'll be pitch dark before we get home, and I am already starved."

"Of course," grinned Pitot. "Wait a moment while I light a cigar."

A brisk wind was blowing, and Grahame held his cap in a way that would shield the feeble flame of Pitot's sputtering sulphur match. As the match flared higher it made a dazzling splotch of light against the blackness of the swamp.

They had just stepped off the bridge. As the flame leaped up they saw a woman standing close beside them. She seemed to have sprung from nowhere, and both men stared in astonishment. She was a young woman, scarcely more than a girl, and she was dressed all in black. Her hair shone like pale gold, and there were little ringlets on her white forehead.

Lying across her shoulder was a tiny babe, sleeping sweetly, its long white dress, with tucks and lace, like a cloud of gauze against the young woman's black gown. She clasped the infant tightly, almost jealously, as though she were afraid someone might attempt to wrest it from her arms.

"Ah, madame, pardonnez-moi!" exclaimed Pitot, seeing that they stood directly in her path. "It is dark—we did not see you coming."

She answered not a word, nor even glanced in their direction. Instead, she crossed the road, stepped to the edge of the bridge, and walked . . . where? There was only one place to go—the water, dark and deep and slow-moving, creeping with the queer night creatures which stared out into the shadows with strange, unblinking eyes, wriggling their slimy bodies along the wet banks and among the bayou plants.

No splash, no cry, no rippling of the muddy waters. And yet—the woman was gone. Had she suffered from some mental agony so keen and cruel that the waters understood and received her soundlessly? Who was she, that she came out here to drown herself and her slumbering babe?

It had all happened in an instant. The two men gaped at each other in bewilderment.

"Now, what did she go and do that for?" gasped Grahame, dropping his cap in his perplexity. "A pretty ending to a fine day's hunting, I should say—watching a woman commit suicide!"

"I never saw anything so quick," said Pitot. "One moment she was here, so close we could have touched her—and then she was walking right into the bayou. We must try to rescue her, Hubert—we can't let her drown like that!"

Dropping his bag and gun, he stripped off his coat and shoes. In a moment he was floundering in the murky bayou, splashing about in an effort to locate the woman. In vain he searched.

"The water's icy," Grahame called from the bridge. "You'd

*She answered not a word . . .*

better climb out and we'll try to get help. No use catching your death of cold—she's beyond help by this time, anyhow."

Finally Pitot hoisted himself onto the bridge.

"I can't imagine what became of her," he puffed. "She went down right here, I know she did, and she never rose. But I never touched anything. Ugh, I'm cold—and the water's a stinking mess!"

He pulled on his coat and shoes, and they started away.

"We're sure to meet somebody," Grahame said. "They'll probably know who she might be. There comes a couple of niggers with a lantern now."

"Hey, boys!" Pitot called. "Come here with your light—a woman's just fallen into the bayou!"

"Yassah," one of the Negroes replied. "Right yere, sah. Bad place on de bridge in de dawk, sah."

"She came along just as we stepped off the bridge," Grahame put in. "Young woman with a baby—bareheaded, too. Know who she is, maybe?"

The Negroes looked up with rolling eyes, huddling close together.

"'Fo' Gawd!" one of them gabbled. "She am yere agin! Come 'long, Teazy—come 'long quick!"

"Was yo' lightin' any match, sah?" the other black boy inquired, his face gray and scared.

"Why, yes—I lit a match. I was going to smoke a cigar," Pitot replied. "Why?"

The Negroes did not wait to answer. Already they and their lantern were flying down the road by which they had come. They did not cross the bridge.

"Well, of all the—" Grahame began.

"Mighty funny," Pitot grunted, trying to sort out his jumble of thoughts. "Looked like they were scared to death."

The two men started on, Pitot wet and shivering. Presently they met a white man carrying a lantern. They stopped him and related the story of the suicide.

"'Twa'n't no suicide," he grinned. "You seen the ghost of the bridge, that's all. Lots o' folks claim they seen it, but me I ain't never took much stock in it. They say you can't light a match near that darned bridge after dark without the spook an' her young 'un appearin' and walkin' off into the water."

"It wasn't a ghost," Grahame snapped. "I reckon we'd know a ghost if we saw one. It was a living woman, I tell you. And we want the loan of your lantern, to see if we can't pull her out of the bayou."

The stranger handed over the lantern without another word, and back went the three. But no trace of the woman could they find.

"And you won't find nary a footprint, neither," the man chuckled. "Look all you're a mind to."

It was true—in all the soft soil at the end of the bridge, and in all the dirt on the bridge itself, there was no print of any woman's shoe.

The man took his lantern and went his way. Grahame and Pitot hurried to their respective homes, amazement tying their tongues. Only once did they speak.

"Tomorrow night," said Grahame, "we'll go to that bridge again. I don't believe it, but it's queer as hell."

"I'll see you tomorrow, then," Pitot nodded. "You're right —it's sure queer as hell."

The next night the two men walked to the bayou bridge and waited. Nothing happened.

"Oh, pshaw!" Grahame yawned. "This is a fool thing for two grown men to be doing. I don't suppose either of us saw a thing last night, except some shadows on the bridge. We scared the Negroes out of their senses, and the white man saw a good chance to fool us. We'd better get on home."

"Wait—I'll see what time it is," returned Pitot. "I'll bet it's one or two o'clock."

He struck a match to look at his watch. In the flare of the light they saw a young woman just at Pitot's elbow—a young woman dressed all in black, with pale gold hair, and a baby sleeping on her shoulder. She glided to the edge of the bridge and stepped noiselessly off into the black waters.

"My God!" Grahame groaned. "It's the same woman!"

"It's a ghost!" hissed Pitot. "That's what they all said, too —it's a ghost! And it is!"

"Was," corrected Grahame. "Let's get out of this. I don't want to see *that* again!"

"We might as well light the lamps we brought, and see if we can find anything," suggested the other. "It seems so utterly foolish just to get scared off, like the niggers were."

So they lit the lamps and peered down into the water and all around. But there was nothing. Within the next few days they called at a newspaper office and related their strange tale. There seemed no solution to the mystery of the "ghost of the bridge."

Then one day a young woman came to the Pitot home. She brought with her a little book, which was the diary her deceased sister had kept. She had found it in the pocket of an old trunk, wrapped in a handkerchief of yellowed lace. Her sister's name had been Anais Bellaumé Renoy.

It seems that in 1857 Anais Bellaumé and Robin Renoy were married in the old Saint-Louis Cathedral. He was twenty-two and she was twenty. They had a modest little house in the Faubourg Marigny, with a flower garden, three canaries, a mockingbird and a nightingale.

"But you are the loveliest bird and the sweetest flower of them all," Robin told his golden-haired bride. "I wish I could give you pearls and silks, instead of calico and muslin."

"I don't need such things," Anais replied. "I have the most precious pearl in the world—your love. That is all I need and all I want."

She was intensely happy, and all the work about the little house was a joy. She hoped there would be a baby after a while—Robin loved babies. Her younger sister, Manette, was always teasing her about having a large family.

Manette visited the little house almost daily. She was eighteen, extremely pretty, and more daring than Anais ever had dreamed of being. She said quick, pert, provoking things in a way which always sent Robin into gales of laughter.

Sometimes Anais wished Manette would not come so often. She began to feel that she was sharing all her days and all her doings with her sister. But when she mentioned it to Robin, he took quite another view of the matter.

"I believe you're jealous of your own sister, Anais," he

chided. "You ought to be ashamed. Manette is the one who keeps things bright and lively."

"Bright and lively"—so that was what Robin wanted, was it? Robin, who had loved her quiet ways and her low voice and her gentle dignity! Robin, who had said she was perfect, and his dream of dreams! Robin. . . .

Anais' days became a misery. She began to hear words she never had noticed before. She caught glances between Robin and Manette. Once she saw them holding hands a moment, when the nightingale was singing.

Manette did not visit them so often as she formerly had. There was a new aloofness about her, too. But Anais had no word which she could speak in confidence. Her sister was no longer her sister—she had become an interloper, a menace, a coiled serpent.

Anais wrote it all down in her diary, which she kept hidden in the pocket of her trunk. It was the only way she had of enduring this agony which had crept into her life.

"Love," she wrote, "was a precious and beautiful pearl. Now I have lost it . . . or else it never was. Perhaps all the time it was only a wax bead. But I thought it was a pearl . . . and now it is lost. . . ."

Robin seemed to sense no change. Sometimes he spoke of a family, happily and naturally. Anais now had a secret, but she did not tell it to Robin. She did not know whether a baby would be welcome to him or not. Once she would have gone into ecstasies over the prospect of a child. Now motherhood looked blank and thankless enough. She grew quieter than ever.

One day Robin came home before noon and asked her to pack a lunch for him. He was in a hurry, and she saw him winding a heavy brass chain around his waist.

"I'm going to set some traps near the lake," he said. "I've got so much to carry that this is the handiest way to tote the chain. It'll be late when I get back."

And that was the last time Anais ever saw him. When he did not return that night, she grew desperately worried. But when her mother visited her the next day and said that Manette also had disappeared, Anais knew well enough what had happened—Robin and Manette had gone away together.

Madame Bellaumé came to live with her deserted daughter and take care of her when the baby was born. The little one arrived in April of 1860, six months after Robin went away. Anais did not care whether she lived or died, but she lived.

When the infant was a month old, Manette came home with her new husband. They had eloped the day Robin disappeared. But Manette had not seen Robin, nor did she know what had become of him. She had been in love with this Jules Avart for some months before the elopement—she had confided in Robin, but was afraid of telling Anais.

So, after all, Robin never had been in love with Manette! They never had gone away together. Anais, his wife, had been misjudging both of them all the time!

But now a great, fierce flame burned in Anais Renoy's heart. Where was Robin? What had happened to him? Why did he stay away? She had kept silent all this time, believing in his perfidy. Now she began to search and to inquire. She asked everybody. She went herself to the woods and the swamps bordering the Lake, walking endless miles, peering this way and that. Once she found his coat, near a sprung trap. She hugged it tightly to her, praying for Robin.

One night she dreamed a dream. She thought she dressed the little one in its long christening robe of soft cambric, all lace and tiny tucks. Laying the baby across her shoulder, where it loved to sleep, she walked out into the wild country along Bayou Saint-Jean. The rough ground hurt her feet and the underbrush scratched her cheeks, but the babe slept on.

She reached a footbridge at the "cut-off," and stood a moment gazing down into the dark water. The stars were out and they dappled the water with a thousand points of light. And suddenly she saw Robin's white face lying under the water. The earth seemed to whirl round, robbing her of a foothold.

She closed her eyes a moment. When she opened them, there was Robin rising up out of the bayou, smiling radiantly and beckoning to her.

"Don't be afraid," he said softly. "I have found your beautiful lost pearl, and I want you to come to me and get it."

She stepped fearlessly off the planks and went to Robin, the water never so much as wetting her shoes. How strong and warm his arms were, how sweet his adoring kisses! The babe lay between them—Robin's son! And there in her hand was a pearl, lustrous and lovely! Robin had placed it there. She thought it must have grown in his heart, it was so alive and flawless. She clasped it tightly, almost forgetting Robin in her great joy and gratitude.

And then . . . she awoke. She knew it had been only a dream. But she wrote it down in her diary, every darling detail of it, so she never would forget. It would be good to read and to remember . . . honey for a hurt heart. But she never told it to anybody.

When Robin's small son was three months old, Anais died They found her one morning, straight and cold in her white bed, a smile on her stiffened lips. The baby died the next week. But they never heard from Robin.

So now, in 1874, Hubert Grahame and Numa Pitot knew whose ghost they had seen on the bayou bridge.

"Do you suppose Anais Renoy's dream meant anything?" Grahame asked his friend one day, when they were talking it over.

"I'd hate to think it didn't," Pitot answered. "I have my own ideas about what happened to Robin. I think he was coming across the footbridge on his way home—they say it was only a few planks loosely spiked on then. That was more than fourteen years ago, you know, and the bridge isn't much even now. Maybe he was careless—stooped to light his lantern, or something—maybe a plank flew up and hit him—and he fell in and drowned."

"But his body would rise," objected Grahame.

"He had a heavy brass chain wound round his waist, the diary said. Supposing it caught on some submerged cypress roots—there are plenty of them along there. That would hold him down for all time. There's really no current there. The faint tides wouldn't dislodge anything of weight."

"We ought to have the bayou dragged there," said Grahame.

And that is what they did. Under a great mass of cypress roots and water plants, lay what had once been the body of a human being. Around its middle was coiled a heavy brass chain. A gold watch was caught in the débris of a rusted lantern. On its case was engraved, *Robin Renoy, 1856.* It was the watch his father had given him on his twenty-first birthday.

'Tis said that when the poor remnants of the body of Robin Renoy were lifted out of the water, a misty figure followed them—the figure of a slim young woman with a babe sleeping on her shoulder. And that, until the body was placed in the family tomb, the slight figure kept faithful vigil beside it.

Drawn by Anais' love and longing, had the spirit of Robin Renoy walked terrestrial ways one starry night, to tell her the grisly secret of his watery resting-place? And did he, with heavenly understanding, that night restore to her eager hand the pearl which she had mourned as lost?—the perfect pearl which is, after all, the only treasure mortals are permitted to possess, through a lifetime of struggle and of tribulation.

True it is, though the ghost of the bayou bridge had walked for more than fourteen years, frightening whomsoever chanced to strike a light there, it never was seen again.

When Denise Mercier received a proposal of marriage from Louis Augarde in the spring of 1866, she was so happy that her older sister, Georgine, knew at once that Louis must finally have made his declaration of love.

"It's about time, too," she smiled to herself. "He's been sending Denise flowers and music until it has become almost embarrassing, and I do think that a box of bonbons twice a week is straining convention. He has given her three volumes of poetry—Christmas, Easter and birthday.

"Personally, I think some of the Browning poems are shocking, although Lord Tennyson himself writes somewhat floridly at times. But that awful Shelley really was an atheist and had children by everybody. I noticed a kissing poem marked, and I've been meaning to speak to Denise about it. However. . . ."

Denise broke the joyful news to her sister after breakfast the next morning.

"I knew it would surprise you intensely," she rippled. "Louis is so sweet, and he's going to build us a new house—think of that! I told him he mustn't be extravagant. But he said he would have had to build a new house for his mother, if she had lived."

"The money was hers—she could have built her own house," Georgine returned crisply. "Of course, I know Louis has inherited more from that Parisian uncle since her death. But if she had lived she would have inherited instead of Louis. Sometimes I think Louis is inclined to boast."

"Oh, how can you be so unjust!" cried Denise, bursting into tears. "You do not know how tender and beautiful he is! Why, when he proposed to me he laid a beautiful white rose against my lips, and then —against his own. He said my lips were too pure for any man to touch, unless I myself asked to be kissed."

"You didn't ask, I hope."

"To be sure, I did! I was engaged to him by that time. It was quite correct. Doubtless you, at twenty-eight, consider kissing light and silly. But it isn't, when one is twenty-three and has just promised a lovely man to become his bride."

"H'm," mused Georgine speculatively. "I dare say he hasn't an idea of how low in funds we are. I dread to tell him, but he must not believe us well off and then find, after marriage, that we are virtually paupers. If it were not for Mother's beautiful wedding veil and white satin gown, I don't know how we could manage clothes for the wedding."

"I told him," Denise rejoined, drying her eyes. "He said he was glad—he wanted to feel that his money was providing everything for me. He loves me so, Georgine—he said he wanted to dress me in satins and velvets and load me with jewels. Isn't it beautiful?"

"It sounds indecent," objected the older sister. "He is thirty years old, and I suppose he thinks of you as a child. But, just the same, you will have to direct his household. This house of ours will soon pass from our hands—there is no other way. We still occupy it, as you know, only because of Judge Jussan's kindly intervention. But everything will go. I shall, of course, find employment."

"Oh, Georgine!' begged Denise. "How can you humiliate me so? Find employment, indeed, like a common working-woman—I shall never live down the disgrace of it! You will live with Louis and me, most certainly."

"Most certainly I shall do no such thing. I can do beautiful needlework, and I can support myself nicely by sewing. I have learned more rigid economy in the last five years than you suspect. The war taught me that much, at any rate."

And, thought Denise, if David Allston had not fallen at Antietam, Georgine would now be happily married, with a home of her own. The knowledge of her sister's great loss always softened the younger girl, even when Georgine's tongue grew bitter. She deemed it wise not to pursue the subject of sewing. Of course, Georgine would live with them in the new house.

"We are going to have a large family," Denise remarked. "Louis thinks large families are beautiful."

Georgine raised her hands in shocked horror.

"You are positively vulgar, Denise!" she exclaimed. "Only young women of loose morals speak of having large families—and you became engaged only last night! I cannot understand you two—talking about babies before you are even married!" And she rushed upstairs to her own chamber to hide her blushes and repair her shaken poise.

As for Louis Augarde himself, he was at that moment breakfasting in his cottage in Columbus street, between Roman and Prieur. The cottage had been his mother's, and its comfortable proportions and arrangement suited him. During the war while he was away, Philo and Gilly, an old colored couple who had been slaves in the Augarde family since he could remember, had kept the place in order and repair.

When he was about twenty, and his mother still alive, he had become enamored of a dark, handsome French girl. Lydie Abbesse, she was, and so she had remained to this day. The girl was of common stock and little education, and it was not a difficult matter to persuade her to accept him as a lover. His allowance was ample and his mother generous. The small house he furnished for Lydie, a half-dozen squares away, served as a pleasant retreat. His mother and friends never suspected him in connection with such a place.

During the war he had no idea how Lydie lived. She could have told him, but she did not. He had been home a year now. At first, he laid the hard lines in Lydie's face to anxiety and hardship. Certainly everybody here at home had been at wits' end during the terrific four years of conflict. Louis was generous in his dealings with her, and he paid all her debts. He felt it was due her to make up, at least in part, for his late financial neglect.

Then he began to tire of her. Occasionally he found her under the influence of gin, and at these times she was loud and coarse. A chance remark gave him an inkling of how she had existed during his absence. She had grown careless about her clothes, too. Once he found a dead cat on her sofa. She explained that it had died during the night, and she had forgotten to remove it. Louis' revulsion was acute.

Lydie had no maid and refused to hire one. She declared she was poor and couldn't afford the luxury of servants. When Louis assured her that he would gladly contribute the wages for a maid, she laughed stridently and said she'd be glad of the money herself. He laid a hundred dollars on the parlor table. In a sudden rage she flung the bills in his face.

"You leave money for me," she screamed, "but you run over to Denise Mercier, in her fine house on Esplanade, and leave her flowers and poetry! Do you think I don't know what you're up to? You may be crawling into bed with her, for all I know—but hardly, with that strait-laced sister of hers. But you would if you could—you smooth-tongued, evil-eyed, lying skunk! I ought to know—I've had seven years of you. You're as full of lies as a goose is of guts. Take your filthy money— I'll live on whatever comes along, like I did for four years, and precious little you'll care!"

Augarde had left her without a word.

Then had begun a series of letters and messengers. Once Lydie even came to the cottage, begging his forgiveness, entreating him to return to her arms. In pity, he again visited her small house. He found everything polished and swept and scrubbed and in exquisite order, herself in a new dimity dress, and a plump cat purring on the gallery.

Suddenly he was again charmed with her. The dancing dark eyes, the mobile mouth, the white forehead, the slim hands—he gathered her to him and called himself a fool for his sulking.

But their quarrels became frequent. Always he had a taunt for her, always she had a stinging word for him. He grew to hate her, but he dared not desert her now, because of what she had been to him. One word of this to Denise Mercier, and his future would be wrecked. He came to know that there was no safety for him any more. Always Lydie Abbesse stood in the doorway between today and tomorrow, leering and threatening.

Slowly and carefully he devised a plan. He thought over it day and night. He revised it and added to it during his solitary meals, with old Philo standing attentively behind his chair. He elaborated on it while he viewed the roses and cape jasmines in his garden. When he pressed Denise to his heart, his plan expanded and blossomed.

He owned a good deal of ground in that section of New Orleans known then as "back of the Second District," below Esplanade avenue. Two squares from the cottage were more than four city blocks which were his property. Most of it was vacant land, with a few magnolias and stunted live oaks growing here and there in the light underbrush.

One day he visited Lydie Abbesse and told her he was going to marry her. She was almost speechless with amazement and delight. His only request was that she keep the plan a secret until the wedding day. He gave her a sum of money for clothes and anything else she might see fit to buy.

"But," she told him simply, with a new modesty which sat queerly upon her, "all I really want is you, Louis." And she spoke the truth.

She always had adored him, desperately and with the certain knowledge that marriage with him never could be for such as she. There were insurmountable barriers. But now he had cast them aside. She was to be his wife.

"I shall build us a new house on some of my ground up the street," he told her. "Workmen have already begun clearing it. Presently I shall take you to see it. We shall be very happy there. And you must never take another drink of liquor."

"I never shall," she promised.

Truly, workmen had cleared away the undergrowth. Louis Augarde himself pottered about one portion of the ground, spading and hoeing, to the increasing anxiety of old Philo who was sure "Mass' Louis" was inviting sunstroke and heart failure and general prostration from such unnecessary labors.

"Him what done got all dat money," Philo grumbled to old Gilly. "An' den spadin' an' shov'lin' an' muckin' round in

de dirt, a-messin' hisselff up lak a ole rivah rat—an' cain't no-
body say nuffin to 'im widout he flare up an' bite yo' haid off.
'Tain't natch'l or lak him. He done got sumpin on de mind,
Ah says."

"I've started the garden myself," Augarde told Lydie the
next week. "I've planted a white althea. Tonight we'll walk
over and you can see how the place is going to be arranged—
where I've planned to set the house and where the garden's
to be. I've sent to Havana for some flowering oranges and other
choice shrubs. You'll be very happy there."

"I shall be very happy wherever you are," replied Lydie
quietly, thinking of the baby she would have next year, and
maybe another the year after that, if all went well. She would
be a good manager, too, and keep the new house sweet and perfect for Louis and his friends.

It was near midnight when he came for her. She put on a
neat dark dress, and they walked at a good pace. The moonlight was bright, and she could smell fresh earth as they turned
into the path leading to the future home. They paused under a
magnolia tree and she turned to look where he pointed. She
could see a tall althea with white buds and a multitude of
shadowy leaves. She wondered how he had contrived to plant it
and keep it so fresh and fine.

At that moment Louis Augarde reached his arm around
her from where he stood, and shot her through the heart. She
sank to the ground without a cry. As she lay still, he took two
long wooden skewers from his pocket and thrust one into each
of her eyes, so deep that he could feel the points strike the
occipital bone. No danger of her ever reviving now. He was
rid of her.

The moonlight was not so brilliant now, and there was
still much to be done. The althea must come out. When the
pit beneath it was so deep that the man could stand upright
within and peer over the rim at the uneven earth, Louis
climbed out and dropped the limp body to the bottom of it.
Then, soaked with perspiration and weary in every muscle, he
replanted the althea tree, tramping the ground down solidly
around it and obliterating every small track of Lydie Abbesse's
shoes.

He would buy the house where she had lived, clear it out and sell it again. No trouble about that. There would be no awkward questions.

Now that the thing was done, he felt as though he had leveled a mountain. Damn the woman, he should have done it long ago! Nobody ever would bother to investigate what had become of a girl of Lydie's morals. Now he could marry Denise Mercier, with no fear of a dénouement.

The next day when he went to potter about in the new garden space, there were blood-red blossoms on the althea tree.

"I thought I planted a white althea," he growled to old Philo. "They cheated me. This one is red."

"De blossoms dey am snow-shite, Mass' Louis," the old Negro declared. "Yo' has wukked so hawd yo' is all tuckered out. Bes' lemme git some black boys to spade an' hoe an' plant all dem fings, suh."

"A red althea," Augarde was mumbling. "I could have sworn it was white yesterday."

"It *am* white," persisted Philo.

Then Augarde knew. It was a white althea. But, because of the scarlet woman whom he had buried deep beneath its roots, its blossoms always would look red to him. He shuddered, and the althea seemed to turn and stare at him, asking him questions he did not dare to answer.

The carpenters came, and the masons and the plasterers. The house was all but finished. It was to be the house where he and Denise would live. He would have uprooted the dreadful, accusing althea, but he did not dare. All the other altheas in the neighborhood were through blooming for the season, but this one's leafy branches hung thick with blossoms. It was a daily aggravation and torment.

One evening just at dusk, when he was walking with Denise and her sister, their footsteps turned toward the new house. The wedding day was already set.

The place was gray and shadowy and very still. The sky looked cold and hard.

"We must put a lamp-post at the gate," Denise laughed, "otherwise our friends might miss their way. We shall have ever so many friends, Louis—everybody will come to see our beautiful new house. I could name fifty people who scarce can wait."

She was very gay, and all at once she turned her attention to the white althea tree.

"Isn't it wonderful, Louis!" she cried, reaching up and picking one of the half-closed blossoms.

The tree flared and flamed like red torches to Augarde. He wondered that the bud she picked did not scorch her white fingers. Each one seemed to have an angry, evil tongue enclosed in its center. The gray-green leaves looked like demon-wings, hovering and gloating and waiting to pounce.

"Don't touch it!" Louis commanded harshly, beside himself with black fury.

"Why, what do you mean?" the girl asked, her eyes wide. "Isn't it my tree? You said it was my tree—that you planted it for me, and because of our love it blossomed as no althea ever blossomed before!"

"Yes, yes, my love!" In an instant he was all penitence. "I thought you had picked a rose and it would hurt your pretty fingers."

"But there are no roses here, Louis."

"That is true . . . I had forgotten, my pet. Do you approve of the gallery railing and the marble steps?"

The moment passed, and Denise forgot it. But Georgine Mercier did not forget it.

"What color is the althea?" she asked casually.

"White," replied Denise.

"Scarlet," answered Augarde, before he thought.

"But," thought Georgine, "scarlet cannot be distinguished by moonlight."

Then a strange thing took place. The althea seemed to gather itself into a cloud—white to the two girls, blood-red to Louis Augarde. It made itself into a shape—the shape of a woman, tall and straight and willowy. It raised a bony finger and pointed at Denise. Then it bent down and traced something in the fresh bare earth. Then it was only an althea tree again.

The moon rose higher, and the place glowed with a soft, full light.

"It wrote something in the dirt!" Denise shivered, shrinking close to her betrothed.

"Nothing, my love!" he reassured her. "Let us get on home. It is growing chilly and you will catch cold."

Georgine was stooping, looking sharply at the ground under the althea tree.

"What do you see?" Denise asked.

"Two letters," Georgine replied. "L and A."

"That is for Louis Augarde," said Denise. "It means that we are to live here and be happy—the Louis Augardes."

"They say ghost-letters mean death!" Georgine thought in alarm.

But to Louis Augarde the two letters meant a different name—Lydie Abbesse. For Lydie Abbesse still lay beneath the roots of the althea tree.

Others saw the strange phenomenon, for the newspapers of the day mention it. But tradition picks up the tale and gives us later developments.

Every time Louis Augarde and his fiancée saw the white althea tree at night, it assumed the strange, glowing shape of a woman, and with a bony forefinger printed "L A" in the soft earth. A month after the wedding, when they came back to the new house from their honeymoon, the tree was still in full bloom. When it rose in a silvery cloud, Augarde one night pulled a pistol from his pocket and shot at it—the same pistol with which he had shot Lydie Abbesse.

Denise shrieked in alarm, but nothing disturbed the apparition. It bent and wrote "L A" in the dry soil, as it had done so many times before.

"Let us have the tree dug out!" Denise sobbed.

"Hush, my love," Louis whispered, holding her close. "It is only our imagination. It does not write at all. The smoke descends from the chimney, and we are foolish."

"But," thought Georgine, when Denise told her, "there was no smoke before the house was finished."

Georgine would not live in the new house. She had heard of Lydie Abbesse, but she never opened her lips.

When the baby came—a little blue-eyed girl—Louis Augarde drew a sigh of relief. Surely now the cursed althea tree would have done. But when he gazed down from the gallery, that first hour after the little one's birth, there the tree stood, its blossoms blazing fiery red, venomous and vengeful.

When the baby was three weeks old, Denise ventured out into the yard. The sky darkened suddenly. All at once a fork of lightning struck the althea tree, under which the young mother sat with her babe. They found her there a moment later, dead and terrible—both she and the infant scorched to black cinders. A breeze was blowing through the althea tree— a demon chorus of triumph and hate.

The next night Louis Augarde shot himself under that same althea tree. It stood soundless and motionless, its white buds rising from the branches like pointed candles of sacrament.

There being no other relatives, Georgine Mercier inherited all the Augarde property. And one night, very late, old Philo began to dig. The white althea came out. Gilly and Ivy helped, with Georgine directing. When Philo had dug faithfully for an hour, he came onto odorous human bones and a woman's shoes. Georgine knew whose they must be. And when Philo handed up the sticky skull, with slimy hair and the skewers still thrust deep into the decaying eyesockets, Georgine knew well enough who had thrust them there.

She had Denise's body removed to the Mercier tomb. And in its place, in the Augarde tomb, went the bones of Lydie Abbesse.

"Because," Georgine said to herself quietly, "that is where they belong. That is where they kept crying out to be laid."

The Negroes kept the secret well. The althea tree, set back into its socket, bloomed and faded, as other altheas do. Each summer it blossomed luxuriantly, and in the wintertime it rested. But never again did it assume the shape of Lydie Abbesse, and never again did a weird forefinger write in the soft soil. It had become only a white althea tree.

# ($1849$-$73$)    *Golden Slippers*

In August of 1873, according to a New Orleans newspaper of that time, two clerks in a store on Common street, near Saint-Charles, worked very late one night, it being twelve o'clock or after when they finally finished.

One of them, Alexander Rogers, went upstairs to get his coat. While he was putting it on, he heard a great commotion on the third floor. Knowing that the upper rooms were used only for storage purposes, he concluded that some thief had crept up there and was rummaging for loot.

Still, the sounds were peculiar. No one person would be likely to make all that clatter—certainly not a thief, who naturally would work as quietly as possible. Even several thieves would take care to avoid a racket of that kind. Young Rogers paused to listen, his hair rising on his cold scalp. The only thing he could think of was great animals in chains, striking out in vigorous but vain attempts to escape, their chains clanking and crashing as they threw themselves about.

Roger's common sense told him that there were no chained animals in Harvey Steiner's store, where he had been employed for some years. He was on the point of shouting to his friend, Malcolm Trask, when he bucked up and decided to investigate by himself. If there proved to be thieves, he could yell for help. Besides, it might be well if Trask were downstairs where he could rush out for reinforcements.

Carrying the lamp which he had brought up from the store, Rogers started for the third floor. Nearing the top of the staircase, he shaded the light with his hand and gazed ahead of him. There, huddled in the wide hall at the top of the stairs, was a group of tall black figures. Their sable draperies swayed as though they stood in a light breeze. So gaunt they were, so voiceless, yet seeming to eye him through and through. The clerk's knees all but gave way under him. What was happening on this third floor, anyhow?

Then the black forms began to walk. Round and round they went, weaving in and out, backwards and forwards. One of them reached for the lamp, took it from Rogers' hand and blew it out. An uncanny wheezing and twittering filled the place, along with a heavy smell of rancid oil and grease and human filth. Something drew him up the last three stairs until he stood in the midst of the black, billowing shapes.

The hand which had grasped the lamp was red and raw and horrible. There was no lamp-light now, but an eerie luminescence lit up the place with a yellow glow. The shapes seemed to be moving the very walls. Rogers' ears ached with the crunching roar they made. He expected momentarily to be hurled to the ground, with every bone in his body crushed amid the wreckage of the building.

And then the shapes shed their wrappings. What Rogers saw sent him into a frenzy of terror. His frozen limbs suddenly came to life. He dashed down the stairs, falling more than running. The lamp came crashing after him. The stairway was pitch-dark, and the frantic clerk's breath came in great gulps.

"What's the matter up there? Did you fall?" Trask was calling from below. "You've broken the lamp. Come on down."

Rogers was down by that time, his face like chalk and his whole body shaking.

"What on earth ails you?" cried Trask. "You look as though you'd seen a ghost."

"I have!" gasped the trembling clerk. "You go up there and you'll see plenty of them!"

"You're crazy!" sniffed the other. "You ran into the broomsticks and things, most likely—the porter keeps his traps up there. You sure made enough noise."

"I didn't make any noise at all—it was *them!*" Rogers rejoined. "You go up and see for yourself, if you don't believe me."

Trask started bravely up. But in a moment he came plunging down.

"There's something wrong with this place!" he panted.

"What did you see?" Rogers asked ironically.

"I saw a red naked woman—and she handed me a pair of yellow slippers—here they are—"

But they were nowhere.

"Why, I had them in my hand—I couldn't let go of them —I was trying to get rid of them all the way downstairs—"

Then the two young men looked at each other.

"This place is haunted, that's all there is to it!" declared Rogers.

"That's enough to it," added Trask, short of breath. "Let's get out before something worse happens."

It took them but a moment to lock the store. Out on the street, they ran until a watchman eyed them.

"We'd better slow down," puffed Trask. "We'll be arrested as burglars or something."

"I'm not going to my room and sleep alone tonight, after what I saw," returned Rogers.

"Nor I," declared his friend. "We'll both sleep in my room. It's nearer, anyway."

It was when they reached the room that Rogers realized he had left his coat on the third floor of the building on Common street.

"They pulled it off," he said. "I expect it's in rags—and it was a pretty fair coat, too."

But he did not tell Trask what the shapes had looked like when they raked off his coat and shed their own shrouds. He was curious about the yellow slippers, but they tried to talk of things more sane and reasonable.

The next day they told the other clerks in the store, and were treated to a riot of ridicule. Ghosts, indeed! Why, hadn't Rogers found his coat on its own peg, where he had quite likely left it? Wasn't the third floor in its usual order, with not even the dust on the boxes and barrels disturbed?

Not a broomstick was out of place—not a mop, not a bucket, not a scrubbing-brush. Not a door was ajar nor a window unfastened. The lamp was smashed, truly—but any scared jackass could smash a glass lamp without supernatural assistance.

"Laugh all you please," snapped Rogers. "But I know I saw ghosts up there. I tell you what I'll do. I'll lay a five-dollar bill on one of the barrel-heads in the third-story rear room, and any of you who is willing to go up and get it after midnight may have it."

The offer was taken up with enthusiasm. When night came the whole force waited until twelve o'clock. Then Flint, the bookkeeper, and Morrison, his assistant, started upstairs. But they came stumbling down, falling over each other in their terrified haste, their eyes bulging and their faces bloodless. The other clerks gaped helplessly.

"What did you see? Tell us!" they chorused.

"Go and find out for yourselves!" groaned the two, their teeth chattering. "Never mind what we saw—we're getting out of here right now!" And home they went.

The next day Rogers found his money where he had left it. In daylight the place held no terrors.

"I'd like to know why those horrible ghosts come here, Malcolm," he said to his friend one day. "I'm going to poke round up there in the daytime a bit, and see if I can find anything."

"I found an old newspaper clipping in my aunt's scrapbook when I first came here," observed Trask. "It said a man by the name of Emile Ducorneau had a shop here in 1849, and it was haunted then. Crowds used to gather in front of it, and the paper advised that they be chased away."

"That was twenty-four years ago," mused the other. "I wonder who had the shop before that."

"A shoemaker named Lucien Feraud," replied Trask. "That's all I know except—"

A customer approached at that moment, and he did not finish.

Later in the summer, after many daytime visits to the third floor, Rogers discovered a loose brick near the great fireplace. He pried it out. In the cavity behind it was a pair of small, golden-yellow dancing slippers with high heels and silk lining.

They seemed to stare at him, as a person might do, appraising him silently and impartially.

He put them down hastily and reached his hand into the dusty hole for the flat, lead-wrapped packet upon which the slippers had stood. It contained a smallish book bound in red Morocco. The pages of fine, pointed handwriting were all in French, which Rogers could not read.

But Mademoiselle Armantine Parseval, who lived on Bourbon street, and whom he expected to marry shortly before Christmas, could read it. She translated it aloud to him, amid much shuddering and many and profuse blushes, and the most solemn exhortations never to let "Maman" know. But the little book was preserved, along with the story of it.

It appears that in Paris, along about the year 1828, there was a clever cook named Gaston Donnet. He was at that time only twenty-three, but his culinary powers were so extraordinary that the management of the Palais Sauvinet, a most excellent and widely-known restaurant, engaged him as assistant chef.

The little book (it had been his private journal) revealed that Donnet took a deep but wisely controlled interest in the affairs of government. Not that he possessed even a trace of aspiration in that direction. But he could remember seeing, as a child, the great Emperor Napoleon. He had heard the mighty one's voice, the beat of his drummers, the sun gleaming on the flanks of his cavalry mounts. He had heard about the golden bees and the wistful violets of Malmaison.

So, later, he subsisted on the crumbs of gossip during the Villéle ministry—followed by the Martignac ministry and then the Polignac ministry. By the time Charles X abdicated in July of 1830, Gaston was head chef at the Palais Sauvinet. In August he built a vast and beautiful cake and called it Le Gâteau du Roi. He waited a cautious hour, and added the name of Louis Philippe.

That same year the celebrated Comte de Tréville and some of his titled companions one day honored the Palais Sauvinet with their presence. To Gaston this was almost equal to a visit from God Almighty. He outdid himself in the matter of succulent meats and delectable sauces and the choicest of other foods.

But young Pierre, the garçon de garde-manger, reported overhearing the distinguished one criticize the crêpes sucrées, which Gaston had prepared with especial genius. Monsieur le Comte had observed that he would have preferred an additional meat dish.

Gaston, insulted and wounded and in a white fury, called all the gods to witness that no chef could have served another meat dish without sacrificing utterly the fine balance of the menu. Everything had been perfect, adorable, divine. And yet that filthy pig, who was only a comte, dared to express a criticism! Nom de Dieu, did the upper crust possess no perceptions at all? So . . . wait until that superior one came again to the Palais Sauvinet—if he ever did! He should be fed scraps and husks and boiled toads!

That night Gaston, after an altercation with the leering Pierre, chased him into a corner of the pantry and ran a knife through him. The boy died on the instant. Suddenly Gaston realized that he had doubtless cut off his own head. He bolted the door and shut his eyes tightly in order to think. The place was closed. There was only one thing possible. After all, what did it matter?

Gaston had, like many another culinary artiste of his time, a tiny personal kitchen which was his sanctum sanctorum. It was here that he created his choicest dishes, building them like ships and universes, smacking his lips and squinting his eyes and clicking his tongue at each matchless new combination of flavors. It was an iron rule that no foot except his own ever trod the snow-white boards of its small but sacred floor. Here was a fireplace, a fearfully hot, forced-draft fireplace. It was as useful for consuming tripaille as it was for hastening experiments.

So now he brought a tub into this petite cuisine, along with the limp body of the impertinent pantry-boy. Of course the blood must be scoured from the pantry floor. . . . A little lye came into use for that.

Back in the petite cuisine, the chef set to work in earnest. Every morsel of flesh was sliced from the bones of the dead youth. He was fat, but there was not as much of him as Gaston had feared. The bones went into the hot little fireplace, with a special extra fire laid under them. In an hour they were charred and sufficiently shapeless. When they had cooled, Gaston gathered them into a sack.

The flesh he prepared in various ways, keeping his mind on young pork and plump capons. He chopped and he seasoned, he pickled and he stuffed. And when le Comte de Tréville and his friends returned the next day, he sent his personal compliments to the chef who could prepare platters of such distractingly delicious meats. One tidbit he particularly enjoyed . . . a little pickled trifle which had been the pantryboy's tongue.

Also, there was a garnish of delicate sausages—saucissons macis de cochon de lait, Gaston named them, with a wide flourish. . . . He hoped the weighted sack of charred bones had sunk permanently to the bed of the Seine. . . . He had been in a hurry, of necessity. . . The boat had been small and leaky and the night had been black as hell's pit. . . . It had been wise to row quite a distance, as dawn was alarmingly near. . . .

With the awakening of the Palais Sauvinet that morning, Gaston had called for young Pierre. Where was Pierre? He was needed for a thousand errands, the young devil. Was he ill? Send for him. . . . But Pierre had not spent the night at home, it developed. Gaston raged and tore his eloquent hair. Wait till that *chenapan* returned—what a beating he would be treated to! That vaurien, that scélérat, that fainéant! Bah!— why must un chef de supériorité be hampered by such worthless trash! A new garçon de garde-manger, and at once! It would be well to keep a garcette hanging behind the door of la petite cuisine for this new one, oui.

But in less than a week that gourmand, le Comte de Tréville, descended from a coach, accompanied by a score of fashionables. They must have another feast, like that one the other day. Oh la-la-la, that marvelous cochon, those heavenly saucissons, that farci, that foie gras, those rognons sautés! Non, non— 'twas too much to expect today—such foods required special preparation, certainement. Tomorrow, then—oui, oui, demain soir. So tomorrow night it was.

Gaston could feel the cold sweat rolling down his backbone. His career was at an end! Le Comte de Tréville had eaten the pantry-boy, oui. But Gaston could not continue to cook pantry-boys. He had personally scoured every dish and utensil in the place with lye. That was bad enough. But to risk another boy. . . . Well, to be sure, this new one, this Georges . . . he was awkward and slow . . . and very fat. . . .

Again the lusty call in the morning for a missing garçon. Surely it was enough to turn one's hair gray, this contending with stupid help. Benêts, rustauds, butors, poux! Where had that other Pierre gone? And now this execrable Georges! Get another—anybody, from anywhere! Monsieur le Comte and his party—so great a distinction, so vast an opportunity—everything must be ready on the instant—the entire occasion must be la perfection en personne—flawless, complete.

Never was there so magnificent a judge of food—never was there so munificent a critic, his criticisms all compliments. His Majesty himself should taste these enchanting delicacies, particularly that luscious pièce de résistance, le cochon de lait! . . . This Gaston must be summoned to the royal kitchens—he should receive a décoration . . . he should be favored by a special blessing from the Pope. . . .

But two mothers were ransacking Paris for two insignificant, loutish pantry-boys. Somebody had found a bloody shoe behind a wine-cask—Pierre's shoe. And somebody else had found Georges' lucky piece in a tub—the lucky piece which the boy's mother had pinned to his shirt.

And the next day came a royal messenger from Louis Philippe, King of the French, commanding the immediate presence of that marvelous chef, Gaston Donnet, whose art had completely captivated le Comte de Tréville. . . .

But Gaston Donnet, listening from the passageway, was suddenly nowhere to be found. The little door in the courtyard led to many directions—all of them away from the Palais Sauvinet. There was a ship sailing in an hour, and its chief cook had been killed in a street brawl. So came one Lucien Feraud, tallow-faced but determined. He was a shoemaker by trade, he said, but he had once been a cook, a quite acceptable cook. . . . It was a small boat and there would be no difficulty. . . .

There were three cogent reasons for the creating of Lucien Feraud. First, there were the persistent mothers; the bloody shoe and the lucky piece would surely accomplish the ultimate downfall of the Palais Sauvinet. Second. Gaston had been compelled to leave one of the sacks of charred bones on the bank of the Seine, for dawn was breaking . . . and the guillotine was still unpleasantly sharp. Lastly, in the palace of Louis Philippe there would be no available pantry-boys and no suitable petite cuisine—he would fail miserably and be compelled to retire from royal favor in humiliation and disgrace. There was no corner of Paris where he would be safe. Better that unspeakable village called New Orleans, in faraway America, of which one heard now and then. . . .

So after some weeks on the turbulent deep, came Lucien Feraud, shoemaker, to New Orleans. During the decade following, he married a wife and perfected himself in the art of making fine shoes by hand. In 1845 he rented the three-story building in Common street, near Saint-Charles. He had living quarters on the third floor, and his shop was on the ground floor. On the second floor was a beautifully appointed salle à manger, large enough for only a smallish party, but serving the most delectable and outrageously expensive foods in the country.

Word concerning the viands at La Petite Coquille crept round the élite circles of New Orleans. Gradually it came about that one must make reservations days in advance. Even then the patrons were picked with a discriminating hand. It was almost a case of, "Will La Petite Coquille permit us to dine there?" But oh, the dishes that were served! The smallest conceivable portions—mere bouchettes—but of so great a variety that the guests were sated before dessert appeared.

That Valéntin Dumèstre, who ran the place—ah, he was the marvelous fellow! Black-haired, thin-lipped—he of the creative soul. . . .

Only Lucien Feraud, the shoemaker (or shall we say Gaston Donnet, late chef de cuisine du Palais Sauvinet de Paris?), knew how and when and why the gray-haired maker of boots and slippers became transformed with wig and wax and the judicious application of certain cosmetics, into the culinary genius known as Valéntin. Soline Feraud, the shoemaker's slow-thinking, heavy-stomached wife, had not the faintest suspicion that the expensive dining-place on the next floor was owned and operated by her spouse.

Feraud (or Valéntin) had now his own priceless petite cuisine. It was not a little room, any more than his salle à manger, La Petite Coquille, was a little shell. It was, in fact, quite spacious, being the room at the back of the living suite. He kept it securely locked and bolted—it was where he drew designs for new and costly shoes, he told Soline. He forbade her ever to enter it, lest she disarrange his patterns and leathers and various precious materials and fabrics, too delicate to keep downstairs in the shop.

Again he was serving those strange and entrancing dishes which had all but turned the head of le Comte de Tréville, and would have turned his stomach had he dreamed what it was he was rolling on his aristocratic tongue. It was Valéntin alone who knew where to buy the cheapest slaves and how to fatten them quickly.

No need now to drop a sack of charred bones into the river. He merely had a false wall built along two sides of his petite cuisine. All he had to do was to climb up on a small extension ladder, pull down a sort of trap door a foot wide and the length of the wall at the ceiling, and drop in the charred bones. They were almost feathery ash, and there was room for millions of them.

He had kegs and jars of meats in choice pickle. One he was especially proud of—it cost his guests the most of any. It was made of slave-tongues, tender and delicate—"fruit de garde," he called it—"fruit that will keep." And there were gently-spiced brains, ribbons of liver, potted kidneys, minced hearts, shiny little saucissons de sang, made from warm blood, slender loins marinated in oil and wine and saffron and bruised almonds. Neat rows of them on spotless shelves. And a narrow secret stair which led down to the tiny, locked Petite Cuisine just off from the main kitchen of La Petite Coquille.

Money was rolling into Valéntin's coffers. And money was

rolling into the battered, dusty moneybox of Feraud the shoe-maker, too. For Negro skins, skillfully and properly cured and tanned and bleached, made the most heavenly dancing slippers for the pretty daughters of rich Créoles living in the Faubourg Marigny. The Americans, too, from the Faubourg Sainte-Marie above Canal street, ordered Feraud's lovely handiwork, frequently bringing unset jewels to be sewn into the exquisite embroidery. Feraud was becoming an institution.

One day Soline grew consumingly suspicious. Her husband was gone night and day. She wondered if, by any chance, he ever visited that restaurant on the second floor. She would just creep down there, dodge in quietly and have a look round. No one would mind. She could say she had made a mistake. She waited until night. Her rooms were so very still and lonely. . . .

It was Lucien whom she saw first, arrayed in immaculate white linen, a chef's snowy cap set jauntily atop his strangely black hair, a waxed moustache (which her Lucien never had had) on his upper lip, and somebody addressing him almost reverently as "Valéntin."

So this was it—this masquerade, which took him away every night while he pretended to be designing patterns for shoes! Her features contracted with white-hot fury, her eyes glazed, her fingers curled like claws. She would scratch that blandly smiling creature, who was her shoemaker husband—she would drag off his starched cap and his black hair and his gay moustache! She would—ah, that son of a pig—

He was smiling at her, his eyes twinkling, his back bent in a courtly bow.

"Ah, Madame la Duchesse," he murmured, in that voice of silken smoothness which even le Comte de Tréville had mentally noted so long ago. "Ah, Madame, we are charmed and honored beyond words! Will Your Grace but step this way with me, and view for yourself the divine morsel you mentioned on the occasion of your last gracious visit to our poor table?"

He was ushering her into the kitchen. And then he was hustling her up the stairs to his own petite cuisine . . . The heavy little mallet which tapped the temple precisely right . . . The five indispensable minutes . . . Poor, foolish Soline. . . .

The incomparable Valéntin was back in the salle à manger, dropping an airy, complimentary remark anent the pleasure and appreciation of the cousin of French royalty, who had never in her life been kept waiting longer than thirty seconds.

Valéntin himself, presently out among his shining cooking utensils, his jars and his bottles and his strainers, was thinking of Jules Cantrelle. Monsieur Cantrelle was a customer of the somewhat uninteresting cordonnier, Feraud. Monsieur Cantrelle had a handsome daughter who desired a pair of more beautiful dancing slippers than New Orleans ever had seen. Mademoiselle Cecile's feet were well-developed, but the slippers must look as small and dainty as Cinderella's. Only Lucien Feraud could do it. Monsieur Cantrelle sighed, spread his hands and shrugged his graceful Latin shoulders—and observed politely that money was absolutely no object.

So now Valéntin, otherwise Feraud, was seeing a dazzling light in the direction of Mademoiselle Cecile Cantrelle's dancing slippers. There would be white skin this time. It could be turned into the semblance of pure burnished gold . . . each pore a repository for the precious dust which Feraud understood so well how to apply and manipulate . . . and at once so soft and pliable and satiny. How it would cling to the warm foot, ironing out every awkward line, making every curve smooth and lovely and of the extreme grace. How they would glisten and shimmer . . . Ah, without doubt it was a stroke of rare fortune that Soline had projected herself into the sacred precincts of La Petite Coquille. . . .

Well, the gifted Valéntin reflected, he was now forty-three years old. Certainly it was high time that he began to count his fortune in six figures. Another month, and he could do so. This was February. Ah, yes . . . March, then. By autumn he would have . . . Ah, well, this was scarcely the moment to be reckoning in detail. Here was a little jar of tongue in almond wine. . . .

The next day Lucien Feraud was busy with designs for Mademoiselle Cantrelle's slippers. A week, perchance two weeks . . . Ah, they would be incomparably exquisite. Those small emeralds and seed pearls, the fascinating silk lining, the provokingly high heels, the adorable curve of the instep . . . and

*. . . so soft and pliable and satiny.*

the gauzy-thin, clinging, shimmering leather, so mysteriously fine-grained, so rich and so alluring. . . .

Feraud was deluged with orders. The gray-haired, stoop-shouldered, nearsighted shoemaker could scarce keep up with them. His wife had gone to visit relatives in Saint-Louis, he said, so he had to get along with the housework as best he could. He would finish all the shoes as soon as possible, he promised . . . "Ah, Feraud, do not kill yourself working, but I beg that you will have the rose-colored slippers done so I can wear them to my birthday ball" . . . Mademoiselle Cantrelle also was having a birthday ball—the last great function before Lent. . . .

It was a day in June of 1848, when Monsieur Cantrelle burst into the shoemaker's shop and flung the shimmering slippers into Feraud's face. A heel struck him on the cheek, and the blood ran down onto the slipper he was holding.

"Your cursed slippers!" Monsieur Cantrelle shouted. "Take them and keep them—they are the shoes of the Devil! All day they jibber and whine to my daughter, saying they are twice worn—that a woman named Soline wore them for forty years! What does such babble mean, Feraud? Who was this Soline, and why does she talk through these cursed shoes?"

"You do me a grave injustice, Monsieur," Feraud protested gently, mopping his wound with a handkerchief and dropping the slippers. "What would I know of any Soline? Slippers cannot talk. What am I to think of a complaint so fantastic, save that you merely wish the return of the money you paid for your daughter's slippers?"

The golden slippers lay on the bare floor, and Monsieur Cantrelle had stalked out of the shop. The shoemaker could visualize his whole following of rich customers forsaking him, the moment they got wind of the tale of the ghastly golden slippers.

And now those dainty creations were tapping themselves across the floor towards him, mincing and squealing and mewing. They moved exactly as Soline used to move, hesitating and uncertain, and they sounded as Soline's voice used to sound when she talked to him through the bolted door of his third-floor petite cuisine. On they came, like teeth clicking and nibbling. They touched his foot, and he shrank back in terror. But they were on him, climbing his back like squirrels, nuzzling at his ears, reaching round to choke off his breath.

He tore at them, flinging them from him like rats. He could hear them squeal softly as they struck the floor . . . as Soline's fat body had done that other night when she slumped on the floor of the petite cuisine. Then they were at him again —up his back, nuzzling under his chin—mon Dieu, what was to become of him!

Up the stairs he rushed, the golden slippers clicking after him like castanets. He slammed the door at the head of the stairs, but they came through, regardless. Into his petite cuisine he flew . . . There they were at his heels, squealing and jibbering and whining in little lisps . . . like Soline. Shuddering, Feraud grabbed them and flung them into a jar of sour wine, clapping the cover on tightly. But they were out again in an instant, drenched with the red of the wine which so resembled blood.

Came a loud hammering at the street door, and the shoemaker turned his distracted attention to this new irritation. He hurried down, the golden slippers but a step behind him.

"I want a man by the name of Gaston Donnet," a burly giant announced in gruff French. "Is he here?"

"But a moment," murmured Feraud. "He is upstairs. I will tell him."

"And," spoke up the giant's companion, "I want a man by the name of Valéntin Dumestre. Can you tell me where to find him?"

"He also is upstairs," bowed the shoemaker. "I shall have the pleasure to ask him to step down to you."

The two waited while Feraud climbed upward. His knees shook like camphor-leaves in a river wind. His breath whistled through this thin nostrils, and his eyes saw nothing—nothing except the hellish golden slippers pattering on before him, as Soline used to go before him up the stairs.

He shut himself into the petite cuisine. And instantly the place was full of shapes. They muttered and pushed and crowded, craning their necks to get a good view of him in his misery and terror. And not an inch of skin on any of them!

Red and raw and oozing with slimy mucus they were, sticky and nauseating. The room was packed with them.

And in front of them all, nearest to him, stood Soline, her skinless cheeks sagging, the roll of soft fat around her ample waist hanging by shreds . . . and in her raw hand, the golden slippers which once had been her own skin . . . She advanced upon him, her awful eyes wobbling in their sockets like oysters.

Feraud gathered his wits. The French authorities and the New Orleans authorities had found him out. Downstairs the officers waited. He had murdered dozens of slaves, two white boys and a white woman. He would be put to death for his crimes. They would drag him away. Perhaps a mob would seize him, tearing him limb from limb. There never could be any end now except death. He was done for.

The terrible flayed shapes were pressing close to him, grinning and mouthing. He picked up a long knife and thrust the point against his breast. But one of the hideous shapes wrenched it away from him, driving him towards that little extension ladder which he had used so frequently. There was a ghoulish roar gathering in the petite cuisine. It drove him, in frantic terror, up the narrow ladder. The stinking shapes clustered about him like huge bats, their noisome hands pushing him and smearing his face with offal.

But the golden slippers were the worst. They perched upon his shoulders, clawing the flesh from his bone, pecking his eyes out, vomiting filth into his yellow ears, peeling his scalp from his skull, wrenching at his teeth, dragging his tongue from its roots, slitting his palate to ribbons, knotting themselves about his Adam's apple, whistling and squealing and mewing. . . .

Finally they pushed him through the long, narrow opening and flapped the trap door shut. The brittle burnt bones of a hundred slaves crunched under his feet. They thrust themselves into his arteries, tore his nerves out like ravelings of silk, pried his joints apart, skewered his kidneys and mashed his liver. Then they squeezed him dry, the golden slippers grown heavy as mountains of lead upon him. And there they perched on him, mocking and crowing and sniggering obscenely.

After a time the shoemaker emerged from the ghastly bone-crypt. But he was no longer the shoemaker. He was Gaston Donnet, young and straight and comfortably plump. He passed through the wall which shut away the discarded bones, in precisely the same manner in which the dark shapes had emerged. The shapes were gone now. Only their obscene giggling and bubbling echoed faintly in the corners.

The lithe Gaston removed a brick from above the fireplace, reached into the hole behind it and pulled out a small red book. He read every page, smiling queerly. He made as though to twist it up and destroy it, but it would not be destroyed. Neither could he erase a word of it. Some force pressed him down into a chair, compelling him to dip his pen into the accustomed inkpot.

So he added two more awful pages, in a bold and strident hand. Sometimes he dipped his pen into the jar of red wine, stained weeks before with Soline Feraud's blood. . . .

When he had finished he turned the pages this way and that, appraising them whimsically. Then he put the book back into its secret place. But before he could clap the brick into the opening, the golden slippers had popped in and plumped themselves on top of the lead-wrapped diary . . . as Soline used to plump herself into a chair after a morning's ironing. And then the whole petite cuisine was a howling nightmare again, with Gaston in the midst of the fiendish shapes, at their mercy —and this time no escape possible. . . .

They crowded upon him, crushing him down and down, the terrible golden slippers beating a merciless tattoo on his raw back.

At the bottom of the stairs (so the diary ran), the burly giant rapped loudly on the street door a second time.

"I wanted to see that Gaston Donnet," he said in French to the other caller. "I have come all the way from Paris. We have had a devil of a time tracing him. Le Comte de Tréville has died and left this Donnet a vast sum of money. Le Comte, it seems, one day dined . . ."

"Oui, oui, Monsieur," sighed the other impatiently, "the shoemaker is annoyingly slow. I wished particularly to consult Valéntin Dumestre. I have an offer for his salle à manger—a great sum of money, out of all proportion to the value of the place, it seems to me. However. . . ."

The shoemaker's body, neatly skinned, was discovered some weeks later. Tradition says he must have done it himself. But that is not what he set down in the diary.

In June of the next year, a newspaper of 1849 tells us, crowds gathered daily on the banquette and blocked traffic.

Twenty-five years after the death of Feraud the shoemaker, the ghosts were still there. Tradition says that there were nights when even the walls cried out in a long wail, like a wolf pack in the full of the moon. So terrifying was it that the Negroes of the vicinity took to their heels and could not be induced to return even in daylight.

As for the golden slippers, Rogers the clerk never could find them again.

But some say that in a Potter's Field of the Old Section there is a sunken grave. And on that grave a pair of luminous golden slippers perch at night, whining and lisping and mewing, until a cloud creeps over the moon. . . .

# (*1915*)     *The Swamp Witch*

On Wednesday, the fifteenth of December, 1915, the Curator of the Louisiana State Museum in this city gave into the hands of his taxidermist the hide of a snow-white deer. It was a buck about two years old, belonging to the family of Louisiana white-tailed deer. Judged by size alone, it could easily have passed for a five-year-old.

It had been shot the day before by a Hammond trapper who had pitched a camp some miles out of Ruddock in order to keep an eye on his traps.

"They called it a 'ghost deer,' " he grinned. "Been calling it that for quite a while. It's been seen all over the Maurepas Swamps between Lake Pontchartrain and Lake Maurepas. Being an albino, the Negroes were afraid of it—sure it was a spook. I brought it down with one shot—and no silver bullets, either. You can see that it's been shot at a number of times— wounds all over one side, two teeth knocked out, and a furrow along its tongue where some bullet's ploughed across it. Pretty close shave, that.

"I don't know how many times I've been warned by Negroes not to go near the swamps at night, or the ghost deer might nab me. They claim an old witch lives there in the swamps—or else they think the witch and the ghost deer were one and the same. Well, the ghost is laid now, all right."

Local newspapers of the following day printed accounts of the killing of the "ghost deer" of the Maurepas Swamps. But a grim tale lay behind those newspaper stories. Gathered from many sources, it pieces together into a weird drama with a still more weird finale.

It seems that, about the year 1880, an Atlanta lawyer by the name of Daniel Weyman was disbarred and came to this city. He was thirty-five, tall and good-looking, and had a few thousand dollars. He had left an unamiable wife in Atlanta, and he proceeded to drink all the whisky he could hold. He never was anything like sober, but he still was brilliant.

One night he met an Irish girl named Kate Mulvaney. Irish himself, he took instantly to this blue-eyed, russet-haired young woman with the white teeth and the wide, laughing mouth. Kate was twenty-five at the time, and able to hold her own anywhere. She was a good girl, with charming manners and a voice like a bird calling. Her father was a bartender— but once upon a time he had been a professor of Greek in Dublin. He never told the cause of the transition.

Kate never did know who her mother had been. She belonged to Joe Mulvaney, and he brought her up with whatever ideals he had left over from the old days in Dublin. She never had seen the inside of a barroom in her life. Joe never took a drop himself. The nuns had educated Kate, and they had done a good job.

Dan Weyman met Kate by the simple method of getting so drunk he could no longer stand, so he sat down on her doorstep in Royal street. When she returned from a shopping trip, she took him into the house instead of sending for the police. When her father came home he ordered the intruder out, and Dan went blithely enough. But he took Kate's heart with him.

She saw him often after that. He made no pretense regarding his married state. His wife refused to apply for a divorce, and he himself had no grounds. He spoke freely of her, referring to her as "X"—laughing at her tantrums and declaring he'd rather be here and a disbarred lawyer, than in good standing and back living with "X." When Joe Mulvaney heard of it he set his foot down. No more of that Dan Weyman.

But Kate was following her heart. Dan still had a little money. Not much, but enough to furnish a small apartment. So they set up housekeeping in a quiet way, without benefit of clergy. Dan drank no more. He read and he smoked, he cracked jokes and laughed at them with Kate, and taught her how to cook and helped her keep house. He called her "Mrs. Weyman," and to hell with "X."

When the money gave out, he grinned and said they'd light on their feet somehow—he always had. So Kate, with terror in her heart, but worship also, beat her brains for some plan whereby she might earn enough to keep them going. She was afraid to apply for work at any of the shops—there would be questions, and Kate had grown sensitive about questions.

She made cookies and sold them; she peddled small bundles of vétiver; she went from office to office seeking secretarial work; she embroidered, she sewed, she made lace and candy and a special kind of ointment; she taught music when she could get pupils. She had headache and backache and earache. But she never complained and she never felt put-upon. She had Dan—nothing else mattered.

Dan was careful with the pennies, and he did most of the housework. He still joked and laughed and called her "sweetheart." But there never was quite enough to eat, new clothes were out of the question, and sometimes there was no fuel with which to cook. During the fifteen years they were together, they were evicted five times for non-payment of rent, and once a part of their meager furniture was seized.

"Things will change," Dan said brightly. "I always land on my feet."

"Yes," Kate replied. But within herself she said, "But your feet are on *me*." It was the first time she ever had doubled back.

"I've got an uncle in Australia," Dan laughed once. "Uncle Tim Weyman. He might strike it rich and die. Then 'X' might die, too. And then we could get married and have a gay time."

At the moment, Kate was too tired even to dream of a gay time. She looked back over the day. She had walked ninety-one city blocks, carrying a case weighing sixteen pounds. And she had earned a dollar and eighty-five cents, if nothing went wrong with her commission.

"I guess I'm no good," she thought dully. "It must be that I'm just a fizzle, after all. *Anybody* ought to be able to earn the little we need."

She was sick in bed for a week, and she could scarce keep her balance when she started out again with the heavy case.

"You'll be all right, honey," Dan assured her. "I'll be thinking of you all the time, and I'll have supper ready when you come home."

"How *can* he let me go out like this?" her heart cried all the way down the street. "If he loves me how *can* he do it?" But somehow she fought through the day. They were already back on the rent and she dared not spare even a few pennies for lunch. "Anyway," she thought, "I'd rather wait and eat at home with Dan."

Suddenly one day he began to find fault with her. She was selfish, he said—self-centered and inconsiderate and domineering. And she talked too much. She was "green." She misrepresented this and that.

Once he said, "You're out all day—how do I know where you are?" She thought of the blistering sun and the drenching rains and the bitter winter winds—her tired feet, her weary shoulders, herself half-mad with worry. Never once had she looked at or thought of any man but Dan Weyman.

She racked her brains—*had* she been selfish and disagreeable and too talkative? She always liked to tell him about her day, to be sure. . . .

Then one day she read in a newspaper that "X" had died. She showed it to Dan, but he merely remarked, "And a damned good thing that she's gone."

Early in 1895 Dan received word that his Uncle Tim was dead. He had left a diamond mine in South Africa and a gold mine in Australia, besides several millions in good hard cash. And Dan was his only heir.

"Now I won't be a burden on you, Kate, as I've been for so long," Dan told her. "You've been a good girl, I'll say that. And I guess you'll be mighty glad to have only one to keep instead of two."

Kate sat very still. Dan was going to leave her. There was no love, after all. She could feel something dying, where her heart ought to be.

"I can't ask him!" she was thinking to herself, making never a sound. "I can't ask for any man's love—not even his!"

The next day he left the dingy little rear apartment. He took none of his clothing. He could buy fine clothes at once, now. And he did.

Kate never had another word from him. She was forty years old now, and Dan was fifty. She smiled queerly, knowing that she was middle-aged. She felt neither young nor old. Just stunned and bewildered. Her father was dead. He had left her a hundred dollars, which she never had claimed. Now she went and got it.

She heard of Dan variously. He was very rich now, of course. He was president of one of the banks, and he had bought a large interest in one of the Central American fruit companies. The next year he married Louise Goebel, a girl of nineteen, daughter of the president of the fruit concern.

How Kate ever managed to live, she did not know. Whenever she thought of those fifteen years with the man she had adored, she smiled grimly and said to herself, "Gift woman—that's what I was. Not even a kept woman. Just a gift woman—gave myself and all that I had, which was little enough. But it was all I could do."

And then she would remember how he had misjudged her motives for this and that, how he had imputed to her things of which she never had dreamed. Green. Yes, she was green. She always would be. But she was clean-minded and straight as a die. She had loved beauty so acutely that sometimes the blue of a flower or the sparkle of rain or the song of a bird was almost agony. Her skin was still soft and smooth and pink, and her hair a bright russet. Her feet always had been quick and light.

In 1897, twin girls were born to Dan Weyman's wife. Exactly what changes came into Kate Mulvaney's life during the ensuing years it is impossible to ascertain. We know that in 1905, when she was fifty, she had smallpox. When the first great scab came off from her face, she held it in her shaking hand a long time. Then she slid it under her pillow.

That was the year Daniel Weyman began his various philanthropies. He was sixty, his wife was twenty-eight, and his twin daughters had just turned eight.

Some time after that, Kate Mulvaney was living in a

shack on the edge of the Maurepas Swamps, with an old mulatto woman. She never talked now, except to the birds and the dragonflies and the swift green lizards. Her skin was a dead white and terribly pitted, and her thin hair was like snow. She herself was like a tall dry weed swaying in the wind. The things she wore were not clothes, they were merely covering. Her hands were shapeless claws, and one foot dragged slightly.

But the wild things came almost at her call. Once a doe died near the cabin, leaving a snow-white fawn. She brought the infant inside and fed it goat's milk. Never before had a buck fawn grown so fast and so fine. His eyes were pink as coral, and he was deaf as a stone.

"You've got wings, little one," Kate whispered to him, patting his snow-white shoulders. "Six white wings, I think, like the seraphim. They were angels of love, you know. Maybe you *are* love . . . come to take me home. You're so very beautiful, White Wings. . . ."

She knew he could not hear her voice, but he seemed always to understand.

"He's part of me," she murmured to herself, "a strange part of me. And I'm part of him. I know. I can feel it."

Sometimes it frightened her. She never named him to anyone else. Lebasse, the mulattress, called him "de white one." Sometimes he came into the cabin, stepping delicately. Sometimes at nightfall he streaked off through the tall marsh grasses, to be gone for hours. But he always came back to Kate, munching scraps of cornbread and certain tender buds she gathered for him. The beautiful pink eyes were sensitive. It was the moonlight he loved.

The Negroes who frequented the swamps for fish and small game occasionally stopped at the shack. They unfolded their problems and perplexities to the strange, still, white woman, and she gave them advice and remedies. The white buck which vanished at their approach began to draw their attention. Was it a buck or a ghost? Was the white woman a mortal, or was she a witch?

So gradually Kate Mulvaney came to be known as the Swamp Witch. Who else could induce wild rabbits to eat from the hand? Who else could call the quail, so that they perched on a knee and pecked at a finger? Who else could raise an arm, and within five seconds find three mockingbirds teetering thereon? To whom else would a wild squirrel bring her young, to make a nest in an old stocking? Who else could mix a salve which would heal a burn in an hour? Who else could compound a powder which would cure asthma? Who else was there to whom you could tell your whole life, and know that never a word of it would be tattled?

"White Wings," she whispered one day to the tall deaf buck, "you're really going to take me away some day, for I'm learning to be like you. I'm learning to fly already . . . in spirit. Six wings . . . yes, six wings will be enough. They'll carry me. My thoughts are light. They'll carry me home, White Wings, and you'll be going with me all the way."

One day in 1914 Kate Mulvaney was walking along the narrow swamp road. She heard an automobile horn, and she stepped out of the roadway to let the machine pass. Not once a year did a motor car venture here. It was a large car, going slowly.

"Oh, that must be the Swamp Witch we heard about," came a girl's shrill voice. "Do let's stop, Daddy, and see what she's like. Maybe she'll tell our fortunes."

Kate turned toward the car. She saw a pretty woman, two girls, an elderly man, and a colored chauffeur. Suddenly she knew the man.

"Dan!" she cried, not knowing what she said. "Dan!"

Her whole soul and the essence of all its agony went into that cry. And he knew her. With all the white leathery skin and the rags—he knew her.

"Don't let's stop here, Dan!" the pretty woman was saying pettishly. "I'm afraid of that horrible creature, and she's yelling at us. Throw her a dime and tell Arnold to drive on!"

"She's that Swamp Witch, I know she is!" screamed one of the girls. "Maybe she'll try to climb into our car!"

"I'll see that she doesn't!" Dan Weyman growled.

In an instant he was out of the car, pushing Kate back into the tall grasses. Almost at once the razor cane hid these two from the machine.

"Damn you!" Weyman was roaring. "You'll dog me, will you? I see you everywhere I go, but this is the worst yet! I never go to a public dinner, I never attend a directors' meeting, I never see a play nor listen to an opera—that you're not there, leering at me! But you're about done!"

He struck her in the mouth with the butt of a heavy revolver. Two of her teeth snapped and fell onto the dry marsh mat.

"Open your mouth!" he ordered, twisting her shoulder cruelly.

She obeyed blindly. He sent a shot between her open lips, and it sizzled away through the rustling grasses. But it tore her tongue. Her mouth was a pool of warm blood. Surely he had held the gun freakishly—if only he had sent the shot through her brain!

"Damn you!" he grunted. "I'd kill you if I dared—but I'm always afraid, at the last. This'll teach you, maybe!"

He gave her a savage push and sent her sprawling into the wet morass just beyond the mat. Then he was gone, and she could hear the car tearing along the swamp road.

Slowly she picked herself up. She felt a cool breath. The white buck was beside her, bending his stately head to her misshapen hand.

"White Wings!" she whispered gratefully, patting him softly as he nuzzled against her. "White Wings . . . you must be letting me use your beautiful wings pretty soon now. I can see them so plainly—they're a glory and a deliverance!" Her arms reached up and held him frantically.

So the two strange companions went back to the cabin. But the buck's mouth bled a red torrent, he had lost two teeth, a deep furrow was ploughed in his tongue, and there were wounds on one of his snowy sides.

"She's growin' wings her own seff," Lebasse whispered to one of the Negroes who came along the next week. "Ah sees 'em plain sometimes. She stan' 'long-side de White One, an' it seem lak she sort o' gits to be mos' pawt o' him—lak a sperrit what b'long in de White One's body, yo' un'stan'. 'Tain't nuffin natch'l lak, but it don't skeer me none. She am dat good, she gwine fly 'way one o' dese yere days, Ah tells yo'. When Ah looks at her, Ah looks at all good, an' dey ain't nuffin else but. De White One he kin hear her wid his sperrit. An' he mos' flies, too."

"Folks dey says he a ghost deer," the darky responded. "Dey says he fly, too. An' dey says yo' cain't kill him, 'less yo' uses silver bullets. Me I ain't gwine try kill dat deer, 'course. But dey's queer fings gwine on. Some white folks says dey seen de White One in de moonlight, wid li'l peoples feedin' him—an' he all shiny lak white glass. An' some o' dem what seen him, dey says smoke an' fire spouts out o' his nose an' ears an' eyes.

"Me Ah cain't say, 'cayse Ah ain't nevah saw him in de night, lak dey says. An' some says when de Swamp Witch she die, de White One he die dat ve'y minute. Me Ah dunno. Ah branged yo'-all two ducks fo' de madam, an' some oatmeal fo' de White One. Now Ah has good luck fo' a month."

But Lebasse never said a word to anybody about that day when the two came in all blood-soaked and besmeared with swamp mud and ooze.

Very early in the morning of December fourteenth, 1915, Kate Mulvaney called Lebasse to the side of her rude bed. She had a big brown envelope in one hand, and she gave it to the mulattress.

"You go into New Orleans today," she directed haltingly. "I'm dying, Lebasse. This packet has got to go to a lawyer named McShane O'Grady. There's something in it—you know what it is. It's got to get there, and you've got to take it. You're the only one I can trust. Don't you fail me, Lebasse—you never have yet. When I die, lay me out straight. When I've grown quite stiff, you bury me in the swamp. Bury yourself, Lebasse. The old swamp's been a good friend to me. Whatever I've got, it's yours. I've taught you how to make the salve and the powder."

She told the old woman how to get to O'Grady's office. Then suddenly her breath stopped, and she was gone. The white buck was standing at the door. Lebasse saw six great beautiful white wings unfold from his snowy back and shoulders, lifting him from the swamp mat where he stood. Then he was gone, and she was there beside a dead woman, holding a brown envelope that must go to Lawyer O'Grady in New Orleans.

A Hammond trapper shot the white buck that morning . . . Or did he? . . .

The next day a weary old mulatto woman handed the brown envelope to Lawyer O'Grady. After he had read the note within, he went to call on the great Daniel Weyman, whose more private business he handled.

"It's something in a box—some keepsake, I suppose," he said lightly. "She's dead, anyway—died yesterday morning, the nigger said."

When he had left, Dan Weyman opened the package. It contained a small, flat tin box, such as cough lozenges sometimes come in. He wondered momentarily if it held the ring she used to wear, playing it was a wedding ring.

"Not a note nor anything," he snapped. "She was a queer card, all right."

Then he opened the box. A single dry, thick scale fell onto his hand. He bent to look closer, smelling a faint and horrible odor, an awful panic clutching at him. Not a letter, not a word—only this. . . .

Some days later the New Orleans papers rushed an extra out onto the streets. There was a seven-column streamer and type three inches tall. The newsboys surged hither and yon, pushing among the evening crowds, screaming the great news:

"Daniel Weyman dies of smallpox on Christmas Day! Daniel Weyman dead! Daniel Weyman—smallpox—all about Daniel Weyman. . . ."